PEARL

TABITHA KING

NAL BOOKS
NEW AMERICAN LIBRARY
NEW YORK AND SCARBOROUGH, ONTARIO

PUBLISHER'S NOTE

This book is a work of fiction. Names, characters, places, and incidents either are the product of the author's imagination or are used fictitiously, and any resemblance to actual persons, living or dead, events, or locales is entirely coincidental.

Published simultaneously in Canada by The New American Library of Canada Limited

Acknowledgments

Excerpts from "The Wraith," and "Give Way Ye Gates" Copyright © 1953 by Theodore Roethke. From *The Collected Poems of Theodore Roethke.* Reprinted by permission of Doubleday, a division of Bantam, Doubleday, Dell Publishing Group, Inc., and Faber and Faber, London, England.

NAL BOOKS TRADEMARK REG. U.S. PAT. OFF. AND FOREIGN COUNTRIES
REGISTERED TRADEMARK—MARCA REGISTRADA
HECHO EN HARRISONBURG, VA., U.S.A.

SIGNET, SIGNET CLASSIC, MENTOR, ONYX, PLUME, MERIDIAN
and NAL BOOKS are published *in the United States* by NAL PENGUIN INC.,
1633 Broadway, New York, New York 10019,
in Canada by The New American Library of Canada Limited,
81 Mack Avenue, Scarborough, Ontario M1L 1M8

Library of Congress Cataloging-in-Publication Data

King, Tabitha.
Pearl.

I. Title.
PS3561.I4835P4 1988 813'.54 88-12541
ISBN 0-453-00626-4

Designed by Julian Hamer

First Printing, November, 1988

1 2 3 4 5 6 7 8 9

PRINTED IN THE UNITED STATES OF AMERICA

This is for my children, the best people I know.

This book owes something to the following people: Marcella Sorg, the forensic anthropologist who provided me with vital information as well as a useful peek at some slides; my sisters Margaret Spruce Morehouse and Stephanie Spruce Leonard, first readers; my sister Marcella Spruce, who helped me with music; and Stephen, for editorial advice. Any boo-boos are my own doing.

There was a body, and it cast a spell . . .

—THEODORE ROETHKE

ONE

1

Learning the other ways into Nodd's Ridge, the back roads, takes a lifetime of living there. Since she was from away, Pearl Dickenson arrived by way of Route Five. The first thing she saw was the view for which the Ridge was famous. One comes upon the skyward folding of the land into the White Mountains as a sudden revelation: all at once the woods open up around the individual houses of the village, standing apart from each other in a community of privacy, their backs to the ancient splendid hills. The lake is a wedge of sapphire in the middle ground between, a blue tear in all that rooted rock and green hallelujah of trees. Pearl forgot she was looking for this very place. Swinging into the scenic turnout, she gawked like a thousand other passers-through.

"Jesus, Mary and Joseph," she said aloud, "I've died and gone to heaven."

A huge, joyful energy welled up in her. She flung open the door of her ancient Dodge sedan and jumped out. She had gotten stiffer than she had realized in the sixty miles since Portland. Putting her hands to the small of her back, she thrust out her pelvis and groaned and stretched agreeably, filling up her lungs with the brisk, tingly air of northern May. Suddenly she felt as if she had just awakened from a very long nap. It was quite inexplicable, this sensation she ought to feel much older than she did.

Paint faded to colorlessness mottled with rust, an aged Jeep truck limped arthritically into the turnout from the opposite direction. It looked as if it were old enough to find its way to the place by memory. It ground to a stop with a loud farting backfire. The old man at the wheel waved and grinned at her, giving her more of a view of what remained of his teeth than she really wanted.

She waved back.

He climbed down from the cab and approached her, still showing her the full glory of his ancient gums and choppers. Clutching a greasy, shapeless fedora, he wheezed up to her like the little train that could, bringing with him a cloud of old-man smell, a rich mix of bean-fart, cigar, old dog, and infrequently changed long johns.

"Welcome to Nodd's Ridge," he said, flinging out both hands as if to gather up the town and present it to her.

Pearl laughed.

Something stirred in the old man, some almost forgotten well of heat. A belly laugh that never did get out of low gear, though it tried, rumbled up out of him in response.

She stuck her hands in her jacket pockets and shrugged in the general direction of the mountains.

"God had a good day here, didn't She?"

"Yes, ma'am," he agreed, her use of the feminine pronoun for the Deity apparently perturbing him not at all. "You taking a snapshot?"

She hesitated, looking back at the view.

"Most folks take snapshots," the old man explained.

"I'm not surprised," she said. "If I were a decent photographer, I'd be tempted. But I didn't come here for the view."

The old man's bushy eyebrows shot up. The tip of his tongue shot out to wet one corner of his mouth.

"You ain't, you ain't . . . ?"

"I am. The woman you came here to meet. Pearl Dickenson." She stuck out her left hand. "You must be Mr. McKenzie, the caretaker. Pleased to meet you."

The old man took her hand in his, his face scrunched up with mental effort.

"Pleasure's mine," he finally decided.

The gap-toothed grin took over his face again like a tattered flag suddenly filling with the wind.

"And I thought," he said with the same grinding of risible gears as before, "I thought you was turned around."

"Turned around?"

"Lost. Looking for Camp Keywadin, prob'ly. The music camp, for kids who are kind of like musical watchyacallums, proda-gees."

She nodded. "Well, I'm not lost. I'm exactly where I want to be."

The old man waved his tired hat at the mountains. "Seen your fill?"

"No. How long have you lived here?"

More gums. "Whole life," he said.

"You seen your fill?"

He shook his head.

"That's what I thought," she said. "Well, I can't spend the rest of my life standing here gawking like Lot's wife. Let's go see the place."

Chortling, the old man pointed across Route Five to where the land rose slowly in a slope patched with meadow and woods. At the top, partially hidden by big old elms and maples in fresh leaf, stood a white farmhouse graced with deep porches. A thousand feet north of the scenic turnout, a town road set off from Route Five up the hillside. In the other direction, a parallel line of decrepit elms, more honored in the gap than by the few still standing, marked the boundary with a rock-walled cemetery.

Pearl stared up at the house. "I thought it would be down some dirt road, out in the woods."

The old man shook his head. "Nope. Pract'cly on the main road. Walk to the post office and the store real easy. You and the folks in the cemet'ry got the best view in town."

"Uncle Joe's up there?" she asked with a nod at the graveyard.

"See that big wild rosebush, white rose, high up there?"

"Ayuh," she ventured. He didn't seem to notice, so she thought she had said it right.

"Joe's right there. He planted that bush hisself for his mother. Josie died of the influenza, nineteen-and-nineteen. Reuben Styles had a hell of a time plantin' Joe on account of the geedee roots, pardon me, miss. Didn't do no damage to the bush, it prob'ly reaches halfway to Chiner. Anyway, Joe only moved next door so we figure he's prob'ly resting comfy."

"Close enough to keep an eye on the place," she said.

The old man nodded and fixed her with a shrewd and watery eye. "Now, just so I can get this straight, you're Joe's sister Gussie's granddaughter, which makes you Joe's grand-niece."

"That's right. I never met Uncle Joe."

"No," the old man agreed, "I bet you didn't," and pulled his hat decisively over his freckled pate.

2

Whatever it is that signals to human beings that a house is empty was clear as a flag about this one even from the distance. It was like a silent alarm, some barely perceptible depth of quiet that declared the house uninhabited. Someone had mowed the grass and had taken pains to maintain the flowerbeds. As if from the vigorously plied crayons of a literal-minded five-year-old, clumps of early tulips spattered blots of primary colors against the clean white of the clapboards. Daffodils and narcissi trumpeted cream and paper-white and yellow.

Walter McKenzie huffed and puffed up the back steps, hauling out a large, noisy key ring hung with smaller ones, like a cheap metal ring puzzle. His thick fingers scrabbled with the rings as if they were a stubborn knot in a shoelace. At last they parted, delivering one cluster into his hands. His knuckles were glossy, the skin of his hands waxy, with an undertone of iris blue.

Pearl was reminded, with a flutter in her stomach, of her grandmother's pallid hands, clutching green crystal rosary beads upon the small, unmoving, ivory-crepe-clad hummock of her belly as she lay at final rest on a bed of rose-petal satin.

Sorting out the proper key required more clumsy jangling while he talked.

"Ain't been inside since I set the mousetraps. I keep forgetting to come back and see if there's any dead 'uns to dispose of. Hope the place don't stink. If there's any in the traps, I'll clean 'em up for you today."

He stopped stabbing the keyhole to gesture widely in the direction of the field that composed what could be called the front yard but was closer to a five-acre field.

" 'Course, I come and mowed or else you'd be on your way to first haying by now."

"I appreciate that."

She touched the handkerchief in her pocket to reassure herself she had something to stifle the stench of a decaying mouse massacre.

At last he got the door open. They went through a short T-shaped shed. Smelling of bark and sawdust and the faintest perfume of cat box, it had a door in either direction. The old man elected the door on the left, which had to be unlocked in its turn. This further fumbling admitted them to the kitchen.

It smelled mostly of sun-heated dust and had as its centerpiece an iron wood-stove, massive and squat as an idol. The sight of it failed to evoke any nostalgia. The stove and the flatiron had been the ball and chain of her grandmother's generation. Good riddance to such overthrown gods of the kitchen. Of course, the cast-iron range had been a step up from the colonial fireplace. Her grandmother had insisted biscuits couldn't be made properly in any other kind of oven. Nevertheless, Gussie had had a gas range and a microwave in her kitchen, not one of these old dinosaurs. Pearl traced the name Atlantic Queen written gracefully in chrome on the oven door. Her nose picked up faded, more complicated oily odors, kerosene and stove polish.

The small electric range and fridge, both not quite old enough to have any particular charm but still noisily functioning, were reassuringly electrical. Dated as it was, the room was basically clean under an understandable layer of dust. From it, back stairs marched tight-lipped upward to the second floor, giving scant headroom to anyone taller than five and a half feet.

Wringing his fedora as if it were a lace hankie, the old man stared at the wooden table.

"Many's the time I've sat at the table with Joe, jawing."

With a huge sigh, he shucked off the cloak of remembrance and turned to the business at hand.

"Well, you like to look around yourself, or you want me to show you?"

His wheezing now seemed to have a distinct distress in it. She wondered if he were uncomfortable in her presence or only troubled by the ghostly past.

The elderly caretaker reverted again to reminiscence.

"Joe kep' his personal business to hisself."

"Never spoke of me."

"Nope." He thrust the small ring of keys at her.

Startled by the number of them, she held the ring in both hands. She'd been expecting what one got when renting an apartment in the city: front door, back door, if any, maybe a spare. Not a baker's dozen or so.

"I thought nobody locked their doors up here, everyone was so honest."

The old man pulled a long face.

"Sorry to say, folks ain't as honest as once they was. Mostly it's folks from away."

The implied slur dawned in his face and he backpaddled.

"No offense to you, ma'am. Lots of nice people from away, it ain't their fault they was borned someplace else. But there's some bad apples come from New Hampshire, Massachusetts. It's really only summertime you can't leave nothing lying around loose. Come winter, those jokers go back to Taxachusetts and New Hampster, where they don't have to chop wood to keep warm and there's more liquor stores to stick up."

Pearl stifled a grin.

"I guess Uncle Joe didn't trust somebody," she said, studying the keys.

"Joe was awful careful. All them keys is labeled. Joe wouldn't leave you a key you didn't know what it unlocked."

He cast a quick glance around the room. There was a finality to it, as if he didn't ever expect to see it again. Perhaps at his age, one fell into the habit of looking that way at everything.

"You need anything, my number's right by the phone. 'Course the phone here's shut off; you'll have to call from the store. Everything else is working; Joe kep' the place like a palace."

"Thanks."

He punched the hat back into a modicum of concavity.

"You won't have no trouble selling it."

"I'm not," she said.

The fedora was arrested halfway to his head.

"Beg pardon, miss?"

Pearl Dickenson's laugh filled up the kitchen. She heard it first, resonating through the eustachian tube, the way we all hear the noises we make ourselves, and then it came back to her from the house, like a greeting.

"I'm going to live here, Mr. McKenzie," she said, and that was the first Nodd's Ridge heard of it.

3

Walter McKenzie drove away, shouting out his open window if she needed anything just to holler.

Pearl watched him go, then set off across the grass, skirting the flowerbeds and the substantial vegetable plot where asparagus was just breaking the mulch. The sound of the old man's Jeep faded away. The canopies of the remaining elms overlapped to make a cool, translucent green roof.

" 'Glory be to God for dappled things,' " she murmured.

Sometimes a great stump like a prehistoric mammoth's foot marked a recent passing as surely as an unweathered stone. Other gaps in the line were like doorways, uneven underfoot as the stoops between unlevel rooms in an aged house, or the hummocking of the turf in a yet unsettled grave. The elms had been giants in the earth, as much as Abraham and Moses. The present generation was now in its last days, the huge old trees being felled everywhere because of the Dutch elm disease. She wondered who had planted these particular trees, which had surely not seeded themselves in a parade line. It was an appealing idea that it might have been one of the Nevers clan, Joe's great-grandfather, perhaps, who had dug holes in the thin soil of this northern ridge and braced saplings in them. While she could expect to eat the apples from an apple tree she planted herself, an elm's coming of age would be a gift to grandchildren and great-grandchildren she might never know. And if the elms connected her to those tree planters she knew only as grave antique faces in sepia photographs and names in her grandmother's Bible, then the extinction of those great trees meant the severing of a connection to further generations. Did the old bones in this graveyard feel the unobstructed sun through the soil or know by the loosening embrace of the rotting roots that an old order was ending, perhaps forever, that God was imagining a new one?

The drystone wall around the cemetery was low enough to climb easily. Making for the wild rosebush, she could see this graveyard had been in use for a very long time, for many of the stones were slates.

The wild rose had seized possession of the family plot, where her Uncle Joe and his parents, her great-grandparents, were at rest. Its buds were still no more than points of punctuation among the tiny newborn leaves, but its thorns were long and brutal. The gnarled dwarf trunk and branches made her think of stone rather than wood. Never mind the roots of the moribund elms, the grip of the rosebush upon the bones beneath it must be unbreakable. Perhaps it was tickling Uncle Joe hello. Uncle Ghost.

Gussie had died the previous winter. Pearl had shipped her grandmother's body to Greenspark to await the spring thaw. On her way through Greenspark earlier that day, she had stopped at the undertaker's to confirm arrangements for the interment tomorrow. Presumably this Styles fellow would be around with a backhoe to dig the grave, disturbing the rosebush once again.

She drifted from one stone to the next, acquainting herself with her neighbors. Among the bones this yard sheltered were some who bore the last name of the gravedigger: SAMUEL and EDITH STYLES, from their dates the previous generation. A raw pinkish granite boulder incised with the name CHRISTOPHER caught her eye. More curbstones identified the Christophers: VICTORIA HAYES/MOTHER, and THOMAS HAYES/SON. The dates on his stone indicated young Tom hadn't lived to grow his first mustache. Some tragedy there.

Then she was among the older stones, the slates, reading the amateur verses. Like old folk songs, the verses contained outright contradictions—sometimes espousing heartfelt loss and then, a few lines later, expressing belief that the separation is not real, that the beloved is still present in some way. Awkward and mawkish and sentimental though some of them were, here and there a line was bluntly honest. Beneath a decidedly puckish-looking angel was engraved:

> Here lyes SILENCE the Wyfe of NOYSE
> Still at last within The Arms of Truth,
> Who kept her Peace and found her Peace,
> Outliving NOYSE, She had The Last Word,
> And this is it.

Pearl laughed out loud and then thought it was good she was alone with the dead. Her living neighbors might think she was cracked, wandering through a cemetery all by herself and laughing.

Silence Noyse, who had held on to life with both hands until the age of ninety-nine in order to get that last word, must have been a firecracker. Something about her autoepigraph made Pearl think old Silence had been stretching the truth about keeping her peace. LYES might even have been a pun. Old Silence sounded like a woman who spoke her mind. If Silence overheard Pearl's laughter at her jokey stone, Pearl didn't think she'd be anything but pleased.

4

Like the old woman gone to dust under her sardonic cartoon angel, the house still waited for her in silence. Pearl wandered through it as she had the graveyard. The parlor with its faded old-fashioned paper memorialized its late owner by omission. Arranged on the plain mantel over the fireplace opening that had been converted to a small wood-burning stove were wedding portraits of her great-grandparents, old Will and Josephine, and of Gussie in her wedding gown with her first husband, Nathan Madden, old Nate looking impossibly boyish, and another of Gussie on her high school graduation. What a beauty she had been, luminous and delicate as a wild iris. There were a couple of group photographs of the three Madden children and then of some of her grandchildren, anniversary pictures. Then a snapshot of Gussie and her second husband, Peter Finley, on the occasion of their wedding, far away from Nodd's Ridge in some place where palm trees grow. All these pale ghosts were so familiar to Pearl from her grandmother's albums that it felt she almost knew them. But of Uncle Joe himself there were no pictures, nor of either of his wives.

Nor was there of Pearl. This did not surprise her. She thought it likely that she had been no more to her Uncle Ghost than a name, a sex, an unimportant and possibly uncertain birthdate. But there was a sad loneliness in the display of Gussie's family and the absence of any of Joe's.

As foreshadowed by the kitchen, the parlor furnishings were solid, well-made, moderately valuable as semiantiques, meaning they were built of solid wood and not on an assembly line, but nothing justifying a call to Sotheby's. Clearly they had been just furniture to Uncle Ghost, kept well-polished, firmly joined, hinges and draw-pulls and locks in working order. Unfashionably darkened oak predominated, upholstered in dated and comfortably worn fabrics. The walls were remarkably bare, sporting only the occasional calendar, unchanged since the owner's demise.

Off the parlor was a sun porch, facing west, that smelled of decades of cigars. It was furnished with a comfortable daybed, some unprepossessing chairs, a wicker rocker, and a magazine stand. Storm windows still sealed its three screened sides against the winter past. In the other direction, beyond the finely turned balusters of the stairs, was a pleasant bathroom that looked as if it might have been a back bedroom at one time, with a shower in it and an invalid's handrail.

Placing her hand upon the smooth, nearly silken solidity of the banister, Pearl paused at the foot of the front stairs, listening to the silence above.

"Anybody home?" she called out softly.

Only silence answered.

"It's just me, I'm home."

She laughed and the laugh came back, from a great distance.

5

Walter McKenzie pulled up to the Texaco pumps.

The garage doors were open on the greasepit where Reuben Styles's younger boy, Sam, was underneath a late-model Chevette, changing the oil. His father walked out of the darkness in the back of the shop, wiping his hands on a rag.

The old caretaker's face was red with excitement and he sprayed the mechanic with spittle.

"Reuben, I just met Joe Nevers' grand-niece, the one inherited his property, and you'll never in a million years guess."

Walter broke into a giggle and slapped at his thighs with delight.

Reuben smiled.

"Want a fill, Walter?"

There was a mournfulness about the mechanic that troubled Walter, and the old man lost his place.

"Eh? Oh, sure."

Reuben saw he had interrupted the old man's train of thought.

Walter struggled visibly to regain the track.

Inserting the nozzle and setting the automatic catch, Reuben waited for him. He had not the slightest curiosity what delicious secret Walter had discovered about Joe Nevers' grand-niece, mostly because he doubted Walter had really discovered anything. The old man was most likely all excited about nothing. Reuben patiently worked the rag around his fingers again.

Walter's face cleared as he remembered his hot news.

"Reuben, she's a Negro."

It was warm and the air was a little thick and smelled of apple trees in flower. Reuben heard him from a distance.

"What?"

"She is," Walter insisted. "Black as old Harry."

Reuben looked closely at the old man.

Walter was all atremble, wringing his old felt hat.

Walter must be mistaken. This was an isolated place with a harsh climate, and the range of ethnic groups was overwelmingly Northern European. Many of Walter's generation had lived their whole lives without encountering more than one or two individuals darker than an Indian. But surely the old man had seen blacks enough on television, to say nothing of the few passing through of a summer, to know black from white. Doubtless the woman had a deep tan like one of those people from Massachusetts who sailed and sunbathed a lot. Walter had never been precise, and these days, he was often confused.

Walter was already doubting himself.

"She's no tarbaby. Lighter'n that. Brown, I mean. Light eyes, too."

He seemed to be visualizing the stranger's features as he spoke, and something was confirmed for him.

"Ayuh. Gussie's eyes. Different color, sort of a funny hazel, you know how hard it is to tell with hazel? Sometimes they're greenish, sometimes they're grayish, sometimes goldish?"

Reuben nodded.

"Well, Gussie had blue eyes, not hazel, but the left one, there was a patch of brown in it, like a tarnish."

Reuben remembered the old woman as he had last seen her, bright blue eyes indeed, the odd bit of color in the left. Same as the little Christopher girl, the one he'd seen murdered years ago, on the lake. In his mind's eye, he could see the canoe rounding the bend, the mother, the girl. The boy in it. He could hear the shot from the woods and see the bullet take her, driving her into the lake, from which her body had never been recovered. Odd how often he remembered the child, thought: Well, now India'd be thirteen . . . now seventeen . . . now twenty. He hadn't eaten a fish out of the lake since 1966.

"Guess she must be Gussie's grandchild then," he ventured. "I never heard one of Gussie's girls married a black. She must just be dark. Some people are who aren't Negroes."

Walter was getting hot under the collar.

"Goddammit, Reuben. I ain't ignorant. I seen *The Cosby Show*, I know a Negro when I see one."

Reuben smiled.

"Anything's possible. Somebody would have said, wouldn't they?"

Walter nodded.

The automatic catch on the pump let go. Reuben squirted in another spurt of gasoline and shook the nozzle off gently.

"Maybe she's adopted."

Walter cheered right up. "Bet that's it."

Reuben didn't care whether the woman was a Martian, let alone black, so long as the old man didn't work himself into a stroke about it.

Walter leaned close. "You know what else, she says she's going to stay. Going to live here."

Reuben glanced up, finally startled.

Walter grunted with satisfaction, then sneaked a peek at the open garage bay, where Sam's high-top sneakers marked his location under the Chevette.

A tool clunked on the concrete floor and Sam said, "Shit," clearly and decisively, then, "Sorry, Dad."

Walter took out his wallet and began to count the cost of the gas into Reuben's hand.

"Seven, eight, and fifty-six cents."

"Thanks."

The old man clambered into the cab of his truck. "Tell you somethin' else, Reuben."

Reuben, picking up the oily rag from where he had draped it on the trash barrel, listened attentively.

"Oo-la-la, I'm telling you. Oo-la-la."

Reuben laughed.

To Walter's delight, there was nothing at all mournful in the mechanic's laugh.

Walter McKenzie fired up the truck and jounced away, still mouthing "oo-la-la" and grinning.

Reuben deposited the money in the cash register, thinking: Oo-la-la. Oo-la-la. He laughed again.

TWO

1

The cold woke Pearl. Mist rolled under the lower sash of the double-hung window she had cracked to admit fresh air before going to bed. Fresh air indeed was what she got, downright out-of-line, pesty air, blind-date-with-Russian-hands-and-fingers air. Shivering, she rolled up tighter in her sleeping bag. Momentarily it was almost cozy. But the damp cold had breached her sleep cycle, the confused dreams of early morning dissipated beyond recovery. Pearl rolled heroically out of the sleeping bag.

Visibility had gone on a toot, nothing to see out the window but bleary fog. The mist had precipitated out of the air upon the wire mesh of the screen window, beading on window glass and sill. She wondered if she were making a mistake and then decided it was only the weather. On the other hand, it was possible that the weather *was* Nodd's Ridge, in which case she might have a problem.

Sweatshirt layered over T-shirt and jeans, she went down to the kitchen. In the cold the old stove had more of an attraction but she was afraid to try lighting it. Something might be nesting in it. Mice, birds, who knew. This was the country, after all. The electric stove did very nicely for the production of a substantial breakfast. Hot food inside her warmed her up, and being warm again boosted her courage and made everything seem possible.

Outside the fog was thinning but the overcast was very low and it was drizzling. A fine day for Gussie to come home. Pearl had much to do. She turned on her radio and found some music. Out of nests of newspaper in cardboard boxes, she extracted Gussie's china and silver. Washing it clean of the newsprint took her back to the packing of it, and further back, to helping her mother with the spring cleaning. She put it out on the kitchen counter next to her coffeemaker. Arranged the silver spoons and dessert forks and cloth napkins. Filled the sugar and creamer and put the creamer back in the fridge to keep cold. There was something missing.

She turned out her slicker and galoshes from her bags, clumped out to the corner of the barn where Uncle Ghost's tools were and located a well-kept pair of secateurs. Rain dripped down her neck while she collected a bundle of flowers. The green glass pitcher from Uncle Ghost's china closet made a satisfactory vase for the red Apeldoorn and red-and-white Peppermint Stick tulips, the big white Mount Hood and smaller, delicate pheasant's-eye narcissi.

The radio reminded her it was nine. A glance out the window showed the weather hadn't changed in the last ten minutes. But it was time she did. Squeaky clean as the china from her shower, she slipped into her black dress and came back downstairs.

As she fastened Gussie's pearls around her neck, she peeked out the kitchen window again. There was a bright spot of color in the drear, a yellow backhoe chugging down the main road toward the cemetery. The man driving it wore a bright yellow slicker trimmed with black, a regular old honeybee. The backhoe disappeared into the cemetery, but glimpses of yellow flashing through the gaps in the leaves telegraphed its position.

Pearl set coffee making, hauled on her galoshes and slicker again, and stepped out into the drizzle. By the time she reached the cemetery bounds, the man had already peeled back the turf and set it aside. She watched the backhoe bite into the damp earth, chew it, tear up roots and rocks. It was an ill-mannered beast, dribbling loose stone, soil, vegetable matter from the sides of its mechanical jaws, but the hole it dug was remarkably neat; the man was very skillful with his overgrown shovel and made short work of the grave.

Backing off to a discreet position, he noticed her standing there watching and nodded. He hopped out of the parked backhoe, his so'wester in his hand. The way the backhoe rose on its springs, watching him unfold and stretch himself, the size of the man came clear to her. The backhoe began to look as if it might have been a tight fit. Only football players and archangels come in that size.

She introduced herself. "I'm Pearl Dickenson."

"Reuben Styles."

He looked to be in his early forties. The hand grasping hers was callused and powerful. He dwarfed her five-foot-five by a little over a foot and outweighed her by at least fifty pounds. Mostly slabs of muscle, but with a comfortable thickening around the waistline, the meat was admirably laid onto a heavy-boned, deep-chested frame. His blond hair might have been fading to silver or perhaps it was only the gloom of the day rendering the thick curls no color at all, the drizzle flecking it with droplets. There was bog-cutter in his face and the serene balance of an honest man.

"Walter says you're Joe's grand-niece."

She nodded.

He reached inside his slicker and pulled out a large, old-fashioned turnip watch on an Albert chain. In an exaggerated Arabic calligraphy, its lid bore the initials SMS.

"Mr. Muller said eleven."

"It probably doesn't make any difference," Pearl said. "I don't expect there'll be many people, with this kind of weather."

Reuben shook his head.

"The old folks are tough, that's how come they're old. Mrs. Madden . . . pardon me, she'll always be Mrs. Madden to me . . . Mrs. Finley may have lived away the last ten, fifteen years, but she wasn't forgotten."

To prove his point, automobiles began to enter the cemetery. Behind the wipers sweeping the windshields, elderly faces craned at them. Within five minutes there were half a dozen vehicles parked on the access road and then the hearse climbed the hill and passed them to draw up close to the grave.

Reuben Styles pointed out a small, round man disembarking from an elderly Olds. "That's Mr. Penny, the Unitarian minister."

Reuben waved at him and Mr. Penny hurried toward them.

"Miss Dickenson," Reuben introduced her.

"Mr. Penny."

Mr. Penny's eyebrows did an instant jig and then he recovered nicely.

"Very nice to meet you finally," the minister said. "I only met your grandmother a few times during her summer visits, but I've heard so much about her."

Reuben Styles excused himself while the minister was making his condolences and crossed to the parked vehicles, conversed briefly with the occupants of each one.

Mr. Penny noticed her watching him.

"Reuben's just telling them to stay in their cars until we're ready for the service," he explained. "No need for the old folk to stand about in this weather any longer than necessary."

"That's very thoughtful."

The minister nodded. "Yes. He's a good man, from all I hear. Not one of my flock. But very thoughtful of the elderly."

Walter McKenzie arrived in the company of a grizzled man wearing a very old Navy peacoat and raggedy discolored bucket hat. Walter tipped his hat to Pearl but did not introduce his friend. The old caretaker instead sought out Reuben Styles for conversation—from his hand gestures, about the business of digging the grave.

The caretaker's companion was thin and hollow-chested as a fork. His slack little beer belly reminded Pearl of the kind of snake that ate a mouse once a month, whose digestion could be judged by the rate its middle bulge shrank. He stood a little back and cast a critical eye over the grave and the preparations of the undertaker's party. Then he gave Pearl a good lookover with bright, angry eyes that found her wanting, with no surprise at all.

She thought he was a man who found the world in general wanting.

He moved off a ways to light a cigarette and have a morose, if damp, smoke.

Pearl had time to examine her grandfather Nathan's stone. He had been Gussie's first husband. Next to him was Uncle Harry's marker. Her mother's brother had been killed in the Korean War and left no issue. Her mother's sister Fran had married a diplomat and now lived in the Southwest. Pearl had never met Aunt Fran's children, her cousins. Her aunt had shown up for Gussie's funeral in D.C., but found it one trip too many to come all the way from Taos to inter her mother's remains.

Pearl shivered in the damp chill, not from being in the cemetery. There was nothing to fear in graveyards, no reason to fear the dead. She had been with both her mother and Gussie at the end. It had been spooky and at the same time inexplicably comforting to witness the abandonment of their bodies by their spirits. The act of interment was a literal laying to rest, giving Gussie back to the very place she had loved in life. Pearl was surprised to feel a vague but unshakable, odd sensation of connection to relatives in the family plot. Though all but a stranger to them in life, in spite of being a stranger, she was flesh of their flesh.

With the efficiency of long practice, the undertaker and his assistants were quickly ready, the mourners assembled around the gravesite, where the coffin sat upon the mechanical bier. Perhaps because he hadn't personally known Gussie, or maybe only because of the weather and his concern for the dozen and a half elderly people in attendance, Mr. Penny was brisk and unsentimental. As Pearl had requested, he ended with an invitation to take refreshment at Joe Nevers' old house next door.

At the door she met them all, introducing herself and thanking them for their effort, receiving in turn their names, their condolences, their wet outer garments, gifts of food, and the first full and open face of their curiosity. She thought she had never been quite so thoroughly and openly gawked at in her life. Once they had each taken a good long look, however, they appeared to be satisfied. More than one of the old women remarked some resemblance in Pearl to Gussie or to Pearl's mother, whom none of them had seen since she was a teenager.

The undertaker and the parson appeared briefly to express the conventional sentiments and left together, discreetly pleading the press of other obligations. Mr. Penny invited Pearl to worship at his church the following day. Pearl thanked him but made no commitment. The sour man who had come with Walter McKenzie never did come to the house, either out of unsociability or because he had conflicting business.

The old people, knowing the place as well as each other, and certainly better than she did, made themselves at home without ado. She dispensed the gifts of food to accompany coffee and tea. The eight women and six men seemed to be old hands at Saturday-morning interment kaffeeklatsches. They settled into telling stories about Gussie and Joe, to Pearl but also to each other. There was a wealth of reminiscence and a great deal of laughing.

Reuben Styles came in and took up a lot of room. One of the old ladies served him tea, another a pastry. Shut of his slicker, he was wearing what was clearly an off-the-rack dark funerals-and-weddings suit from some place that specialized in Backhoe-Size Gents. She did not think he had ever heard of the concept of dress-for-success. He kept sticking his finger between his shirt collar and hauling at it—too small for him, no doubt. He had to be an eighteen collar. His wife was no seamstress; the hem of his right coat sleeve was coming undone. He made his manners to her.

"This is the happiest wake I've ever attended," Pearl told him, and laughed softly.

2

Reuben stopped chewing, his mouth fell of mincement square, his great head swiveling about to fix unwavering, suddenly intense blue eyes on her. He swallowed hard.

"I've got to get the recipe for these things," Pearl remarked. "They're wonderful."

Taking her by the arm, Walter McKenzie asked, "Gussie ever tell you about the time . . . ?"

Relieved, Reuben picked up a filled cookie. His taste buds instantly recognized Ruby Parks's baking. Best filled cookie in town. Walter had indeed exaggerated. Pearl Dickenson wasn't anywhere near as black as old Harry, he thought. Black hair, to be sure, the kind of black that has blue highlights, thick and glossy and wrapped up neatly at the back in the kind of fold some sea shells had, the way Grace Kelly used to wear her hair in the movies she made for Alfred Hitchcock, he couldn't remember what that particular hairstyle was called. French twist, maybe. It was curled up where it had escaped its pins around her face. But her eyes were light, as Walter had reported, the actual color hard to determine and so called hazel, when "anybody's guess" would be more accurate. And her nose was distinctly un-Negroid, a strong, almost beaky shape that hinted at an Indian in the woodpile too. It must be a crowded woodpile. Her lips were undeniably full and sensual, but that was nothing unique to blacks. He'd seen a picture in a magazine once, while waiting for a haircut, of a ballerina so white she looked like angel hair on a Christmas tree, whose lips were a little like Gussie's mysterious granddaughter's. Whatever Pearl Dickenson was, though, she wasn't white, at least as Reuben Styles understood the term. One of Gussie's children had unquestionably had doings with someone of a darker tribe.

She laughed again over some witticism of Walter's and it vibrated right through him. If he were a man who believed in such things, he'd be worried she was throwing a hoodoo on him. He worked himself around to get another look at her eyes. The patch in the left eye was assuredly there, a dark smudge in what was gray iris this rainy day. It reminded him, as it always had when he had seen Gussie, of the biblical passage constraining us to first pluck out the beam in our own eye before we railed our neighbor for the mote in his. A mote it was, a familiar . . . no, familial mote, the very observation a familiar one.

It was not hard for him to understand why she had come to Nodd's Ridge to stay. He couldn't understand why the whole world didn't want to live in Nodd's Ridge, but was grateful that it didn't. What he wondered most was what she was going to do here.

She came back to him, offering him more tea.

"That reminds me," he told her, "I've got Joe's truck and wagon on blocks. Bring 'em over for you later today, if you want."

"Okay. How do they run?"

"The Eagle's fine, almost brand-new. The Ford wagon's got sixty thousand on it but it's been well-maintained. If you want to sell either one, I can find you buyers. There's a plow attachment for the Eagle, you could sell with it or separately, as you choose."

"Thanks. I'll have to look at them to be sure, but the one I actually want to sell is my old Dodge."

"The one in the driveway?"

She nodded.

"I'll take it in when I bring the other two around, look it over, give you a price," he offered. "If you want."

3

Business coming up reminded him of work pending. He finished off another pastry in two bites, another cup of tea in a couple of gulps, said thank you kindly, and left.

It made Pearl smile to think to herself she could almost feel the house rising on its springs as the backhoe had done as Reuben Styles stepped off the back step.

Late in the afternoon she was back in her sweats, cleaning out the old sedan in the driveway, when she heard cars coming in. Weak sunlight filtered through clouds that were trying to break up. The drizzle passing had left sweet air and the ground wet underfoot.

Reuben Styles dismounted an AMC Eagle with JOE NEVERS/CARETAKER lettered on the door. Directly behind him, a slight man with a permanent x-crease between his eyebrows, marking a steady state of perplexity, slipped out of a well-preserved Ford wagon with the same logo on its door. An oversize teenager boy of unmistakably Styles paternity exited the passenger side. The boy came forward shyly and was introduced as Sam. Pearl thought he must be eighteen or nineteen. The other man was named Jonesy and he was even shier. The trio cast professional glances over the old Dodge.

Reuben handed Pearl two sets of keys, she gave him two sets for the sedan.

"I believe Joe used to keep spare car keys in a locked drawer in the garage."

"I'll look," she promised.

"I expect your phone isn't in. Okay if I let you know a price on Monday?"

She nodded.

"You want Joe's sign taken off the doors, we can do that for you. Match the paint and do the whole door, you'll hardly notice it was ever there."

"Eventually," she said. "I thought I'd drive them a bit, see if I want to keep both of 'em or not."

Reuben Styles agreed this was a prudent course.

"How much do I owe you?"

He blinked and smiled. He had a lot of large, healthy-looking teeth. "All paid up, Miss Dickenson. Billed the estate by the quarter. This quarter's on me, encourage you to do business with me."

She laughed. "Why, thank you. That's very nice of you."

"My pleasure."

She watched the Q-tip-shaped rear lights of the decrepit Dodge leaving the yard with a pang of nostalgia for it. It had carted her around long enough for her to be attached. She surveyed her two new vehicles, another part of Uncle Joe's estate. He'd left it all to Gussie, who had promptly turned toes up and left it all to Pearl. At times, she felt a little disoriented, as if she had won a state lottery. More and more, as she took possession, it all felt natural, as if she were a piece of puzzle that had fallen to the floor, only to be searched for, found, and put in her proper place with a flourish.

Uncle Joe, whom she had never once met, seemed to be still a presence here. She touched his logo on the truck's door. JOE NEVERS/CARETAKER. Some vocation, Uncle Ghost, she thought. Taking care. Skinny old white man, keeping the back of beyond tidy and safe. What do you think about having a black woman living in your house, driving your wheels, hugging herself in your driveway? You having a laugh of your own in that boneyard?

4

Sunday was fair, cool from the rain, a beautiful day. She did some driving around in both vehicles and was satisfied with Reuben Styles's maintenance. On her return, she found a Post-it note stuck to the back door, offering her book on the sedan, what she had hoped to get out of it and not a penny more.

On Monday morning, she headed down Route Five for a mile-and-some-odd and pulled into the gravel lot of Needham's Diner. It was an L-shaped single-story building with a two-story facade like something out of an old oater, with a loading bay at the rear. It hadn't seen a coat of paint in too many years, the windows were too dirty to see through, and the steps were springy with rot.

Inside it was dim and warm, thick with the smell of hot overused grease, coffee, and cigarette smoke. A line of stools at a thirty-foot length of L-shaped counter was fully occupied by workingmen, most of them substantial, at least in the beam. The stools had seen hard use and needed cleaning but didn't seem to be having any trouble supporting, in several instances, considerable meat.

She paused to let her eyes accustom themselves to the difference between bright sunlight and interior gloom. There was a beer and soda cooler along one wall, a newsstand rack, heavily stocked with glossy skin magazines sealed in plastic, and an assortment of fly-blown dry goods on rusty shelves. Pearl helped herself from an open bale of Portland dailies next to the newsstand. When she turned around, a heavy man in green workclothes was dismounting from one of the counter stools, his coffee mug clutched in one hand.

"Siddown here, ma'am," he said, "I'm just slurpin' up my coffee. Some of us," speaking to the room at large, "can't hold down one of these stools all day. Some of us has to work for a livin'."

The line of men at the counter gave up a rumble of amusement from behind coffee cups, cigarettes, the grinding of heavy jaws.

"Don't sweat too hard, Sonny," one of them said. "Two much air pollution already. Leave some of them trees standin', will ya?"

This witticism received a louder round of laughter.

"Thank you," Pearl said to him.

Sonny knocked back the rest of his coffee and slid the cup onto the counter.

" 'Welcome, ma'am," he said with a shy smile.

"Watch it, Sonny," the wit remarked. "You swore you was all done with good-looking women after Heidi booted you out."

Pearl slid onto the stool amid snortings and guffawing.

Sonny leaned past her to drop money onto the counter.

"Don't mind them, ma'am. They're a buncha ignorant shitkickers."

He exited, with heavy dignity, to hoots and catcalls.

Scrambling eggs and spilling pancake batter onto the gas grill was the sour man who had accompanied Walter McKenzie to her grandmother's interment. Sweating freely, he wore a strappy T-shirt that emphasized his hollow chest and draped the round little gut. Military service was implied in his tarnished white brush cut, made explicit by the tattoo of the Navy Seal on his right bicep. Ash dripped from the end of the cigarette cliff-hanging on his lower lip.

Assisting him behind the counter was an extravagantly nubile young girl in tight blue jeans. A black T-shirt hammocked her unrestrained breasts.

Hooeee. Granny Dickenson would have taken one look at her and said, "Years ago, we'da married that one off quick." Her coloring, the ponytailed blond curls, the face so like young Sam Styles's but feminized into beauty, declared that she must be also a Styles. Sam's sister, Reuben Styles's daughter.

It was mildly surprising that the men at the counter were so well-behaved toward her. Surely teasing and ribbing were to be expected from an all-male audience in the presence of a female this hot. She could see they were looking, every chance they got, but otherwise treated the girl with almost exaggerated politeness. The men called her Karen, said thank-you to her a lot. Perhaps the thought of Reuben Styles's wrath kept them in line. Poor man. Pearl, for one, was intensely grateful that the girl was not *her* daughter.

The girl was good at her job, Pearl noted approvingly, kept the coffee cups filled, delivered the right plates to the right customers. Karen thunked a mug down in front of Pearl and filled it.

"What'll you have?"

Pearl glanced up at the slotted menu board high on the wall over the counter.

"The Lumberjack."

Karen nodded, handed a slip to the cook, and continued her serving.

Pearl watched the cook closely. No wasted motion. He had been at this business awhile. The potatoes he was frying were processed frozen cubes, the bread was mass-produced white. She wondered which his war had been, World War II or Korea; he would have had his twenty in by Vietnam. She found the coffee strong but quite acceptable, the eggs a bit damp, the toast too tasteless to trouble eating, the sausage cheap and greasy, mostly filler under a camouflage of chili and paprika. The pancakes were a greasy spoon-grade mix bought and sold by the fifty pound. The prices posted on the menu board were more than competitive but it was a bare-bones operation. Paper napkins, jelly in little packets, the flimsiest Styrofoam cups for the takeout, and the owner dripping sweat onto the grill. No tables, no table service. After watching a stoolmate dunking a doughnut, she asked for one, was surprised to find it tasty with cinnamon, nutmeg, and vanilla light but unmistakable, with a heavy-cake density she had never before encountered. She could get to like Yankee doughnuts.

Pearl looked up to find Karen's gaze on her. The girl smiled. The population on the stools shifted, there were some women now, and a steady trade in takeout coffee and pastries.

Pearl made way for another customer.

5

Coming back at midmorning, she found the cook alone, doing the tidying-up in the lull between breakfast and lunch. He looked at her speculatively.

"Coffee," she said.

He poured it from a pot she was sure from the smell had been sitting there half-finished since the end of his breakfast rush.

"Are you the owner?" she asked.

He laughed harshly. "Yup."

"Mr. Needham?"

He nodded. "The one and only."

"You lookin' for a buyer?"

He stared at her. There was an incredulous gleam in his eye, as if after years of lusting after the town librarian, he had been offered a blow-job among the periodicals. It was as good as a look at his accounts.

"Just about give it away, you want the truth. I'm so sicka the smell of eggs I like to puke."

She nodded.

"Lunch-counter business'll wear a body down."

"You think you're up to it?" he challenged her.

"Yes, sir."

He looked her up and down.

"You're young and rugged, I guess."

"What do you want for the place? Maybe we can do business."

He nodded and poured himself a cup of coffee. He took a pencil out of a cup near the register and turned over a paper bag to work some figures. A few minutes later he grunted and shoved the bag her way.

"This is what I do a week."

He tapped one figure with the eraser end of the pencil.

"This is the expenses. This is what I figure I got to have."

Pearl studied the figures.

"Fifty-five. That seems high. What about the liquor license?"

"I included it in the expenses." He scrawled another number on the bag. "That's how much."

"I don't want it. It's worthless to me."

He stared at her and tapped the pencil on the paper.

"Honey, you're crazy."

"Don't call me honey," she said. "My name's Pearl Dickenson."

A mirthless grin stretched the man's mouth, revealing his military teeth.

"Miss Dickenson. Gussie's granddaughter. Beg your pardon."

It was as patently insincere an apology as she had ever received.

"I won't pay for a liquor license," she said. "Won't pay for something I'm not going to use."

He threw down the pencil.

"You're asking me to throw away the thing that costs me the most and brings in the most cash. I can't sell it to somebody else like a pop cooler."

"Sorry," she said.

"Well, the hell with ya," he snarled. "What's your problem, you some kind of Temperance Christer?"

"You've run the place down to next-door-to-a-dump. It isn't worth twelve. I'll give you twenty thousand, lock, stock, and barrel."

"To hell with ya," Needham shouted. "This place ain't for sale. Not to you, it ain't."

Pearl smiled.

"Cash. You change your mind, you know where I am. My phone will be in tomorrow, you can get the number from directory assistance."

As the screen door slapped shut behind her, she heard him complain loudly, "S'pose I'm s'pposed to wipe my ass with my frigging liquor license."

6

She stopped at Styles's garage.

Reuben looked up from the desk in the office and leaned over to flick on the pumps.

She jumped out and had the nozzle in the intake before he reached the island.

"I'll be happy to do that for you," he said.

She laughed and accepted the rag he offered her to wipe her hands on.

"Little petroleum never hurt anybody. Could you recommend some people? I need a roofer, a carpenter, an electrician, and a plumber."

"Sure. You won't check the oil or the tires or wipe the windshield or anything while I go back and get some cards for you, will you?"

She promised she wouldn't. She leaned against the truck and watched him come and go. He hadn't gotten any smaller since the last time she'd seen him. Karen must have gotten her stature from her mother, as she was on the small side, except for those centerfold knockers.

He came back with a small fan of business cards.

She took them and he finished gassing the truck.

She showed him a card.

"How do you say this guy's name, the plumber?"

He grinned.

"Onesime Rossignol. French name. We call him Rossie for short. He won't cheat you too bad."

She hooted.

"What kind of recommendation is that?"

"Yankee."

She laughed.

"Thanks."

" 'Welcome," he said.

He took her money.

"Thank you, Miss Dickenson. I'll bring around the paperwork on the sedan and a check."

She hung on the Eagle's door a second. "You have a daughter working at Needham's Diner?"

"Karen."

"She works hard. She's good at it."

"Glad to hear it."

He looked into some middle distance.

"The boys were easier, somehow. Frankie, my oldest, he wasn't any trouble, just didn't know what to do with himself. Been in the navy a year and seems fine. Sam's a good kid."

"I'm not a parent," Pearl said. "Looks like hard work to me."

Reuben nodded.

"Sometimes."

Just what she thought. That little girl was trouble in tight jeans, all right. There wasn't any sign of her mother giving any help reining in the kid. Reuben's wife must be a sack of marshmallows.

Karen was a good little waitress. She'd keep her on to start, assuming the girl wanted to stay on the job. The old man was probably paying under the minimum wage, from the figures on his paper bag. Must have been asleep during the sermon that mentioned the laborer is worthy of her hire. But if there was any trouble, the very first trouble, out the door, and sorry, Reuben, but that's how it is. Too bad Granny Dickenson wasn't around to get the girl married off quick.

THREE

1

When the telephone man left, Pearl hooked up the answering machine to the one in the kitchen, taped a brand-new message, and inserted the tape, which she regarded as the equivalent of the silver card plate by the Victorian front door.

"'Miss Dickenson,'' she announced to herself, "is now at home, after wintering in Monte Carlo.''

With a tall glass of iced tea and a stack of postcards picturing views of the White Mountains as seen from the Ridge, she settled down on the daybed on the sun porch to notify her friends and relatives of her new telephone number. Looking at her address book, she was suddenly struck with the thought it was a kind of time machine: each of the names in it was a doorway of memory to a time and a place she had left behind her. Well, she was thirty-five, approaching middle age; she supposed an occasional attack of nostalgia was only to be expected, along with the first white hairs.

It was dark when the phone rang for the first time.

"I got to have fifty and that's final," Roscoe Needham said without preamble.

"No," said Pearl. "The new roof, the flooring, the siding and paint will cost me twelve thousand if I'm lucky and the sills don't turn out to be rotten."

She had, in fact, checked the sills with a penknife during her Sunday-afternoon reconnaissance and knew them to be sound.

There was a strangled roar at Needham's end of the line before he slammed down the receiver.

With a soft laugh, Pearl flicked on the answering machine, drew herself a soaking bath in the pleasantly deep old-fashioned tub upstairs. As she settled into water fragrant with almond bath oil, the phone rang once and the machine cut in. She smiled. Squeezing her sponge down her back, she moaned and groaned and generally carried on with the simple physical luxury of hot water and scent.

He rang again at six the next morning. Pearl was sitting at the kitchen table in her kimono, her hands around a mug of coffee.

"I've got to have forty-nine," he said. "What the hell do you think I'm going to live on the rest of my life, I let it go to you for chicken feed?"

"The Social Security and military pension you've been double-dipping for fifteen years," she retorted, "and the savings you've taken out of the business at the expense of maintenance."

"By the Jesus," Needham shouted, "if you think I'm a sick old man you can jew out of his life savings, you got another think coming, lady."

She waited for him to settle into breathing hard.

"Mr. Needham, all you've got to sell is location, your central location in the village. It just happens there's a service station standing empty two miles south on Route Five I could turn into a crackerjack diner for ten thousand less than I'd have to put into yours. You don't want me to do that, because I'm a better cook than you are. You'll be feeding my overspill in three weeks. From my point of view, ten thousand bucks is a lot to pay for location."

She listened to the old man's angry wheezing. The pause while he thought it over was encouraging, at least to her.

"Bullshit," he finally countered. "You'll never make a go of it. People around here won't eat grits and black-eyed peas or any of that Southern coon food."

She laughed.

"Mr. Needham, I don't let anybody's bigotry or bad manners stand in my way. Believe me, on my worst day I'm a better cook than you are on your best. The customers will come to me."

The phone came crashing down on a volley of curses.

"You're nothing if not consistent," she said to the dial tone without rancor. "Foul-mouthed old shit."

She was still moving in, spreading herself around in the house, taking possession in her own time. She wanted to savor this, the first house she had ever owned all by herself. Her vision of the diner and the changes she would make in it were detailed and immediate. But she felt little need to alter very much about the house. She had decided to do no more than thin out the furnishings, shift the odd piece slightly, salt her own few possessions among Uncle Ghost's. Wallpaper, curtains, new appliances could wait upon later reflection, when she had lived in the house awhile. It was certainly adequate as it stood for a single person of undemanding tastes. The worn, even frowsty, upholstery of the parlor pieces, the plain, faded curtains, the threadbare hooked and braided rugs were homely in the original sense of the word.

Today she had set herself the pleasurable task of culling his books, to make room for some of her own in the bookcases in the parlor and bedroom. Uncle Ghost had had a taste for sleazy, rather datedly lurid novels about sexual high jinks in small towns, or perhaps they were his last wife's and he had never bothered to give them the heave. She had remembered *Peyton Place,* which had been back in print very recently to commemorate its original publication, but she had forgotten *Tobbaco Road* and *God's Little Acre,* books her stepfather had kept on the highest bookshelf in his study, out of (he thought) her notice but not quite out of her reach. There were plenty of westerns and thrillers and the entire *oeuvre* of Alistair MacLean but relatively few hardcovers. Uncle Ghost had obviously been a man who had thriftily waited for the paperback. The acquisition of several Michener epics and Travis McGee mysteries by John D. MacDonald in hardcover must have come by way of the Christmas tree and, indeed, when she opened the covers, she found inscriptions to Joe in Gussie's hand, dated one Christmas or another. As she handled the books, she was struck by how badly the paperbacks were aging. Brittle, crumbling, the ecru-colored pulp pages escaped their glued bindings and floated free to the floor as she picked them up. The cheap inks of their covers were blurred with fingerprints, the pages dog-eared. Those that fell apart most easily and sadly bespoke frequent handling, likely Uncle Ghost's favorites. She was gentle with them, setting aside the Travis McGees to keep.

In the mid-evening, the phone produced the insipid computerized ring that the new electronic phones all had, every single one of them, so half the time you couldn't tell if it was your phone or one on the tube that was summoning you. She marked her place in *The Lonely Silver Rain* and trotted to the kitchen to turn off the answering machine before it could start its mechanical routine.

"I won't let it go to you for less than forty-five, and that's without the fixtures," she said.

She laughed softly.

"My final offer is thirty-five. Ten thousand dollars is too much to pay for location and a liquor license I don't want. The stock's negotiable. Most of yours is worthless anyway. I'll keep what I want and you can haul the trash off and keep or sell what you can. I imagine you could unload that pancake mix on the county jail. Jails aren't too particular what they feed the inmates."

She held the phone away from her ear while he swore. He quieted down in a couple of minutes and then there was the scratch of his match and the air-suck of his cigarette igniting.

"You're crazy," he said. "I might as well give the place away as sell it for that kind of money."

"That's what you'll have to do if I buy that service station. I'll be talking to the guy who owns it tomorrow at nine. Good night, Mr. Needham." She hung up gently and put on the recorder.

"Now we're talking," she said to herself, and went back to Travis Magee.

The phone rang at five-forty-five A.M. She was waiting for it.

"I'll sell you half of it," Needham said, "for thirty thousand. You waste your money fancying the place up and run it. I'll retire, get out from under your feet, and you give me half your take for as long as I live. If you fail, I'll get your half back, before all your creditors, and I won't be responsible for any of your debts. If you make a go of it, I'll leave you the other half in my will. I ain't got anybody I care to reward for neglecting me, so I jist as soon dispose of my remaining half interest to you or the Salvation Army or I don't give a shit."

Pearl was glad he couldn't see her face. The old coot must have stayed up all night thinking out his offer.

"No."

"Well, the hell with ya then."

2

His resistance tickled her. The last offer was ridiculous. She wasn't going to support the old goat for the rest of his natural span, which could easily be another twenty years. But it was interesting that he was thinking in terms of barter. She put a good night's sleep between them and dropped into the diner around ten.

"Git outta here," he said, plugging a cigarette into the corner of his mouth. "We got nothing to talk about and I don't care for the look of your face."

Astonished at the seemingly unprovoked display of spleen, Karen nearly dropped a stack of plates.

"Coffee," Pearl said to her, "please."

Karen looked at the old man for some signal of what to do.

He blew smoke angrily. "Give her the goddamn coffee. She'll prob'ly have the govamint down on me for refusing service to a nigger."

The girl blanched. But she managed to pour the coffee, though a little sloppily.

Pearl gave him a long, calm look and then laughed.

"Mr. Needham, you sure are a tough nut."

It must have been the right thing to say. After a thoughtful silence of his own, Roscoe Needham laughed too, further astonishing Karen. He waved his cigarette in Pearl's direction.

"This high-riding bimbo wants to buy the place," he announced to Karen. "What do you think about that? 'Course she wants it for nothing, and she ain't"—he beetled his brows at Pearl—"gonna get it."

Karen turned a dazed stare from Needham to Pearl.

Pearl nodded confirmation.

"Well, there," Pearl said. "We're making progress. I've gone from nigger to bimbo in less than five minutes."

She threw the racial epithet back into his face coolly and deliberately to show him it had no power to inflame or intimidate her.

Cod-eyed, he stared at her a few seconds and then chortled cockily.

"Gimme a cup of coffee," he ordered Karen. "Then go on. I'll see you at eleven-thirty."

Somehow it was not surprising he had the girl on a split shift. Probably stole her tips from her when she wasn't looking.

He hooked his head toward the end of the counter. "Miss Dickenson, come on around and I'll give you the ten-cent tour. You don't understand what good shape this place is in." A grand seigneurial wave took in the shelves of dry goods. "Used to have tables, then I couldn't get any women to wait on 'em."

"Karen's a hard worker," Pearl said.

"Aye. Don't look as if she'd be good for anything but starting fights, does she? Surprised the hell out of me. And she *is* a hellion. Has been since her mother and father broke up. She's grayed Reuben's hair some, I'll tell ya. But I told her I didn't want no fracases in here and to meet her boyfriends out in the parking lot. Couldn't get her to wear a bra, though."

Interesting as all this was, it wasn't getting them anyplace.

"You buy this cooler new or used?" Pearl prodded him.

She could see the scars of at least two moves in the fixture's enamel.

"Practically new," he lied.

They went over the place with the attention to the same detail but at cross-purposes. Pearl's eye was turned as for compromising evidence of a crime, while Needham's effort was to divert her. They returned to the counter, where he refilled her mug and his and lit up a butt from the coals of his last. He offered her one. She shook her head. He waited expectantly.

"Mr. Needham, I'll tell you what I'll do."

His eyes glittered.

"I'll give you thirty thousand."

His thin shoulders started to tighten up.

"Cash. Not my personal check, a cashier's check. That's as far as any bank is involved, because I'm not taking a mortgage. Transfer of deed, the necessary fees, that's it."

He froze. The glitter in his eye confirmed what Pearl had suspected: here was a dedicated tax cheat.

"You keep that beer cooler. You ought to be able to resell for a nice little piece of cash. And," she added, "I'll feed you two meals a day for the rest of your life, or as long as I own the diner, which I intend to do for at least as long as you're likely to live. Call it twenty-five years."

He started to open his mouth.

She held up a cautionary palm. "Just think about it a minute. You'll never have to cook breakfast or lunch again, all you'll have to do is come in here and sit down."

His head sank upon his knotted knuckles.

"Why not three squares a day?"

"I don't intend to do a supper trade. Breakfast and lunch only. I'm willing to go to work when the sun rises but I won't let the sun set without trying to see it. It's against my religion to let the day go by without noticing it, Mr. Needham."

He snorted incredulously.

"You'll never make a living without selling dinner too."

She smiled at him and the disbelief drained out of his face. He squinted, as if to help himself think.

"You're a deep one. I dunno," he went on slowly. "I dunno. It don't seem like enough."

"Tell you what. You think about it. I'll come to your house and cook you supper tonight and you can let me know tomorrow, after you've had time to digest."

His thin lips stretched over his nicotine-stained false teeth in a rictus of a smile as he tumbled, Pearl guessed, to the realization that at the very least he would be getting a free meal out of her. He slapped a palm onto the counter.

"Well, I dunno what's wrong with that."

"What time and where?" she asked.

"Eight-thirty. I won't be shut of this place until then. I'll write down the directions. Women can't follow directions unless they're writ down."

He hauled out a paper bag and laboriously recorded the way to his home.

"Never mind the telephone number in case you get lost. You get lost, the hell with you."

And she thought *I know a trick or two, too, old man.*

3

Making notes on his paper bag of mileage and features she could count on after dark as she made her way, she drove directly there. The way to his ramshackle farmhouse was by a maze of back roads that one would almost need to be born in the town to navigate with any confidence in daylight, never mind at night. Thoroughly testing the shocks of Uncle Ghost's Eagle, she did more silent swearing than she had done since her single encounter with her Aunt Fran over her grandmother's body. Seemingly more by chance than with any real comprehension of how she had gotten there, at last she rolled into Roscoe Needham's yard.

Trash was littered like nuggets in a gold field, awaiting only the serendipitous find that would set off the Rush. Broken-down automobiles of amazing vintage rusted like crashed spaceships among saplings and shrubs as the woods crowded in. A big old lilac spurting air roots like a wall of thorns was greening by the back porch. The barn, looking like an ark turned turtle, its roofbeam become the broken keel, had fallen down and Needham had not bothered to clear away the remains. Sheds and ells sagged, roof and wall, trying to break away from the main body of the house. It didn't look as if Roscoe Needham had put his hard-earned gelt into this place either.

More than likely he had buried rolls of cash in mayonnaise bottles all over the yard or possibly papered the walls of the parlor with it. In the shade of the lilac a very old, nearly toothless collie was chained to the porch rail. The dog staggered to its feet and attempted a growl that turned into a yawn, as if he had forgotten before he opened his jaws what he was doing. Then he lay down and panted at the effort. Pearl paused long enough to make his acquaintance. The poor beast was pathetically grateful for a scratch under the chin.

Finding her way back after dark was almost the adventure the day trip had been. She had several sweaty moments when she was sure she had gone wrong. But she managed, somehow, to arrive only seven minutes late.

With the ancient collie at his feet, Roscoe Needham was sitting on the back porch in the dirty light of a naked bulb hanging from the porch ceiling. He had put on a frayed plaid wool shirt over his strappy undershirt. He didn't rise to greet her but the collie did, with enormous effort, scrabbling down the steps. Needham reluctantly pushed himself out of his chair.

"See ya found the place," he muttered, banging open the screen door for her.

She finished a quick scratch of greeting under the old mutt's chin and stepped into the Needham abode.

"That's Jack," Needham said. "He's older'n I am."

She laughed and put down her string bag with her groceries in it. Roscoe Needham appeared to be the sort of ex-military man who went to the other extreme in civilian life. The kitchen was so full of accumulated junk, there was hardly a place to stand. A glance took in heaps of brittle old newspapers, paper sacks filled to overflowing with discarded beer cans and bottles, dirty boots and shoes, dirty dishes, and a cat box next to a huge oil range. With relief, she saw she was not going to have to cook on that; there was also a small, though appallingly filthy, gas range. She wrinkled her nose at the strong smell of over-be-shat cat box. And nicotine soup. In convenient places around the room were several rusty coffee cans in which old cigarette butts were marinating in water. She counted five full-grown cats prowling various surfaces, obviously princes of the kitchen. If there was a Board of Health in Nodd's Ridge, someone should tell them about this dump. With a sigh, she took an apron out of her handbag and rolled up her sleeves.

"Wanta beer?" Needham offered.

"Sure."

He took two cans of Pabst out of an old fridge and handed one to her.

She popped the tab and had a long, cool swallow. It took away some of the gritty smell of the room.

"So you ain't a Baptist dry after all," Needham observed.

She shook her head. "Just don't care for the trouble of selling the stuff. I'd have to keep a baseball bat under the counter to handle the ugly drunks. It doesn't seem worth the aggravation."

He nodded. He was a man who understood about setting limits on aggravation. He took his own beer to the kitchen table to do the heavy looking-on.

Firmly strangling the little voice inside that was shrieking, "Oh my God, the *germs*!", Pearl pushed enough clutter out of the way to make space to work. Was the diner this dirty where no one could see?

Behind her, the rasp of a wooden match informed her Needham was lighting up.

Opening cupboards, she extracted various pots and pans, dishes and utensils.

Needham cleared his throat. "I heerd you inherited from Joe by way of Gussie. So how come Gussie Nevers left you all a his and all a hers? Thought Gussie had four or five grandchildren to spread it around amongst."

She could tell him to mind his own business, but on the other hand, it would give him some gossip to retail to the village. He would feel beholden to her. She stopped to sip her beer.

"That's right, I have four cousins. They're all my Aunt Fran's children. Aunt Fran married a wealthy man and her kids all went to Ivy League schools and are making money as fast as the government can print it."

Needham chuckled, sharing her amusement at how some people get born with bank accounts and others have to open and try to fill their own.

She poured peanut oil into a battered old stock pot and lit the gas with a little snap.

"I went to college too, but it was on my own stick. I worked my way through the University of Colorado. That's where I learned to speak Northern."

He guffawed.

"That ain't North, that's West."

"Well," Pearl said, "I guess I mean not-Southern. It's all relative, isn't it? To the people in Quebec, Maine is South, right?"

Relativity was not a concept that interested Roscoe Needham, who was the unshakable center of his own world. Nor did he give a shit about the goddamn Canadians. He had led his life without giving the slightest thought to Quebec or any other Canadian province and saw no good reason to start now.

"I noticed you don't talk like a Southerner, nor one of them Northern nig . . ."—he backed and filled—". . . Nigras from Detroit or someplace like that. I knew a lot of Nigras when I was in the Navy and some of 'em I could understand right away and some of 'em I *never* did catch on, but there were crackers I couldn't make head nor tail of, too."

No doubt he had picked up the use of "Nigra" from the rednecks in the Navy. She offered him a piece of celery.

He looked at it warily, then shook his head.

She bit a chunk off the stalk and chewed it thoughtfully, then went back to chopping.

"I'm not properly a Southerner. People in Florida don't think they're part of the South, you know, except when they're watching *Smokey and the Bandit*. I was born in Key West. I'm a Conch, is what I am."

"I'll be goddamned," the old man said, on a crest of excitement. "I was stationed in Key West from 1950 to 1952."

Pearl grinned at him.

"That so? Well, we overlapped, then. But I was still in diapers when you left."

"How about that?" Needham marveled. "The world sure is small."

This discovery so amazed Needham that he sat there for several minutes repeating *How about that?* to himself, in wonder.

A little later when she had things cooking, Pearl picked up her story.

"Anyway, my grandmother took ill about two years ago. I went to live with her in D.C., to take care of her. I guess she appreciated it enough so she decided to leave everything to me."

"Fair enough," Needham said. "Smart thing for you to do, too."

Pearl didn't look up.

In a deliberately neutral tone she said, "I would have taken care of her for nothing. As far as I was concerned, I was. I didn't know she left anything to me until after she died."

"Oh." Needham shifted in his chair, discomfited by Pearl's sincerity. He looked a bit shamefaced.

"Well, I ain't saying you just did it to get in her will. I s'spose I'm just always amazed when anybody treats one of us old goats decent.

Hell, I knew Gussie when she was a girl. She was always a nice woman. She deserved to have somebody to look after her."

"Thanks," Pearl said.

"Well," he said, now anxious to get away from that subject, "I didn't think anybody'd be crazy enough to swap Key West for Maine."

"How come you're not in Key West, you think it's so great?"

He shifted uneasily, took a swig of beer.

"Well, it don't matter. I fetched up where I belonged, I guess."

"Maybe that's what's happening to me. Maybe I'm fetching up here because this is the right place for me."

He nodded.

"Anyway, there's lots of places in Key West where the food would make you think you were in heaven. But here, Nodd's Ridge, right now there's my kitchen and yours, tonight. You sell me the diner, then there'll be Pearl's."

He laughed out loud with her.

"I'll tell you, lady," he said. "I'm beginning to think I'd like to see you try."

A while later he said, "You say you went to college. You get one of them food-service degrees?"

She shook her head.

"No. I've got a Master of Library Science."

Needham grunted.

"Didn't know there was no science in running liberries."

He shook his head.

"And now you want a diner? You ever run one before?"

"Yes. My stepfather had a place in Key West. He was a small businessman, sold some real estate, and over the years picked up a few places as investments. He had two apartment houses, a small motel, for coloreds, of course, a launderette, and this diner. For years, he had a friend of his, from when he was in the service, yeah, Navy"—she looked up from her cooking to share the laugh with him—"this guy named Dick Halloran, run the diner in the winter. Dick used to work summers in a resort in Colorado. Summers in Key West, nobody came there back then, except diehard fishermen and drunks like Hemingway, maybe there's no difference, huh?"

Again they laughed together.

"Well, I worked around the place from the time I was nine, bussing up, you know? and then I learned to waitress, and the winter I was a freshman in high school, Dick taught me to cook."

She tasted the batter she was making, and kissed off the tip of her finger.

"God, could that man cook!"

She grinned at Needham, who was absolutely rapt, and she realized how lonely the old goat was, really lonely.

"Why, if he'd been white, the restaurants in New York would have offered him a fortune."

She pointed a spoon at him.

"Dick was a lovely man, too, always had a couple of girlfriends, had a taste for fast women, strippers and dancers and scat singers. He used to bring 'em by the morning after for coffee. My God, some of those women were beautiful. Anyway, Dick taught me the business and the next winter he told Dad he didn't need him anymore, I could run the place myself, and I did, right through college. Paid for both degrees. Dick's dead now; I still can't help keeping an eye out for him to breeze in, come December, ready to feed up the customers and chase those fast women."

"How come you ain't running it now?" Needham demanded.

"Well, I had those degrees and I loved the work. My stepdad had his own children to look out for too," she said. "He turned the place over to his oldest son. Seemed more than fair to me."

"You ain't worried you forgot how, with all that fancy education?"

"I dream about it," she said. "Fry chicken in my dreams."

He chuckled in wonder. "Dream about it, huh?"

4

He didn't say word one, just hunched there and ate, chewing up cornbread and coleslaw and piece after piece of fried chicken, grunting once in a while like a dog with his muzzle in the dish. She stopped being the least bit anxious when he went for the second drumstick. At last he pushed back his chair and belched.

Pearl got up and flicked on the coffeemaker she had all set to brew, and took his plate.

He took a toothpick from a glassful on the table and started poking at his gums.

"You gonna sell fried chicken?" he asked.

She nodded.

"That's the best I've had since I was last south of the Mason-Dixon Line."

She smiled. "Got room for pie?"

"You bet."

She unwrapped it and after she served him, she sat down with him.

"Tell the truth," he said, "I ain't et this well in years."

"Well, think about it."

Putting down his fork, he gazed regretfully at his plate and then peeked at her a little shyly.

"I 'pologize about calling you a nigger. I guess I had a hair across my . . . my butt."

"Mr. Needham," she said, "I don't concern myself with the motes in other people's eyes, only with the beam in mine own."

"I knew you was some kind of Baptist."

She laughed.

"No. I'm not any kind of anything. I'm just me, Pearl Dickenson."

He nodded. "That sounds like something Joe Nevers woulda said. Is it okay if I say you're a hell of a cook?"

"Yes. It is."

They sat on the back porch awhile and listened to old Jack wheezing.

"Look," he said, "I ain't so sure I'm ready to sit here and rot, you understand?"

She reached down to scratch old Jack's chin. The collie slobbered gratefully over her hand.

"S'spose you'd ever need an extra hand?"

She laughed.

"When don't you, in a diner?"

"I don't want to work *regular*," he emphasized. "Like to go fishing, ya know. What you said about seeing the day go by without noticing. I think I'd like to notice some before they cart me off."

"No argument from me."

"Good," he said. "Good. You say the cooler's mine?"

They got down to the hard bargaining.

5

At a quarter to six the next morning, the helmetless long-haired rider of a Honda Shadow, with Karen Styles riding pillion, her arms wrapped tight around his leather-jacketed chest, rode into the diner's parking lot. The back of the biker's jacket bore the legend BRI in silvery studs. The bike passed across the gravel with a grating, edgy noise.

The girl hopped off, the handsome rider grabbed her arm, and the two fell into a passionate kiss while the bike idled. At last the girl broke away and started across the lot toward the diner. Grinning and puffed up with possession, the rider watched her. Her forward motion pulled her long, disheveled hair away from her face and back over her shoulders. But the girl's brisk stride slowed as she approached the diner, and she went up the three steps to the door almost hesitantly. She turned to beckon the rider, who rode the bike over and squinted at the hand-lettered sign tacked to it.

CLOSED TODAY, it read.

"Christ," he said. "Do you suppose the old bastard kicked it or something?"

Karen shook her head, her cheeks reddening with anger.

"How the hell am I supposed to know? Somebody coulda called and told me something."

The rider grinned.

"If you'd been at your dad's last night to take the call."

The girl turned on him.

"You shut your mouth, Bri."

"What'd I say?" he asked. "What the fuck I say?"

She stuck her hands in her armpits and hunched up as if somebody had rabbit-punched her in the stomach.

"Don't you understand this might mean I'm out of a job? How the hell am I gonna be able to afford the trailer?"

Bri was silent for a moment.

Karen started to rock to and fro. A tear escaped the inner corner of one eye and started to track down her cheek.

"So you'll have to live at home awhile longer, it won't kill ya," he said. "Hasn't slowed you down any lately."

"It'll be like being in jail."

"Look, you want him to get off your back, he wants you to promise not to see me, promise it. You don't have to keep it. He can't watch you all the time. He hasn't got any right to tell you what to do."

"The court'll make me go live with my mother and the Preacher," she said. "All he has to do is say he can't handle me."

Bri shrugged.

"Hey, stupid. He won't do that."

Karen swung out wildly at him.

"Don't call me stupid," she shrieked.

"Bitch." He drew back out of her range and revved the bike. "I don't need this shit." He roared away.

The girl watched him go. Her hands went back to her armpits and she hunched over again.

"Oh, oh, oh," she moaned, "you goddamn old bastard, Roscoe. You better not be dead. I want that trailer. If you're dead, I hope you *are* dead. You and my mother and that goddamn Preacher."

FOUR

1

With an almost visible cloud over her head, Karen Styles trudged along the side of the road. An empty pulp truck passed her; she recognized Sonny Lunt driving it. He waved at her cheerfully. Carefully he swung his rig well into the middle of the road to give her a wide berth. She watched him pass. In a minute he would be standing at the diner's door, scratching his head in puzzlement.

Once he was gone, though, the quiet was striking. A woodpecker in the woods beyond the ditch nailed a tree. She was walking uphill, a long steep rise of the road. The gravel margin was hard to walk on, the big stones making their edges and points known even through the thick crepe soles of her sneakers. Slipping fluidly out from under her, the finer stuff was like beach sand, and the more she struggled to dig into it, the harder the going went, making her ankles roll. Insect buzz became loud; she had attracted a horsefly and suddenly there were minges all around her.

"Shit," she said, "shit, shit," her voice rising higher with each expletive, until she actually screamed the last one and sticky tears washed her face.

At the height of the storm of weeping, her father's Chevy Suburban appeared over the crest. She wiped at the moisture on her face, all the more frantically because she knew it was useless; there would still be traces and he would know anyway from her red and swollen eyes. The weeps gave way to rising anger at him for blundering along in her moment of weakness.

He met her glare with his usual wildly provoking calm, made a U-turn, and fetched up beside her. He leaned over and popped the door.

She crossed her arms and refused to look at him.

"Get in," he said, smiling at her.

"Go to hell."

The smile faded. "I've got a message for you, kitten."

"So? And don't call me kitten."

"Roscoe called last night to say you shouldn't come in until eight. He's not going to open for business today; he wants to do an inventory."

"Great. I could have slept another hour and a half."

"I waited up to give you the message."

She blushed furiously.

"Listened all night for you to shinny up the maple tree and climb in the bathroom window. Be quieter if you just used the door."

Her lower lip pouted out and went trembly, her eyes filling up again with tears that were still ready to spill. She blinked rapidly.

"Come on," he said, "I'm hungry. I haven't eaten breakfast yet."

She climbed in and sat as far from him as she could get, tight up against the door.

"Why's Roscoe want to do an inventory?"

Reuben took his time.

"Storekeepers usually do an inventory when they're going to sell their businesses. I imagine Roscoe's thinking about selling."

Karen sat up and knuckled one fist into the other palm.

"The old bastard. He said he wasn't going to sell to her, but he is. He's selling the diner to Pearl Dickenson!"

He smiled.

"I thought maybe. She asked me about contractors the other day. At first I just thought she's remodeling the house. Then I heard she was asking about second-hand booths at Linscott's in Greenspark. Made me wonder."

Karen rolled her head against the back of the seat.

"She'll keep me on, I'm pretty sure."

Reuben nodded.

"Daddy, I'm moving out. There's a trailer for rent on the Pigeon Hill Road."

He sighed.

"If you wait four months, you'll be seventeen, and you'll save me a lot of aggravation."

Karen crossed her arms and looked out the window.

"I knew you'd say no. I'm going to anyway."

"Karen, as soon as your mother finds out, she'll complain to the court that I've lost control of you, which"—he gave her a grave look—"I have, and I'll have to pay for the lawyer to go in and say you're practically at your legal majority so you should be allowed to do what you want. Your mother will make a scene, and Sam will stop talking for a couple of weeks. Please, Karen. Surely you understand by now that what you do has a lot of effect on the rest of us. If you don't care whether you hurt me, please think about Sam. You know he goes all to pieces when we have one of these family wars."

She chewed at her lower lip and blinked away a fresh onslaught of tears.

"I don't give a shit if Mom has a shit-fit or what it costs you for a lawyer, and if you're so goddamn worried about Sam, you shoulda kept Mom away from that frigging Preacher to begin with. Anyway, it's my life. I'm sorry about Sam. He'd be better off leaving home too."

Reuben took his eyes from the road long enough for a quick glance.

"Four months, Karen. You can't put up with another four months for Sam? Look, you're out all night most nights and nobody says boo to you about it. You only come home to change your clothes and run a wash, anyway. You better shower before you go to work today, you smell like an ashtray full of marijuana."

"Jesus Christ, get off my back," she snarled. "It's better than smelling like Texaco Sunlite."

"Gasoline's legal," he said. "When your mother makes her complaint, I won't defend. Maybe you'd be better off living with her. She can't do worse than I have."

"I won't!" Karen shouted. "I won't live with them!"

They had arrived home. Reuben slowed and turned and let the Chevy roll along the driveway.

"I don't want Sam to hear shouting. Get a grip on yourself, Karen. You want to be treated as a grown-up. Fine. The first thing you'll have to do is grow up. Your actions are going to have consequences and you will have to live with them. But I warn you, I will do anything I have to do to minimize the damage to Sam."

She stared at the house, not seeing it, blinking back tears but refusing to look at him.

"Come on," he said. "Let's eat some breakfast."

In the kitchen, Sam looked up from the sports page.

" 'Home is the sailor, home from the sea, and the horny from the pillion of a Honda Shadow.' "

Karen slammed through the kitchen.

"Shut up, you big shit."

"Got your period?" Sam yelled after her, his voice heavy with mock sympathy. "That should be a relief."

"That's enough."

Reuben put the teakettle on.

"She didn't come home last night, did she? Never mind, don't answer."

Reuben eyed the front page but pushed the paper away a little distastefully, as if it were fish going over.

"You'll be late for school, you don't go soon."

"Yeah. I'll do the brake linings in that Buick after school, if you want."

"No, I'll have time to do them. Roscoe's apparently going to sell the diner."

Sam looked up from the newspaper.

"No shit."

"I'm getting tired of 'shit this' and 'shit that' from you and Karen."

"Sorry. I'll watch it but I can't do anything about Hotpants."

Reuben cleared his throat.

"It appears Miss Dickenson is Roscoe's buyer."

Sam sat up straight.

"No sh—" he started to say, and hastily amended it. "Really? Wow!"

He grinned.

"I can see I'm going to develop the habit of eating breakfast at the diner."

"Just so long as you get to school on time," Reuben warned, but he was grinning too.

2

The diner's front door was locked when Karen came back, but Roscoe, on the other side of the window, gestured to her to go around to the service bay. Inside all the lights were on and the old man and Pearl Dickenson were already grubby. Pearl had her hair tied up in a bright cotton scarf and Karen was fascinated at how exotic it made her look, like something right out of the *National Geographic* or a James Bond movie set in Jamaica or Rio.

"Look what the cat dragged in," Roscoe said.

Pearl just smiled in a distracted way. She stooped and poked her pencil deep into the back of a shelf.

"Mouse droppings!"

"The hell you say."

He shoved a pen and a lined steno notebook at Karen.

"You write down everything behind the counter and how many or how much of it. Can you work all day?"

"Sure," Karen answered.

It might just make up for today's lost tips. She was thinking of the trailer on which she had already put down a cash deposit.

"How bad a mouse problem do you have, Mr. Needham?"

Pearl seemed momentarily to tower over the old man but it was really only Needham cringing.

"That little bit a poop?" he scoffed unconvincingly. "That ain't nothin'."

It crossed Karen's mind that she could pay the old bastard back for all his abuse and his cheating of her by telling Pearl Dickenson exactly what a rest home for field mice the place was. Common sense came to the fore; it was in her best interest to have the place change hands, as long as she went with it.

"Miss Dickenson, Mr. Needham . . ."

"What is it?" the old man rasped irritably.

"What about me?"

"What about ya? I ain't your father, thank the living Jesus. You can shit or go blind, I don't care. Ask Pearl. Places's gonna be hers, not mine."

"Is there gonna be a job for me?" Karen asked her.

"I can't do this on my own, Karen. It would be a pleasure to have you on board."

Karen hugged herself. "Thanks, thanks a million."

Pearl made a moue of distaste and thrust her pencil in the general direction of the recently discovered mouse droppings. "This place'll have to be scrubbed top to bottom. Then we'll set some traps. I'm not serving any uninvited furry little guests at my table."

3

Walter McKenzie stopped at Reuben's pumps. He had his tank filled by the time the mechanic was able to slide out from under the Buick.

"Reuben, you know what that Dickenson woman is doing?"

"Buying Needham's Diner."

Walter was deflated.

"You prob'ly heard from Karen."

Reuben nodded, taking Walter's money.

Walter was not one to linger over a disappointment.

"I never thought Roscoe would retire."

"Me either."

"More things change," Walter observed inappropriately, "the more they stay the same."

Reuben patted the old man's shoulder.

"How's Jean?"

"Oh, she's fine. I keep trying to get her to go out more but she always has something she's got to do at the house. She ought a get married again, I told her so myself. I said Jean, you oughta get married again, young woman like you, but she come back, what would I do without her? and I say same as I did for all them years when she was married to Nighswander, but she don't hear me."

Walter peered slyly at Reuben.

"Now, when are you going to settle down again? A young man like you oughta have a wife. Why, you got time to have some more kids."

Reuben laughed. The old man's matchmaking was outrageous. There was a stretch of thirteen years between Jean and himself; she had been his sister Ilene's classmate. And Jean looked twenty years older. She was a dim, sad, empty potato sack of a woman who was frightened, almost literally, of her own shadow.

Diplomatically, he made response only to Walter's last remark.

"Still got my hands full with the ones I've got."

"Sam's no trouble, is he? Hard worker. You oughta tell Karen to wear a brassiere, though."

He pronounced it "bra-zeer."

"She's too big on top to be bouncing around in one of them thin shirts. I see her riding around on a motorbike with that Spearin boy. That's Paul Spearin's boy, Brian, ain't it? The one got the dishonorable discharge. He needs a taking-down, that one. If she was my daughter, I think I'd show that one the open end of a shotgun and tell him the Cannucks is still taking draft dodgers."

Reuben listened patiently. He repressed the impulse to tell the old man that getting a brassiere on a teenage girl who doesn't want to wear one isn't the same thing as pinning a kid's mittens to her sleeves.

"Kids don't listen too much to what their parents tell them."

Walter nodded vigorously.

"That's true, that's too true. I told Jean she ought not marry Nighswander but she did, to her sorrow."

Reuben suspected that there was more wishful thinking than accurate history in this assertion about Walter's daughter's unfortunate second marriage. It was generally held to have been a marriage of convenience. Jean had been a penniless widow with a feebleminded son, and Nighswander the widower of a suicide, who had needed, apparently, a housekeeper and a bedmate.

"Well"—Walter rubbed his hands together—"I expect that Dickenson woman can cook."

"Why's that?" Reuben asked, remembering that Sam had expressed a similar belief.

"Well, she's colored."

Reuben laughed.

"Aren't you afraid it'll be chitlins and you won't care for it?"

Walter laughed too.

"Nope. She's been living with Gussie, she must know how to cook white." As Reuben marveled at this deduction, the old man added, from the depths of his wide experience as a man of the world, "Besides, woman with that much ya-know oo-la-la couldn't be a bad cook. One goes with t'other."

Every time Reuben thought of the conversation with Walter all day long, he had to laugh again. Sam heard him break out into bellows of laughter from under the Buick. Several times, Sam asked his father what was so funny, but Reuben just shook his head and laughed some more. Sam did make out his father muttering "that much oo-la-la" several times, just before another outbreak. It cheered Sam to hear his father laughing; it meant his little twitch of a sister hadn't completely succeeded in ruining Reuben's day.

4

Pearl Dickenson stopped by the station as Reuben was locking up.

"Just leaving, Miss Dickenson," he said, approaching the truck with his keys in his hand. "Did you need gas?"

She had already slipped out of the cab and leaned against the truck's door. She shook her head.

"No. I just wanted a word or two. And call me Pearl."

"Pearl."

She grinned.

"Karen told you yet I'm buying Needham's Diner?"

"No. I haven't seen Karen since this morning. She doesn't tell me much anyway. But I guessed."

"Well. I'd like to keep her on."

"Good."

"She'll be working six to three-thirty, six days a week, at least through the summer."

He nodded.

Pearl hesitated.

"Did you know Needham's only been paying her three dollars an hour?"

"Yes. I did."

"Is paying under minimum wage common practice around here?"

"Well," Reuben said carefully, "it isn't unknown."

"Excuse me saying so, but I'm surprised you'd consent to the arrangement."

He met her gaze levelly.

"Frankly, I thought Karen needed to find out what kind of jobs are available for a high-school dropout."

Pearl started out of her slouch against the truck.

"What? Karen dropped out of school?"

"Quit right after Christmas."

Pearl whistled softly through her front teeth.

"I'm sorry to hear it. I thought she was nineteen, anyway."

"She'll be seventeen in September."

Pearl shook her head disbelievingly.

"She's only sixteen? What possessed her to do that? I mean, she strikes me as a bright girl."

"Mixed-up is what they call it, isn't it? I let her because I thought a dose of the hard old world would cure her. I guess"—he looked at the pavement—"I was wrong."

"Look. I'm on your side. I'll do my best to encourage her to go back to school, even if I lose my right hand. I promise you."

Reuben nodded.

"Another thing, I was really looking forward to a garden. I'd thought I'd have all this time to put it in because it would take me a while to find the right place for the diner. Now everything's falling into place too quickly and I've got too much to do. The garden really should be tilled now and I don't have time to do it myself. I hate to ask Walter McKenzie."

"No trouble, I'll do it or have my boy do it. Give you the bargain price since you've got your own tiller attachment for that mower. Walter will probably be relieved not to have to try to do it. The old-timers always figure it's a person's absolute right to award a job to suit themself. It'll save his pride not to have to tell you he isn't up to it."

"It's just," she said, biting her lip in a way that Reuben wouldn't have minded watching her do awhile longer, "I don't know what to say to him."

"Tell him Sam asked for the job. Walter'll just laugh. He's only out twenty bucks and a chance at a stroke."

"Okay. That's a relief."

"Don't worry about planting, you can't put anything in the ground here without cover much before June fifteenth."

"Ooo, this is North, isn't it?" She smacked her forehead lightly with her palm. "Lord, I'm stupid. You'd think I hadn't lived in the foothills of the Rockies for six years. I ought to have taken the altitude into consideration."

Reuben smiled.

"The Ridge isn't Denver but it's uphill from the Atlantic."

"What about the cool-weather stuff, peas and spinach?"

"You can plant them but you'll have to cover them. If a late frost doesn't get them, you'll have a salad bar for the bunnies and chucks."

"Bunnies?"

"Big white ones with pink eyes and big teeth."

His face was perfectly straight.

"You'd be surprised. Been so many people had domestic rabbits get loose, the wild ones around here are all interbred with fancy city-bred."

She laughed. If it was a leg-pull, it was innocent enough. She climbed back into the truck.

He closed the door after her. One big hand closed over the edge of the open window.

"Thanks. About Karen, I mean."

"No trouble," she said, and then realized she had adopted not only his formula but also his accent. "No"—she smiled—"no trouble."

He laughed and waved at her as she left.

5

When Pearl arrived home the next day, the sun had set without her notice. The garden had been tilled and the air smelled of open earth. There was a damp newspaper-wrapped parcel on the stoop and a Post-it note stuck to the back door. FIDDLEHEADS, it read in neat printing. ALL WASHED. COOK THE SAME AS ASPARAGUS. GOOD HOT OR COLD. REUBEN STYLES.

She opened it on the sideboard. When the damp newspaper was spread open like the petals of some night-blooming exotic, she found a mess of deep green curlicues. The smell was swampy, much stronger than asparagus. Photographs of the Yankee delicacy was as close as she had previously come to them. She bit into one. The taste was as pungently swampy as the smell, ferny but more strongly so than asparagus. The crisp texture made the domesticated fern seem bland and slick in memory. She dumped them immediately into a pot and steamed them a few minutes, then ate them, plain, right out of the very pot. Then she made a note on the chalkboard she had installed on the kitchen wall, next to the phone. CORNBREAD FOR R.S.

6

Passing papers was unusually fast and easy because Pearl wasn't taking a mortgage. Roscoe Needham crowed to his customers that it went "like shit through a goose." He had reopened for business as usual as soon as they had completed the inventory, which had taken them a day and a half. The diner buzzed continually with discussion of the change.

Pearl and Karen could be seen through the windows every night after Roscoe had closed, hard at work cleaning the place. It was noted that Karen had taken to tying a scarf around her head à la Pearl.

Days, Pearl was on the run, attending to the paperwork, meeting contractors, mapping out suppliers, obtaining a temporary victualer's license. She made several forays to neighboring towns to inspect second-hand equipment of one kind or another and was successful in obtaining a second deep-fat fryer for chicken but not in locating the booths she wanted to install. In short order, she had acquired a local reputation as a hardheaded but scrupulous bargainer. It was said of her that she worked as hard as a man, harder than most. Everyone knew, mostly through Roscoe, who had never before had anything quite so entertaining going on right in front of him day after day, that Pearl intended taking over and running the counter trade under, inside, and on top of all her planned repairs to the building.

On Memorial Day, at six o'clock in the morning, in the middle of a steady drizzle, Pearl stuck a new neon-look sign in the front window. The glass was the cleanest it had been since its original installation. The lettering clearly and unmistakably read PEARL'S. Roscoe solemnly shook her hand, held up the keys for a last smug look at them, and dropped them into her palm. Karen clapped. Pearl did a brief joyous dance while Karen clapped harder and cheered and Roscoe laughed. Outside, Sonny Lunt peered into the window and made desperate coffee-drinking motions. Pearl reached over and flipped the cardboard sign in the door's window from CLOSED to OPEN and flicked back the snub on the lock.

When that first day's work was done, she had something to do. She went straight home, pulled on galoshes, and went into the graveyard. Gussie's grave had settled a bit. The sods were beginning to blend into the rest of the green. Pearl checked the potted geranium she had left on the grave. The soil was thoroughly soaked, the plant giving off the musky scent of its green leaves. She had a satisfying sniff at it and arranged some stones under it so it would drain properly.

Colors at the periphery of her vision drew her attention to the tokens on other graves. She wandered from stone to stone, examining them. People had left everything seasonable and imaginable. The lilacs and pussywillows on Edith Styles's marker, the spray of red roses and the sheaf of lilies on Victoria Christopher's were typical. The petals were beaded with the rain. The perfume was heady. The big rosebush was thick with white blossoms. She turned to look at the mountains, through tattered veils of mist and rain. The dead had the best view in town.

7

There was a steady business based on curiosity the first couple of days, and after that it was just word of mouth: if you ain't et there yet, you've missed something. It took a while for people to get used to the place not being open for supper, but Pearl stuck to the three-thirty closing.

Roscoe was there more than he was not, eating heartily and basking in his indolence. But when he showed up the first Sunday to work, he was edgy.

Understandably nervous about working for her, Pearl thought.

He tied on his apron and then fell to hunting for something.

"If you're looking for a coffee can to use for an ashtray," she said, "I threw them all out. You can use a real ashtray on your break."

His mouth fell open and he stared at her.

"You can't smoke while you're working."

His jaw snapped up and his eyes smoldered. "The fuck you say," he snarled. He tore off his apron, threw it at her, and stalked out.

She reached for the phone. His reaction didn't surprise her. Karen had already said she would give up her Sunday if Roscoe put his back up about the new rule.

Karen arrived fifteen minutes later.

"Thanks," Pearl said.

"No trouble."

Pearl repressed a giggle at the sudden flash of Reuben in Karen's face and voice.

After she closed up, she went to see Roscoe.

He was sitting on his back porch, with Jack at his feet.

Pearl crouched to scratch Jack's chin.

"Look, Roscoe, I know it's tough for you to give up being the boss and doing just what you please. When you were in the Navy, you lived with more demanding rules than this one, I know you did. Maybe you decided you didn't want any more rules. If you did, maybe I'm here on a fool's errand. But I think you're a reasonable man, a little hotheaded maybe, I can understand. I'm a little hotheaded myself. You might as well know, I'm not going to give in about it. But I'd really like to have your help. You're a rock and I'm a hard place. So what are we going to do about it?"

Rocking steadily, he heard her out. His mouth worked and his eyes glittered. "Nothing. Nothing. You do what you want and I do what I want. I ain't lived seventy years to be told what to do by some smart bimbo."

She gave Jack a final pat and stood up.

"Okay, Roscoe. I'll see you at breakfast."

Roscoe had only just begun to fight. He showed up the next morning with his chin out.

"This tastes like shit," he said loudly, and shoved his plate across the counter so hard it went over the other edge and shattered.

Karen, at the other end of the counter, jumped a foot.

"You miserable old shit," she muttered.

Customers exchanged looks.

Pearl looked calmly up from the grill.

"Sorry you didn't care for it, Mr. Needham. Would you like another of the same?"

"Goddamn right."

A few minutes later, Pearl put the plate down in front of him.

He tasted it and spat it out.

Silently Pearl removed the plate.

Sonny Lunt had been watching.

"Something stinks around here."

He stood up and lumbered up to where Roscoe was sitting. He sniffed the air.

"Just what I thought."

Gently he patted Roscoe's shoulder.

"Fuck off, Sonny," Roscoe said.

Sonny shook his head.

"That's no way to talk with ladies present, Roscoe."

Sorrowfully Sonny picked the old man up. Roscoe thrashed out at him and swore, but Sonny had him firmly caught. Sonny carried Roscoe outside and gently put him down. Roscoe screamed and ranted. Sonny turned his back on him and came back inside the diner.

"He's pretty riled up," he told Pearl.

"Pearl forbade him to smoke when he was working and took away all those filthy old coffee cans," Karen said.

Sonny paused to scratch his head.

"He's a pretty old dog to learn new tricks, Miss Dickenson."

"I know," she said, "but I can't serve my customers an old dog's cigarette ashes."

The customers present nodded and agreed this was so.

Roscoe slammed back in.

"I ain't had my breakfast. You owe me my breakfast, you nigger bitch."

Suddenly the diner was completely silent.

Sonny Lunt stood up again.

Pearl put down her spatula and wiped her hands.

"I'm afraid you'll have to leave, Mr. Needham."

Sonny nodded and picked up Roscoe again, wrapping his arm around the old man from behind.

"She's right. You're outta line, Roscoe. You can't be saying something like that to Miss Dickenson."

Roscoe swore and kicked but Sonny removed him anyway. He carried Roscoe to his truck and heaved him inside.

"Go home," Sonny said. "Don't come back until you can show some manners."

"You ain't got no right to take me outta my own place," Roscoe screamed at him.

"It ain't yours anymore. You took the money, old man. Now shut the fuck up and be a man."

Roscoe flinched as if Sonny had hit him. Tears began to run down his face. He fumbled for his keys. It took him a while to find them and insert one in the ignition. The old truck itself protested going.

Finally it turned over, and Roscoe drove away slowly, his face still glistening with tears.

Sonny sat back down at the counter and resumed eating his breakfast.

"Don't fret about him," he said calmly. "He's tougher than one of his own pancakes. You're right, you know, Miss Dickenson. I've et my share of his cigarette butts and they don't add a thing to the flavor. He oughta be ashamed, talking to you like that."

FIVE

1

One afternoon in the middle of the second week, Pearl found herself returning home with no errands to run, nothing to pick up in Greenspark. She had finally looked at every second-hand booth in a twenty-five-mile radius. It was the first time in a month she was going to be able to notice the day passing.

Walter McKenzie was mowing the grass on the riding mower. He swayed a bit too much making a turn and she looked closer as she passed. Under his raggedy straw hat his face was slack and pallid. He looked as if he might be going to faint.

Pearl went into the house, poured a glass of iced tea for the old man, and hurried back out again.

He had stopped the mower and was just sitting there, weakly fanning himself with the hat. What remained of his hair was plastered to his skull by sweat, running over his face in rivulets. He was wheezing noticeably.

"Why, ain't you nice?" he said, his voice as shaky as the hand he held out for the glass.

She was afraid to let go of it completely and kept her palm underneath it while he drank. She managed to catch a bit of what he dribbled out the sides of his mouth with a hankie plucked hastily from her jeans pocket.

"You look beat. You'd better stop."

He wiped his brow with the back of his arm. He seemed just a little less shaky and she was glad she had paused to load the tea with sugar.

"Tell you the truth, miss, I'm afraid I ain't up to this anymore."

He had to take breaths in between the words.

Pearl held on to his arm.

"You'd better come in the house and lie down, Mr. McKenzie."

He allowed himself to lean on her as he dismounted the mower.

"You want me to call the doctor?"

He shook his head.

"No, no. I'll jest rest a minute in the shade over there," waving the hat vaguely at the nearest tree.

She helped him the few yards to the shade of the oak and sat down on the grass next to him until he had drunk up the tea and his color and breathing improved.

"Sun got to me, miss. Didn't mean to alarm you."

He heaved himself more or less vertical, not being too proud to accept her helping arm again.

"Are you sure you're okay?"

"Oh, sure. But I guess you ought a get somebody else to cut the grass. I hate to let you down but I guess I can't take the sun anymore. Reuben's boy'll do a good job."

His voice gained strength as he put some distance between the admission of his own weakness and the problem at hand.

"I'm sure he will. Sure you wouldn't like to come inside and rest awhile?"

"Nope. I'll jest go along and put my feet up at home. Sit on the porch until the sun's down."

"You do that."

He struggled a bit more than usual climbing into his Jeep, causing her fresh alarm, but he did make it into the driver's seat, took a minute to rest, and then drove slowly away.

She watched him go, wondering if she had been right to let him try to get himself home. Well, he was old because he was tough, that's what Reuben Styles had said, and probably Reuben was right. But of course nobody was tough forever, which was why there was a graveyard next door.

She took her own iced tea and flopped down on the fresh-cut grass just outside the sun porch. The sun-warmed air was thick as perfume with the scent of the fresh-cut grass. She was physically very tired indeed and more wound up than she liked to admit to herself. The old man's spell had provoked a violent surge of adrenaline in her and now it had ebbed away and she felt drained. She lay back on the grass. The luxuriant, wonderful green-grass smell whirled around in her head. She felt herself drifting.

2

The angry roar of the mower starting woke her violently and she sat bolt upright. The sun was setting luridly. Reuben Styles looked up from the mower's ignition and waved, rather distantly, she thought.

Her mouth felt wet and she realized she had drooled a little in her sleep. Her iced tea had fallen over and wet a patch of her blouse.

"Shit," she muttered, jumping up and hurrying into the house.

Freshened with a shower and change of clothes, she peeked out the window and saw Reuben was cutting the last few yards of grass. She ran downstairs and stuck her head out the door of the sun porch.

He had dismounted and was cleaning the blades, a man who left his tools clean, even when they were somebody else's.

"Iced tea?"

He looked up and nodded, then turned back to the work.

She brought the iced tea out and sat on the front steps while he finished with the mower. He sat down next to her.

"Walter stopped and told me he'd had a spell."

"He scared me."

"He's getting on. Happens to us all."

Pearl nodded.

"Thanks for finishing for him. It could have waited. I didn't expect—"

Reuben held up a hand.

"No trouble."

The light was going fast.

There was a longish pause and then Reuben said, "Sam rushed over here to do the job. He came back all tongue-tied. He found you sleeping on the grass and, well, he's shy."

"Oh."

She didn't know what to say. It was a bit comical but she knew Reuben hadn't told her to make fun of the boy. He was telling her to be careful of the boy's feelings and modesty, she supposed.

"I'm sorry. I didn't mean to embarrass him. I just fell asleep."

"No big deal. Fifteen is an awkward age. Women are a big mystery he wants to solve." Reuben laughed ruefully. "More luck to him. But it's intimidating to him too. I'm not saying this very well."

"No, no," she assured him.

He stood up, between her and the faint light remaining in the sky. She was struck by how damn big the man was.

"Anyway, Walter said he was going to tell you he couldn't do the caretaking anymore. He was only looking out for the place because Joe died so suddenly and somebody had to do it and the lawyer asked him. You planning on being here, you don't really need anybody checking all the time, but if you'd like a regular check when you're away, or help with the groundswork or maintenance, be no trouble for Sam and me to take care of you. Last couple of years, we've gradually taken over most of his and Joe Nevers' old jobs anyway. Keeps us during the winter."

"Must keep you busy. Why don't you have a sign on your truck, like Uncle Joe did?"

He shrugged.

"Waiting for Walter to officially retire. I don't want anyone thinking I'm in competition with him."

"Real kind of you, I'm sure. Either I let this front field go to hay or have some help, or else I'll do nothing all summer but ride that mower."

"I'll drop off our schedule of rates. Thanks for the iced tea, and the cornbread and chicken last night."

"No trouble."

She laughed.

And so did he.

"Good night, now."

She sat listening to the croakers after he had gone, thinking Sam had come by his shyness honestly. Nor was it much of a surprise to discover that Reuben Styles and his son had quietly, almost secretly taken up her Uncle Ghost's business. She had overheard enough remarks to know that soft-spoken and shy or not, Reuben Styles cast a long and respected shadow in this little bitty town, no trouble at all.

3

Reuben stopped at the diner Saturday morning around ten. Except for the sign in the window, the place looked no different from the outside but was so clean inside he had to blink. The old shelving was gone, piled up on the loading bay under a tarp, and the beer cooler too, leaving more than half the diner empty. The senescent linoleum, its pattern worn to a ghost, had been torn up, exposing the old pine floor Reuben had last seen twenty-five years earlier when the building had been transmuted from a small grocery store to Needham's Diner. One of Reuben's earliest part-time jobs had been laying the dust on that floor in Partridge's Store with used oil. Now the disturbance to the floor had released a faint scent of the old oil. Brand-new lineoleum was rolled up at the far side, awaiting installation.

The offerings on the letterboard menu were different, the prices up, but not unreasonably so, especially if you had ever tasted Roscoe Needham's cooking and then Pearl's. A few customers lingered over their papers and coffee at the counter. The biggest surprise was that Walter McKenzie and Jean were among them.

"Hi Walter." Reuben patted the old man's shoulder lightly. "Jean."

Jean blushed. It was not what she did best but she did it often.

Walter looked up from what for him must be the first brunch of his very long life and grinned.

"Best biscuit," he enthused, "I've had in a month a Sundays."

"I told Dad," Jean blurted, "we oughta have a treat. Everybody says the food's so good here."

"Thanks." Pearl looked up from cleaning the grill.

She gave Reuben a big smile and he went a little dry in the mouth and hoped he wasn't blushing the way Jean did, all the time and over everything.

Karen came out of the storeroom with an open carton of Maxwell House coffee. His daughter, whose lovely face had not given him anything but severe weather warnings for months, actually beamed upon him.

The pleasure on Reuben's face at being greeted by his daughter with something besides anger was a sudden revelation to Pearl of why he never came into the diner: he didn't want Karen to think he was checking up on her.

"Isn't it incredible? You should have seen the paper towels we cleaned the windows with, Dad. And the light fixtures, there was a pound of flyspeck on every one of them."

Pearl laughed.

"Was there?"

Pearl confirmed it.

"At least."

"Want a cup of tea, Dad?" Karen asked.

Pearl's eyebrows ticked up and she caught Reuben's eye.

He wrinkled his nose with interest.

"Is that rhubarb pie I smell?"

Pearl displayed it with a flourish.

"Ruby Parks's recipe. She swapped it for my key lime pie."

"Rhubub? I want some of that," Walter said.

"Dad," cried Jean. "You know rhubub goes right through you."

"I don't care. I want some rhubub pie."

"How you feeling, Walter?" Reuben asked.

"Full a piss 'n' vinegar."

"Dad," Jean protested weakly.

"Tell you what," Reuben told Pearl, "Sam's waiting for me to bring him a treat. Could you wrap up a couple pieces?"

"Sure."

The door darkened briefly as Reuben exited. A man in dark glasses coming in stepped aside to let the big man pass.

"Hello, Reuben."

Reuben stopped to shake hands.

"David, you gormless whelp of the devil. Nice to see you back."

"Nice to be back. You ever going to get your growth?"

Reuben laughed. "Don't you know it's hard work and a blameless life?"

"I believe you, Reuben, but don't carry it too far. The world's scaled for lazy sinners like me."

"That explains why you've got all the money and I do all the work."

The two men laughed. But as if he had been reminded he had work to do, Reuben patted the other man's shoulder and went on his way.

The newcomer stepped inside. As he entered, he swapped his

sunglasses for a pair of dark-rimmed clear prescription lenses. That accomplished, he came to a sudden full stop.

"Jesus," he said. "The Board of Health finally catch Roscoe pissing in the coffee?"

Walter McKenzie guffawed delightedly.

"David, you young cuss. How'd you get through the state-police barricade we throwed up to keep you outta town?"

The man called David shook the old man's hand and sat down next to him on the other side from Jean.

"I know ways in that you've forgotten," he said.

The old man snickered some more.

"Karen," the young man continued, "are you still here breaking hearts and zippers?"

"You'll have to mind your manners now, David, this is a nice place. Meet Pearl Dickenson, the new owner."

Pearl wiped her hands on her apron and reached over the counter.

"David Christopher," Karen said. "He likes to provoke people. Don't pay any attention to him, he leaves big tips."

"How do you do?"

David Christopher held her hand a fraction of a second longer than he needed and frankly studied her face.

"Better every second. What storm washed you to this odd little island? Don't answer that, it was nosy of me. Somebody'll tell me before the day is out."

"Joe Nevers left her his property," Walter said, "and she jewed Roscoe Needham out a this diner."

"Dad!"

"See?" David Christopher was contented.

Pearl smiled and waggled a mug in his direction.

He nodded. "Please."

"What'll you have?"

"Number Three. And a bran muffin."

Jean plucked at the old caretaker's sleeve.

"Time to go, Dad."

Wheezing, Walter hitched himself off the stool.

"G'bye David. Did I tell you I'm retiring now? You'll have to get Joe Nevers to look after your place for you."

Jean looked apologetically over the old man's shoulder.

"He means Reuben," she confided.

"Boy, Walter's getting soft." Karen leaned on her elbows on the counter.

"He seems to have failed a bit," David Christopher agreed.

"Dad's doing all his jobs now."

"What's Roscoe doing?"

"Pissing and moaning."

" 'The more things change, the more they stay the same,' " he quoted. "What'd you use on the place, a fire hose?"

"Just about. Guess what?" Karen asked him brightly.

"What?"

"I quit school."

"You ninny. I'm so disgusted I'd like to paddle you."

"Screw it. I wasn't doing anything but killing time."

"Somebody dropped you on your head. You're going to wind up divorced with two kids by the time you're nineteen."

"Up yours. What do you take me for, an idiot?"

"Yes. Your father should give you a whaling."

"My father's screwed up his own life; he hasn't got any right to tell me what to do."

David Christopher stared at her and shuddered.

"God spare me parenthood."

"Amen, brother."

Pearl put his plate down in front of him.

"Karen, that dishwasher wants unloading."

David Christopher tasted his eggs carefully and waggled his eyebrows at her in approval.

Pearl poured herself a cup and pulled up a stool on the other side of the counter.

"You've been coming to Nodd's Ridge awhile?"

"All my life. Can't seem not to come."

"Fatal attraction."

"Maybe."

He ate heartily.

Karen, passing, caught his eye again.

"Karen, if you don't start wearing a bra you're going to be able to swing those tits of yours over your shoulders and tie 'em in the back."

Karen waggled her tail at him mockingly.

"It's the fresh air," he speculated, "or the water or something. The girls up here don't have tits, they have udders."

"I don't notice you averting your eyes."

He winked at her.

"Self-defense. Just looking out I don't get punched in the eye with one of them."

When he was done, he wiped his plate clean with a piece of toast.

"Wonders never cease. I never thought I'd eat a meal in here and like it. Have they voted to change the name of the town after you?"

Pearl laughed.

David Christopher leaned back lazily and admired her as frankly as he looked over Karen.

"Do that again."

"What?"

"Laugh."

Karen came out of the storeroom.

"What a line."

David counted out his money and laid it down. "You could take a lesson from Miss Dickenson in deportment, you silly cow. She's a grown woman of subtle and exotic charm."

"Get him."

"You"—he reached over the counter and chucked Karen's chin—"are a generic teenage sexpot of surpassing obviousness."

"Brat," Karen said disgustedly to his back.

"Now you've got the idea."

He smiled brilliantly from the door and was gone.

The diner was suddenly quiet, empty of customers.

Karen leaned on the counter, staring after him.

"Isn't he the most beautiful man you've ever seen?"

Pearl smiled. "Well, yes, now that you mention it."

"You know what he is?" Karen was incredulous at the waste. "He's a poet."

"No. You don't say."

"He's a lot older than me. He's got to be thirty if he's a day."

Pearl turned away, fighting the giggles.

4

Roscoe Needham was splayed in a ratty hammock on his back porch. Reuben shook him into a vague consciousness.

"Lemme alone," Roscoe muttered.

"Roscoe, you don't wake up, I'm going to pour a bucket over your head. I might anyway, you're drawing flies."

Roscoe groaned and fell out of the hammock.

Reuben helped him up.

The old man mumbled a steady stream of curses as Reuben propelled him into the house. The bathroom stank almost as badly as Roscoe, who stood weaving over the toilet. His hand shook violently as he searched in his flies for his penis and while he held it. Most of the wavering stream of piss wound up on his well-holed socks.

"Whew."

Reuben opened the window and flicked on the shower in the metal stall.

"Come on, Roscoe."

Still dribbling pee down the front of his trousers, Roscoe attempted to leave the bathroom. Reuben picked him up and shoved him into the shower, still clothed.

Roscoe erupted in violent cursing.

"Take off your clothes and pass them to me."

This took a lot of effort. Reuben got soaked helping Roscoe with his buttons. He found a garbage bag and put the wet clothes in it while the old man finished washing.

"You better have some good reason for busting in here and treating me like this," Roscoe said as he dried himself with a ragged piece of toweling.

"There's a nukular war on and the President's waiting for you to go to his bunker with him."

"Ha fucking ha."

Roscoe was shivering.

Reuben found some shorts for him.

"Sonny Lunt told me you called Pearl Dickenson a nigger bitch and he had to throw you out of her place."

"*Her* place," Roscoe shrieked.

"Her place. You owe the lady an apology, Roscoe."

"So what."

"So you can't go apologize to her smelling like you've been on a three-day binge."

"The hell you say. I ain't apologizing to her."

Reuben sighed. "You want me to button those shorts for you?"

"No. Gimme some pants."

Reuben watched him struggle into a clean pair of pants.

"So Pearl Dickenson doesn't want you to drip any more cigarette ash into the eggs. You ought to be grateful you got away with it for so long. There's nothing wrong with your willpower. You can stand ninety minutes at a time without a butt, can't you? Whole town's laughing at you, Roscoe. Want them to stop laughing, you're going to have to act like a grown-up and stop whining."

Roscoe stared at Reuben.

"I don't care who laughs at me, fuck 'em."

Reuben leaned against a cluttered highboy, crossed his arms, and laughed.

"Hear me laughing, you old fool. I'm laughing because you're drinking yourself to death to spite Pearl Dickenson. That'll teach her to be mean to you."

Roscoe's chin trembled. Suddenly he sat down on his bed and put his head in his hands.

Reuben went and got him some aspirin.

Roscoe swallowed the pills with some effort and drank some water.

"I guess I've been an asshole. I get drinking, Reuben, I don't think straight."

Reuben patted his shoulder.

"I know. All the years I've known you, you've had that rotten temper. You waste an awful lot of energy on being angry, Roscoe."

Roscoe nodded.

"Do I have to 'pologize to Pearl in front of everybody?"

Reuben laughed.

"Call her on the phone. She's a real fine woman, Roscoe. She'll take it however it's given."

5

That second June Sunday didn't so much happen as it exploded. It seemed as if Pearl flipped the CLOSED sign to OPEN and the lock snub up and everybody in the world decided to have breakfast and buy their Sunday newspaper at Pearl's, every last soul at the same time. As inspiring as the sound of money jangling into the till was, there were moments when she was almost literally juggling plates in the air. The first occasion she had a chance to catch her breath, it was past one.

The screen door slammed shut behind the last straggling customer.

Lighting up his first cigarette in ninety minutes, Roscoe Needham said, "Praise be to Sonny Jesus. This is how every jezzly Sunday'll be until after Labor Day. The geese is laying golden eggs."

"Glad you were here," Pearl told him. "I couldn't have done it by myself."

Slumping onto a stool on the other side of the counter, he exposed most of his gums in a rictus of a grin.

"Guess I ain't forgot everything I ever learned."

Pearl took a small notebook from her back pocket and made a few hasty notes.

"The muffins really went. I could have a lot more backup in the freezer."

She opened the fridge and ducked down to check the level of the orange juice left in the pitchers on the bottom shelf.

"Here comes Golden Boy."

Roscoe was far more interested in who was coming in than in how many more dozens of blueberry, corn, and bran muffins ought to be on hand or the quantity of orange juice ready to be poured.

At the sight of Roscoe at the counter, David Christopher halted on the threshold.

"Shit."

"Is that any way for a collidge graduit to talk?" Roscoe demanded.

Pearl straightened up and closed the refrigerator door.

"Good morning, Mr. Christopher. Are you any relation to that butler who used to deliver the checks for John Bearsfoot Tipton?"

He laughed.

"My favorite show. Fantastic plot device, wasn't it?"

He stepped as daintily as a cat around the splayed plastic wrapping that had once contained *Boston Globe*s and *Portland Sunday Telegrams*, now littered with torn scraps of newsprint.

"Papers all gone, I see. Glorious summertime. I forgot how quickly they go."

Pearl reached under the counter, hauled out a copy of the Portland paper, and dropped it in front of him.

"All the conveniences of McDonald's. It's a little dog-eared but Roscoe managed to keep 'em from sneaking off with the sports section."

"Thank you kindly."

He exchanged his sunglasses for a clear pair of lenses and shook out the front page.

"I'll have more next week," she promised. "Could have sold another two dozen this morning."

"Going to carry the Sunday *New York Times*?"

"So many people asking for it, I guess I should. You want one?"

"No. I just like to watch the civil wars over it."

Roscoe snickered.

Pearl raised her eyebrows in question.

"Really," David explained. "Perfectly civilized upper-middle-class people will tear them right out of each other's hands. Most of the stores around here won't handle the *Times* anymore because of the battles."

Roscoe confirmed it.

" 'S true. I seen folks bin next-door neighbors for twenty-five, thirty years stop speaking to each other over who got the last copy of the geedee *New York Times*. You'd think there was treasure maps in 'em. Maybe them summer people ought a go to church Sundays instead of reading papers. Nothin' but lies in the papers anyway."

"Spoken like the devout Christian you are, Roscoe," David applauded. "I know there's a poem in the Sunday *New York Times* wars but I haven't been able to get it out. I keep thinking a fresh outbreak of hostilities will turn the trick for me."

Roscoe cackled and sucked lustily on his cigarette, then flicked it into a coffee cup and stood up to begin clearing the counter.

David nodded in his direction.

"What's he doing here? Almost ruined my appetite seeing Roscoe dripping cigarette ash into the dirty dishes when I thought he was now a fabulous chapter in the culinary history of Nodd's Ridge."

"Working," Pearl answered, "so Karen can have Sundays off. What about you?"

"Breakfast. I don't need a job, thanks."

Roscoe sniggered. "Don't mention work around David. He don't know what it is."

"People have been trying to keep it from me for years," David confided.

Roscoe retreated to unload his dishpan into the dishwasher.

David stirred his coffee lazily and watched Pearl turn his eggs deftly.

"Nice of you to give Karen Sunday off, but you must know it's a futile exercise in liberality. Future Divorced-Cocktail-Waitresses-with-Two-Kids of America don't waste their Sunday mornings in church. Those precious hours are set aside for interaction with whomever she shacked with last night—in other words, we're talking the Battle of Big Hangover."

"You're sharp-tongued enough today to be hung-over yourself."

"Not him, David's teetotal."

Roscoe clunked and chinked dirty dishes into a Rubbermaid dishpan for punctuation.

"Sit all night at the Hair a the Dog on the same flat gingerale. Sorta customer drives a barkeep to Amway."

"Roscoe, I'm a student of human nature."

"That'll give you a dirty mind," Roscoe retorted.

The younger man smiled.

"You'd know better than I would."

"I'm hard put to think up something more useless than a rich teetotal poet."

"Whereas Roscoe here has cured cancer and brought us peace in our time."

Glowering, Roscoe opened his mouth to snarl back, but Pearl distracted him.

"That must be your lady wants to take a look at those shelves," she said, indicating a lumbering old van just rolling into the parking lot.

Personal gain took precedence over social intercourse.

"She's late," Roscoe grumbled, but took himself off to bargain with her.

It was a while before David spoke again, as he was eating his breakfast.

"I did see Karen last night at the Dog, with that loathsome little shit who is currently enjoying her extravagant favors."

"I take it," Pearl said, "the Dog is the local nightspot."

David smiled seraphically.

"Only one in a twenty-five-mile radius. Once in a while the Dog has a local garage band or some alcoholic wreck from the glorious past of rock-'n'-roll washes ashore there, and it's worth putting up with the drunks and the druggies. Actually," he confessed, "I went last night because I thought you might be there."

Pearl didn't look up from pouring herself a long-deferred cup of coffee.

"You did?"

"Yes. Perhaps you'd like to go sometime with an experienced guide who speaks the language."

"Maybe. There's a lot to do right now."

"All the more reason to take an evening off. What did you do with your Saturday night, if I may be so bold?"

"You may. Worked in my garden."

"Jesus. You must have been eaten alive by the blackflies. You know, all this sweaty hard work won't do it."

"Do what?"

"Convince these people you're a Yankee."

Pearl frowned thoughtfully. "Don't do that."

"What?"

She grabbed a broom and a waste can and came around the counter. She began to pick up the plastic wrapping from the newspapers and stuff it into the can.

"Play that snotty little game. Send me a lot of cute little messages that you and me have this little joke together which is that I'm up to some kind of con. That shit's for insecure little pricks."

David laid his fork carefully down upon his plate.

"I was doing that?"

Pearl nodded.

He made a church steeple with his hands and collapsed it.

"I'm sorry. I ought to know better. It *is* insulting."

"Close your eyes."

"What?"

"Go on, close your eyes."

As solemnly as a kid playing hide-and-seek, he did. Her hand came down gently over his and moved it along the countertop, then withdrew. At once, the sensation of heat informed him she had placed his hand in a patch of sunlight, and he exclaimed delightedly.

"Hush. Just be still."

So he sat there, with his eyes closed, feeling the sun on his hand and forearm. In the quiet, he heard the gentle swish of her broom, her moving behind him. Then she was close again, right behind him, smelling of the kitchen, butter and fried eggs, bacon and coffee and cream, and also of musk and spices. Vanilla, he thought, and cinnamon.

Next to his ear, she fluttered paper and then quickly ripped it, several times.

He laughed.

"Keep your eyes closed."

Then the torn bits of newsprint began to fall onto his hair and face and down behind the frame of his glasses, where they sat on his nose. He sat very quietly, letting the paper fall.

"You can open your eyes now."

"Thanks," he said. "Thank you."

6

Roscoe Needham came out of the storeroom as David Christopher left. Pearl was sweeping up the newspaper confetti she had made and scattered.

"She squealed some, but she took 'em."

"Good."

Roscoe looked her over speculatively.

"David don't drink, you know, on account of his mother was an alcoholic."

"Oh." She straightened up and pressed the small of her back with both hands. "That happens sometimes."

"A course it happens sometimes. Lotsa women drink. I knew an old lady used to doctor up her tea every afternoon with checkerberry extract. Nobody ever had the gumption to tell her old Baptist heart the stuff had a higher proof to it than vodka outta the greenfront."

"Greenfront?"

"State liquor store. Years ago, their fronts were all painted green."

"Oh. I meant, sometimes the children of alcoholics become teetotal."

"Some of 'em become drunks, too. Did you know it was David's mother's house ol' Joe died in?"

Pearl almost dropped the broom she was hanging up.

"No."

Roscoe beamed with pleasure at being the first to retail this information to her.

"Ayuh. Geedee ol' fool had a heart attack trying to dig her Caddie outta a snowbank she put it into when she was in the bag. She managed to get him back into the house, drunk as a coot as she was, and he died in her bed."

Roscoe's eyebrows semaphored the likely significance of that fact.

To keep herself from giggling, Pearl started wiping the counter, which didn't need it.

"She's dead now, a course. Cancer. Riddled with it. David's the sole survivor. She had another boy, Tommy, the ballfield's named after 'm. Killed by a baseball. I seen it happen."

Pearl gave up and sat down with a cup of coffee to give all this her full attention.

"And there was a girl too, murdered on the lake back in sixty-five or sixty-six, I forget which. Your Uncle Joe and Reuben was there and seen it. So did David, just a kid then. I know for a fack Reuben ain't et fish outta the lake since."

Roscoe shook his head in ritual sorrow at the perfidy of the world.

"Don't doubt it for a minute, David ain't never been quite right, since. Something wrong with a healthy young fella with a bundle a money who sits around writing poetry instead of chasing girls. The only kinda pomes I ever liked was the rhymin' kind with a story in it, like *Gunga Din* and *The Ballad of Sam McGee,* but I ain't ashamed to say there's lots I don't know nothin' about, nukular physics and women's fashions and so on. I read one a David's pomes once, though. Joe showed it to me; it was in *The Maine Times,* which I don't usually read. Why the hell anybody wants to read reviews about dancin', ballet, and stuff is a mystery to me. The women ballet dancers is all ugly bags a bones and the men dancers are queer, 'cept for a coupla Russkies that slipped their leashes. There's that one used to live with the actress. I guess he's left pecker tracks all over, but I don't understand how a regular man can wear them tights. Anyway, David's poem was about picking raspberries, anybody coulda understood it. Didn't have no rhyme, I guess that's against the rules now. On the face of it, though, I don't think there's any danger of anybody putting a statue a David Christopher up in Portland like the one they got there a Henry W. Longfellow. Now, there was a fella knew how to write a rhyme."

" 'Life is real! Life is earnest! And the grave is not its goal,' " quoted Pearl. "Did I get that right?"

"By God, you did. That ain't my favorite line, though. I like the one about the thoughts of youth is long, long thoughts. It's bullshit, a course. Youth hardly thinks at all. It's old folks think the long thoughts. Did you know Rudyard Kipling used to live in Vermont?"

"No."

"Wrote that story about the mongoose there. I read it in *Yankee* magazine."

" 'Rikki-Tikki-Tavi.' Wonders never cease."

"Goddamn right," Roscoe agreed. "Nor never will."

SIX

1

Coming down the back stairs into her kitchen at five-thirty the next morning, Pearl heard what sounded like the world's shittiest old car in the driveway. A quick peek out the window revealed a Plymouth Fury of leprotic, undescribable color. Karen Styles proudly slid out from under the wheel.

Pearl opened the screen door, saying, "If you paid more than ten dollars for that piece of shit, you got taken."

Karen's smile crumbled.

"Pearl, I never heard you swear before."

Pearl walked slowly around the car, shaking her head. "It isn't swearing, it's the make of this heap."

Karen bit her lower lip.

"I didn't pay an awful lot. I really needed a car."

"I guess you did."

"Now I don't have to ask Bri for a ride to work."

"Wouldn't your dad give you a ride?"

The girl shrugged.

"It's outta his way."

It wasn't. He had to pass the diner to get to the Texaco. Pearl held her tongue.

"Besides," Karen went on, "I didn't get my own place so I could always be asking Dad for favors."

Pearl sighed.

"You want a cup of coffee? We've got fifteen minutes."

"Sure."

Opening the door to let Karen go first, Pearl looked back over her shoulder at the car and grimaced. Oh, it was wonderful not to be almost seventeen and trying to make it on her own.

The girl had shown the sense to continue to observe Roscoe's rule that no boyfriends ever darken the door of the diner. She'd overheard Karen bitching about it to Bri on the phone in the storeroom. But when Pearl walked by, Karen had flashed her a look of conspiracy that said *Listen to me bullshit him, Pearl.* The rule, Pearl realized, made the diner a refuge for Karen from Bri's overbearing possessiveness.

"Listen, honey," Pearl said on her way to the coffeemaker, "don't let that thing eat you out of house and home."

"Dad calls it half-bucking you to death. He'll hate the car but he and Sam'll keep it running."

So much for independence. Well, it wasn't her place to point out the contradiction to the kid.

"Speaking of being eaten out of house and home. I found some more mouse poop in the storeroom last night."

"Gross. I thought we got 'em all."

"Guess not. Or else it's a new family."

"I just wish we didn't have to kill 'em. They're so tiny."

"I had Roscoe set some traps this afternoon. Be careful you don't put a finger into one."

"As long as he empties 'em." Karen shuddered.

"It's almost worth what he eats," Pearl said. "Getting him to take out the dead mice. Maybe I ought to kill two birds with one stone and feed them to him."

Karen laughed. Pearl glanced out the kitchen window at the old Plymouth and wished she heard that laugh oftener.

2

With Karen's help, Pearl had salvaged the cobwebbed old tables from the cellar. Cleaned and repainted, they did for picnic tables, arranged on the grassy verge in the shade of a pair of maples on one side of the parking lot. The new flooring went down, the new sign outside up. But she hadn't been able to find the booths she wanted, so half the diner remained empty. Because every roofer in the area was solidly booked, she was still waiting for the roof repairs, checking the sky each day anxiously, every good day that passed distressing because it was wasted. The sider had come and left materials and apparently gone fishing for a couple of weeks.

As with the local people in the first weeks, she began to sort out the faces of the summer people, remembering who liked English muffins and who always wanted bacon and sausage on the side, even caught a name or two. They tended to come in later than the locals.

Nodd's Ridge was a place without any major beach, state park, or other amusement to attract the general public, so there were few day-trippers. People came to spend a month or the summer. The noontime a family of Asian-Americans stopped in on their way somewhere else, it struck Pearl she had not seen a nonwhite face in weeks, except on her television screen. For all her refusal to classify herself as one thing or another, it made her momentarily uneasy to realize what a whitebread world she was inhabiting.

Roscoe had plenty of gossip to retail about summer people as well as locals, but she rarely had the time to listen. From her side of the counter she often wondered, as the old man sat there hour on hour, gossiping and sucking on coffee, just who had made the better bargain. But on Sundays when he filled in for Karen, or in the tight spots when he came around the counter, washed his hands, and hung an apron around his neck to pitch in, he was more than worth the cost of his meals.

On a Tuesday morning, the sky closed in and heavy rains turned everyone damp and crabby. Pearl could hear the roof leaking into strategically placed pots over the sounds of a breakfast crowd which lingered long to avoid going back out. The construction crews were morose, losing money as the world turned to mud. The old people were as touchy as their arthritis.

Karen developed a wretched case of what Roscoe called the dropsy, smashing cups, plates, and rattling everyone's already strained nerves.

When Sonny Lunt, in an elephantine attempt at humor, asked if she were having her period, the girl nearly went over the counter at him.

Pearl worked harder trying to cheer people up and ease them past real crankiness than she did cooking. By nine-thirty everyone except the construction workers had gone off to their daily round or to hang out at the post office. Roscoe had gone home. Pearl looked up from starting a new pot of coffee to see Reuben Styles filling up the doorway.

He took off his sou'wester shyly.

"How do, Reuben."

She let her pleasure at seeing him show.

Ears pricked up along the counter.

"Pearl. Got something for you."

He brought his right hand out from under his slicker. In it was a seal-point Siamese kitten half the size of the hand that held it.

"Oh, my." She held out her hands to receive the kitten.

A grin spread across his face.

The construction workers made noises of approbation.

Pearl was intensely aware their interest was only marginally in the kitten.

"Karen said you were still having mice problems."

"Thank you. Karen!"

Karen came running out of the storeroom, drying her hands on a towel.

"Look what your dad brought."

The girl cooed in delight, reaching for the kitten.

"I remembered Mrs. Cobb said her Petunia's litter was ready to sell. She owed me for some minor bodywork, so I discounted it," Reuben said.

"I owe you one, then."

"Well."

He took his left hand out from under his slicker. "I figured you'd need another one for the house."

A second kitten slithered out of his hand onto the counter.

Laughing, Pearl scooped it up. "So I do. Guess I owe you twice."

"Anybody know where I can get me some kittens?" one of the construction workers said.

Pearl and Reuben ignored the guffaws this witticism evoked.

"Boy and girl," he told her. "They're ready for their shots."

"There's a vet in Greenspark," Karen put in. "Right on Main Street."

"Karen, run down to the store and get some kitty litter and we'll make 'em a box."

"No need," Reuben said, producing a five-pound sack of kitty litter from the folds of his slicker.

"You thought of everything," Pearl said.

"No trouble. Thought I'd save you the trip."

Elbows dug into love handles, and there were shoulder-shakings and head-tuckings going on among the audience. Nobody dared any more verbal barbs at Reuben's expense, but even their delicacy was heavy-handed.

Ignoring them, Reuben had taken off his slicker and sat down at the counter to watch the kittens skitter around the big open space that still lacked booths. Karen crouched down, teasing the kittens with a piece of string.

The men at the counter swiveled around too, seemingly intent on the playing kittens. Admittedly it was a boring morning for the construction workers, but the kittens wouldn't normally be that fascinating.

Karen was wearing an oversize T-shirt that not only covered her breasts but also hid her bottom in her tight jeans. For once there wasn't much for them to ogle. At that moment Karen looked about twelve. She stood up, tugged the hem of her shirt to straighten it, and came around the counter to wash her hands.

"Can I get you something, Reuben?" Pearl asked.

"Tea'll do."

She slid the mug along the counter to him.

A man down the counter waved his cup at Karen and she took the hint, taking the new pot along with her to warm up the coffee of everybody who wanted it.

"Roofer still hasn't got to you yet?" Reuben asked.

Pearl shook her head.

"Nor the sider."

As far as they were concerned, the idled workers were participants in the conversation. They hung openly on every word.

"Curley had a gallbladder attack, Miss Dickenson," said one, "didn't nobody tell you?"

"No. Is he okay?"

"Ayuh, be back at work the first clear day. He just had too many fried clams, is all."

The phone rang and Pearl walked the receiver around the corner into the storeroom, as was her custom. It was the meat man alerting her that the weather was slowing him down and not to panic, he would be there by lunchtime.

3

Pearl had been planning on doing errands in Greenspark anyway that afternoon, so she left Karen to close up after lunch and took the kittens with her. The vet was as easy to find as advertised, in a trim little office on Main Street.

As she stepped into the empty waiting room, a bell tinkled somewhere, apparently triggered by her opening the door. She heard women's voices and thought she had probably interrupted closing up for the day. But a handsome woman came into the waiting room from the back with a welcoming, if artificial, smile.

"Rotten day," the woman said.

Pearl agreed.

The receptionist wore a smart tailored uniform and a pin with her first name. BELINDA. Slim and well-tanned, with a lot of obviously pampered dark hair, the vet's assistant quite openly took a good, appraising look at her.

"You must be Pearl Dickenson," Barbara said, holding out her hand.

There was an assertiveness that bordered on the imperial in her carriage.

"I'm Belinda Conroy." She pointed at her name pin to clarify the point. "Roscoe Needham is my uncle, my aunt's husband, really."

"Oh."

Pearl wondered why this woman thought she needed to know about the relationship, tenuous as it seemed to her.

The Conroy woman laughed lightly.

"Roscoe's quite a character, isn't he? My mother never could stand him. He's such an old reprobate. I've been dying to meet you. I just wish my mother were still alive so I could tell her Roscoe'd met his match."

"Really?"

Pearl felt nearly as insulted for Roscoe as she did for herself.

At the sight of the kittens, sleepy from the ride, the woman gushed.

"Look at them! Aren't they cute?"

"They need their shots."

The receptionist handed her a couple of forms and told Pearl how much the shots cost.

"I'll take care of them while you fill these out."

Picking up the kittens, she carried them off.

Pearl picked up a pen and filled out the forms, putting down *"Boy"* and *"Girl"* in the space for names.

Belinda Conroy reappeared in a few minutes.

"All done," she sang out, taking Pearl's money.

She told Pearl when they would need their next shots and when they could be neutered, if she wanted.

Outside Pearl breathed deeply. The air outside seemed extravagantly pure. She felt herself unwind a little and decided she was overtired and grouchy. So she treated herself to an ice-cream cone and went home.

4

Keeping them together to ease the separation from their mother, Pearl left both kittens at the diner for the night when she stopped to check that Karen had closed up shop properly. The clouds were breaking up to make a lovely twilight as she arrived home. The cloudiness in her spirits lifted. When she opened the back door, an envelope which had been stuck in it fluttered to her feet. It was an ordinary business-letter envelope with her name typed on it.

Sliding a nail under the flap to break the seal, she took out a single page. On it was a poem.

The Sunday *New York Times* Newspaper War

"Mine, Mine."
We rip the newspaper to shreds,
tear words letter from letter,
and toss them overhead, to float
and flutter and lastly swoon earthward.
Black and white and read all over,
the newspaper winter falls
upon us
in the shape of a map;
X marks the spot where
something is buried.

She sat down and read it again. Then she picked up the phone book and called David Christopher.

"Thank you."

He was silent a moment and then said, "You're welcome. You don't have to say anything else."

"I wouldn't know how. Not the first thing."

"It's just a first draft."

He seemed to be embarrassed at the impulse which had led him to leave a poem in her door. So she asked him if he wanted to meet her at the Dog for a pizza. He seized the invitation as if he were a teething puppy being offered a rag to chew on. They made an appointment for seven.

Her phone tape whispered and clicked in a rapid series but there were no voices. Someone had called and not left a message. Brother Bobby, she thought. He hated talking to a machine. She wondered where and how her stepbrother was.

Pearl had had a soak and was just changing to go out when she heard a vehicle coming in.

The door banged open downstairs and Roscoe Needham shouted tremulously from the kitchen.

"Pearl!"

She ran down the back stairs in her stocking feet.

The old man was standing in the kitchen, his mouth fallen open and his Adam's apple falling and rising in distress.

"Roscoe, what's wrong?"

"It's Jack," Roscoe said. "I think he's dying."

Pearl grabbed her galoshes and slicker and piled out after the old man to his ancient truck.

Jack lay on the front seat loosely wrapped in a hairy old blanket. The old dog's eyes were rolled up, there were flecks of foam around his muzzle, and his sides heaved with the effort of breathing.

Pearl stroked his head gently a moment.

"Roscoe, you'd better take him to a vet."

Roscoe was shaking.

"He's dying, I know it. He's dying."

She put an arm around Roscoe.

"He might be. He's old, Roscoe."

"I never seen him like this."

The old man seemed to have aged another decade since breakfast. His hands shook, he looked frantic. He was in no shape to take the dog anywhere by himself.

"Let me call the vet."

She was back again in three minutes.

"Dr. Beech is going to meet us at his office. Come on, you hold Jack, and I'll drive."

Roscoe nodded dumbly and did as he was told.

During the drive to Greenspark, Jack had several convulsions, but Roscoe, perhaps because he was able to concentrate entirely on the dog, seemed to pull himself together a little more with each seizure, as if the holding and soothing of the animal gave him strength.

"Jack's been sick a long time. I knew he was ready to go. I was selfish."

"People get attached. It's hard to let them go."

Roscoe sat up a bit.

"I didn't expect nothing when I got him, but Jack turned out to be a natural rabbit dog. Why, one year, musta bin October of seventy-nine. . ." Roscoe wandered off into reminiscence. At the vet's door, he simply stopped talking in mid-word, ". . . that piebald buck was the biggest rab . . ." and slid out from under the dog.

Pearl wasn't sure he had the strength to carry the dog, but he summoned it.

The vet admitted them to his office. He was a young man, thin, with freckled skin and sandy hair that was already in retreat over his pate.

"This way," he said, and led them into an examining room, his eyes never leaving the dog.

Pearl introduced herself as they went in and the vet shook her hand casually and said he was Dr. Beech.

Roscoe laid the dog on the examining table and the vet stroked Jack's head and ran his hands along his slack old body. The convulsions had stopped and the dog's ribs heaved upward, fell inward, struggled upward again.

"Well, Mr. Needham, Jack's in very bad shape."

The old man cringed. He was trembling.

Pearl put her hand on Roscoe's forearm.

"I shoulda shot 'im," Roscoe suddenly blurted.

He wiped under his nose savagely with the back of his hand.

"I shoulda done it myself before he got so bad."

Pearl noticed a box of Kleenex on a table and passed it back to the old man. He blew his nose loudly.

The vet patted Roscoe's shoulder.

"Mr. Needham, I know this isn't easy for you."

Roscoe blinked.

"I know it's time to put him down."

The vet nodded.

"Would you like a moment with him?"

Roscoe straightened up and shook his head.

"No."

He held the dog's head.

"Do it, this has gone on too long already."

It was over very quickly.

Pearl put her arm around Roscoe's shoulders again.

"There'll never be another Jack, will there?"

The vet patted Roscoe's shoulder again and the starch went out of the old man. He burst into tears. Within a few minutes he had mastered his emotions, however, and insisted on helping return the dog's body to the truck. But he was very quiet until they were back at Nodd's Ridge.

"I'll get me and Jack back home on my own, Pearl. You get out at your house."

A quick glance assured her he was very calm.

"You sure?"

Roscoe nodded.

"I'd ruther be by myself now."

He thanked her when she got out. His voice shook slightly and he wiped at one eye hurriedly but held on.

"You're a good woman, Pearl."

"Call me if you need me."

She watched him drive away, hunched over the steering wheel as if somebody'd punched him.

5

The phone was ringing when she came in.

"David," she said to herself.

She dove for it.

"Did you get lost?"

"No, no, I'm sorry. Errand of mercy came up suddenly."

"They do," David said. "Come up suddenly, I mean. You don't have to tell me what it was."

"I had to rush Roscoe and his dog Jack to the vet's."

"Oh."

"I couldn't let Roscoe drive, he was too upset."

"That mangy old collie? What happened?"

"He died."

There was a pause.

"Too bad for Roscoe. Really. I mean that."

"Yes. 'S hard to get old."

"You realize, if I may be so indelicate, you stood me up for a dead dog?"

Pearl laughed.

"I said I was sorry. Take a rain check."

"Okay. You can't help being a nice person."

"Thanks again for the poem. Last poem anybody gave me was in the third grade."

"Well?"

"Well what?"

"It do the third-grade poet any good?"

"I let him ride me home on his bike. Next day he fell in love with a little redhaired girl."

The way he laughed, she thought he had forgiven her for standing him up for a dead dog.

6

Karen drove in early the next day as Pearl was dressing.

The girl let herself in and called up the back stairs, " 'Morning."

"Right down," Pearl called back, and pulled on her jeans.

When she came into the kitchen, she found Karen, a cup of coffee already poured, reading the poem Pearl had left on the kitchen table.

Oops.

"Wow," Karen said. "Nobody ever wrote a poem for me in my whole life."

"It's not a love poem," Pearl pointed out hastily. "He didn't write it for me, anyway. He just gave it to me to read, that's all."

"I can see that. I don't understand it but I can see it's not a love poem."

"Maybe you quit high school too soon," Pearl said, hoping to divert her.

Karen dropped the poem on the table.

"I don't think I'd understand it if I had stayed in school."

"Actually, I'm not sure I understand it myself."

Karen giggled.

"Well, I think it's just incredibly romantic, getting a poem. What's going on, anyway? Are you two going to have an affair? I ran into David last night at the Dog and he asked me if I'd seen you. I got the idea he was expecting you and you didn't show."

"We were going to have a pizza, that's all. But I had to take Roscoe and his dog to the vet. Jack died."

"His old collie? Roscoe's had that dog ever since I can remember."

" 'S shame. The vet seemed like a nice fellow."

"Dr. Beech? He's a sweetheart."

"Hey, time to go to work."

Pearl hustled them on out with relief at having at least momentarily distracted Karen's nose from her business.

Roscoe was waiting for them at the diner. He didn't look like he had slept the previous night.

Karen hugged him, and he was so startled, Pearl had to suppress a grin. It was clearly a first in the relationship between those two natural antagonists.

"Sorry about Jack," the girl said.

Roscoe shrugged.

"Ya live long enough, everything dies on you."

The kittens were frisky but hadn't killed any mice.

"They're so little," Pearl said, "probably a mouse would scare 'em."

Karen laughed. "Don't you ever think it. I've had kittens kill mice as big as they were. There'll be dead mice around here this week, I promise."

Finding no new mouse trace but no dead mice, Pearl decided if all the kittens did was scare away the vermin, she'd be happy. She made Roscoe his breakfast but he just picked at it.

The early-morning customers wandered in. Karen's whisper to Sonny Lunt was somehow transmitted, *sotto voce,* to each. Pearl was moved to witness the brief pats on the old man's shoulder, the murmured condolences. They were all people to whom a dog meant something.

Roscoe had no banter, not even spleen. He left early.

Reuben dropped by, looking for Roscoe. Sonny had stopped at the station long enough to inform him that Roscoe had lost Jack. Reuben stayed long enough to have a cup of tea and examine the kittens critically, peering into their eyes and ears and mouths as if he were checking for alignment, before saying he had to get back to work, as he was expecting a delivery of gasoline from his distributor and Jonesy was nervous about dealing with the deliveryman. He

bought a doughnut and coffee for Jonesy and said he would call on Roscoe later in the day to make sure he was okay.

Pearl was closing up when she realized David Christopher had not come in all day. Well, she had nothing invested. He was an amusing man, certainly attractive, but she was too old to expect anything from any man who wasn't ready to give it, whether it was friendship or more. If he was having an attack of the shys, he would have to get over it on his own.

Karen, however, had also noticed.

"Don't worry," she counseled Pearl, uninvited. "He's probably a little pissed off at you about last night. He'll get over it."

"I'm not worried about it."

But Karen was too busy fantasizing to pay any attention to Pearl's disclaimers.

"You know, if I didn't already have a honey, I'd be jealous. David's just about the most gorgeous man I know. I bet you never in your wildest dreams thought you'd meet somebody like him out here in the boonies."

"No."

Karen just rolled on. "It's just like a soap."

As she watched Karen drive away, Pearl didn't know whether to be amused or irritated at the kid's runaway romanticism.

7

She went directly to Roscoe's and found Reuben there before her. He and Roscoe, who was red-eyed and drunk, were sitting on the back porch, shying pebbles into the dirt. A raw patch at the bottom of the steps next to the lilac revealed Roscoe had buried the dog in Jack's favorite spot.

She showed Roscoe the bag she was carrying.

"Brought you supper."

Reuben took the bag.

"Smells good. Smells great, actually."

"You eat it then," Roscoe said, and then, looking away from Pearl apologetically, "I ain't got no appetite, Pearl. Thanks anyway."

Reuben and Pearl shrugged at each other.

"I'll put it in the fridge."

Reuben took it inside.

Pearl sat down next to Roscoe.

"Wanna get drunk?" he asked her.

Pearl squeezed the old man's arm.

"Tough to get up at five-thirty, hung-over."

"You ain't just talking to hear yourself talk."

Reuben came back out and handed Pearl a beer.

"But I'll drink to Jack's memory," she said, popping it.

Solemnly they raised their cans to Jack.

"Throwed my back out, planting Jack," Roscoe said. "This Bud's all I got for painkillers."

Reuben teased and scolded.

"I'd have been glad to do it for you. Why didn't you ask me? You don't take care of your back, it can turn into a real misery."

The old man stared bleary-eyed at the dog's new grave.

"Guess I can plant my own dog, even if I was too chickenshit to put him out of his misery when it was time."

Reuben nodded. Roscoe had rolled himself up around his mourning like a threatened porcupine. There wasn't much anyone could do for him but put up with it.

A Country Squire wagon rolled in behind Pearl's truck and Belinda Conroy got out. She waved at them and then opened the rear door and straightened up holding a black Labrador puppy.

Pearl and Reuben looked at each other in chagrin.

Roscoe laughed his most unpleasant, chalk-scratching laugh.

"Uncle Roscoe," the Conroy woman cried, "look what I brought you."

Roscoe tossed back the last mouthful in the can, crushed it in one hand, and tossed it over the porch rail onto the ground.

"I don't want it. I ain't having any more goddamn dogs."

Belinda Conroy continued inexorably across the yard with the puppy lolling in her arms.

"Why, hello, Reuben."

With a toss of her head, she dismissed Pearl as an intruder.

"Pearl. What a surprise to find you here."

Pearl thought about telling her she was Miss Dickenson to her, but the woman was like a tank.

"Now, Uncle Roscoe, Jack was very old. It's all to the best, he's out of pain."

"Oh, fuck off, Belinda," Roscoe said.

Pearl had to fight off a grin.

Belinda's mouth pursed.

"I know you're upset, Uncle Roscoe. But you need a puppy, Uncle Roscoe. First thing. Like getting back on a horse that's thrown you. Lots of old people," Belinda rattled on, "when their old dogs die, don't get another one because they're afraid the animals will outlive them, but I don't think you should concern yourself with whether they will or not. I mean, somebody will always take care of an animal if the owner dies"—a statement of such rank untruth that Pearl could barely contain herself—"and what's important is, old folks need animals so they won't be lonely. Now, this little guy is one of my own, Desdemona's pups. You know what a terrific dog Desdemona is. I get three hundred dollars apiece for her pups. You couldn't find a better-bred dog in the state."

"I'll tell you what," Roscoe said. "I'll write you a check for three hundred dollars and you keep the goddamn dog."

Belinda Conroy struggled visibly to damp the anger in her face.

"Oh, Uncle Roscoe, you are so stubborn. You just don't have any idea what's good for you."

Suddenly she shoved the pup at Reuben, who scrabbled to hold on to it.

"I know you think an old dog can't learn new tricks, but it's time you learned how to take a gift when somebody gives you one."

She turned on her heel and strode back to her car.

Roscoe struggled to his feet, his face purpling with rage.

"I don't want any goddamn dog," he shouted. "You hear me, Belinda!"

She was already starting her car.

Reuben looked helplessly at Pearl and she rolled her eyes.

Belinda Conroy backed out with a squeal of tires and was gone.

Roscoe, spewing obscenities, headed for the porch rail as if he intended to go over it after Belinda.

Pearl caught him, and all the strength went out of him.

He began to cry.

"The bitch. The goddamn bitch."

Pearl and Reuben put him to bed. Roscoe either passed out or fell asleep with the help of the beer almost instantly.

"You want to eat Roscoe's supper?" Pearl asked.

"Somebody ought to," Reuben said and went out to see the puppy.

Pearl had a place on the table cleared and set for him when he came back in.

As he washed his hands at the kitchen sink, he told her, "The pup was already digging at Jack's grave. I tied her up on the other side of the porch. She's as stupid as a doorstop." He laughed. "Belinda's brought him, out of the kindness of her heart, the runt of the litter. She's breeding mother and son, and half her litters are untrainable idiots. She gets her three hundred a pup from people who buy dogs by what's on a piece of paper. That bitch out there is as close to nothing as a dog can get."

Pearl turned lasagne out onto a plate for him and sat down with him. "Roscoe won't keep her, will he?"

Reuben shrugged. "I don't know. I wouldn't put it past him to shoot the thing and leave it on Belinda's doorstep."

"Ugh."

"Roscoe's got a mean streak in him," Reuben said, as if he were observing the weather. "Belinda's got a meaner one. It's not in the blood, he's her uncle by marriage, that's all. His wife, Rita, she never cared for Belinda either. Not too many women do."

"Doesn't he have any other relations?"

"No, just Belinda and her kids, who are grown up now and have kids. He doesn't have anything to do with them from one year to the next."

"She makes a handsome grandmother."

Reuben looked up from the lasagne, into which he had made admirable inroads.

" 'Handsome is as handsome does,' " he quoted Roscoe's favorite saying. "'Belinda's hung three husbands out to dry."

"You want another beer?" she asked him, getting up for both of them.

"Please, and thank you."

When he finally sat back, he asked, "What about you, what are you doing about supper now I've eaten Roscoe's?"

"Think I'll go home and work in the garden."

"It's coming along, I noticed."

"Uncle Joe built that soil up something lovely." She stood up. "Think Roscoe will be okay?"

"Roscoe's been taking care of himself for seventy or so years."

"Maybe I better take the dog, if you think he'll shoot it?"

He laughed.

"You don't want that dog. It's mostly brain-dead already. Don't concern yourself. He just put one dog down and it hurt him. I don't really think he'll do away with it. Push comes to shove, he'll leave it with Evvie Bonneau, the animal-control officer."

He went out with her and opened the truck door for her. There was a second when they just looked at each other, and then he smiled and closed the door for her.

"Well," he said, "you don't need another kitten, do you?"

She laughed and he stood back, savoring it.

She drove away marveling. Not a man worth a decent meal in three years, and now she had a choice. Never rains but it pours. She giggled and pounded the horn with the side of her fist, lightly, so it made a noise like a chuckle.

SEVEN

1

The following morning the rain had come round again, in a system that seemed unable to raise enough energy to move on. Looking very much worse for the wear, Roscoe slunk in only a little later than usual. He poured his own coffee and claimed his place curtly.

Walter McKenzie and Jean came in.

Walter had to sit down before he had enough breath to converse.

"Roscoe, sorry about Jack."

Having had enough of condolences, Roscoe ignored him.

Walter didn't notice.

"Every day I come downstairs expecting to find Fritzie stone-cold dead in the morning. I figger it's between her and me which one of us is gonna find the other one dead as a doornail."

"Dad." Jean used her elbow to dig hard into Walter's side.

"Quit pokin' me, Jeannie. Anyway, Roscoe, Jack was a good dog."

He peered closely at Roscoe.

"You look like shit."

Before Roscoe could snarl at him, Pearl lightly touched Roscoe's shoulder and laughed.

"Morning like this, everybody feels that way."

The most reliable deflection was always provided by the weather. Everybody wanted to opine on it.

Sonny Lunt banged in, carrying the Labrador pup Belinda Conroy had given Roscoe.

"Lookit what I found running loose on the Main Road."

Roscoe suddenly found the newspaper very interesting.

The kittens skittering around the floor backed up, hissing. The little dog struggled wildly to escape Sonny. He nearly lost her once or twice but finally established a firm grip on her. Her eyes were little chips of bright glinting obsidian.

"Got some rope?" he asked. "I'll tie her up outside."

Karen ducked into the storeroom and came out with a length.

Sonny came back in shortly.

"I believe that's one of Belinda Conroy's. Stupid as a fried Popcicle. You want to call the dog officer, Pearl?"

"Roscoe," Pearl asked, "you want to call the dog officer?"

Roscoe crushed his newspaper angrily.

"I'll do it," Karen said, but Pearl put out a restraining hand.

"Roscoe. Do you want Karen to call?"

"Go right ahead. I don't give a shit."

About ten minutes later, Evangeline Bonneau, the animal-control officer, charged in. She was a small, wiry woman of indeterminate age.

"Roscoe," she said, "I'm sorry about Jack."

Roscoe nodded.

Evvie Bonneau gestured toward the door.

"That bitch's so stupid she's got to be one of Belinda's. You know how the hell she came to be here?"

"The hell, Evvie. She ain't mine. I don't want her."

Evvie paused, tapping a finger on the opposite arm, and planted her feet. Making up her mind, she nodded crisply.

"I figure the way this pup got here was Belinda gave it to you, without asking if you wanted it, to replace Jack. Well, you can't just turn it loose. I won't let you."

Roscoe's red-rimmed eyes watered.

"You take it back to Belinda. It's her lookout."

The room had grown quiet, the customers listening and exchanging looks that Pearl could only half-read.

"Roscoe," Evvie said quietly, "you know Belinda's got an injunction against me. I can't deal directly with her."

Roscoe had sunk on the stool to where his head was hanging only inches above his arms and the counter.

"Miced all fuckin' Chryty," he muttered.

"I'll put the dog in your truck."

Evvie nodded again, taking her leave, and strode out.

"Evvie tried to stop Belinda breeding and selling dogs, and Barbara got an injunction against her," Walter told Pearl. "Evvie's dog officer here, but not in Greenspark, which is where Belinda lives, legally. Her place is right on the border. Belinda ain't doing anything illegal, see. It oughta be, but it ain't. Evvie's a lot better with animals than she is with people."

"Give Evvie credit," Sonny Lunt said. "I believe she'd probably save a cat or a dog from a house fire before she'd save a person, but she's no fool. She knows animals ain't stuffies. She's as interested in regulating breeding as she is in collecting up starving strays."

"Why don't you put a sign up offering to give the dog away?" Pearl suggested.

Roscoe brightened a little.

"That's what I'll do."

Walter approved.

"Somebody probably like to have that dog."

Several people observed they didn't want her.

Outside, the yipping and yapping rose hysterically as a vehicle passed by on the road.

"Anybody's got a gun," Sonny Lunt said, "I'll go shoot the goddamn thing right now."

Most of the crowd found this amusing, but nobody volunteered a gun, if anyone had one.

Roscoe leaned over the counter.

"Shoot Belinda too and I'll lend you mine."

Sonny grinned.

"Just get her to stand in back of Evvie's truck."

This provoked an uneasy ripple of amusement as the door slammed behind him.

"Oh," said Jean McKenzie, fluttering like a hen being nipped at by a dog. "I don't believe a word of it."

Karen snagged Pearl's sleeve and murmured, "Evvie's supposed to have backed over her common-law husband and killed him."

Pearl blinked in disbelief.

"What?"

"'Few years ago," Walter said.

It was amazing how his hearing improved when there was dirt going around.

"One of them Broncos that was s'posed to slip outta gear. Nobody ever proved anything. He was a useless son-of-a-bitch, anyway."

"Dad," Jean scolded. "That's just gossip."

Walter was unperturbed.

"You don't see anybody rushing to prosecute her, do you?"

"Must be somethin' in the water," Pearl muttered.

"What?" said Karen.

"Pearl said must be somethin' in the water," Walter explained. "Makes people around here act out. Fack is, people live in each other's back pockets around here. Nothin' goin' on here ain't goin' on in New York City or Boston, Taxachusetts, or the pope's house. Just we know about it sooner, is all."

"I'll tell you what," Sonny Lunt said. "One more day of this rain and *I'll* be out mowing people down with my truck."

Pearl nearly kissed him. Back to the weather.

2

At five-thirty the next morning, Pearl had a visitor. She knew it wasn't Karen's car rolling over the wet gravel of her driveway because she could barely hear it at all. Looking out the window, she was startled to see David Christopher's little Mercedes. The sky was brilliantly blue and clear, as it often is after rain.

Characteristically removing his sunglasses and putting on his clear ones, David climbed out of his sports car and came to the screen door.

"So this is morning. Are you in charge of making the sun rise?"

She let him in.

"How'd you guess?"

He dropped into a chair at the table.

"Couldn't sleep. It happens to me once in a while. I suddenly realized that you were probably awake too."

"Well, I'm a morning person."

"It's some gorgeous." He pronounced it "sum gawjus" in mock Yankee. "It's going to be hot enough to fry eggs. Want to have a swim and a picnic supper at my house?"

She put a mug of coffee in his hand.

"Why, that's very nice of you."

"It's the only way I could think to get you away from Roscoe and Karen."

She laughed again and sat down with him.

"I'm sorry. Karen saw that poem. It gave her ideas of which I have not been able to disabuse her."

"Good," he said. "They're probably the same ideas as mine." He laughed. "I can't believe I was so clumsy as to leave you that poem. It's only a first draft and I'm afraid it's never going to be a very good one. But you leave me tongue-tied, Pearl."

"If you're tongue-tied, I'd like to hear you loosened up."

He smiled.

"Off my place is the deepest part of the lake. It's cold. I mean that seriously. A deep Maine lake can stop your heart, except for the first week of August, assuming a scorching July. Usually it rains the first week of August."

"What can I bring to the picnic?"

"Your bathing suit. But only if it's very small."

"You sure you're not a morning person?"

He stood up and stretched like a cat.

It was a pleasure to watch. But when she glanced at her watch, she jumped up.

"Look at the time."

He caught her round the waist.

"What about being morning people?"

She pushed his hands away.

"I have to go to work."

"Now I know you really are Joe Nevers' grand-niece."

"And what's that supposed to mean?"

Another car could be heard rolling over the gravel.

"Here's Karen," he said, and grabbed Pearl.

She was too startled to even begin to resist as he kissed her hard, and then she was so surprised by the sudden response of her body that it took her several irretrievable seconds to reassert control.

Karen stood round-eyed at the door, staring at them, as Pearl broke away and whirled around.

"Karen."

Pearl barely contained a violent surge of anger. It had been a clumsy, arrogant pass and, worse, she'd responded to it. She ought to have slapped his face.

"We'll talk about this later," she said through clenched teeth.

"Yes, ma'am."

David was perfectly sober and correct, slipping his sunglasses back on. He walked out.

Karen stepped aside to let him pass, her mouth open.

"Shut up," Pearl said before the girl could say anything, and went to get her keys.

3

Karen managed to contain herself for the first three minutes they were inside the diner.

"Nothin' goin' on, eh?" she said as she put the coffee on.

"Look at that!"

Karen peeked around the corner and squeaked. The pair of kittens was strutting around their kill, displayed on the storeroom floor.

"Good kittens."

Pearl picked them up to cuddle them.

"Good little mouse-murderers."

"Can I leave them for Roscoe to clean up?"

"I'll do it." Pearl handed her the kittens. "Give 'em a treat, will you?"

The kittens had gotten what looked like most of a family, the smallest one so tiny Pearl felt a momentary flash of extreme guilt. She sighed and swept them onto a newspaper, then started filling a floor pail to swab the floor where they had died.

Roscoe crowed when he saw the newspaper on the top of the trashcan.

"Kittens earned their keep, did they?"

Pearl handed him a cup of coffee.

"How's the pup? D' you take her back to Belinda's?"

Roscoe began to purple with rage.

"Shithead dug Jack up yesterday afternoon. I like to kilt it but it got loose and ran away. If I got any luck left in the world, somebody's already kilt it on the highway. If Evvie catches it again, there'll be hell to pay."

"What a shame, Roscoe. Why don't you take it back to Belinda?"

"Why the jezzly Christ should I have to make a trip to Greenspark to take back something I didn't ask for?"

"Oh, Roscoe." Pearl patted his arm. "Take it easy. I'm on your side."

He subsided.

The screen door slammed open and Sonny Lunt came in carrying the pup.

"Roscoe, your goddamn bitch about kilt me running in front of my truck."

Roscoe stared at Sonny and the dog briefly and then turned his back on them and lowered his head into his hands.

"Got some rope?"

Karen was already going for it.

Pearl reached across the counter to hand Sonny his coffee when he came back in.

"Thanks. Probably you need this."

"Guess I do." He grinned. "Roscoe, that mutt's as stupid as a dead perch."

"Smarter'n you," the old man snapped, "for botherin' to stop."

Sonny laughed. "Don't you know a dog that stupid can't be kilt? There's a special guardian angel, ain't there, for stupid dogs and mean dirty old drunks. Dogs like that, they kill drivers, not the other way around."

Roscoe nodded morosely.

Pearl smiled to herself, imagining Sonny as the special guardian angel of stupid dogs, or at least of this one.

"Can I call Evvie to come over and ream you again?" Sonny asked. "I just love listening to that woman give people a hard time."

Karen snickered.

"Just don't get in an argument with her when she's got the car keys."

Sonny sobered up and leaned over the counter.

"I knowed Cross, Evvie's common-law, and she oughta have a medal. She saved the taxpayers' money. Probably the only way to get the bastid off unemployment."

Karen laughed.

Outside, the dog was not only making irritating noise, it appeared to be lunging on its rope at arriving customers.

"Sonny," Pearl asked, "would you tie her up out back, by the loading bay, before she bites someone and I get sued?"

"Sure. I shoulda thought of that when I tied her up out front."

"Roscoe," Pearl said, "you want me to take the dog back to Belinda?"

"No. You stay out of it. This is between me and her."

Sighing, Pearl turned to her customers.

4

David Christopher lounged in for a late breakfast. "Did you know there's a small black dog strangling itself out by your loading dock?"

Roscoe stood up, swore vigorously, and stalked out.

"Sorry about Jack," David said to him in passing.

"Me too," was the curt response as he left.

"Belinda Conroy gave him that dog to replace Jack," Karen told David. "Just dumped it on him. I guess she thought it would help him get over Jack."

"Wish I'd been there to see it. It must have been rich."

"Roscoe was drunk," Karen said. "Otherwise, I don't think she would have gotten away with it."

"Can't blame him for not wanting it. It's a pretty poor excuse for a dog." Pearl kept her tone carefully neutral.

David looked at her sharply.

He chewed his lower lip a little and then said, "So the puppy's hanging herself on a piece of rope and Roscoe's choking himself on his anger at Belinda."

"You got it."

Karen was hovering and getting on Pearl's nerves.

"Go do something," Pearl told her.

Karen pouted and twitched away to the storeroom.

"Your fault." Pearl shook her head in the direction of Karen's retreat. "Show-off."

"Pardon me," he murmured, slouching guiltily over his coffee mug. He pretended to be interested in the activities of the kittens, who were once again, now that custom had fallen off, chasing each other and their growing collection of toys across the floor.

"They got some mice last night."

"I'll have scrambled eggs, thanks," he said.

Pearl burst out laughing and David basked. When Karen floated back out from the chores in the storeroom and was coy, Pearl was still in such a good humor she hardly noticed.

Roscoe came back in.

"Why don't you just shoot it?" David asked.

"I oughta." The old man slunk moodily onto a corner stool. "She digs Jack up again, I will. Like to charge Belinda for the bullet."

"Why don't you shoot Belinda?"

It was interesting that so many people seemed to regard the Conroy woman in a degree of cold-bloodedness usually reserved for mass murderers of the Bundy stripe.

The thought of murder cheered Roscoe up rapidly.

"Set me right up, but I'm too old to go to Shawshank. First-degree murder's a seven-year rap in this state and I doubt I've got the seven years to spare." He spoke with genuine regret.

"Well," David said, "there's plenty other people who'd like to shoot Belinda. You can always hope."

Roscoe laughed, the first time since Jack's death Pearl had heard from Roscoe's milder side.

Outside, horseshoes clattered on the gravel and two girls on a pair of Appaloosas hove into view.

"Them's Ansel's girls," Roscoe remarked. "That older one, you can hardly tell her butt from that mare's, can ya?"

David laughed and Pearl chided, "Now, Roscoe, they're nice girls, those two."

Nancy and Liz, the daughters of Ansel Partridge, the town's most successful farmer, came chattering in. Tightly packed into their jeans and T-shirts, they were just what they looked to be, farmgirls in the bloom of their youth. With double-D-cup bosoms and legs like pianos', they had a comfortable choice of boyfriends among the rural lads. No rumor of punk had apparently reached their shell-pink ears, hung with turquoise and silver in the Navaho fashion favored by horsey people. Nancy wore her hair in a ponytail, her sister wore hers in a permanent frizz. Neither painted her face from one prom to the next.

Karen regarded them with amusement as unregenerate hicks and puzzled over what the boys found attractive in those fertility-goddess boobs and thighs. In turn, she mystified the Partridge girls, who thought she was as beautiful as any model in *Seventeen* or actress on the soaps. They envied her figure and clucked over her reputation as a wild 'un, but chiefly they pitied her because she didn't like horses.

"Hope there's some blueberry muffins left," Nancy cried. "I'm hungry enough to eat a bear."

Much of what passed for witticism in the Partridge household revolved around what various family members were hungry enough to eat.

The girls' voices covered the sudden cessation of the little black bitch's continual chorus of yips and yaps.

David, his breakfast consumed, turned on his stool to face the front of the diner. He saw the two gray horses, tied to the railing on the steps, flicking at flies with their tails. Suddenly there was a streak of black whipping around their feet.

"Roscoe," he said, "dog's loose."

"Fiddly fuck." Roscoe turned himself around to peer out the window. "Pardon me, girls."

Everyone in the diner also turned to watch the dog.

It flashed through Pearl's mind that that was the purpose of the revolving stool, to allow people to gawk at whatever might be happening.

Just as Roscoe reached the screen door, one of the horses lifted its tail and a fall of manure began to bounce off the puppy's head. She danced under the horse's tail and began to eat the hot greenish horse apples.

"Jesus Horatio Christ," Roscoe said in disgust, "a shit-eatin' dog. If there's anything I hate, it's a shit-eatin' dog."

Everybody was laughing too hard to be able to speak.

Roscoe put his hands on his hips and smiled nastily.

"There. Now I got a name for that dog. I'm gonna call it Belinda."

They all laughed themselves nearly sick, but Pearl, fortunately, was not called upon to perform the Heimlich maneuver on anybody.

5

Business was booming at lunchtime.

When Reuben came by to pick up an order he had phoned, he found Walter McKenzie and Jean sitting out at a picnic table in the shade at the side of the parking lot. He stopped to say hello.

"Isn't this the nicest thing?" Jean said. "And the chicken is just lovely, isn't it, Dad?"

Walter, working on a drumstick, nodded.

"Miss Dickinson is an excellent cook," Jean went on. "I regard her as a very valuable addition to the community."

"Karen thinks the world of her."

As if she had heard her name, Karen came out of the diner with a pitcher of iced tea. When she saw her father, she came directly to the McKenzies' table.

"Hi, Dad. Your order's just coming out." She refilled Walter and Jean's glasses. "How is it?"

"Excellent," Jean said.

Walter nodded sagely and then said, "Karen, them jeans is so tight I can see—", which observation of exactly what Walter could see was interrupted by Jean swatting hard at her father's hand.

"Dad! Mind your own business."

Karen, blushing, backed away. "I've got to see who needs refills." She hurried away to attend the customers at the other tables.

Reuben watched her go.

Jean leaned over and patted his hand.

"She's a lovely girl, Reuben. She's just going through a stage."

Walter was sulking.

Jean looked sternly at Walter.

"I can't think what I'm going to do with you, Dad."

"Girl's goin' to chafe herself," Walter insisted, provoking Jean to further, weaker hand-swatting.

Reuben patted Jean's arm and went in to claim his chicken.

Inside the diner the air was hotter than outside, and muggy from the fryers. Reuben watched Pearl while she packed the order for him. No wasted motion. The smell of the chicken was heady. She smiled brilliantly at him and greeted him, but clearly had no time for banter. Still, when she saw him, her face did light up and she did smile that smile that made the diner seem quite a lot hotter, made him tug at his shirt collar.

He bought a takeout container of iced tea and drank it down as soon as he was back in the truck, thinking about Walter and Jean and himself and Karen. One of these days he was going to be an old fart like Walter. Maybe a lot like Walter, maybe fat and wheezing and garrulous. He remembered Jean, in her youth, the friend of his sister Ilene. Once she had had a bloom, had not always been the faded, dim creature she was now. The unexpected course of his own life had taken away any assumptions he might have made about how happy the lives of his children would be. It was entirely possible that Karen might come back home to him, manless, childless, bereft of looks and youth and hope, routed by the world like Jean. Maybe she'd be swatting at him every time he opened his mouth and embarrassing truths and prejudices fell out. It could happen to him, to Karen.

Need a wife, he thought, knowing perfectly well that a wife was proof against nothing at all. *No. I need a woman.* He threw back his head and laughed, turned on the truck, and drove away.

6

The road to the Christopher house was cool and green. Pearl relaxed into the seat of the truck and breathed deeply of forest-flavored air, the breeze from the lake cooling her off. She caught glimpses of the lake through the trees, patches of blue in the dark green of spruce and pine, the lighter greens of the deciduous trees. She had wished for hard work and her wish had been granted; she was tired. Good and tired. The water in the air promised her the lake's caresses.

Around a corner, it was suddenly there, house under trees at the edge of the water, at the bottom of a steep driveway. Basking in the late-afternoon sun, the house was a surprise, looking like it belonged to Malibu. She supposed she had been expecting something old because at the back of her mind she was aware David's family had come to Nodd's Ridge for their summers for generations. Parking behind David's car, her beach tote in hand, she knocked at the back door.

Inside was all shadows and she could almost feel the house exhaling coolness. David materialized out of them from somewhere, barefoot, in shorts and an unbuttoned crinkled gauze shirt, its long sleeves rolled up to the elbows. Despite the interior shadow, he wore sunglasses.

"Welcome."

Solemnly he flung open the door. It cracked smartly against the siding and he caught it as it came back, sparing Pearl an ungraceful jump over the stoop to avoid the door spanking her calves. He led her through the dark entry hall past a galley kitchen.

Abruptly the house opened into the living room, three stories high, with a wall all of glass facing the lake. It was a breathtaking wedge of space that dwarfed the two of them, an alien intrusion of right angles into the natural world of forest, lake, and mountain, and yet in scale with the enormous old pines, the vast containment of the lake's water, the leap of the land toward the sky that made the mountains reach.

Pearl turned around slowly in a complete circle, taking in the room. An open stairway rose and turned along two walls in a gallery to reach the upper stories. The walls were hung with jigsaw puzzles and were pierced with a series of niches obviously built to display some collection. But at first glance, the things in them had nothing in common. There was an old softball in one, a glass bowl full of marbles in another, a discarded red tie and a chunk of quartz in a third. Perhaps the oddest was the ancient Raggedy Ann doll folded fetally into the niche.

"Stations of the cross," David said. "My mother had a bunch of bones and pottery shards and old shit, I mean seriously old, in those boxes. Some of it actually did stink. I gave it all to Harvard. Now I don't know what to put in the boxes. They don't like to be empty so I try things out in them. Sometimes the boxes like the found objects and sometimes they don't."

Pearl couldn't think of anything to say so she didn't. He didn't seem to expect anything. He took her by the hand and brought her out onto the deck that seemed a continuation of the openness of the living room. The chaise David had apparently just abandoned to answer her knock was in the shade of an overhanging roof. There were books and papers heaped around it, a tape player with earphones, a glass of ice water on the deck next to it.

"You smell like fried chicken," he said.

"Thanks. I did shower."

He dropped an arm casually over her shoulder.

"Down, woman. You smell good enough to eat."

"Oh." She looked around frankly. "This is your summer home?"

He nodded.

"Like to see where you live in the winter."

"An apartment. A perfectly ordinary apartment. Can I get you something to drink?"

"Water would be nice. I've been drinking iced tea all day and my mouth's a little puckery from the lemon."

"I do have drink. Be happy to get you a beer or a glass of wine or your choice of hard stuff."

Pearl shook her head. "Maybe I'll take a glass of wine later."

The kitchen was a wall-laid-out galley and it was very clean.

"The lake's been waiting all day for you."

"That's all I've thought about all day. Getting into the water."

"There's a bedroom down the hall if you'd like to change."

It appeared to be the master bedroom, with a beautiful mahogany four-poster with elegant simple lines. Though the windows were open, it was hot, heated by sun coming in from skylight and window wall, with an occasional whisper of breeze from the lake. No visible air conditioning. And no draperies or sheers in the windows, but the bed was tented in mosquito netting, the only concession to the normal privacy of the bedroom. David Christopher either led a blameless life or was a raving exhibitionist. Of course he had the option of the other bedrooms; the place must have two or three more anyway. Perhaps he used each in turn. She laughed at herself for being thoroughly dirty-minded.

When she came back out, David was standing at the deck railing looking at the deck. He was still wearing the shorts and open shirt and his eyes were hidden behind the dark glasses. Her gut tightened with apprehension. She hoped she wasn't going to have to cope with any more adolescent come-ons.

"Aren't you going to swim?"

"No," he said shortly. "I've got my period."

He barely looked at her. His face was tight and closed and he bopped his clear glasses lightly against the rail. Perhaps he was having his own second thoughts, his own attack of cowardice.

"Ouch," she said, trying to inject good humor.

Now he looked at her and smiled and a little of the tension went out of his shoulders.

"I'm sorry. I'm touchy about swimming. I usually deal with the problem by not inviting guests."

Impulsively she covered his hand on the railing with hers.

"I'm honored, then."

He was still too tightly wired, looking at her unreadably behind the sunglasses. Then he seemed to come out of a trance. He smiled and patted her bottom affectionately.

"Go swimming."

It was a short walk from the deck across lawn to his beach. She tried not to be self-conscious. The water smelled good to her, essence of cool in the heat, knowing he was watching her. She wanted to feel it flowing over her skin. Breezes wrinkled the water, emphasizing its silkiness, the meniscus of surface, the water's own skin. She dove into paralyzing cold. Breaking the surface, she screamed and heard David laughing.

Swimming steadily, she warmed herself from the inside out. Eventually her joints stopped resisting the cold and began to feel oiled. The goose bumps went down and her skin felt burned with the cold. As soon as she was out again, she broke out in violent shivering. Wrapping herself in a towel, she staggered back to the deck.

"You put the ice cubes in the lake?"

David handed her a mug of hot tea.

"Two trays."

"I never swam in colder water in my life." Her teeth chattered punctuation.

"I understand it's cold enough to induce hypothermia, so if you drown in this lake, there's a good chance of revival, especially if you're a kid."

"Really?"

"Yeah." Behind the dark glasses, he seemed to be staring at the lake. "I think a lot about how people can be brought back from the dead now. Second coming. Like we're cats now, with nine lives to lose."

She listened, fascinated.

"I have a dream, sometimes, that I'm standing at this railing, looking at the lake, and suddenly I see my sister floating on the water. I swim out and rescue her and she's blue and cold but she's not dead, she's in a hypothermic state. She's still a little girl, still wearing the white cap she was wearing that day. A helicopter comes to take her away to a big hospital where she'll be revived."

Pearl realized she had been holding her breath and let go. She reached out to touch him.

"David."

He straightened abruptly at the rail and flinched away from her.

"I'm sorry, Pearl. That was unforgivable."

"No. No, it wasn't."

He pulled himself together visibly but couldn't seem to let it go.

"Your Uncle Joe was on the roofbeam, with Reuben. Reuben was all long legs and arms and big hands and feet, like a half-grown puppy, back then. Did you know he had an affair with my mother?"

Pearl shifted in her chaise. She didn't want to know anything more, it hurt too much to receive all this pain of his, but she understood he was struggling to find a way out of the story of his sister's death. Even if she got some rope burns, she had to throw him a line. So she shook her head no.

"Roscoe told me Joe died here. He implied there was something going on, but you know Roscoe. Uncle Joe was an old man and your mother was sick."

David laughed softly.

"No, that's ridiculous. Joe was like a father to my mother. He looked out for her. I meant Reuben."

Pearl started. "Oh?"

"My mother was a beautiful woman and she was alone, really, even before my father died. She was an alcoholic, you know, and there were times when she went to bed with people drunk when she wouldn't have sober. I'm sure it was her initiative. Reuben was too shy, back then, to ask a girl to dance. I'm not judging, I'm glad if they both got something out of it. God knows my mother never had anything after, and Reuben's marriage was a disaster."

Pearl sipped her tea.

"How do you know they had an affair?"

"Surprised them in the woods one day." David grinned.

She could see the tension draining out of him as he talked. They had finally gotten away from his sister's death.

"It may be a boy's misperception but my memory is that Reuben Styles is a well-endowed farmboy."

Pearl nearly choked on a mouthful of tea. She held up one hand defensively and laughed.

"Don't tell me things like that. I won't be able to wait on the man without sniggering."

"Hey, why do you think I put my sunglasses on every time I see him?"

"Now I'm going to laugh every time I see you wearing shades."

David started poking around with a hibachi.

"Reuben's wife left him for a fundamentalist minister about five years ago, just as Karen was coming into puberty. It was an unholy mess, I'll tell you. Karen's been wild ever since and Reuben seems like he's been poleaxed."

"I'm sure Roscoe would have given me the dirt on it, except Karen's around most of the time he is."

"Roscoe's almost but not totally without sensitivity," David observed.

He grunted in satisfaction as the coals flared up.

"There, did it with two matches, always a good sign. Of course," he continued, "the biggest reason for Roscoe's reticence on the subject is Reuben Styles. He may be a rural oaf but he's one of ours and Reverend Elmer Gantry sure the hell wasn't."

Pearl smiled. "Elmer Gantry?"

David dropped back onto his chaise. "Or Reverend Dimmesdale. I've been meaning to ask you, did your mother name you Pearl after Hester Prynne's baby in *The Scarlet Letter*?"

Pearl burst out laughing. "I don't know. I've wondered that myself. She had a copy of the book, if that's evidence. And she had an odd sense of humor. It would be just like her."

David seemed enormously pleased with the idea. "Anyway, you'd think these preachers could think up a more original sin, wouldn't you? They seem to be fixated on sex. Don't seem to be able to get off at all unless it's illicit. Whereas when it comes to the money, they don't linger over Thou Shalt Not Steal. Anyway, the word 'prick' was invented to describe the Rev. He's a bullet-headed, mean little ex-con who got Jesus in the joint and has since made his living sowing dissension among the more hapless rural Christians. It happened during the winter when I was away, but the general consensus seems to be that the Reverend Richard Smart cold-bloodedly busted up the Styles family. He was minister to a small church in the next small town over, Grant. Little mill town, notable for its grimness. He began to proselytize across the town line, dirty pool around here. He got a hold on the wife. Laura demanded Reuben and the kids accept Jesus as their personal savior and the Reverend Dick as their personal Führer. Reuben declined. When it was clear Laura was prepared to choose the pastor over the family, the kids came down on Reuben's side. Laura kicked up the shit, a judge removed the kids to a foster home, and then the Rev heroically punched out the foster mother, a woman with a heart condition, in an attempt to reclaim the Styles kids for Laura. That's when things got serious.

"Seems this was not the first time the Reverend Dick had pulled a family apart. There are a fair number of farmers and pulp cutters around who have grievances against the Rev. Some male relatives of the foster mother took offense. People began to carry chains and guns and there were several public incidents of pushing and shoving and punching out, all revolving around the Rev. The state police were called in to restore order. A number of citizens, including the Rev, found themselves serving brief terms in the county hoosegow for assault or public disorderliness. Reuben, I'm proud to say, maintained his dignity and had nothing to do with the civil disorder.

"Then things got really amusing. Laura was living with the Rev and his official wife, 'as a sister.' There was talk otherwise but no proof, until another woman, a former member of the congregation, whose husband was among the combatants who had gone to jail, accused the Rev of practicing a little Christian *droit du seigneur*. You may not care to know this, but I don't think the Rev's a likely customer of yours, so I'll tell you: the word on the street is the Rev is not as impressively hung as Reuben. Chicken Dick, the locals were calling him. Perhaps he has other qualities. His congregation finally gagged on his refusing to turn 'sister' Laura out. The Rev and his ménage have since removed to a larger town about fifty miles from here where the pickings are richer. Laura's some kind of deaconess.

"There was enough of a stink so that Reuben obtained full custody of his kids, but by then the damage had been done, at least to Karen. She hates the Rev and her mother about equally. I have a suspicion the Rev may have, as they say around here, 'bin at her.' I don't think Reuben has the faintest on that score because there is an end to his patience and the Rev wouldn't still be alive if he did."

"Please." Pearl's tummy hurt from giggling. Poor Karen. Poor Reuben. Poor Sam. "No more." She shook her head. "I thought I had a lurid family history."

David rolled over and checked on the coals in the hibachi.

"Tell me," he said. "As soon as I put on the fish."

EIGHT

1

It was still hot in a way the coming of dark would not diminish by much. Pearl's bathing suit had dried on her body and her upper lip was damp with sweat. Relaxing into the chaise, she savored the heat and the luxury of having her feet up. Boats moved on the lake, Sunfish with sails dipping and belling, motorboats plowing, canoes drawing their placid threads.

The glass of iced chablis David put into her hand was shockingly cold, raising goose bumps on her arm for a second or two. The wine's aftertaste was faintly oily and metallic, like an olive. Holding the glass to the light, she admired its scant color.

"Supermarket Special Reserve. How extravagant of you."

" 'We buy no plonk before it's on sale,' " David intoned, peeling paper towels from a pair of coral salmon steaks and displaying them for her delectation.

She clapped her hands together. "*Saumon*, marinated in something peculiar and grilled on a bed of coals so expensive they are almost diamonds, the *saumon* then decorated with a day lily and a feathered leek!"

"Please, *mademoiselle*." David took mock offense. "Spare me your flippancy. This is not food, this is *nouvelle cuisine*."

"Sorry, I can't eat that without a sauce, it's against my religion. I got *roux* in my veins instead of blood."

He rocked on his haunches. "Rue?"

"R-o-u-x. R-u-e is an herb and sometimes an emotion."

David snatched a notebook from among the books and papers beside his chair.

"Hold it, let me write that down." He pretended to pout when she laughed. "Please, I'm a poet. Words are my life."

"Do tell."

He dropped his notebook and took up his spatula. "No, it's your turn to tell me."

"What?"

"I knew it, you never were going to tell me."

"What?"

"Your lurid family history."

"Oh, that." She waved it away. Under the influence of the chablis, her hands were beginning to do a lot of punctuating.

"Figure of speech. It's nothing unusual, really."

"I've been very polite." He dropped onto the chaise next to her. "And I'm feeding you dinner. The least I expect is to find out how Joe Nevers' niece happened to have a black baby."

"I'm not black. I'm a very nice shade of mahogany, and I was conceived in the usual way, by sexual congress. Since it was already well-known that human beings of various shades are able to mate outside the laboratory"—she took pains to pronounce it "la-bore-a-tore-ee"—"there was no media coverage. I thought," she went on, "Walter and Roscoe functioned as Gossip Central. You bucking for the job?"

"Smart-ass. There is a story in it, isn't there?"

2

When she was little, the world was populated by people of nearly every imaginable shade, from blue-black to espresso to bitter chocolate to coffee-and-cream to cinnamon, amber, ivory, and bisque. Many of her schoolmates did not match one or both of their parents and sometimes not their siblings. Why, then, should it be remarkable that little Pearl did not match her mama? Yet the contrast with her own skin caused her to regard the color of her mother's as beautiful. The time when she would realize her own color would make the world more troublesome was yet to come.

She remembered an intense green distance, deliciously cool between her naked toes, and the colors and shapes of flowers—the velvety gem-colored bellies of snapdragons, the airy, spidery cleome and fairy-capped columbine, the doubled butterfly wings of pansies, bachelor buttons, like small ruffly improbable blue-violet parasols, and bleeding hearts, dangling upon their bows. And then her mother's arms and bosom, the silkiness of her mother's petaled blouse sleeve, and a peony with petals of creamy silk against her mother's face, the color and texture of her skin, as the two of them sniffed ecstatically at the flower. One day she knew the fabric of her mother's blouse had been crepe or silk-crepe, and the name of the peony had been *Paeonia albiflora*, probably the variety called Doris Cooper.

It was not their garden unless it was somewhere they had lived when she was very small. Their tiny rented house in Key West had no yard in which to make a garden, only an enormous banyan tree which was extremely good for climbing. But for the overflowing porch and window planters, their garden was all indoors, a luxury of growing green that countered the poverty of furniture and decorations. In this picture-book library of her mother's plants, Pearl learned the alphabet of gardens. She looked all over Key West at various times in her childhood and could not find the broad green lawn with the huge flower garden and the peonies in it. She acquired the conviction it was somewhere else, perhaps on the mainland, ratified by the eventual realization that neither peonies nor most of the other flowers she had seen in that mythic garden could grow in the alternately saturated or dehydrated cat-box soil of the Keys. They were Northern flowers; the garden must be somewhere North.

By the time she was seven, in the second grade, she had the primer lessons of Color down pat. In any situation, the first thing to establish was who was what Color. She and her classmates were called Colored or Negro and her mother was called White. Sorting the lighter shades of Nonwhite from White was easy; there the difference was in attitude. Coloreds acted one way, Whites another. White was the rarest flower in the rank, impoverished garden of her limited world, the few crowded shabby blocks of very small houses; its most obvious bloom was her mother.

They lived on a small island called a key, one of a bunch of keys connected by causeways all the way to a mainland called Florida or Miami. She was in the third grade before she had sorted out whether Florida contained Miami or the other way around. It was extremely interesting to her that the device her mother used to lock the door of their tiny house was also a key. Pearl carried into adulthood the punning, metaphorical image of the islands shaped like keys upon the key ring of the causeway.

At seven, she was perfectly aware that Key West was not shaped like a key. She and her playmates knew its outline intimately, for it was there, on the shore and in the shallow water, that they grew up, rather than in the narrow dusty streets that did for dooryards. Many of them grew up in and on boats, the children of fishermen or men who crewed for others. Much of their play—crabbing, clamming, fishing—also put food on their families' tables. There were White kids who lived the same way—who had their hair cut inexpertly at home and dressed as they did, in hand-me-downs and make-dos, and went barefoot, like them, most of the time. Their nets and fish lines were also homemade. But the groups didn't mix even when they were only feet apart and doing the same thing. Sometimes it seemed as if the White kids couldn't see them, dark as some of them were, standing right next to them. Pearl was aware her kind always gave way, yielded the best places to the White kids, silently, unasked, just moved out of the way.

Then one day her best friend, Lila, informed her that she was a bastard.

"I am not," Pearl retorted. "We don't belong to no church."

Had her mother heard her, she certainly would have corrected the use of the double negative. Pearl would have said, "Yes, ma'am," and gone out and used it again because that was the way her friends talked.

Lila, hanging from the banyan in the backyard, laughed cruelly.

"I mean," Lila said in her thickest drawl, "you ain't got no daddy."

Pearl didn't know what to say. Of course, she had noticed that most kids had fathers. But some didn't; she was one of those. It really hadn't seemed very remarkable. Finally she decided upon the issue of relevance as the proper response to Lila's attack. She thrust out her chin.

"So what?"

"So," Lila said, inexorably logical, "she's a whore."

This was also a new word.

"I told you," Pearl said crossly, "we don't belong to no church."

Lila's laughter was rusty and ragged as an old cross-saw.

"Don't you know what a whore is?" she twitted.

"Well," Pearl ventured, "if it means where she's from, she's some kind of Yankee. She used to live someplace it snows a lot."

"She did?" Lila said momentarily distracted. "She ever build a snowman?"

Pearl nodded. "There was so much snow it reached over her head and she could build forts out a it and have snowball fights."

Lila was impressed. "Luck-ee."

Pearl held her head up. Here, it appeared, was a safe brag. She would bring it up to the other kids too. *My mama built forts outta snow, there was so much of it. Higher than her. She went right insida it.*

"What's a whore?" she asked Lila cautiously.

"A whore is a woman that mens pay for lovin' 'em up."

"My mama don't love no men up," Pearl said quickly.

Lila thought about this.

"But she did, or you wouldn't be borned. Only White woman who'd love up a Colored man is some kinda whore."

Pearl was growing desperate.

"But my mama's a waitress. She gets paid for waiting on table."

"A waitress in a Colored diner," Lila countered. "A White woman with a Colored kid's a whore. Whites won't let no White woman with a Colored kid live in their part of town. That's why you live on our street."

"You're a liar." Pearl calmly punched Lila in the mouth.

Lila came out of the fight with a swollen upper lip and some scratches. Pearl cut her knuckles up on Lila's teeth and acquired an impression of Lila's overbite on her upper arm. Her mother made her apologize to Lila and Lila's parents, who listened grimly and then forbade the girls to play together for a month.

The first day of the interdiction, Pearl took out her crayon box and crouched on her knees over the kitchen table, silent and intent. She covered paper with tight whorls of her black crayon, her brown crayon, but when she tried to scratch the color off, there was always a stain upon it. Color was more powerful than White, it blotted White out. Yet White, unblotted White, owned the world. It was inexplicable. There was some great knot in this logic that the grown-ups must understand better than she.

3

Pearl's mother had not always worked at the diner. She had waited table in other establishments. Sooner or later the owners of those other luncheonettes, restaurants, bars, and grills found out about Pearl and then there were terrifying times, in which her mother wept with her head in her hands over her open pocketbook, with the meager pile of bills and coins counted over and over next to it. There had been one awful time when her mother had had pneumonia and Pearl thought she was going to die. But she didn't. She got well and shortly after found the job in the diner.

The All-Night Diner was owned by a prosperous Colored businessman who had come from the Keys but who presently lived in New Orleans, where his wife originated. His several small businesses were tended to on a day-to-day basis by trusted relations. The diner was the exception. In the off season, summer, the night manager was in charge; winters the All-Night was managed by a cook named Dick Halloran. It was Dick Halloran who hired Pearl's mother. Within a few weeks, he asked her to take over as night manager.

One evening, Pearl realized her mother had left her umbrella at home and it was raining hard. What if her mother caught a cold? Colds went right to her chest. So Pearl put on her only jacket and raised the umbrella over her head and set off for the diner. She hesitated outside, for she was strictly forbidden to visit her mother's places of employment. But it was late at night and raining hard. She could see there were only one or two people inside the diner, she could see her mother, see the cook, who must be the man her mother called Dick Halloran, laughing. Pearl knew she was going to catch it anyway, for being out of the house so late at night on her own, for coming to the diner, but she had to bring her mother the umbrella or her mother might get sick and die. She decided she would slip the umbrella inside the door and lean it against the wall. Maybe her mother would think she herself had brought it after all. Slowly and quietly Pearl opened the diner's door just enough to insert the umbrella and her arm. She closed her eyes with relief when she had it propped against the wall and started to withdraw her arm. Then a hard hand closed around her upper arm and she gasped. Her eyes flew open and she discovered herself in the grasp of the cook. She was too terrified to scream or even peep. Dick Halloran opened the door the rest of the way and scooped her up.

"Your mother know where you are, kid?"

Pearl managed to move her head in single negative side-to-side.

"Yes, she does." Pearl's mother came out from behind the counter.

Surprise opened Dick Halloran's face, but only for a second. He put Pearl down.

"You forgot your umbrella," Pearl said faintly. She snatched up the umbrella again and held it out.

"Thank you." Her mother's voice shook.

Pearl was in agony. She had done a terrible thing coming here.

Her mother's hands fell upon Pearl's shoulders.

"Dick," her mother said in a stronger voice, "this is my daughter, Pearl. Pearl, this is Mr. Halloran."

Dick held out his hand and slowly shook hers. "Pleased to meet you. You better have something to warm you up now you're here. How 'bout some cocoa?"

She twisted her neck to look up at her mother. Her mother's hands relaxed on Pearl's shoulders.

"Okay. I'll take her out in the kitchen."

"Let her sit on a stool, cocoa tastes better you can turn a stool around while you drink it."

Pearl liked that idea. It turned out to be true. Dick knew a lot of silly jokes. She finally fell asleep in one of the booths. In the very early morning, her mother walked home with her, hand in hand. She didn't catch a scolding. A day or two later, Dick Halloran said she could come to the diner anytime it was okay with her mama and he would let her bus the tables. Her mother said after school and weekends, not nighttime. Pretty soon Pearl was at the diner as often as she was home, oftener. Dick Halloran acted like she belonged there, so she figured it was okay if she acted that way too.

She missed Dick when he went away but her mother made more money, which was a small compensation. Dick wrote to them and his letters were almost as good as having him around the diner. He sent her postcards of the Rocky Mountains and snapshots of himself in the kitchen of the hotel where he worked summers.

It was a summer evening when a tall coffee-colored man with a smooth, naked egg-shaped skull and a deep, rumbling way of laughing came into the diner and introduced himself as Mr. Norris Dickenson, the owner. He smelled very nice, of what she eventually learned was Old Spice after-shave, and wore a suit like a salesman or a preacher. He made her mother nervous, Pearl saw, and so she did her best to make herself scarce without actually leaving the place, but she kept feeling he was looking right at her. He was, he announced, moving back to Key West. It seemed that his wife had died a few months earlier. Mr. Dickenson had decided to return to his hometown. He had made some money and thought he could make more while looking more closely after his aged parents and renewing his ties to two brothers and a sister. It took some years for Pearl to sort out all Mr. Dickenson's relations, but his immediate family included a grown-up son named Harry, who had a wife pregnant with Mr. Dickenson's first grandchild, as well as two teenage daughters named June and May, and a ten-year-old son, Bobby. Pearl's mother told her bravely she thought Mr. Dickenson would keep her on as night manager but not to be surprised if he decided to make changes.

Mr. Norris Dickenson began to call regularly and Pearl could see he pleased her mother very much. In the fall her mother told Pearl that Mr. Norris Dickenson was going to be her stepfather. The wedding was in a small Roman Catholic chapel, dark and thick with the scent of beeswax, of oils and incenses, and hung about with darkly colored and mysterious images and pictures. Most prominent was a statue of the mother of Jesus holding her baby; she was a white woman in white and blue robes, and her baby, also white, was nearly naked. Afterward was a lawn party at Mr. Dickenson's new large house. Dick Halloran was there. It seemed to Pearl the whole town must be there, though it was really only *her* whole town, the Colored part of it. In the backyard, several times bigger than the house in which Pearl and her mother had been residing, a band played Cajun reels and New Orleans blues and the dancing went on long after Pearl had fallen asleep in her new bed. Several times that night she woke enough to hear it, the music and people laughing, and somehow it got all tangled up with her dreams.

Pearl thought Norris Dickenson was God. She adored him, and the adulation was returned. She was not too old for him to carry on his shoulders, her long legs crossed on his broad chest, so she had to duck, screaming with delight, under doorways. The breast pocket of his suit was a treasure chest kept filled for her, boxes of Junior Mints, smooth loops of brightly colored hair ribbons, marbles and seashells and smooth pebbles.

In his much larger house Pearl had her own small bedroom, once a nursery, under the eaves. For the first time in her life, she had three new dresses, a white one with a blue sash, a blue one with brown horses galloping around the hem, a red one with white dots all over, hanging in the tiny closet of her room. She had a pair of black patent-leather Mary Janes for dress-up, and a pair of brown lace-up for school, as well as her sneakers to play in. She had a white straw hat with a blue ribbon to wear to church. They went to church every Sunday now and she sat next to her mother, with Bobby on the other side, and listened to Mr. Dickenson sing baritone in the choir with June and May.

Every Friday evening he made her hold out her hand and close her eyes while he pressed two cool, bright dimes into her hand and closed her fist around them. On Saturday morning she would walk two blocks to a little neighborhood store and buy a green-glass six-ounce bottle of Coca-cola and then she would nestle in the banyan in the backyard and drink it, the coldest, sweetest nectar on earth. On Sundays he often took the whole family to the beach and he would throw her into the ocean ahead of him and race her through the waves until they were both exhausted, while her mother shouted encouragement from the sand.

June and May wore lipstick and had nylon stockings and garter belts like her mother did. In a small cupboard in the bathroom, they kept their own boxes of the soft, snowy white rectangles that played some vital role in the female mystery of *monthlies*. She was not supposed to know anything about the contents of the cupboard, but if she happened to see them open it to put away a new box, they would become, over the top of her head, all wise and ironic and sophisticated to each other.

June had a bottle of Evening in Paris perfume on her dresser, and a boyfriend, and May had *two* boyfriends. May also had a record player in a leatherette-covered cardboard suitcase, and sometimes, behind the closed door of their room, the two big girls danced to bebop recorded on the race labels, Chess and Dot and 'Gator. She could hear them singing with the records and giggling. She didn't even mind them occasionally treating her like an ignorant baby, for they were so glamorous it was like living with movie stars. She was nearly transported at the sight of their ankle chains and their enormous crinoline petticoats under their taffeta party dresses.

Even Bobby, after an initial period of reservation, treated her like a little sister and not some unfortunate appendage of her mother's, like the mysterious bag her new grandmother wore under her clothes that Bobby whispered was a "klostme bag."

Pearl was expected to help June and May clean and cook for Mr. Dickenson's parents. Pop was bedridden and Grammy was frail. Pearl learned to feed Pop his oatmeal and wipe his chin for him, and helped June wash Gram's hair in a basin. Sitting in an itchy horsehair chair, she would read the Bible to the old folks, and if she did it well, Gram would press a penny in her hand.

Mr. Dickenson gave her a piggy bank.

With one thing and another, she saved enough money to acquire a raggedy blue second-hand bike and Bobby taught her to ride it. He helped her paint it red, clipped old cards to the spokes for a dashing percussion sound. On her next birthday, he gave her reflectors. She felt like she was Mr. Dickenson's own child.

4

June and May and Bobby grew up. Harry and his wife had more children. Gram and Pop, each in their turn, died. Mr. Dickenson's business ventures prospered, and so, it seemed, did his marriage to Pearl's mother.

Pearl went away to college. When she was home on holidays and during the summers, she worked in the diner. One summer evening, when she had just finished showering away the sweat of a long day's labor in the diner, she heard her mother cry out to her. She found her lying on the ground in the garden, having a seizure. Her mother's eyes had rolled up, spittle flew from her mouth, she made a noise like *egg, egg, egg,* and there was a sharp smell of urine in the warm night air.

"Aneurysms," was what the doctor called it, as she sat in his office with Norris Dickenson. "Inoperable, nothing we can do."

In her own mind Pearl always called it *egg, egg, egg*.

The next day, her mother looked up from her hospital bed, her face as white as the sheets, one eye full of blood, and said, "My family name is really Madden. I come from a town in Maine called Nodd's Ridge. I would like you to write to my mother and tell her. Tell her. Tell her I would like to see her."

Pearl knew there was not enough time to write. She called, obtaining the telephone number of her mother's parents through directory assistance. A woman answered the phone and Pearl asked for Mrs. Madden.

"Speaking."

"My name is Pearl Dickenson. I am your granddaughter."

There was a fractional pause. "Oh, my God. Is Elizabeth all right?"

"No," Pearl said, "no, she's not."

The woman cried out in anguish and Pearl burst into tears.

Pearl and Norris Dickenson met Gussie at the airport in the late morning of the next day. The pain in the eyes of the old woman was nearly unbearable but Pearl had cried herself out by then. She could barely speak, her throat was so tight. Her guts churned with rage at her. It must be this old woman's fault if Pearl's mother had not been able to tell her the truth in those wretched moments of her pregnancy two decades past. It was a delusion Pearl was not able to sustain for very long.

"Did you forget," Gussie asked Elizabeth, "that I love you?"

So Pearl came to understand that it was possible to sin as deeply in the name of love as it was in anger or hate. She was not, after all, her mother's sin, or only her mother's sin, or her mother's only sin. The price of this knowledge was high. But there was a new gift of love, the unflinching and unquestioning love of Gussie. Love, it seemed, like matter itself, was never entirely annihilated by death or forgetting or mutual sins, but was merely transformed.

5

But Pearl did not tell any of this to David Christopher, not then. "How do you know where to start a story or where it ends? I know a lot of things about my mother and about Gussie, and some of what I know is very important. To me, anyway. But there's so much I don't know, can't know, never will know. 'We see through a glass darkly,' doesn't just mean we don't know what God does, it also means we don't know half what we think we do about ourselves and each other. All I feel safe in telling you are bare facts—my mother ran away from home when she was seventeen, and somehow came to grief. I am the bastard child of Elizabeth Madden, who later married Norris Dickenson and died in Key West in 1973 of an aneurysm. Maybe those facts aren't all that important, or even true. I am also the daughter of Norris Dickenson in every sense but the biological. My mother is dead but she has never died in my memory. She never told me who my father was or why they didn't marry or if she loved him. She held her secrets tight. I've had to accept that how I came to be born is a mystery I will never solve. I doubt it matters, really. What surely does not matter to me is the color of my skin. It's just my skin that holds me in."

David had listened acutely and without interruption and now he touched her wrist lightly and smiled. " 'Such music in a skin!' "

"That's quite a line," she said.

"Not mine," he confessed. "Roethke."

"I thought I'd read it somewhere. Well, I don't mind if he doesn't."

"He'd think it was appropriate, and that's what matters."

She laughed, patted his hand and went into the house to change back into her shorts.

When she returned, David cranked up the volume on the stereo system in the house and she picked Paul Simon's *Graceland* out of his tapes as dinner music. They ate potato salad and salmon and fresh peas, with white wine for Pearl, on the deck.

Pearl started to feel pleasantly tight. When David reached for the wine bottle again, she covered her glass.

"Enough. I've got to drive home."

"I'll drive you home. You've got two cars, you'll still get to work in the morning."

"Are you trying to get me drunk?"

"My mother always swore by it," David said gravely, and got them both giggling. "Come on, let's dance."

He caught her hand and pulled her, protesting, to her feet. After a brief rummage in the tapes, he put on one he wouldn't let her see.

"Oh, Sue," sang Michael Douchet, and the sound of a Cajun fiddle returned Pearl instantly to the night of her mother's wedding.

"Oh, how did you know?" It occurred to her she really had had one glass too many.

"Know what?" David asked, drawing her into the first steps of a reel and catching her when she almost overbalanced into a stagger.

Drunk too much indeed. No wonder the old Puritans considered dancing a sin. At least she had eaten heartily. A full stomach was a drag on both drunkenness and lust.

" *'Oh, Sue,'* " they sang together. " *'Oh, Sue, baigne pas dans le bayou,'* " as she ducked under the arch of David's arm, " *'Cocodril va te manger tout cru.'* " *Oh, Sue, don't swim in the bayou, the gator will make a meal of you.* He brought her back as the fisherman's rod bows back to its original arc and drew her close, much too close, with one arm tucked behind her under his control. They looked at each other with speculative eyes and again broke out laughing. He looked so amused she kissed him, thinking *drunk too much, you fool.*

It was a long, frighteningly hot clinch and when they came up for air, the tape had fallen silent.

"We're stopping here," she said.

He let her go, peeking at her bashfully from lowered lashes. In silence he offered her another glass and she shook her head.

She hugged herself, realized what she was doing, and managed a bitter chuckle. "Look at me."

"I am." He went to the fridge, poured iced tea for her.

She was, she discovered, very thirsty.

"I don't want to stop," he said. "You don't want to stop either."

She went out onto the deck, where it was darker and a little cooler, and leaned over the rail. Clotted clouds were backlit by the sinking sun like smoke. The colors were draining out of the sky, the woods, the mountains, seemingly into the water of the lake, a caldron of deep and dark glinting gold and red and purple.

In a minute he followed her out. She turned her back to the rail and he planted a hand on either side of her and kissed her again. This one was soft and searching, and in its own way, much harder to stop.

"Thank you," she said, "it was a lovely evening."

She picked up her beach bag and he caught her hand.

"First date. Never."

He sighed. "What about true love?"

She laughed and put down her beach bag again. Still holding his hand, she dropped onto the lounge chair and patted it. He sat down on the edge of the other.

"David, I'm not prepared."

"Oh." He was thoughtful for moment. "Why not?"

"Because I'm not going to bed with you on the strength of one dinner and a Cajun reel. Besides, women shouldn't have to do all the contracepting."

He smiled and she thought she must be crazy to pass up a good thing.

"Of course not." He kissed her hand.

"Stop that." She pulled it away. "You're just a horny poet."

"Poets need sex too. Probably worse than other people."

She thought he might actually laugh her into bed if she didn't watch out, the problem being that was exactly what she really wanted.

"So do cooks," she countered.

"I'll still respect you in the morning," he said with a sly grin.

"Your mother didn't paddle you enough. It's been eighteen months and six days since the last time I had a man. You'd be taking advantage."

"Shocking," he said. "I'm a lot more desperate than you. I haven't had a woman in three years and thirteen days."

They laughed themselves nearly sick.

"David," Pearl finally gasped. "What I want to know is," but she couldn't finish the question because the giggling got the upper hand again.

"What?"

She sobered up enough to talk. "When's the last time you went to bed with a man?"

He sobered at once. The silence stretched out. He looked at her defiantly.

"Three years and ten days."

Neither of them laughed.

She put her hand out to him at once. "David."

He pushed her hand away. "I know what you're afraid of."

He was beginning to be angry at her so he wouldn't be angry at himself or all the complexities of existence over which they neither of them had any control. She didn't know why people wanted things to be simple; they hardly ever were.

She sighed. "David, I'm afraid of lots of things."

He peered at her intently. "How much does it matter to you that I find men as well as women attractive?"

She shook her head. "If sex was all I was interested in, not at all. I find men attractive too."

He smiled again. "Is it so obvious? What I am?"

She wasn't going to tell him when and where and how often he had revealed himself, the tiny things that alone might be nothing but put together were too much to ignore. Nobody really wants to know that about himself.

"Nothing's obvious, David. I'm older than you, I've been around awhile. I've developed the kind of antennae a single woman in her thirties had better have grown, so she doesn't waste any more breeding time on impossible situations. Look, I don't know whether you're hiding or being discreet. Do you think it matters here, will it get you run out of town? You can't be yourself here?"

"No, I don't care what people here think, but this is my place, I don't bring anyone here."

"You invited me."

He smiled. "Be flattered, then."

"Oh, I am."

He reached for her and she shivered, pushing his hands away.

"Don't. I'm too old to go to bed with someone 'cause I had too much to drink and I've been too long without. I don't actually care whether you respect me in the morning, though I hope I never do go to bed with someone who wouldn't, but I have to be able to respect myself, minimum."

"I was afraid of that," he said, and laughed, and she knew it was okay between them, they were still friends.

He carried her beach bag for her and slung it into the cab of the truck. She circled his neck loosely with her arms, raised her face for a good-night kiss, and discovered he had not cooled down at all. One hand in the small of her back pressed her urgently against him. She was perfectly sober.

"David," she protested weakly, knowing they were not, after all, going to stop.

"Shut up," he said, and picked her up bodily.

6

The bedroom was completely open to the night air. It was as if she were in some magical wood where the forest floor was pillowed. The air was heavy with pine pitch and the scent of water. The absence of curtains did not now seem exhibitionistic or shameless; the mosquito net's gauze was private enough, the material reflection of the absorption in each other that clouded their awareness of anything but sensation. The violence and depth of her first coming stunned her. In its lee, she heard a wild, strange hooting and cackling and sat bolt upright, clutching the sheets to her breasts.

"Jesus!"

He laughed. "The loons."

They listened to the bizarre chorus for a little while.

"What are they talking about?"

"Soap operas," he said. "They like *The Young and the Eggless* best."

She could not believe it was possible to giggle and make love at the same time, but then, there were a lot of things she was discovering, delicious and wild, that she'd forgotten or never known about herself.

" 'She laughed me out, and then she laughed me in; in the deep middle of ourselves we lay . . .' " David said.

She tweaked his nipple. "You do go on. What you gonna do when you run out of Roethke to quote."

"This," he said.

He seemed awfully pleased with the inarticulate noises she made in response.

At last, somewhere between exhaustion and terror, she left, insisting she had to have some sleep, she had to work in the morning. True enough, but still not quite the truth; it was flight. Going home, she was intensely conscious of what she had been missing in her abstinence. She was bemused at how and why she had gone so long without; it was as if she had thrown out all her spices and cooked herself meals of sawdust and mud.

7

Her house, looming lightless and dark in the warm night, seemed like a refuge. The bedrooms would be hot with the heat of the day collected in them under the eaves. Open to the night as David's bedroom, the daybed on the sun porch was in her mind.

The smell of strawberries greeted her as she put her foot to the back steps. The screen door was propped open by a small box of woven peeled wood full of tiny aromatic berries. Automatically she glanced at the door, but the expected Post-it note was not there. But she had not the slightest doubt who had gifted her with the berries. She couldn't help a brief flit of guilt. She pushed away any consideration of what Reuben would think of her if he found out she and David had become sexually involved. Man hadn't spoken *except with his little gifts* came back the answer *as loud as words*. She shook off the frisson of guilt; she owed him nothing, not on the strength of kittens, ferns, strawberries. *Then why are you hoping and praying he doesn't ever find out where you just were and what you were doing and whom you were doing it with? Are you telling yourself you can get away with a summer fling with your poet and not change whatever might be sprouting between you and the man? The hell with him, the man might never collect up enough to do more than mooncalf over you.*

Picking up the box of berries, she popped one in her mouth and the explosion of taste and texture was exquisite. With a soft moan she abandoned them on the kitchen table and went upstairs, where she stepped out of her clothes and slipped a thin short nightshirt over her head. While she brushed her teeth, she gave thought to a long shower and came to the conclusion she was dead on her feet and it could wait until morning. The early morning would be cooler. She could run the water as hot as she could bear it and would be all the better for anticipation.

Suddenly ravenous, she took the berries with her onto the sun porch and dropped on the bed with a purely animal grunt of satisfaction. God, they were good. She was exhausted and replete. She lay back and savored the taste. It was wonderfully intense, much stronger than cultivated berries. She turned on the small lamp on the nearby end table and examined the fruits. They were so small, they bled upon her fingers and stained them.

It had been, undeniably, a hell of a day. She refused to allow herself to think about the chances she had taken. If she thought about it, she would have to scold herself, and she was not only too tired, she was frankly in a state of sexual satisfaction that it would be both hypocritical and difficult to regret. She felt too damn good to be banging her head against the stone wall of her conscience. But more obstreperous than stone, her conscience was still there, muttering as crudely as drunken moaning and thumping from the other side of a cheap motel-room wall *what if you get pregnant, if he gave you something, never mind what, never mind if this little romp kills you, what if—*

"Shut up," she muttered. She turned off the light again and closed her eyes, leaving the box resting lightly on her stomach.

And the sound of an engine, the crunch of wheels over gravel, made her open them again. The headlights of a vehicle, a truck, were coming up her driveway from the road at the bottom of the hill.

She flicked the lamp on again and drew the single sheet, all the heat of the night required, around herself in a foggy attempt at modesty, wishing she had brought down a robe. No surprise, somehow, at who had come to call, only bemusement and the sense that a puckish star was now ascendant in her life.

When he opened the door of the truck's cab, something fell out and rolled tinnily upon the gravel.

She watched him shamble from the truck to the sun-porch door. She wasn't the only one who'd been drinking this evening.

He knocked politely at the screen door.

"Come in, Reuben, it's open."

"Pearl, you're up late," he said, flashing her a grin that was just a wee bit slowed with legal anesthetic. He breathed a yeasty zephyr over her.

"You too. Excuse my dishabille. Thanks for the berries."

"It was too hot to sleep," he explained.

She struggled to keep a straight face.

"Actually," he said shyly, "those are your berries. I picked 'em on your land."

"Do tell. Sit down."

He pulled up a straight-back chair, turned it around, and sat down with its back for an armrest.

She offered him a berry and he popped it into his mouth with great relish.

"I shouldn't. I ate a lot when I was picking 'em."

She giggled. "I remember picking strawberries at a farm as a kid and eatin' too many."

He grinned. She was looking at the way his mouth hitched up ironically when he did that, and not thinking about the box of berries, and she sat up. The box spilled and they both reached for it and came up with each other's hands. *Oh, man, why couldn't you have waited till the fall, when poets fall off the trees and get swept back to the cities?* Her stomach tightened up, partly in panic, partly in a nearly hurtful arousal. It seemed David hadn't satisfied her after all, but only awakened her to what she had been missing.

Such a look came over him, so full of hunger and joy, she was a little frightened. He came around the back of the chair and gathered her up. Amazed at herself, she lunged back and the two of them rolled onto the daybed, which protested with a big huff. The berries got crushed among the sheets and against her nightshirt and down inside her nightshirt, and their perfume tartened the night.

What difference did it make she was unprepared, her diaphragm still unpacked? Amid the jumble of sensation and emotion, the stony, ironic Pearl sneered at her: throw a red scarf over the night lamp on the table, woman, and put up a price list. But what did it matter; who in the world cared whether she was loose or a dried-up spinster?

She was so soft, even bruised, everywhere, intensely open to him. Surely if he had not been a little bit drunk and if it was not a first time it might have seemed remarkable to him that she responded so precipitately, so violently. Or perhaps he merely assumed she came to him in the state he came to her, not just long unsatisfied but deeply hurt, guilt-ridden by a sense of failure deeper than the merely physical. She had thought herself exhausted, and now exhaustion itself played a part, she gave herself up to it, to a kind of savory, incredulous submission to sex and the man and the summer night.

NINE

1

The racketing of the Plymouth's engine brought Pearl bolt upright on the daybed. Moaning a half-articulated curse on herself, she struggled to her feet. Her nightie was nowhere visible. She snatched the sheet off the daybed and slung it around herself.

As she charged into the kitchen, the screen door slapped gently behind Karen and interrupted the good-morning on the girl's bee-stung lips. Pearl snatched her key ring from the kitchen table and tossed it at an astonished Karen.

"I overslept." Still moving, she called over her shoulder, "Open up for me, I'll be right there."

Past the girl and starting up the back stairs, she was congratulating herself on retaining some shreds of dignity when she tripped on the sheet and, letting go of it to save herself from falling, left her entire rear out to the wind.

"Damn." She ignored the muffled giggle behind her.

A shower that started scalding and ended dead cold flushed away the last grogginess. When she stepped out, she was awake as a dog straining on its chain after a burglar. Her skin felt as if it could walk and talk on its own, a feat it might have to perform before she had hope of rest again. Hauling open dresser drawers to snatch out underwear, she hopped one-legged over much of her bedroom trying to get her panties on. She considered a pair of clean cotton slacks, shuddered, and pushed them aside to burrow further for gauze harem pants. They would be cooler than slacks and, most importantly, looser, not that anyone would even notice what she was wearing under her apron.

Bolting from the house, she left the slutty (and that was the appropriate word, she chided herself) mess of damp towels, unmade bed linen, and dirty clothes on the floor. The way things were going, the pope would call today. And he'd probably be horny.

At the diner, Karen had the coffee brewing, Roscoe was opening the bale of newspapers, and Sonny Lunt was already parking his wide load on a stool.

Moving at a speed she hoped would deflect anything but a curious glance from Karen, Pearl slung her handbag into her tiny office off the storeroom and grabbed her apron.

As Pearl passed her again, Karen murmured, "Musta been some date."

"Get Sonny his coffee. He's waitin'."

It was a little unfair, as the coffee was still dripping, but Karen took the hint.

Pearl felt like someone had tied weights all over her during the night. But there was work to do, and after a while she was too busy to be tired.

At the height of the morning rush, Pearl was trying to follow a conversation at the end of the counter.

"I like her," one woman was saying to another, "but she drives like there was money waiting for her on the other end. She come barrel-assing down Pigeon Hill and just about took the front of my Subaru off—"

The door crashed open and Evvie Bonneau came in, leading the black retriever pup on a chain with the hook-screw still attached. She waggled a finger at Roscoe.

The old man swore but nevertheless all but rolled over and showed his belly. The little bitch was also well under the animal-control officer's control, heeling loosely, though with tongue lolling and bright eyes still empty of anything except puzzlement.

Evvie handed the rope leash to Roscoe.

"She was out on Route Five chasing trucks. I pick her up again, I'll cite you. Don't forget to register her and get her rabies inoculation when she's six months old."

She had turned on her heel and was gone even before the breakfasters had finished elbowing each other and snickering at Roscoe's chagrin.

The dog immediately tore after her and came up short on the rope.

"Jesus Christ."

Whether Roscoe spoke in praise or in hope of redemption or in despair was unclear. He took the pup outside to tie her up.

On his return, he confided gloomily to Pearl, "Beshatted bitch dug Jack up again. I put him down again, deeper, and soaked the ground with ammonia. That ought a take care of it. But that goddamn bitch took her chain right outta the wall, screw and all. I don't know what I'm going to do to keep her chained up."

"Maybe you ought to take her back to your niece."

Roscoe seemed be giving it serious consideration as he stood in a favorite contemplative pose: his fingertips on his hips, head cocked to one side. But finally he shook his head negatively and went back to work.

When David walked in around ten, Pearl broke out in a nervous sweat. She could feel Karen's antennae going up, the girl's eyes tracking the both of them. Pearl sent out frantic telepathic messages: *Behave, behave, or I'll kill you.*

David's demeanor was perfectly sober; perhaps he was receiving her messages. He went through the little ceremony of changing eyeglasses, picking up a paper, settling onto a stool, and said good morning absently.

She replied in a low but unremarkable tone she would have used with any regular customer who was also a friend.

His glasses had settled at the end of his nose and he peered owlishly over them.

"How are you?"

"Can't complain."

She took his order as briskly as he gave it, blessed him silently, and went about her business. She felt a certain savage triumph over Karen's curiosity and then was mildly ashamed. Kid couldn't help it.

Sometime later, she stepped into the storeroom to discuss a change in her meat order over the phone. Suddenly David stood up and came around the end of the counter and through the door after her, so smoothly and quickly some of the people eating at the counter might have missed him. She had almost forgotten he was still there. She was so completely startled, she started to cry out, and he stifled the sound with the back of his hand.

She bit him and he snatched it back.

He sucked at his hand like a child. "Ow. You didn't have to do that."

"Get on back where you belong. Right now."

He nodded agreeably and then kissed her hard.

She fought him off, banging at him with the receiver of the phone.

He let go, pinched her bottom in passing, and slipped away as quickly as he had appeared, putting on his glasses as he made the turn around the end of the counter.

She caught her breath and said, "Excuse me," to the meat man.

Karen's knowing expression inspired Pearl to wilder heights of fury at David. The hope that nobody else had noticed his little foray past the sign that clearly read EMPLOYEES ONLY was punctured by the sly glint in Roscoe's eye as he noisily sucked up coffee.

As she was cashing up, Karen approached her tentatively. The girl stared at the floor and picked at the polish on her nails. "Pearl, I need to work Sundays. I can't afford to take 'em off."

Pearl slammed the drawer shut.

"If you think you can do it, I need you. Roscoe and I just about drowned last week."

Karen unwound instantly.

"Great."

Pearl watched her peel out of the parking lot in her oil-burner. Kid had a big grin on her face, obviously thought she'd solved her money woes. Well, it was a long winter up here in the North. You had to pick when the money came ripe.

Place locked up, she hauled herself wearily into her truck. She worked at counting her blessings. Surely something was going her way. At least Reuben had made himself scarce. She had a groggy memory of having pushed him out in the wee hours with the flannel-mouthed warning that Karen would be by early. As much as she wanted to go home and fall into bed, she didn't. She turned the truck in the opposite direction and headed for Greenspark.

2

The roads were mostly empty. It always struck wonder in her to drive these miles and hardly ever see another vehicle. The ones she did see were mostly trucks. More trucks up here than she'd seen since she lived in Colorado. The two-lane blacktop, some of it potholed, some of it maintained like avenues, passed through woods and past farms and across the Pondicherry Causeway that seemed so perilously level with the plane of the water. Not much more than a line of huge white and pink rocks divided the pavement from the lake. She turned on the radio but the music immediately made her head ache so she punched it hastily off and drove in the silence.

She needed to think, to make up for how cockeyed—again the appropriate word—her thinking had been the previous night. She was angry with herself and depressed at having been so unbelievably stupid; she had never in her life been sexually *irresponsible*. Her conscience was insistent—*oh, boy, are you going to be sorry, you big dumb cunny*. At the same time, her body was enormously pleased with itself, in a way she had forgotten it could be. It was not talking at all; it was purring. All of a sudden, the tension overcame her. She pounded the steering wheel and laughed hysterically.

She knew why.

The summer of her sophomore year in college, she'd taken eight weeks off from the diner to cook at a girls' camp in the Blue Ridge Mountains. One night she and the counselors, all college girls, had gotten tight on sweet cheap wine and gone midnight skinny-dipping when they knew the college-boy counselors at the boys' camp on the other side of the lake were having a poker party on their beach. She remembered the feeling of power and freedom, the sound of the boys whooping and calling to them, the bodies slicing into the midnight water, the cold shock of it, the scurry into the woods to evade the guys, then huddling, shivering and giggling, under the blankets in the cabins and passing around the bottles to get warm again. She had wondered since how close they had come to a sexual free-for-all.

It came down to thinking she was getting away with something. But she wasn't a college student anymore, proving to equally callow friends that she didn't buy all grown-up, middle-class dicky-shit morality about paying taxes and having kids and kissing some fat ass to keep a crappy nine-to-five job, she was a . . . rebel. Someone who had seen through the hypocrisies and shallows of the conventions.

Well, it was a rush to drive real fast, do something somebody said don't do. There were lots of rushes to be had. But they all cost. Look at old John Belushi, frantically having such a good time it killed him. It had to be one hell of a good time to die for it. Truth was, you never got away with anything. You played, you paid. No free lunch.

The shrieks of laughter petered off into weeping. She wiped her eyes, dug shades out of her glove compartment to cover the damage, and blew her nose vigorously and decisively at a wide place in the road outside of Greenspark. *There*. She pulled herself back together. She was so damn tired.

3

As Pearl swung into the parking lot of the Greenspark Shopping Center—supermarket, pharmacy, dry cleaners, feed store—she saw Reuben's Suburban, but it was too late. Man himself was coming out of the pharmacy and had seen her. She smiled distractedly at him and was grateful for the invention of sunglasses. He smiled dazzlingly back and she was compelled to remember the large, hard teeth as her tongue knew them, causing a rueful and dismaying jolt of unadulterated lust in her tired, hard-used body.

He reached her as she gingerly lowered herself from cab to pavement.

She bit her lip.

"Hi," she murmured.

She felt utterly inane, like a teenager again, too shy and sex-stunned to be able to string two words together intelligently.

He had his planned out.

"I want to apologize. Jumping on you like that. You deserve better."

She was astonished. Her stomach flip-flopped and she felt tears welling and had to blink rapidly to keep them back. Every bit of condescending amusement she'd taken from his awkward courtship now embarrassed her acutely. She had been worse than clumsy, she had been dishonest. He was the one who deserved better.

"I married the only woman I ever courted before," he went on, "and that was a good many years ago. But being out of practice is no excuse. I beg pardon, Pearl."

"It's not owed," she said very quietly.

He nodded. "I'd like to start over and do it right. You care to go berrying later?"

She sucked in a breath. "I can't. Not today."

"What about dinner and a movie this evening?"

"Damn. I'm sorry. I've got so much to do . . ."

Now it was awkward. He was starting to back away.

"I need a night's sleep," she blurted.

He smiled, very slowly. "Well, I guess I do too." He tapped the end of her nose lightly, affectionately. "You . . ." He couldn't find whatever it was that was on the tip of his tongue. He filled in. "Weather holds, you want to pick berries tomorrow?"

Deep breath. "Yes." By then, she'd be rested and have her head straight. She'd be honest with him. Maybe he'd give her another chance. She had to hope so.

He hesitated.

"Another thing. Karen and Sam. When you're a teenager, sometimes your parents take a dislike to whom you're dating because they'd just as soon you weren't dating at all. When you're grown-up, it's your kids who are apt to take dislikes."

She raked her lower lip lightly with her incisors to keep from laughing.

"You need to be discreet; I understand."

"Do that again," he said softly, "or let me do it."

"What?" She was bemused.

"Bite your lip."

She covered her mouth with her hand.

"Meet you in the apple orchard behind your house," he said. "Four okay?"

She nodded. He touched the tip of her nose again and she left him quickly. She was conscious he was watching her go, and she tried not to walk as awkwardly as her extensive tenderness, complicated with long, hot hours of not giving in to it, demanded. She glanced back. He was still there. He waved and then his face changed and she realized she was going to walk into something or someone and hauled herself up short. She was just able to save herself from colliding with a woman at the entrance to the pharmacy. The woman checked her with a defensive arm even as she caught herself. She found herself looking into Belinda Conroy's dark and cynical eyes.

" 'Cuse me," Pearl muttered, brushing past her into the store.

It was mercifully dim (in part because she kept her sunglasses on, thinking she probably looked as foolish as she felt) and cool inside. The aisles were piled high with both the normal drugstore stock of nostrums and cosmetics and a wide variety of the kind of dry goods suddenly required by people in Winnebagos abroad in unfamiliar territory. Pearl grabbed a carrier basket from the stack by the door and ducked into the comfortingly anonymous consumer maze.

The Conroy woman, entering the pharmacy just after her, disappeared toward the back of the store, where a separate counter and register served prescriptions. Good. Maybe she was picking up something with nasty side effects. She'd be out of Pearl's way, anyway.

She moved quickly, on the theory that the faster she moved, the less likely she was to have to speak to Belinda Conroy or be noticed by anyone else. She picked up a box of baking soda for the long cool soak she had planned, then a jar of Vaseline, a can of contraceptive foam in coy packaging, a tube of K-Y for her diaphragm, the one she was going to unpack as soon as she got home and wear every day and every night for the rest of her life and be buried in if God would please spare her from her previous night's folly and make her need her next purchase, a package of tampons. Holding her sunglasses down with one finger, she peered furtively around, didn't see anyone, and snatched several packages of condoms from the display. She started away, hesitated, reached back and plucked several more. Her headache was throbbing, so she grabbed a huge bottle of Excedrin with a shocking price tag on it and hurried to the checkout. She didn't see Belinda Conroy around. Pearl breathed a sigh of relief. The bitch must have left, no doubt with a prescription for uppers so she could ride without a broom.

As she spilled her basket on the counter next to the cash register, there was a sudden nasal uptake of air from the clerk. She looked up into the tightening face of a slight middle-aged woman who wore both her glasses and her cardigan on black cords, perhaps fearing they would try to get away from her. The woman flinched back from the pile of intimate products on the counter as if someone had just deposited something nasty there.

From Pearl's elbow, in cool, amused tones, Belinda Conroy asked, "Going into business?" She had a bottle of hair mousse and a small bag that presumably contained a prescription.

Pearl stared at her, itching to snatch her bald and make the woman eat her own glossy coiffure. Instead, she laughed, bringing it up deep and dirty.

"No," she said with excessive sweetness, "these are party favors for an AIDS benefit. Would you like to make a donation?"

Belinda Conroy's incredulous tinkle of laughter raked Pearl's nerves.

The clerk was hurriedly punching in Pearl's bill and shoveling the nasty items clumsily into a large bag.

"You must find us awfully provincial," Belinda Conroy said with a huge, sharky, bogus smile.

Pearl spilled money onto the counter.

"No," she said with brittle nonchalance. "It's your good manners that are the big thrill."

The two women bared their teeth at each other once more.

The clerk thrust Pearl's bag at her as if it were full of something catching.

As the pharmacy door closed behind her on its pneumatic hinge, Pearl heard the clerk's only line: "Well," the woman said in strangled tones, "I never."

"Me either, honey," Pearl murmured, and dove into her truck as into a hidey-hole.

4

Reuben started forward, not that it would do any good, when he saw she was going to collide with the Conroy woman, but Pearl recovered herself nicely, tired as she was. He could see she was dead on her feet; he ought not to have even asked. It wasn't considerate. Not the least of her charms was she was a hardworking woman.

He hauled himself into his truck, thinking he could use a night's rest too. Well, he wouldn't turn it down, but actually, he was decidedly randy, that part of his nature like a big powerful beast out of hibernation and come into its rut. The remnants of a slight hangover he had worked off. Still, he was not nineteen anymore. Except maybe when thoughts of the previous night insisted on being thought.

Much of the day, he had distracted himself with a side issue: his kids at home, and how much and what and when they needed to know about this part of his life. It went against his grain to hide it, for while he had a strong sense of personal privacy, he was also loath to practice deceits. It smacked too much of his former wife's dishonesty to him. He was an adult and free, doing nothing of which he had any reason to be ashamed. Moreover, he was quite simply in love, and that was not a thing one ought to have to hide. All his instincts urged him to announce it, declare possession and commitment. It had been difficult, even necessary, to cover up the anger, the depression, the grief that the end of his marriage had brought, to nurse his wounds privately, but it was going to be a tough trick to pretend he was not as happy as a pig in a mud puddle. But he had grown wary of Karen's anger; she seemed to perceive his every breath as stealing the air. Sam might go either way.

When he arrived back at the service station, he sent Jonesy on his way and Sam home to start dinner. He meant to close up shortly, but first he rolled himself under Ruby Parks's old Plymouth Valiant to check what Sam had said about the condition of the universal joint. Reuben didn't like to have to tell Ruby the Valiant had had it unless he was dead sure nothing could be done.

Outside, a tight-ass Cadillac rolled up, not to the pumps but right in front of the open garage bay. A woman stepped out. Even after all these years, he'd recognize those ankles anywhere. Not the trimmest he'd ever seen, but with a nice turn to them, all the same. The ankles were headed his way. With a sigh, he rolled himself out from under.

Laura looked down on him, her face tightened up with a frown. Her arms were crossed. Her chin was starting to go, he suddenly realized. There was a definite doubling there.

"I always hated the grease," she said.

She was wearing a tailored but virginally white sleeveless dress that was oddly asexual; she had always had a boyish figure that was still unsoftened in middle age, and the dress seemed to emphasize the smallness of her breasts, the angularity of her hips. Karen had gotten her front from his mother, a full-bosomed woman, not from Laura. His ex-wife's thin primness was a dramatic contrast to Pearl's dark lushness. He had to think his way back down to Laura's ankles to find something even comparable, and then he concluded Pearl's were better too.

He rolled himself upright and picked up a rag.

"I won't offer to shake hands, then."

"I wouldn't shake your hand if you offered."

He shrugged. "Suit yourself."

Turning his back on her, he headed for the office and started to cash up for the day.

She followed him, her heels clattering angrily on the concrete floor. "Karen's living in a trailer. You never let me know she'd moved out of the house."

"I figured it was her business to tell you. Besides, you found out, didn't you?"

Laura was so furious she was ready to hit him.

A while back, he would have been hard put not to be equally angry at her.

"It's a violation of the custody agreement."

He just looked at her. "What do you expect me to do, Laura? Chain her up?"

Laura led with her chin (*chins,* he amended) thrust out at him. "I'm taking you to court, that's what I'm going to do."

"Fine," he said. "Now get the fuck out of here, I'm closing up."

She slammed out, doing her best to break the glass in the door.

He didn't watch her go, just listened to her peeling out, abusing the Reverend's Cadillac. She never had been any good with cars. He hadn't loved her for a long time now, not since he'd seen what she'd done to their kids. It was the oddest damn thing, but just then, he realized he was glad, for the first time, that she'd left him. He was, suddenly, entirely free.

5

There was a long narrow florist's box by the back door. From it, Pearl spilled two dozen white roses onto the kitchen table. "Oh, my." She sniffed ecstatically at them. "Oh, my."

The tiny card inside read simply *Pearl,* but there was another envelope. Inside was a single sheet, and written on it, in gorgeous calligraphy:

my pearl in hand is more
like skin than even watered silk
or pussywillow plush;
the warm and glowing magical oyster stone,
a friable accretion—
scar tissue—
as words and poem also,
smoother than the birthed unbroken skin,
the wounds become belated genitalia
opening the body to the sex of pain.
she is the sonnet of oyster,
sea-tasting haiku of clam and mussel.

Suddenly she could hardly see for headache.

Finding a vase nearly by feel, she blindly removed the plastic stem-vases, clipped the stems, and arranged the roses.

"What have I gotten myself into?" she mumbled to herself, and realized she was sniffling again. "Stop it." She blew her nose defiantly into a handkerchief.

The bag of drugstore items sat accusingly on the table amid the scattered clippings from the roses.

She picked up the phone, flicking the Rolodex on it to David's number. But she didn't get a chance to dial it.

There was a click and David said, "Pearl," calmly and assuredly, as if he had known she was about to call him.

"David, we just crossed lines. I was trying to call you."

Over the line, his laughter came back to her delighted.

"Thank you for the poem and the flowers. I don't know what to say."

"I want to come over to your house right now," David said, "and throw you on your bed and make you scream for me to stop."

"Oh, David."

"If you didn't work for a living, you could do it all day long."

She giggled tiredly. "I need some sleep."

"Just tonight. I hope all your dreams are wet."

She snorted laughter as he hung up.

She had to give it to having an affair with a poet; he knew how to be romantic. Who among her previous lovers had ever troubled with flowers and poems?

Pearl had not had uncounted lovers; she was not, despite what she had done the previous night, a promiscuous woman at all. Never had there been a one night stand or a casual pickup. Never had she taken a risk on an unplanned pregnancy or on venereal disease. She did not know what to make of herself. She had thought herself sexually fulfilled. What had suddenly rendered her wanton? Whatever it was, the inside Pearl spoke up, you get it under control, you stop *right now* thinking with your cunny. Send that boy on his way; there's no place in your life for a boy who's five or six years younger than you to start, and bisexual to boot. You don't need the trouble a possibly shiftless neurotic poet with too much money and a push-me-pull-you sexual identity might be. Roses and poems are romantic, but life ain't a romance. You want a substantial and monogamous man; you want a simpler, less chancy kind of man; be satisfied with Reuben, who'd never look at another man and have his flag start to flutter. Reuben's more like you; he works hard, he's got no temperament, he's a decent, kindly man, not a horny Byron who'll want to live in some city in the winter, want to support you, want you to give up what you're building for yourself so he can, at least as long as he's in love, build castles and plant walls of thorn for you. Be done with David. Be honest, kiss him good-bye, and show him the door. He'll live. Just the wrong time for the two of you, you made a mistake getting involved, so now you back out. He'll live. That one's been in love before and he'll be in love again, sure as ten dimes make a dollar.

The message light was on but when she played back the tape there was nothing but those irritating clicks. Dammit, Bobby. Say something.

Wearily she gathered the sheets from the daybed, discovering her missing nightie tangled into them, collected dirty clothes and towels, and threw everything into the washing machine. It was too hot to sleep upstairs, but she turned on the old-fashioned standing blade-fan and hurled herself onto the bed anyway.

It was dark when she woke again. The phone was ringing.

" 'Lo," she managed.

"What the hell you doing asleep at nine-thirty?" Bobby said.

She sat up. "Bobby, some people work hard for a living."

"I called last night, you must have had some good time. You got a boyfriend already?"

"Where are you, Bobby?"

"You mean, 'Are you messed up?' I'm just fine, thank you, ma'am."

"Bobby, you mind letting me do my own talking?"

"Ha, I step on your toe, Sissy?"

"I would just like to know where you are. I know you're messed up already."

"I forgot you went to college. I can't get nothing past you. What's a smart woman like you doing slinging hash for Northern rednecks? I believe you be the one messed up."

"Spare me the jive, Bobby. I thought we'd agreed you'd live your life and I'd live mine."

"Yeah, that's right. That's right. You don't need my help to fuck up, and I sure don't need yours."

"Bobby, let's start over."

He was silent a moment.

"Bobby?"

"Aw, shit," he said. "I shoulda known better. You still trying to be white like your mother."

There was a click as he hung up.

"Screw you, Bobby," she said to the open line, and slammed down the phone.

She hugged her knees and let the tears flow. When she was cried out, she got up and washed her face. She was violently hungry. Raiding the refrigerator, she stuffed herself full of potato salad and chicken from the diner and a huge quantity of iced tea. Then she put the wash in the dryer and went right back to bed, where she fell asleep immediately.

6

She woke up thinking *It's Father's Day*.

Norris would be up this early, sitting by the phone, with his cup of coffee and chicory and two slices of dry rye toast to eat, very slowly. He'd be walking to church to hear Mass in another hour, would stop at the corner store for his Sunday papers on the way back, would spend the day reading them, watch *Meet the Press*, poke in his garden.

He picked up on the first ring.

"Pearl, how you doing?"

"Dad, how'd you know it was me?"

"You the only one of my chirren who ain't a slugabed. You get that from me."

She laughed. He'd never had any patience with anything less than the King's English. Thought jive was just affectation, patois was acceptable only when everyone present was native to it. Funny how he'd fallen back into the idiom and usages of his childhood, like "chirren" for "children." At least he did with her, maybe to intensify the parent-child relationship.

She wished him a happy Father's Day.

"Thank you kindly," he said, "it's been all pleasure, far as you go, honeypie."

"Oh, Dad, I gave you plenty of trouble."

"No, no. I cain't make a single complaint. You make me proud."

The sudden tightness of her throat surprised. Honestly, Pearl, you're turning to mush.

"You heard from Bobby?" he asked.

Pearl's heart lurched. The occasion was reminding Norris of the child who was still a worry.

"Sent him a postcard with my new telephone number to the hospital in Philly." She tried to sound casual and cheerful. "I expect he'll be in touch anytime. You know Bobby, he hates to write."

Bobby had good reason to hate writing, as his left arm was a stump. The taxpayers had purchased an artificial arm and right leg for Bobby but he had thrown the arm into the waters of the Gulf in drunken frustration. The leg he did use, though it was a favorite bitter joke—all Bobby's jokes were bitter—that it wasn't hollow. The taxpayers also owed Bobby a new bladder, several feet of intestines, and a set of testes. Bobby didn't have an identical twin with a spare testicle, nor were the other items in supply. He was supposed to be in a veterans' hospital in Philadelphia, neither the first nor the last of those institutions in his life. It wasn't just the little problems that arose from stepping on land mines that plagued Bobby; he had brought home a monkey on his back from his three tours of Vietnam as well. Bobby's joke about that was: Wait'll you see what this country does to the *bad* niggers.

Pearl fumbled for something to distract Norris from Bobby. She inquired about her other step-siblings and he did have news to tell her. Then he wanted to know about the diner.

She told him about Roscoe and the dog. He laughed hard and it cheered her up to hear him do it. When she had to go, she knew she had left him in good spirits.

It had occurred to her to invite him to visit her for the Fourth of July. Maybe it was too crazy this year, with the diner just underway. But she knew Norris would be taken with this place, the house, the town, the people. He'd be pleased she'd found her place in the world. She had an unspoken hope that once he did come to visit, she could seduce him into staying for good. It wasn't just she owed him; she dearly loved and missed the old man. He was the only parent she had left. She wanted to take care of him as once he had taken care of her, and of his own parents. Her stepbrothers and stepsisters wouldn't be resentful; they figured she owed him too, in the cynical bookkeeping way blood children can sometimes view the outside child. But Norris might not care to leave the Keys, or might not be able, in part because his grown kids and grandkids were there. She wasn't sure she had a right to ask. What if he didn't really want to come and did because he thought she needed him? It wouldn't be fair, after what he'd done for her, to take him away from the place he was most comfortable, where his roots were, and force a whole new world on him, to say nothing of a harsher climate.

7

When Karen's Plymouth drove in, in its usual cloud of black stink and rattles, Pearl had coffee on.

The girl looked her up and down critically. "Better."

"Watch it. Want some coffee?"

Karen snickered and took the proffered mug. "Why didn't you just stay there? At David's. You're both free and legal. You don't have to put up any front."

Pearl frowned over the edge of her mug. "Karen, that's none of your business. Okay?"

Karen hung her head and looked hurt. "Well, this is a real small town. You'd better get used to people minding your business for you. They've been doing it for me since I was a baby."

"Then you must understand a desire for privacy."

Karen nodded, a little shyly. "Really, Pearl, I'm just happy for you. And David. He's had a lot of bad things happen in his life." The girl leaned forward, propping her face on the balls of her hands. "And he's stinking rich too."

Pearl laughed. "I got enough money, honey."

So much for persuading Karen to mind her own business. Anyway, there was work to do. Devil take the hindmost.

TEN

1

The heat had collected under the eaves, intensifying the voluptuous scent of the open roses. While shucking her working clothes, Pearl played back the tape in her phone recorder.

Multiple clicks. Bobby. Pushing her buttons.

David's voice: "Gawjus, I'm keeping the lake cold for you."

The hell with Bobby. She dialed David's number.

"Pearl," he said on picking up, before she could so identify herself.

"Are you psychic or am I the only person who ever calls you?"

"Both. Want a swim and supper here?"

She closed her eyes. It would be as good a moment as any. Look him right in the eye and say it was unforgettable and she was glad it had happened but from now on they'd have to be just friends. It wasn't as if friends were so easily come by that you could dismiss a one of them as "just," meaning "mere."

"Seven too late?"

"No, fine. Be a nice sunset."

In passage from flower to leaf, the orchard was redolent, the trees in their petal-shorn crookedness beseeching and lonely. Pearl flopped upon a particularly thick hummock of grass under a tree and closed her eyes. A feeble breeze booted the odd remnant petal over her, tickled her nose, caught in her hair, touched her so lightly she thought she was dreaming. Then one brushed over her lips and clung to them, as if one of the trees had stooped down to steal a kiss. Then the tree made bold to touch her breast and she woke up, to find the name of the tree was Reuben.

"It's you."

He gave her a hand up, saying, "I couldn't wait the hundred years."

She had to shake her head to get the wool out, and then she realized he was referring to the fairy tale about the princess who pricked her finger and subsequently slept a hundred years before a prince's kiss woke her, all because her parents had failed to invite a certain bad fairy to be her godmother.

Brushing petals from her hair and clothes, she said, "That's okay. I'm no princess. A doze is as good as a night to me, a night as good as a century."

He led her out of the orchard through the graveyard and into the woods on the other side. They passed the opening of the old woods road where Reuben had discreetly parked his truck in deep shade. The woods were dim and cool, patched with openings and clearings where real heat poured in. Holding hands, they dawdled along the paths, savoring a sensual progress of cool soothing shadow and splashes of dizzying feverish sunlight that made the hair on the top of her head hot to the touch. The sheer and unexpected variety of species entranced Pearl.

"Look at that," she said, pausing to caress the gray, ridged bark of one notable specimen. She craned to take in its whole height, but it stretched a hundred feet above her head.

"It's a balm-of-Gilead. Don't see it too often anymore, let alone that big," Reuben told her. "Over there, that's a dwarf willow."

She crouched over the matted hummocky shrub. "My, my. Never heard of it, Reuben."

"It's a real strange one. Main branches and trunk are underground. What you're seeing are air roots."

"It's upside down."

"Near enough so it makes no difference."

She was suddenly suspicious of his grave demeanor. It was a little too poker-faced. "You having me on?"

"A little."

She whacked at him playfully. "Oaf."

"There's a lot of things in this woodlot that are rarities now. Joe never said what he was doing but I believe he was trying to preserve some of the varieties that had been clear-cut about everywhere else now. He had this woodlot from his father and grandfather. Kept it like a palace."

Walter had used the same phrase about Joe's house. Suddenly she wished fiercely she had known the man, her Uncle Ghost.

"Thanks. I've been meaning to take a walk in these woods since the day I got here. Got too busy too fast."

" 'Welcome. I owe you anyway for all the berries I've stolen from you."

They stepped into a small clearing and the heady perfume of wild strawberries. With every step, they trod upon strawberry plants.

Dropping to her haunches, Pearl peeked under leaves. In modest green shadow, the small berries hung upon their stems like droplets of bright red blood. The smell of the fruit was rich and gorgeous.

She popped one in her mouth, then offered it to Reuben, who was hunkering himself to her level. He snapped it up, exposing his incisors like a pup going after a treat. They looked at each other lasciviously and then, snickering, collapsed onto the carpet of strawberries. They did a little tentative smooching. But the kisses kept breaking up into giggles and snorted laughter.

"So much for picking berries."

"I haven't been grassing since I was twenty," he admitted.

"Me either."

She propped herself up on one elbow and fed him a berry.

He turned serious. "I meant it when I said I wanted to do this right."

"Reuben, you don't know anything much about me—"

He sealed her lips with two fingers. "Everything I need to know."

She looked at him from under lowered lashes, her throat tightened up with both shame at how she'd played (there was no other way to describe it) fast and loose and fear of his rejection if he found out. It was startling how much she suddenly dreaded the loss of this man's regard.

He took his hand away and relaxed. "We're not teenagers, we've got histories. You know I've been married once, a woman your age could have been too."

"I have been," she interrupted.

He nodded. "It doesn't matter to me, so long as you're free now. I'm free now. Seems to me the two of us are in new territory and there's nobody here but us."

It was as if she were a small boat in strange waters and that qualifying phrase "as long as you're free now" was like a submerged rock. It made a hollow thump against her heart. She pushed herself hastily away from it.

What a generous man he was, or perhaps only sensible, if the word only wasn't too much of a diminution of that quality. Impulsively she took his hand and kissed his fingers one by one.

He drew her closer. "We're not getting much berry-picking done. Like to go back to your house and go to bed?"

"No sweeter sheets back there."

He seemed pleased at the answer. But now a little shyness came into his face. "I never asked you—last time, it never crossed my mind. I was a little foozled. I s'pose you're taking the pill, since you didn't say anything either."

She chewed her lip a bit. That wasn't the only thing she'd forgotten to bring up. "Well, actually, I'm not."

They were both blushing.

"Oh. Christ, that was a bonehead stunt, then, wasn't it?"

She nodded.

He took her hand and squeezed. "I'm sorry too, and it's just as much my fault as yours, more really." He chucked her under the chin and made her look him straight in the eye. "What're the odds?"

She shrugged. "Even."

He laughed, shaking his head at their folly. "Well, it'd be embarrassing to rush to get married at my age, but I guess I'd have earned the chaff. I'd rather not have the complication, but I'm already clear in my head about you, Pearl. D'you know that?"

She evaded that last question. She knew, and it gladdened her and frightened her. She had not come to Nodd's Ridge looking to get married, let alone become a mother. It was a little alarming how rapidly the former idea was gaining the force of decision, never mind getting her mind around the latter possibility.

"It's not all your responsibility."

He sat up straight and his mouth tightened. "I guess maybe it would be half mine. I couldn't stop you, you know. Just, you wouldn't go off and have an abortion without at least consulting with me, would you?"

His distress tightened her up inside again. How could she have gotten the two of them into such a stupid, adolescent situation? Angry with herself, she lashed out at him. "Good God, Reuben. I'm a bastard myself. My mother didn't abort me."

He drew her close again. "It's funny, in a way."

It took her a minute to get back the good mood that had been disrupted, but she agreed: if you looked at it from another light, it was funny.

"No more of a joke than we deserve. Now, as to locking the barn door after the horse is out—"

"I've got my diaphragm."

He had already taken a condom in foil packaging from his shirt pocket. "—well, I went to the drugstore. Shouldn't be all your lookout."

They burst out laughing.

"Very thoughtful of you," she told him, and then produced hers from the pocket of her shorts. "I brought one too."

Reuben looked at it, puzzled. "But you just said—"

"There's other things to protect against than pregnancy," she said quickly.

He was suddenly very quiet. "Things have changed since I last went courting."

She snuggled up to him, put her arm around his neck. Too true. "So far as I know, I've no reason to alarm you."

He put the tip of his pointer finger to the midpoint of her upper lip and began to trace, lightly, the whole outline of her lips. She caught his hand and held it at the corner of her mouth. "I have to tell you this." She leaned closer and murmured, "I love to feel *you* inside me. I don't want to use those things."

For a moment he was quiet, holding her, thinking it over. "I'll take a test if you like, but if I'm carrying that particular bug, it'll be the first case of catching it from your own hand."

She dissolved in giggles. A little breathlessly she finally managed to say, "But I could have been exposed, you see."

They looked at each soberly a long moment and then he sighed and pulled her very close and laid her head on his chest. He chucked her chin up, tipping her face to his, and kissed her. He tasted of strawberry, the real intense sweet and tart of the wild strawberry. She left off nibbling and sucking his lower lip and slid down a bit, tracing the midline of his body from collarbone to belt buckle with her tongue. He caught her chin and lifted her face with an incredulous and unmistakably satyric gleam in his eye.

"Pearl," he said in astonishment.

She blew him a kiss from her open palm.

When she took him into her mouth, he sucked in his breath sharply, signally an unmistakable virginity of a kind.

Sometimes we bear a resemblance to the boar snuffling for a truffle. The boar is after the truffle's perfume, very like the scent of a sow in heat. When he finds it, he tosses it violently into the air with his snout. But at the end of his hunt, the boar is cheated of both truffle and sow. He does not think back upon the ecstasy of pawing in the earth, any more than he thinks, when he is tearing up the forest floor, how wonderful the cool and musky mold and mulch and soil are, or how glorious the texture and flavor of the truffle. He is not, in short, a gourmet. Poor pig.

Reuben shouted when Pearl tossed the truffle.

Then he hauled her up violently by her armpits and all but

devoured her face, until they were exhausted and lay dazed in the heat, in the lee of each other.

"Reuben . . ." she said, rolling onto her stomach and propping herself on her elbows, ready to continue serious talk.

Casually and easily he knocked one elbow out from under her and flipped her on her back. The breath huffed out of her. She gasped. It was her turn to be the truffle. She stopped thinking about what was happening and let it happen.

So much for appetizers. The main meal was under way, with huge hilarity, when suddenly something black and hairy and clawed was scrabbling over them with open, slobbering jaw and hysterical baying. As they tore themselves apart, they realized simultaneously the small black-and-furry, four-legged missile shooting off into the woods was Roscoe's bitch Belinda.

Out of the shadows of the woods from which the retriever had come stepped Evvie Bonneau. There was a brief hesitation, and then, as she passed them, she looked Reuben over straight-faced.

"Why, Reuben, if you'd showed me that in a berry patch you wouldn't've spent the last five years on your lonesome."

At Reuben's bellow of laughter, the woman did let her lips twitch once.

"Good day to you, Miss Dickenson." She ducked back into the woods.

Pearl was still laughing when Reuben simply took up where he had left off.

2

Later, he asked her if she wanted to go out to dinner or something.

She looked him in the eye and said, "I've got a date with David Christopher. He asked me over for a swim and supper."

Reuben paused, gave her a careful look, and nodded. "You like David."

"Yes. Yes, I do."

Reuben characteristically took a moment to consider what he said next. "Sharp as you are, I doubt I'm talking out of school to mention

David's a little confused about whether he likes girls or boys best. You probably knew anyway, you've lived in big cities."

Pearl had to suppress a giggle. Here David was getting such a kick out of the whole business of being taken for one thing and secretly being another, and it was transparent to Reuben, of all people, Reuben, all face and no lock on his heart at all. She wondered if the man had ever in his life successfully told a lie, or had even tried.

"You know about his family, what happened to his little sister. When we gave up looking for her body that night, I held him while he screamed. He was going to find her if we couldn't. Doc McAvoy didn't dare give him another shot of trank after the first one, David didn't weigh but eighty pounds. So I can't help it. I worry about him. Doesn't much matter to me either whether he's sheep or goat, he's alone too much. He does need a friend and a good levelheaded woman like you, for sure. Take care, now, Pearl," and he kissed her, the careful kiss she was beginning to recognize.

"Sam'll be home soon anyway. Went to his friend Josh's to work on Josh's old car with him. Josh's got an old Maverick they've been getting street-legal. He was out with Josh Friday night, going to a dance at the high school in Greenspark, and slept over at Josh's house. Josh brings him out some, gets him to ask the girls to dance. Wish I could be there and see it."

There was real wistfulness in his voice, that hinted at a bittersweet aspect of parenthood that had not occurred to childless Pearl. "They don't want their folks watching 'em try their wings."

It was the most he had ever spoken at one time, and it made her uneasy to realize he had talked as much about David as he had about Sam.

"Good for Josh," she said.

"I'll call you tomorrow, maybe we could get out on a real date."

She was glad to kiss him good-bye at his truck and not have to invite him into the house. He had not wanted to come in anyway. If he'd come in and she'd brought him upstairs into her bedroom, she might have had to explain those hothouse roses. She'd already moved them to her bedroom, along with the poem, now in the bottom of her jewelry box, to keep them from Karen's prying eyes. Reuben might begin to worry more about Pearl-and-David than just David-on-his-lonesome. He apparently found it entirely natural that David might have a thing for Pearl but he was presently either too dazed with his own infatuation to perceive any threat, or else so puffed up with conquest for it ever to dawn on him that he might not be in clear possession. No sooner thinking this than shamed by it, Pearl rebuked herself: no, the man was too honest to suspect she might be capable of such a thing when he wasn't.

But the roses reproached her, silky perfumed petal to stem and minuscule thorn, for having again slipped the chance of telling him she was not, exactly, as free as he thought. But how did one gracefully explain: *Ah, the night you knocked on my door, you were taking sloppy seconds. Don't worry, it was only the once, and it'll never happen again.*

Their sweet stink seemed to summon a small and ugly, trollish demon, who curled up on her shoulder to whisper *You're not married to the man, so you're not accountable to him. There's no need for you to tell him you've bedded David. Just once, for all that's holy, and before he made his own move. What fraction of a percentage of all your previous fornications with other men is that? It don't signify. Far as that goes, you haven't signed any exclusive contract with the man, the two of you have had a couple of damn nice interludes that might, and might not, turn into something substantial. Why should you start wearing a gold band when you haven't even got an engagement ring?*

Enough. Pearl, stripping, dumped the strawberry-speckled clothes into the hamper and dropped the lid decisively, as if it were a cage for the wanton imp.

Clean again, after a second shower, and in fresh clothes, she spent some time with her account books; then, firm in her resolve to do the honest thing, she drove to David's.

3

Reuben heard the thump of Sam's ZZTop through the shower and knew the boy was back. Astoundingly, the boy somehow heard his knock at the door above the din.

"Come in," he shouted.

"Welcome home," Reuben shouted back, and continued to his own room.

The noise stopped suddenly. Sam came down the hall after him, full of excitement.

"We put a new fuel pump in the Maverick and I think that did it.

All we have to do now is put a new muffler on her and get a sticker."

"Did Josh come up with the money for the insurance?"

"He's going to bale hay for the Partridges, figures that'll put him over the top on it."

"Baling hay for horses so he can feed his horsepower?"

Sam laughed. "Yeah. You go berrying?"

Reuben concentrated suddenly on zipping his fly.

"Where'd you get those scratches?" Sam wanted to know. "You got some good welts on your back."

"I know. Stung some in the shower."

"You want me to put some disinfectant on 'em?"

Sam was already out the door and into the medicine cabinet in the bathroom.

Reuben leaned on the windowsill and looked at his garden. The spinach was starting to bolt; he ought to pick what was good.

The scratches stung cold and then hot under the disinfectant swabbing by Sam.

"Tree branch whipped back and bit me. I zigged when I should have zagged," Reuben lied, hoping the boy would take the color he could feel heating his face as embarrassment at clumsiness. "Dropped the berries, too."

Sam was unperturbed. "That patch by the birches is ripened up. I'll pick some tomorrow. Make us a strawberry shortcake."

"Be nice." Reuben tried not to wince as his shirt settled over the welts.

"That goddamn dog, sorry, Dad, that dog of Roscoe's, chased us halfway home. I wanted to stop and leash her, take her over to Roscoe's, but Josh wouldn't stop. Said he wasn't going to have anything to do with a dog he didn't know, he saw *Cujo*, read the book too. I said she ain't a St. Bernard, she's just a stupid little Labrador bitch, and Josh said, fuck that, he said it, not me, Dad, fuck that, she's foaming at the mouth. I couldn't see if she was."

"I doubt she's rabid, probably just dehydrated from the heat. Stupidity ought to be proof against something. Try Mrs. Bonneau on the CB, why don't you? Just let her know where you saw the dog."

So Evvie Bonneau hadn't caught up with the dog. It was funny, most animals came to Evvie just like that. Well, if he wanted to worry about something, he could worry about the dog now. It was the dog's nails that had torn up his back. If the dog was rabid and had infected him, it might be the first case of rabies that could be counted as a venereal disease. No, he guessed not. People got poison ivy all the time from grassing and they didn't call it VD. The hell with it. The world was too complicated. He just wanted to roll around in berry patches with Pearl and be left alone. He went out into the garden and picked spinach.

4

It was later than Pearl had arrived the last time, closer to sunset. The astonishing peacefulness of the place immediately affected her. It was as if it were hidden in the center of a garden or a maze, walled off and inaccessible to the world. Once again, David appeared at her knock, out of the shadowed hall on the driveway side of the house. He embraced her so enthusiastically he lifted her right off the floor.

"Hey," she yelped, but he was burrowed into the hollow of her throat, which tickled, and holding her so tightly she could hardly breathe. She whacked at his shoulders and back until he put her down.

"Control yourself, Pearl," he said sternly, and led her into the kitchen, where he grabbed her around the waist and lifted her onto the counter next to the fridge. Besides his sunglasses, he was wearing, again, shorts and an open shirt and was shoeless. The simple clothes emphasized his long and loose-limbed body. He wore his body as casually as he did the clothes. Popping the fridge door, he showed her a pitcher of iced tea. She nodded, and he poured her a tall glass and dropped a chunk of lemon into it.

She took a long pull on it. "Good."

"Old family recipe," he said. "Pour boiling water over a bunch of tea bags, steep, remove bags, chill infusion in icebox. Garnish with lemons."

She had to giggle. "Sounds like *nouvelle cuisine* to me."

He shook his head negatively. "For *nouvelle cuisine,* you use Lapsang-souchong tea leaves and garnish with some kind of fruit with a bizarre combination of consonants in its name, that looks like it came from Arcturus but really grows in New Zealand."

"Oh. I see."

He hooked his sunglasses down his nose and looked her up and down lasciviously. "Wanna fuck?"

She nearly choked on her iced tea. "No wonder you haven't been able to get laid for three years."

"Not unable, just too picky," he countered. "Anyway, you do want to tell me we made a terrible mistake and you'd just like to be friends, right?"

She slid off the counter but he didn't move, so she was tightly sandwiched between the counter's edge and David. He had her pinned within his arms.

"Back off." She tried to push him away.

"I like it where I am." His face was perfectly straight but he was having a good time, she could tell. In fact, it would be difficult for her not to notice how good a time he was having.

"Last time somebody tried this on me," Pearl told him, "was on the subway in D.C."

"Tell me about it. Was it fun?"

Pearl smiled. "He was wearing sneakers. I was wearing three-inch spikes. I nailed him right where the metatarsals meet the phalanges of the toes. As he hunched up screaming, I drove my elbow into his Adam's apple."

"Oh, God, I think I'm coming."

She ducked underneath his arm and slipped out. He sighed and let her go.

"Smart guy. You tell me why I'm here to tell you we made a mistake."

"Come sit on the deck," he said, and then made a production out of walking with an erection.

She picked up a good-size art book and whacked his bottom with it.

"More, more," he cried.

The lake was extremely quiet, with only an occasional boat passing in one direction or another. As the sun lowered, the light was pooling in patches on the water, surrounded by depthless, formless darkness, as the solid edges of the world dissolved.

"Silky as a teddy bear's armpit." David gestured toward the water. "Makes me want to take a swim."

"Me too." She turned from the lake to look at him. Same reaction. His physical beauty drew her with the same seductive power as that body of water that managed to look the way the private skin of human beings feels.

"You're scared," he said. "You're a sensible, practical woman who's been taking care of herself for a while."

She felt her cheeks warming at the double meaning implicit in "taking care of herself."

"You think lovers should know each other well first."

She nodded.

"Well, it's safer," he said. "The times are with you, Pearl. You might even be right."

"David . . ." But she didn't know what else to say.

"Whatever you want. You'll be responsible for a great deal of self-abuse, but I'll do it your way."

She touched his shoulder and he backed away.

"You better start with the cold water right now. Go take your swim. You'll let me watch, won't you? The male of the species responds to visual stimuli, you know, and I'd be so very grateful."

"I didn't bring my suit."

"All the better."

She laughed and he cheered up.

"There are spare ladies' suits in the bottom drawer of the dresser in the bedroom. They're a little dated but I'm mother-fixated anyway, it'll just be a little more kinky for my fantasies."

All this sweet reasonableness was a little breathtaking. Two civilized men in one life was almost more than a body could take. She smiled at her own double-entendre.

The bathing suits in the bottom drawer were dated indeed, ten years old, at least, cut to cover real breasts, not the mosquito-bite bubbies of anorexic models, and not requiring the shaving of pubic hair as a sop to modesty. She would actually be able to swim in one of them without falling out. And checking herself in the mirror, she thought the gold one was rather sexy, really, with a suggestion of the lace-up satin corset of the turn-of-the-century courtesan.

David fell on his knees to beg mockingly, "Oh, for a pair of silk stockings."

With a giggle, she sashayed past him. The evening air was moist and cool and she breathed deeply, feeling almost deliriously freed. She dove into the lake eagerly. The shock was no less than the first time, but this time she reveled in it. She swam further out and, curious to see what lived in the clear, frigid water, dropped below the surface. The cold was almost painful on the surface of her eyeballs but soon the sight of living fish moving fluidly in their own medium entranced her, with the same kind of soothing wonder that an aquarium provides. She returned to the surface for air and paddled a bit. The remaining light was silvery, sky and water blending subtly. She dove back under the surface. And again. The lake seemed empty now, the boaters off the water to take supper or dinner, depending on whether they were locals or summer people. All the things that had been worrying her were forgotten. She lost track of the time, immersing herself in the sensations the lake offered. She dove again, watched the fish undulating like flags in a cyclical wind. Her lungs at last protested and she returned to the surface and paddled lazily in. The water felt cold again and she shivered. It was still muggy, and there was a distant crackling of heat lightning. While she had been gamboling, it had become night. Without a moon, there was but meager light, lights from cottages, glowing here and there. She was rendered color-blind as a cat.

David admired her goose bumps. "You *are* a masochist."

Sinking onto the lounge chair, she realized she was actually clenching her teeth to keep them from chattering, in a humid heat that felt more like the Keys than she had ever expected of Maine.

David reached over and touched her arm. She started at the contrast of the warmth of his hands.

"Christ, you're cold. You stayed in a little too long."

Abruptly he moved from his lounge to hers, nudging her onto one side, then drawing her close against him the whole length of their bodies.

"David."

"Old Eskimo trick," he said, making her laugh.

He nestled against her cold skin and she felt him shiver, as if she had transmitted the chill to him. She found herself observing, piqued and curious; the coldness of her skin was having a galvanic effect upon him. And that was having a similar effect on her.

He shifted about so he was nearly on top of her. "Tell you what, let's be just friends tomorrow, okay?"

To herself she murmured, "I can't believe I'm letting this happen."

"You're not letting. You're doing."

"Wait a minute. No bareback, my friend."

"I almost forgot. No problem. I went to the drugstore."

She laughed but didn't explain why and he didn't ask, his mind on more urgent matters. He threw the mats from the lounge chairs on the deck to use for a mattress. Every gap in the planks was still transmitted to them, and the mats smelled of heated plastic. Bugs snapped, crackled, and popped in the buglight with a disturbing clarity.

Later, they ate a huge meal and went to bed again. The night went on and on, hot and confusing. Thunderheads rolled in, and after an hour's pyrotechnics, rain slashed down. They listened to it bouncing off the deck and it sounded like corn popping. Or bugs frying in the blue coil of the buglight, she thought sleepily. Then it was cooler and they were able to sleep. It was very nice, comforting, to be making spoons with him while the world outside took a drenching. She rolled her head to one side to look at him.

His eyes seemed bruised as if the darkness bore heavily upon them. His breathing evened out and he slept; she could see the rapid eye movement underneath his lids as he began to dream. She lay back and tried to go to sleep too. David's hands, slack upon her body, suddenly clenched and then his whole body jerked, as if he were falling. A tiny moan escaped him and he muttered unintelligibly, but the gibberish was clearly terrified. His dream was going bad; he had slipped into a nightmare. She thought of the roots of the word "nightmare," how appropriate it was. David was overboard in night seas. He moved restlessly, seeking some route out. He began to weep, totally unnerving her. Shushing him as if he were a frightened child, she tried to hold him but he reacted violently, struggling frantically to escape her. Then he quieted again. His face was wet with sweat and tears and the moisture beaded the edge of his upper lip. Impulsively she licked them away, and his lips parted for her, met hers. He grasped her as violently as he had minutes before tried to escape her, and rolled onto her so quickly he knocked the breath out of her. Fully conscious, almost painfully aware, she felt as if he had dragged her into his night seas. He was extremely hard and she gasped with every movement. It was as close to a battle as it was to lovemaking, but there was not the slightest sense of rape, for she was taking him with as much wildness as he was her. Everything seemed to give way; nothing was held back. She gritted her teeth against a climax that was very like a blow and found herself washed ashore still in a state of hyperawareness. Every hair on her head hurt to its roots, every weary muscle was exhausted, yet she was electrified, strung out.

Holding her quietly, David murmured, teasing her, "This is terrible. Not safe at all."

She sat up. "We didn't use anything!"

David pulled her back down. "I forgot." He didn't seem at all perturbed. "Anyway, I hope I got you pregnant."

She sat up again and stared at him, astonished. She was so angry she was shaking. "I don't believe you said that. You got something to prove, some fantasy of your own, find somebody else to do it on."

There was shock in his face. "I'm sorry," he stammered. "That was stupid. I didn't mean any of that. I was trying to say something else."

She swung her legs over the edge and started dressing.

"Anyway, forget it. I'm wearing my diaphragm."

There was a long, frozen moment. Then he spoke quietly. "You were wearing it?"

"Damn right."

"I'm confused."

Pearl sat down. "Me too."

"What was all that let's-be-friends for? Were you playing some kind of game?"

An angry *No* was on the tip of her tongue. She really had not intended to have sex with him again. Been cocky enough to think it would be as easy as saying so. She had just forgotten about the diaphragm. She had a wild impulse to tell him about Reuben, but something in her rebelled or was too cowardly. "So maybe I wasn't sure." Must not have been. They hadn't just been shaking hands.

He punched up pillows to lounge on, crossed his hands behind his head, and watched her dressing. "You don't have to go."

Her hair felt as if it were trying to crawl off her scalp. She was all goose bumps. "I do. Give me a little time. I need to think some things out."

He bounded from the bed and kissed her on the tip of her nose. "Call me when you're ready."

5

Glass exploded against the cheaply paneled wall. Shards sprayed over the bedroom. Karen, naked, snapped into the defensive curl of the porcupine.

The rain had not eased the heat inside the stingy one-bedroom trailer on Pigeon Hill. The room was barely lit with a single low-wattage bulb in a bulkhead lamp. Karen sobbed into her hands, her hair falling forward to cover her face.

The sound of Bri's zipper was loud and angry against the background of hard rain pelting the metal skin of the trailer.

"You're such a stupid bitch. You haven't got the brains that frigging bitch of Roscoe's has."

He grabbed her by the hair and jerked her head back. She screamed and lashed out at him and he threw her down again. Bri picked a plastic bag off the floor and stared at it disgustedly. The cocaine inside had melted into a hard lump.

"I can't believe anybody could be so stupid as to leave three grams of coke in a tin box where the sun would turn it into an oven. I ain't no fucking chemistry ace, I don't know what the fuck you can do with a lump a melted coke. You got any ideas, you dumb cunt?"

Karen shuddered and hid her face again.

Suddenly he tore the bag open and the lump fell into his open palm. He leapt onto the bed and straddled her, grabbing her by the hair again. She wailed, flailing her hands at him in self-defense. He shoved the lump into her mouth. "Eat it, you bitch," he shouted.

She fought it frantically with her tongue.

He clamped her mouth shut and then pinched her nostrils closed.

She heaved underneath him, coughing and choking. He watched her coldly for a moment, then let go of her nose, drew back his hand, and punched her in the solar plexus. She whooped and he felt the coke going down her throat as she swallowed convulsively. Her frantic eyes first glazed and then rolled back in her head. She went limp.

He grunted with satisfaction and got off her. He turned her over and punched her again, twice for good measure, in the kidneys.

Karen heard the door slam. Failing to latch, it kept on slamming as the wind caught it repeatedly. She lay there woozily, her head and stomach both reeling. Sliding from the bed to the floor, she crawled and crabbed her way to the toilet, where she sicked up and sicked up. She didn't want to look at it but she knew there was blood in it. Hugging the toilet, she passed out.

ELEVEN

1

Once inside the cab of the truck, Pearl felt oddly safe. She was back in control and calm again as soon as she was up the hill on the road.

It was drizzling and not noticeably cooler than yesterday, promising a depressing, humid day. But the damp air was fresh, its cool passage over her face and arms savory. So green, this place was, densely, thickly green, greener than anyplace she had ever lived. Trees grew here like dandelions in other places. The woods made a narrow corridor with only occasional glimpses, like puzzle pieces, of cottages, lake, mountains, of a road going somewhere. They walled in the dirt road to Route Five, effectively erasing the rest of the world, making the way out self-contained. Breaking out onto Route Five felt like escape.

Weary and nerve-racked as she was, she had to admit a degree of physical contentment she had never before imagined. She could feel what Dick Halloran used to call a Chessie-cat smile trying to break out. It was almost worth everything else, the confusion, the guilt. She had to wonder if she had ever before been truly sexually satisfied. She had thought she had, but must have been mistaken.

The most sensible course would be to tell each man bluntly she was seeing the other. Was *sleeping* with the other. And tell them if they couldn't handle it, it was their problem. It was one way to sort things out. Let them decide.

She hung upon the wheel, feeling like a zombie. She was old enough to know the body makes it declarations as well. Maybe she was not meant to be a wife to anyone.

Or maybe it *was* something in the water. It was worth a tired laugh.

2

The phone was ringing when she stepped out of the shower.

Karen said hoarsely she was sick and couldn't come to work. Flu, she rasped, and hung up.

Pearl looked at the phone a second. Flu. Sounded like she'd been crying. She glanced at the clock, saw there wasn't time to go to Karen's place and check on her before work. After work, she promised herself.

Back behind the wheel of the truck again, she couldn't turn her mind from the problem. If it had been a mistake to sleep with David to begin with, she had now compounded it, and with the foreknowledge that sex doesn't stop in bed. She remembered too clearly for comfort her first impression of Johnny Caswell.

They had met on a flight from Chicago to England she was taking to attend an international conference on computerizing libraries. A man with *The Wall Street Journal* tucked into his armpit had looked at his boarding card, then at the seat next to her, and stopped to pop the overhead cupboard open in order to stow his briefcase. He evoked an immediate reaction of distaste. Maybe it was the satisfaction with which he looked her over, telegraphing his delight at having a good-looking woman to hit on instead of a knitting gran'ma or a fat guy who would take up all the elbow room and fart a lot. His clothes were expensive, too expensive for tourist class; he must have had to settle for the last seat. He sported an equally pricey haircut and glove-leather shoes. The sudden electrifying scent of an expensive European after-shave assured her he would at least be a pleasant-smelling seatmate. His briefcase with its built-in-combination lock made her want to giggle. She never believed such accouterments really contained anything of earth-shaking importance or value. Probably it protected the current issue of *Playboy*.

She didn't like his face. He had too much chin, with a fat dimple in it. Big dimples creased his dark cheeks. His mouth was wide but thin-lipped and tight. His eyes were a little too far apart, brown eyes with heavy, sensual lids. His nose was long, narrow, and twice bumped and had large flaring nostrils. Obviously there was a large and dominant portion of ugly white man somewhere in this upscale black man's ancestry. And he had a self-assurance in his posture that hinted at how lucky she was to have such a big handsome successful brother man sitting next to her.

Why was she reacting to this guy as if she were coming down with a particularly bad period? Honesty compelled. There was her well-established prejudice against the brothers. Back in college, she had had her fill of black men who explained away all their warts as the fault of white oppression and emasculating black women. She had about as much control over whites as she had over a billion Chinese, but she did run this black woman's life. She elected self-protection. If they wanted to take politics to bed they could go with white women, or white men, or each other. Maybe someday she'd meet a Norris or a Dick Halloran. But in the meantime, the brothers of the world could call some other black woman "bitch." On the surface, it might seem inconsistent, even remarkably racist, to reject a whole class of people on the basis of color. But she reasoned that she was reacting to the variety of black male racism that classed *her* by color and sex.

Of course this fellow next to her was a peacock. Full of himself. Such creatures are always irritating to an independent woman. She froze a smile on her face and shook his hand carefully when he introduced himself, thinking if she had to listen to this guy tell her all about how much he'd grown as a consequence of his divorce for the next six hours, instead of reading the Travis McGee adventure she had saved for just this trip, she would puke on him and blame it on airsickness. In fact, she would rather *be* airsick for six hours. *One Fearful Yellow Eye* was in her lap, just retrieved from her tote bag,her finger marking the first page.

Then he said, "That's a good one, I read it when it first came out," and held up the hardcover of *The Green Ripper* he had had tucked inside *The Wall Street Journal*. "You like ol' Travis?"

He laughed before she answered. It was an easy, attractive laugh. "I tell you, I'm a terrible sailor, I get seasick looking at the dentist's goldfish, but I read about Travis on his old houseboat and I start thinking about taking a cruise, deep-sea fishing, that Hemingway trip, you know?"

Three weeks later, she was amused to discover Johnny Caswell had become handsome in her eyes, and she knew it was just sex, nothing but sex. Chemistry. Body talk. She had much yet to learn.

Three months later they were married and buying a house in the suburbs. They agreed they would start a baby in a few years. They were young yet and wanted to save some money.

When she realized Johnny wore jeans as awkwardly as most men wear black tie and tails, it seemed funny. He didn't own any until she came along. But his new role as a property owner with a gas barbecue grill and wife who liked gardening seemed to require them, and he was a great believer in dressing the part. His jeans fit perfectly, never acquiring the softness and patina of long acquaintance with the body. He always looked in them as if he thought somebody would take him for a field hand.

Several years went by and they were still only talking about having a baby. The increasing distance between them, she put down as the inevitable discovery of flaws and differences that intimacy brings. She knew the honeymoon didn't last forever. It wasn't that at all.

Johnny was never original enough to give the going thing a skip, but it was a while before she noticed his Adidas sneakers had gone to the back of the closet. He had gone right from jogging to the razor blade and the mirror. When she first discovered he was using the stuff, shortly after their fifth anniversary, he insisted it was casual and social. She threw a hissy fit and threatened to leave. Sulking, he said he would stop. Maybe he did, for a while. But things were never really right between them again. He grew secretive and spent little time with her. She didn't bring up babies again. She realized he was doing it every day, starting his day with it, the way she had a cup of coffee. Things clicked into place. The sudden attacks of impotence that were always her fault for being too demanding. Insomnia, mood swings, complaints of intestinal upset. Shit.

The day came when she told him it was her or the coke, he could take his choice. He had called her a bitch. And her vision cleared. All at once he wasn't even remotely handsome. Just a dandy with a particularly ugly white man's dominant genes in his ancestry.

Seven years of marriage blown away in a puff of cocaine, and she felt like a fool. She had a bad taste in her mouth. Gussie needing her was a relief.

Roscoe came in as she was lighting the grill. It huffed nicely and she grunted back at it.

"I need you on this side. Karen called in sick."

He grinned and kept on coming right around the counter to put on an apron and go to work. He liked it when she made him feel needed. It set him right up.

"You don't look too rested yourself."

She was busy, shifting into higher gear, filling the coffeemaker. "The heat's been something awful."

He squinted at her over the door of the refrigerator. "I guess so."

Sonny Lunt came lumbering in.

Pearl was grateful for the distraction. "Good morning, Sonny."

Sonny brightened right up. " 'Morning, Pearl. Don't know what's good about it, though."

"No snow on the ground," Roscoe said. "That's something."

"Hah. Roscoe, you bin working too much," Sonny chaffed.

"What'd you know about work?" Roscoe came back, waving a spatch at him.

3

It continued to drizzle off and on all day, and the humidity remained oppressive. Too many people hung around with nothing to do except drink too much coffee and get acid and bitch about the weather. Normally Pearl enjoyed a good bitching session. Natural as it was for her to extract what she could out of anything, she also liked listening to people expressing their varied prejudices and accumulated wisdom, telling stories and jokes. People were always revealing themselves, mostly unconsciously, sometimes shyly, sometimes slyly, and she was often surprised and delighted. It was one of the perks of the business. But today everything and everyone was flat and exhausted.

David came in late and picked at his meal. He wore his dark glasses despite the gloom, like a woman hiding swollen or blacked eyes.

Pearl thought he's probably just forgotten which pair of lenses he was wearing. What a dark day he must be having.

"It's not so bad," she said softly as she refilled his cup.

He slid his glasses to the end of his nose and looked at her gravely. "You're not a poet. We all have Pathetic Fallacy Disease. It clouds up and we rain."

"Is that anything like getting a period?"

She was successful in teasing a smile out of him.

"I wouldn't know, but if it is, you have my sympathy."

Walter McKenzie and Jean came in as he was leaving.

David stopped to shake Walter's hand. "Did you order this weather, Walter, to try to get me to leave?"

Walter grinned. "Did not. You musta left the tub runnin' upstairs."

"I don't bathe. It wasn't me."

Walter sniffed. "That you? I thought it was me."

The old man and the young one shared a quiet laugh and David took his leave.

Jean tugged at Walter's sleeve. "Come sit down, Dad."

Walter huffed onto a stool and then the old man spent a long time peering closely at everyone sitting there, as if he weren't sure who they all were, or they had all changed faces overnight. Then he plucked a menu shakily from its holder and squinted at it.

"Dad," Jean asked impatiently, "what do you want? Pearl's waiting on you."

"Oh, shut up." His voice trembled. "Leave me alone, can't you see I ain't even had time to read the menu?"

Jean's face turned scarlet and her eyes filled up with tears. She snatched a hankie from her purse and dabbed frantically at her eyes.

Pearl patted Walter's hand. "Take your time." She spoke with a cheerfulness she did not feel.

She patted Jean's hand too.

Jean sniffled bravely in response. "I didn't mean nothing," Jean whispered.

Walter looked at her as if he weren't too sure who this faded middle-aged woman next to him was.

"Eh?"

4

The lunch trade was depressed; no one was going to the beach. Sam blew in with his friend Josh in tow.

"Where's Karen?"

"Called in sick with the flu," Pearl told him. "I thought I'd check on her later."

Sam was quiet. Josh was noisy in compensation. They were both hungry.

"Maybe we better go see Karen?" Sam finally said to Josh.

Josh shrugged. "If your dad doesn't mind us getting back late, I don't care. I don't want to go over there if you're just going to yell at each other, though."

"What are you talking about? I can talk to my sister."

Josh raised his eyebrows. "You can? I never heard it."

"Don't be an asshole." Sam, blushing, muttered the last word in a paroxysm of embarrassment at having used it at all. He stared at his hands with the expression of a man who had realized for the first time that they were unbelievably ugly, or had six fingers instead of five, and were covered in warts.

The two boys left, insulting each other cheerfully. The day went by.

Pearl locked up and drove to Karen's trailer. The sight of the Plymouth in the yard and the tiny battered trailer was enough to send her none-too-high spirits nose-diving. The rain trickled down her neck as she stood on the stoop.

To her surprise, Sam flung open the door. His hair was wild, as if he had spent the time since she had last seen him tearing it. By way of confirmation, he proceeded to rake it some more.

"Thank God it's you. She's in the bedroom. She won't talk to me, but that son-of-a-bitch did something to her."

Pearl hurried after him as he lunged toward the single bedroom at the other end of the trailer.

"Where's Josh?"

"He had to go home. Dad left Jonesy at the station, he's out somewhere working, I can't find him. I left him a message, though."

He stood aside to let Pearl pass.

Karen was under a sheet, one arm up over her head hiding her eyes and half her face. She was ghost-white and holding her stomach.

"She's been puking her guts out, the bathroom stinks of it."

Pearl bent to feel Karen's forehead. She was cool to the touch and clammy.

"Karen, what's wrong? Did Bri hurt you?"

Tears started sliding down Karen's face. "Please, I don't want my father to know about this."

Sam exploded. "It's too fucking late for what *you* want."

Pearl pushed him out of the bedroom and closed the sliding door after him. There was hardly room for three in the stingy space anyway. She sat down on the bed and held Karen through a further storm of tears and slowly pried the business out of her.

"It was my fault," Karen cried at one point.

Hearing her, Sam punched the flimsy door. "The hell it was," he shouted. He stomped around outside. Things crashed and thumped.

Pearl came out and closed the door behind her. "Who's your family doctor?"

"Dr. Hennessey. In Greenspark."

"Where's the phone?"

Sam pointed to it.

"Phone book?"

He found it and handed it to her.

"This is private. Go outside a minute, will you?"

Sam wandered disconsolately out.

A few minutes later she stuck her head out the door and asked him back in. "I called the doctor. I'm going to take Karen to Greenspark. You want to come?"

Sam wouldn't have it any other way. He called Jonesy to leave a message for Reuben and then he carried Karen to Pearl's truck.

5

Reuben caught up with them at Dr. Hennessey's office in Greenspark.

"Let me do the talking, okay, Sam?" Pearl murmured, and intercepted Reuben on the door stoop. She deflected him from his path. "Outside."

"What's wrong?"

"Karen called in this morning, saying she had flu." Pearl put her hand on his arm. "You be calm now."

Too late; he was already taut as a guy wire.

"Brian punched her around some."

His face changed and her heart sank.

"I'll kill him," he said flatly.

Wearily she hung on to him. "No, you won't. Beat the shit out of him, if you want. But you're not killing him."

Something in Reuben let go a little. He cocked his head slightly, acknowledging her win.

She hesitated. "The reason was, she left some coke in the sun and it melted."

Reuben's face twisted in anger and his fists clenched tighter.

Pearl took a deep breath. "And he made her eat it."

The big man spun away from her and she stepped back involuntarily, fighting for balance against his torque. She had forgotten his sheer size and density. It made her feel frail and helpless. Then he visibly regained control.

He looked back at her. "Is she okay?"

"I don't know. And Sam doesn't know about the coke."

"You sure I can't kill him?" The ironic glint in his eyes was just this side of tears.

"If it was up to me, I'd probably help you."

A smile ghosted in her direction.

Reuben came back to her, caught her by the arm, and led her into the office.

Sam was pacing the room. Reuben wrapped an arm around him briefly and the two of them seemed to steady down, calming each other.

They didn't have a chance to sit down before Dr. Hennessey, a bearded fortyish man who looked as tired as most doctors do, summoned Reuben. Reuben's eyes asked her if she wanted to go with him, but she shook her head and stayed with Sam.

Sam started pacing. She got up and paced with him, to keep him company. Suddenly he came to a dead stop.

"We're wearing a rut in the carpet."

Pearl laughed softly. "Want to pick out another route?"

He shook his head. His mouth went all funny and Pearl threw her arms around him.

"Oh, Sam."

He held on to her tightly.

She wept too. She was very tired. Exhausted.

Sam caressed her hair with a shaking hand. His hands were so big, big as his father's already. They swayed gently together and worked their way back to sniffles. Eventually they parted with an awkward little laugh and shared a box of tissues.

Reuben came out with Karen in a wheelchair. The girl looked half-dead, all pale and wobbly. Reuben didn't look much better.

"Dr. Hennessey's putting Karen in the hospital for some tests. We're going to take her there now."

Outside, Reuben picked Karen up and put her into the truck.

"It doesn't seem like it now, but you were lucky. You'd be dead by now if you hadn't been."

Hugging herself, Karen turned her face away.

Sam got in next to her.

Reuben walked Pearl to her truck.

"Thanks. He did her a favor, punching her. It made her toss the poison. Not much appears to have gotten into her system. Enough to make her good and sick, and that might be more from the cut than the coke. There's some bleeding in her stomach. And kidneys—he rabbit-punched her too. She's going to have some tests that will make her sick. But it could have killed her, she came that close."

"What about Brian?"

"I know where he hangs out. If I don't find him at the Dog, I know where he works and what time his shift starts in the morning."

"Oh, no."

"If I don't do it, Sam will, and Sam'll get hurt."

She hadn't thought of that. "Then I want to go with you."

"No. Go home. You look exhausted. Go get some rest."

6

Early on a dirty Monday night, the Dog wasn't doing much more than keeping the alcoholics from the DT's and a dispirited trade in takeout pizza. Some of the after-work beer drinkers were lingering on, putting off going home. A few had minimal hopes of some action.

Reuben recognized Sonny Lunt's pulp truck in the lot, next to the ambulant wreck of an Oldsmobile belonging to Sonny's housemate, a long-faced man who had been christened Melvin Mullins but who had been known as Lurch since his high-school days. Lurch Mullins, like Sonny, was divorced and lonely and more than halfway to being a drunk. There were other vehicles he recognized automatically—Belinda Conroy's Country Squire, for one. She'd be picking up takeout; it was the wrong night for slumming. In another corner of the Dog's parking lot, one of a covey of motorcycles, was Bri Spearin's Honda Shadow. It looked as if a handful of Bri's buddies were with him.

Inside, it was dim but not cool. The proprietor's idea of air conditioning was to prop the back doors open to the evening breeze, and if there wasn't one, people could sweat. They bought more beer when they sweated. The place smelled powerfully of beer and pizza. It turned Reuben's stomach. Or maybe it was the cold fury he was in.

Sonny looked up from the bar and bellowed, "Reuben! Buy ya a beer, old hoss."

Sonny was feeling no pain. Lurch joined him in bellowing inarticulate welcome.

There was a little stir around the table where the motorcycle contingent was lounging.

Reuben locked onto Bri Spearin, who was already rising, cocky defiance fighting queasy panic in his handsome face. Spearin made six feet of height and lifted weights, but he didn't have the mass to go against Reuben and he knew it.

Sonny was not too far gone to register what was happening.

"Shit-a-goddamn." He gave Lurch a vigorous poke.

Reuben's big hand snaked out and caught Bri even as the younger man ducked back and away. Bri tried to round on him, and Reuben shook him out, just once. Then Reuben let go of him, and as Bri tried to get his balance, the big man's hands slapped around his face, *wap wap*, like tentacles.

The Dog's proprietor, from behind the bar, shouted, "Take it outside, boys!"

Sonny Lunt opened the door and Reuben casually tossed Bri out onto the parking lot. Bri opened his mouth to yell obscenities and then he was facedown in the mud and gravel, eating it.

The crowd spilled out into the lot. Bri's buddies hung back. It wouldn't be their fight unless he started winning.

"Kin I help?" Sonny volunteered. He was not alone. Lurch and a number of other men were eager to take sides with Reuben. Some of them had grudges against Bri Spearin, others just thought he was a nasty piece of work and it would be a public service, as well as fun.

Reuben shook his head and picked Bri up. He brushed the gravel and mud off him. "I should have done this a long time ago." Suddenly he brought his knee up into Bri's crotch.

Bri's eyes glazed and a strange little sound dribbled out of his mouth. He fainted.

Reuben held him upright by his shirt. He looked at Bri thoughtfully, then let him go. Bri curled up and retched.

The proprietor had come out on the stoop to watch. He liked a good fight as well as the next man, but this was beginning to look like something else. Nervously he wiped his brow with his bar cloth. "Sonny," he muttered, "this is getting outta hand."

Sonny grinned. "What d' you care, Fudgy, it's free entertainment."

Sonny gazed over the transient population of the roadhouse, which was now entirely outside the bar. Everyone appeared to be having a good time. In fact, some of them were having too good a time. Sonny nudged Lurch. "Check out Belinda. She's creamin' her jeans."

Belinda Conroy's eyes were glittering dark stars.

Sonny and Lurch were almost distracted from the main event.

Reuben stooped down and picked Bri up. Bri wobbled like a tulip on a broken stem, his eyes rolling. Reuben wondered, with clinical detachment, if Bri were in shock. Shock could kill a man. He didn't want to go to jail for this piece of garbage. On the other hand, Bri had it coming, and it was done. Almost. He hauled him to Sonny's truck and dropped him. Reuben popped the hood on the truck and hauled Bri upright again. He tugged Bri's hands out of his crotch and held his wrists over the apron where the hood fitted down. Then he reached up, grabbed the hood, and slammed it down on Bri's hands before he could pull them away. Bri screamed and the hood bounced up and Bri fell down.

"Oh, Christ-in-a-handcar," the proprietor said, and hurried inside to the telephone.

Reuben caught the hood on the way up and slammed it shut. Without looking at Bri again, he walked away.

The crowd had gone quiet. Sonny and Lurch turned their attention back to Belinda Conroy. She couldn't take her eyes off Reuben, who had gotten into his truck and was just sitting there.

Sonny and Lurch were so overcome with merriment they had to hang on to each other, and chortled beerily in each other's faces.

"I better call Reuben back," Sonny said. "He must have enough of a head a steam left to throw a fuck into Belinda."

Lurch shuddered and sputtered. "Me first. I need it worse'n he does."

"Fuck you do," Sonny advised him. "Not from her. We used to call ol' Reuben 'Hosscock,' but you ain't got nothing to spare. I hear she don't leave nothing but pencil shavings."

They had to hold each other to keep from falling down laughing. The two of them staggered back into the bar, along with the rest of the patrons, leaving Bri's buddies to tend to him.

"I ain't seen anything like that," Lurch confided to Sonny, "since Parrish give Laimbeer the lip. I never seen human arms do that before. Laimbeer was spitting teeth left 'n' right."

Both Sonny's and Lurch's eyes were misty with the cherished

memory of the Celtics' center's encounter with the Pistons' guard in May. Belinda Conroy, salivating over Reuben, was nothing to that great moment in pro-basketball history.

"Yeah, Parrish just sorta came from behind Laimbeer and give him a little facewash with them hands. What d' you think them handsa Parrish's go, foot across?"

"At least," Lurch agreed. "I figure his arms are four feet long."

"Maybe five." Sonny drained his beer mug. *"Wap wap wap.* That's just all there was to it."

The Conroy woman stood briefly next to her car, staring at Reuben's truck with the sweat standing on her face. At last she took a deep shuddering breath and crossed the lot.

He saw her coming and rolled his eyes.

She licked her lower lip and laughed a little embarrassed laugh. "Good job," she said huskily.

"Go away, Belinda. I don't need any runaway bitches in my life."

She slapped him and stalked away.

He wiped blood off his lip, then threw back his head and laughed.

A Rescue Squad ambulance was on the scene in fifteen minutes. The garage where it was parked was two doors down from the Dog, but it took ten minutes to get a crew together.

Two sheriff's deputies arrived as it was leaving. One of them glanced his way, and Reuben recognized him for an old high-school classmate. The other, Jeff Deluca, was much younger. Reuben had once cured a balky motor in a county cruiser for him.

Reuben waited patiently while the Dog's proprietor delivered a high-pitched, profane, and self-important account to the deputies.

Reluctantly the deputies shambled over to him. Reuben got out of the truck.

"Hi, Reuben," said Tom Clark, his old classmate. "Old Fudgy over there says you committed an assault on that peckerhead Spearin."

"Tom." Reuben shook his hand. "Jeff." The younger trooper was deeply distressed. "I did."

Tom Clark laughed. "Probably the state oughta strike a medal for you, but there's no justice, you know."

Jeff Deluca cleared his throat and fingered his holster. "You like to tell us about it?"

"He used his hands on my daughter. I decided he couldn't be allowed to do that again."

Tom Clark took out a pack of cigarettes and offered him one. Reuben declined.

"So you busted his wrists and his balls. You always were a direct son-of-a-bitch." The deputy laughed rustily. "Don't blame you a bit. But you can't fight your kid's battles for her, Reuben. She shoulda called us, made a complaint. 'Least we could have put an order on him, mighta been able to jail *him* for assault. Instead of you. The way the law sees it, Reuben, is two wrongs don't make a right. You know that."

Reuben nodded. "She's not seventeen yet." He paused. "He's been fucking her since she was fifteen."

Arrested on its way to the cigarette, Tom Clark's match flared and flickered in the damp air. The deputy couldn't remember ever having heard Reuben say "fuck" before, not even back in high school, nor during the hooraw over his wife and the minister.

"Statutory rape. One of Bri's favorite tricks. He likes hanging out by the high school." Jeff Deluca dug the gravel with his toes.

The older deputy took a lusty suck on his cigarette. "Your daughter testify against him on either charge, statutory or assault?"

"I think so. The assault anyway. If it would keep me out of jail."

"Okay," Tom Clark said. "We have to take some names and so on here, and then I'll make my report. You go home. I'll call you tomorrow, talk to your daughter. She seen a doctor?"

Reuben nodded. "She's in the hospital."

"Good, really need the medical testimony. Look, Reuben, we might be able to work a trade-off. Keep you outta jail, keep that useless scuzzbag outta jail and away from your daughter." Tom Clark tossed his cigarette away. "God, I love them things and they're nothing but a death sentence." The deputy sighed. "Do me a favor and keep your nose clean, Reuben."

Reuben shook the deputy's hand. "Thanks."

"G'wan home now."

7

Pearl let herself into the house. It seemed emptier than the very first time she had ever come into it. Nearly night now, the day closing fast; she had let it go by without noticing it.

The message light was on. She flicked on the playback.

"Pearl," David said, "I'm pregnant. Please call me."

She laughed and picked up the phone. "It ain't mine," she said when he answered. "I know what kind of tramp you are."

"It was a false alarm. You work too much. I want you, but I imagine you need some sleep."

"Well, I do. That's very considerate of you."

"Selfish, really. I need to grow some new skin where it's all rubbed off."

"Poor baby. Weather still getting you down?"

"I'll live. That's the depressing thing, not the weather. Actually I sort of enjoy a dark, nasty day. Keeps people off the lake. I can hear the loons."

"What they talking about today?"

"*Howard the Duck.* They didn't like it. One said it was miscast. Danny DeVito should have played Howard. The other one said, 'You stupid son-of-an-egg, DeVito's too Italian.' "

She couldn't help giggling. "Go listen to the loons some more. I'll talk to you tomorrow."

There was nothing else on the tape but more of Bobby's silences.

8

Reuben stopped on the Pondicherry Causeway and walked down to the water's edge. There was little to be seen. The clouded sky seemed to suck up all the light from the cottages scattered along the shoreline. The deep black water was silent and secretive as ever. This was how it had always been. He had grown used to it, and had learned to take a species of comfort from it.

He drove home and found Sam watching TV.

"You get him?"

Reuben nodded. "Go to bed, Sam. We'll talk in the morning."

Sam was too pleased to argue. The tension he'd been carrying all day, making him lead with his head and shoulders all bunched up ready to butt something, went out of him. He shambled off to bed.

Pearl had dozed off, waiting for Reuben. She hadn't thought she would. Tired as she had been and still was, she had also been wired. The daybed shifted and she snapped out of a confused and sweaty dream. Reuben was sitting on the edge.

"Hi," she said sleepily. "You okay?"

He smiled. "No."

She held out her arms.

Later on, he brought them a couple of beers from the fridge and told her what he'd done.

"Well, was it fun?"

He looked at her. "I'm not proud of myself, if that's what you mean."

"Then why'd you do it?"

"Partly so Sam wouldn't try, and partly to get Bri to leave Karen alone. If it scares him off, it's worth it. I should have done it a long time ago, when I found out he'd been at her."

" 'At her'? Reuben, I know the guy took advantage of her, but Karen's—"

"Karen's got a grown-up body but that doesn't mean her emotions are. I know I haven't been much of a father. I should have looked out better for her."

"What could you have done?" Pearl asked. "You can't lock a girl up and throw the key away."

"Beaten the prick up right at the start. Made it cost him."

"Huh-huh. And what would Karen have done?"

Reuben didn't have to think about it. He sighed. "Taken his side. Thought I was a shit and that he was just wonderful."

"Right. Anyway, the best parents in the world can't protect a child these days. Will she take him back?"

Reuben shook his head. "I think she's cured. Of this one, anyway. But this isn't likely to be the end of it."

"I didn't want to be the one to say so."

Reuben cuddled her comfortably. "If you weren't here, I don't know what I'd do."

"Probably the same."

He smiled and ruffled her hair and leaned over to turn off the lamp.

She slept heavily, didn't know when he left. It was still raining when she woke. "Complications" was the word that formed itself in her mind. Things were no forwarder.

TWELVE

1

Sam's radio-alarm clock suddenly blared at a decibel level sufficient to cause an adult with normal hearing to leap, cursing, upon the device. If not quite enough to wake the dead, it might have caused some of the dear departed to roll over and fumble for the no-longer-in-reach alarm's off button. It was not loud enough to wake a fifteen-year-old male.

Reuben rapped on Sam's bedroom door, though he was certain his knock could not be heard above the din. Opening the door, he looked in on a room as dark as the inside of a tent, all shades drawn down tight against the slightest intrusion of light. Sam splayed over his bed like an insectile sculpture. Reuben reached the alarm clock just as the boy's hand closed over it.

"Sorry," Sam mumbled blindly.

"Shower's yours. Breakfast in ten minutes."

Slicked and shiny, Sam came into the kitchen and collapsed into a chair at the table. One hand fell upon a piece of toast, the other upon the fork by his plate.

Sam gobbled the toast, swallowed mightily, and asked, "So what'd you do to the bastard?"

Reuben opened the newspaper. "I put him in the hospital."

The boy vaulted out of his chair with a whoop.

Reuben looked up at him. "Put a lid on it, Sam. It's nothing to cheer."

Sam sat down again, a little abashed.

Reuben sighed. Sam was so easy to abash.

"I'm looking at an assault charge," Reuben said quietly. "I don't want you looking at one too."

Sam slumped. He blinked at his scrambled eggs as if they had just sprouted there on the plate.

"Bri committed an assault on Karen. If she'll make the charge against him, and if we're lucky, we'll be able to trade off and call it even, at least in the eyes of the law."

The boy nodded.

"So no more trouble. When Karen comes home, I'll need you to stay with her. Keep an eye on her in case she gets sick, be around if Bri's brother or any of his gang wants to take this any further. Maybe Josh would hang out with you. I don't want Karen left alone."

Sam sat up straight. "Sure. We can look out for her."

"Just make sure nobody hassles Karen and she gets her rest."

"Okay." He attacked his breakfast with renewed appetite.

In fact, Reuben didn't think Karen would be subject to any more open attacks, but he knew Sam needed to protect her, having been denied the opportunity to take on Bri Spearin personally.

2

Leaving Jonesy at the service station, Reuben went directly to the hospital in Greenspark. Hennessey was on his early-morning rounds and passed a word with him: she seemed to be okay and could be released.

He found Karen's room and sat down on the edge of her bed.

Stirring, she peered at him from under heavy lids. She propped herself up on one arm and hooked the other over her brow to shade her eyes from the daylight.

"Good morning. How are you?"

"Okay." She was hoarse.

He offered her water and she took it eagerly.

"Dr. Hennessey says you can go home today. I'm going to have Sam stay home with you. Until you're feeling ready to look after yourself."

She nodded.

Reuben hesitated. "I hurt Bri last night, Karen."

She stared at him and then collapsed back onto the bed with a moan of distress.

Then, sullenly, she asked, "How bad?"

"Broke his wrists. Busted his lip. And I imagine he's got a damn sore sack this morning."

Karen snorted bitterly. "Oh, no."

It was passing strange to be sitting there discussing the state of his daughter's lover's sack with her, but he didn't feel the embarrassment he'd thought he would. Maybe it was their first real conversation as adults and equals. Pearl would appreciate the irony.

"I'm in trouble," he said.

She struggled up onto her elbows again.

"He could have me brought up on a charge of assault. The only way out for me, and even that's an outside chance, is that you could make the same charge against him."

Karen stared at him for a long moment and then sank away, rolled over, and curled up with her back to him.

"Whatever you want. Now, leave me alone, will you? I'll be ready to go as soon as I get dressed."

3

"Wap wap," Sonny Lunt repeated for perhaps the eighth time since he had planted his rear end on the stool and his elbows on the counter to leverage cupping his mug. "Parish and Laimbeer, I tell ya."

Roscoe chuckled nastily. "I wouldn'ta minded watching it."

For the second morning in a row, Pearl attended her business more closely than it required. When Roscoe finally caught her eye, she realized it had been a mistake as far as he was concerned. To fake him out, she ought to have been more interested, more surprised. Being busy and disinterested made it an easy guess for him that she knew all about it before Sonny ever dropped his jaw and spilled it. But at least from then on, through the whole day's repetition of the story, she didn't have to do any acting, just listening.

For once, the weather was ignored. Considering how long the rain had hung on, everybody was clearly grateful for the distraction. The gossip seemed to transfuse new life into Walter McKenzie. The confusion, disorientation, and irritability people had been shaking their heads over was completely gone. It was as if his mind had slipped back into focus again.

"Golly, I wish I'da been there. By God, Reuben oughta done it a long time ago. I tole him so, way back."

It was a commonly held sentiment.

"Fudgy's wishing he'd sold tickets," Lurch Mullins said.

"To what?" David, coming in, wanted to know.

"Don't you know?" Walter asked excitedly.

"There's lots I do and more I don't. Maybe you could be specific."

Walter immediately proceeded to a lively, if inaccurate version of the night's events. Periodically he would cock a bushy eyebrow at Lurch and ask, "Ain't that right, Lurch?"

And Lurch would hem and haw and venture a careful correction or two.

David was so enthralled that when he realized he had cleaned his plate unconsciously, he started. "Pardon me, Pearl."

"Not at all."

"Well, there," Walter said, "I guess mebbe Karen's seen the last of that young lout. There's your chance, David."

Walter's surprise when everyone except David laughed made it clear the old man had not intended it jokingly.

"Please, Walter. Not even the delectable Karen could be worth the health of my gonads and the use of my hands. Pardon me, Jean."

She was red in the face but she tittered loudly, as she had several times already. It was clear she was having an enormously good time.

Walter teeheed but he was not to be put off. "Fack is, you'd never give him the occasion. You was raised a gentleman, God rest your mother and father. You wouldn't hurt a woman even if she gave you cause."

"Thank you. I'm flattered."

"Well, don't be. It's only behooving." Walter brought his contribution to the conversation to a close with a noisy fart.

"Dad!" Jean was mortified.

"Pardon me, Pearl." Walter picked up his hat. "Fellas. It's an ill wind that don't blow someone some good."

"Dad!"

Pearl turned quickly to hide a grin.

David suddenly dove into his newspaper. The pages trembled suspiciously.

Lurch was not so discreet. He simply guffawed.

Roscoe poured himself a cup of coffee and pulled up a stool opposite David. "Walter's an old woman, always trying to marry people off. Surprised he didn't try to foist Jean off on you. He was trying to get me interested in her the other day." He snorted with contempt.

David folded his newspaper and remarked dryly, "Lucky Jean."

Roscoe ignored him. "If Reuben had taken a hand with Karen five, six years ago, none of this woulda happened. You don't take a strong hand with your yowens, they'll go wild every time."

David laughed. "How many kids have you raised, Roscoe?"

"Jesus," Roscoe cried, "you don't have to be Eye-talian to make spaghetti. Look at you, healthy young fella sitting around moping and writing poetry and thinking about sex all the time. Raised too easy, is why. You had to work for a living every day, you wouldn't have so much lead in your pecker."

David choked on the last of his coffee.

"I didn't know work took the lead outta your pecker," Lurch said. "Guess I'll give notice."

"Better find a woman desperate enough to have you, first," Roscoe said. "As far as I'm concerned, it ain't worth the bother. Sex ain't bin nothing but trouble since Adam and Eve was kicked outta the Garden."

David folded his newspaper with a snap. "Amen, brother."

The Needham marriage must have been a barrel of laughs. Pearl had an impulse to ask Roscoe if his wife had predeceased him out of frustration or boredom. Instead she bit her tongue and loaded the dishwasher.

4

Arriving home with dinner for Reuben and his family in one arm and the female of the two cats, having decided she was old enough to be separated from her brother, in the other, Pearl had to step over the envelope that had been slipped under the door. It contained two calligraphed sheets. She sat down at the kitchen table to read them.

Reliquary

Among the artifacts recovered from the pirate ship *Whydah,* the wreck of which was recently rediscovered off the coast of Massachusetts, was a small woman's high button boot,
which still contained the foot bones.

pearl upon my tongue
draws me fathoms deep
into the sea of skin,
where sudden buoyant memory,
from the *Whydah*'s pillaged grave,
yields into my thought
the booty of a kidskin boot
still holding, like a pirate's hand,
the relic dainty bones of a dainty woman's foot,
some ugly pirate's mary's toes,
once counted by his kisses
and tickled by his beard
while she breathless bucked and rode,
the heel she pressed
upon his cat-scarred spine,
the foot that trod his shoulders
while he dove deep and urgent
for the salt-slick pearl hiding
neath the bony roof
of her cave of tides
whereto he did drownd his bones:
X
marks the spot
where love lies buried
who ever had practiced so
at how to be drownd,
hanging upon each other's necks,
and so do lie together still
with bones still woven
and with and like
their clothing scattered all about
the wreckage,
as when they had rushed to bed,
to pitch and yaw upon the fatal bottom.
do I remember, romance, dream, or prophesy?
The truth is on my tongue.

"Oh boy," she muttered. Chin on her left knuckles, she smoothed the sheets on the table and stared at them blankly. She read them again. The phone rang.

"Pearl," David said in a quiet voice. "Did I get it right?"

She closed her eyes. "I don't know. I don't know anything about poetry."

"It's not about poetry."

She was quiet for a few long seconds. "I know."

"Good. It's very important that you know."

She couldn't think of anything else to say. And after a moment, there was the very soft click of David hanging up.

5

After she refrigerated the food, she carried the pages upstairs, refolding them, unfolding them again, finally refolding them and shutting them quickly inside her jewelry box.

A couple of hours later, clean and feeling competent after attending to her accounts, she went to Reuben's.

Sam and Josh were in the kitchen, hulling strawberries at the sink. From the excessive delight with which they greeted her, she took it they had had a long tense day waiting for nothing to happen.

"How's Karen?"

Sam pointed her in the right direction. "Go see for yourself."

Karen was reading. She dropped her book and held out her arms. "Pearl!"

Pearl hugged her and then looked at her critically. The girl was still a little pale but seemed much herself again.

"Did you hear what Dad did?" Karen asked in a low voice.

Pearl nodded. "What do you think about it?"

Karen picked at the bedcovers. "I don't know." She sounded very lost. "I don't know how I feel about Bri. I think I still love him."

Pearl expelled a long exasperated breath. "He punched you out. He damn near killed you, forcing that shit down your throat. And you think you still love him."

Karen hid her face, saying through her hands, "Please, Pearl, don't be angry at me."

"I'm not angry with you." Pearl bit her lip. "Well, yes, I am. How can you love somebody that hurts you like that?"

"Haven't you ever loved somebody who hurt you bad?"

Pearl grabbed the girl's hands and pressed them together between hers. "I stopped loving him when he hurt me that bad, Karen. It's called self-preservation."

"But you're so strong, Pearl."

Pearl didn't feel strong. The competence she had been riding when she left her house was galloping away in the distance. She could almost hear it laughing, the way horses do, snorting and blowing. The girl literally made her tired. She felt like a wrung-out dishrag.

"No, I'm not. I've been as stupid over men as any other woman."

Even as Pearl waned, Karen was brightening up. "Didn't you ever want to get married?"

Pearl shook her head wearily. "I was married, for seven years."

Karen's eyes widened. "Oh. It didn't work, huh? So you don't think you'll ever marry David?"

"What?"

Pearl was surprised at how panicky that out-of-the-woodwork thought made her feel. Weak and woozy and scared.

"I think," Karen said confidently, "you two are really, seriously in love. I mean, I've seen the way you look at each other. You've changed, too. You've got a glow about you. You're a happy woman, I can see it."

"You see too much, kid. I think maybe you're confusing satisfied with happy." She meant the blunt assertion of sensuality to distract Karen, but wondered if she were also trying to convince herself.

"Maybe I shoulda tried him." Karen was sly.

"You *shoulda* stayed in high school and learned better grammar. And less about sex."

The girl laughed hoarsely. "You've been outta high school awhile. It's different now."

"They tell me. You say so. The older I get, the less certain I am I know anything."

"You know," Karen said, "you're the only grown-up who treats me like an equal. Daddy can't seem to understand I'm not his little girl anymore."

"Karen." Pearl paced the room irritably. "If you're still thinking about adults as *them*, how can they treat you as an equal? You're defining yourself as not-grown-up. Aren't you making as many assumptions about how *they* think and feel as they do about you, without bothering to find out if it's so or not?"

Karen was quiet a minute. "I never thought about it that way," she said in a small voice.

Pearl bent over and hugged her again.

She was just leaving when Reuben arrived. He pulled his truck up between her and the house, slid across the cab, and exited from the passenger side.

"Pearl," he said, and she leaned back against her truck door to collect a hasty kiss. Between the trucks, it felt a little like the tunnel of love at a carnival, or maybe stealing kisses in the corridor outside some college classroom. She wondered if they could be seen from the house. Probably not, or Reuben wouldn't have. Something had gone well. Some worry dissolved. The tenseness had gone out of him and he was playful again.

"I brought supper over and checked on Karen. She seems fine."

"Thanks." He let her go, leaned back against his own truck. "You know the deputy I mentioned last night, Tom Clark?"

She nodded.

"He stopped a few minutes ago and said he's seen Bri in the hospital. Seems it gave Bri a serious pause when Tom mentioned that Karen might charge him with assault. Tom thinks Bri's going to roll over without Karen even making the complaint." Reuben smiled. "What Tom actually said was, 'Bri's like a skunk that's had some close calls. The judges in this district already know him by smell.' "

Pearl laughed and climbed into her truck. He closed it gently after her.

"I'd like to see you tonight," he said. "But I should be here."

She nodded. "I need a solid night's rest anyway."

They left it at that.

At home, the atmosphere of the bedroom was rich with the smell of the dying roses. The bed seemed empty, a phenomenon associated with an ongoing affair. When she wasn't involved, her bed seemed perfectly cozy. In fact, her bed was far too full. She'd need a bigger bed and a shoehorn to accommodate three. When the kitten jumped up and curled up next to her, she was glad of it, a silky little bundle of warm, living being, its purring as good as a lullaby.

6

"We still taking the Fourth off?" Roscoe wanted to know the next morning.

"You bet." Pearl was cracking eggs over the grill with élan. She felt like a new woman. A good night's rest had made a huge difference. "Even the slaves don't work on the Fourth."

"Whatcha gonna do?"

"Beat up on my garden. With the rain, it's turned into a jungle."

"S'sposed to give it up today."

" 'Bout time," Sonny Lunt grumbled.

"Amen," Pearl agreed.

The phone rang and Pearl picked it up and stepped sideways into the storeroom.

"Pearl," Reuben said with a distant snap of newspaper, "I think I found your booths. Fella in North Conway, just retiring, giving up a place I remember. The booths were comfortable and he kept up his fixtures. Want to look at them this afternoon?"

"You're on. And thanks."

"No trouble. Pick you up at three-thirty at the diner?"

"See you."

She hung up and looked out over the empty space where the booths would be installed, imagining them. It gave her goose bumps. It would be nice to have some time alone with Reuben, uninterrupted and private. She could talk to him. The prospect of putting things right calmed her.

David came in during a lull. He came right around the counter and walked into the storeroom. Pearl whipped around after him and ran straight into him with an *ooof,* when he came to a sudden stop and turned around. All he had to do was circle her with his arms, as if they were playing *London Tower* in the schoolyard and she were being taken prisoner. It was uncanny how he seemed to know before she actually moved what she was going to do, as if they were engaged in some uncharted dance.

He peered at her over the top of his sunglasses. "Hi."

"What did I tell you about coming back here?" She tried to be mad at him. "Can't you read? This sign says *Employees Only.*"

"So hire me."

"Okay. Now you're fired. Out." She shook off his embrace and pointed at the door.

Leaning back against a stack of cases, he crossed his arms. "How would you like to go out tonight? Put on a dress and go to the movies and dinner. I'd take you dancing but it's Tuesday and there's nothing but canned music in the roadhouses."

"Love it. But I can't. I have to go to North Conway to look at some booths."

David stood up straight and pushed his glasses up his nose. "Christ, first it was a dead dog and now it's *booths.* I'm doing something wrong."

She nudged his foot with the toe of her sneaker. "For starters you're in my storeroom where you don't belong, and keeping me from my work. "

"Roscoe can keep those three cups out there filled without even breathing hard."

"Nevertheless," Pearl began, and stopped. "You're right," she said, smiling.

She gave the door a tap off its wedge and it sighed slowly closed. Reaching back, she clicked the lock.

He smiled and pulled her close.

David went out first, adjusting his glasses, sat down at the counter, and opened a newspaper.

The three customers had left and the place was empty.

Roscoe rudely shoved a mug of coffee at him, leaving a trail of spill along the counter.

"Good morning to you too, Roscoe." David didn't lift his eyes from the paper.

Pearl came out, noticed the spillover, and wiped it up in a single quick swipe.

"What'll you have, David?" she asked.

His quick look over his glasses made her want to giggle.

You he mouthed.

Her tongue flicked lightly over her lips and then she realized what she was doing and turned hastily away.

Roscoe leaned toward David and muttered, "Already had it, David?"

David ignored the remark. "How's your dumb dog, Roscoe?"

Roscoe turned purple and stalked away.

Pearl watched him go, looked quickly at David. David shrugged.

Roscoe sulked all day. At first she ignored it, but after a while she began to feel uncomfortable. It drained the excitement out of her, the fun out of what had happened in the storeroom, and brought out the uneasiness she had felt about it even as she did it.

"What's bugging you?" she asked him as she locked up.

He exploded. "You know goddamn well. You going off in the storeroom with that goddamn spoiled pretty boy. You think I wouldn't notice?"

She let him blow steam for a few seconds before answering, in as neutral a tone as she could manage, "I thought it wasn't any of your business, Roscoe."

He snorted. "It ain't *your* business, is the point. Your business is cooking, running this diner. You want to make giving blow-jobs to spoiled rich boys a business, you oughta take it out on the street where it belongs."

Her face grew warm and she was ashamed of the sudden rise of anger against Roscoe, the vaulting rush of self-justification.

"I'm sorry."

"You're goddamn lucky I didn't walk outta here on the spot. What the hell's got into you, woman? Never mind, I know *who*'s got into you. He drives a little toy car and talks a good game to empty-headed women looking to get their heads turned."

"Don't blame David. I'm as much to blame as he is. We got carried away."

"I don't give a shit," Roscoe snarled. "It's your private life. Just keep it outta my face. Have the decency to do it in your goddamn bedroom and keep your mind on the job. Bleeding Jesus, I'd expected somethin' like this from that girl of Reuben's. I thought you had more sense."

She nodded, her throat tight.

Roscoe walked stiffly away to his truck.

7

Reuben swung into the lot.

Roscoe looked at him, looked back at Pearl. The expression on his face was one of incredulity mixed with utter contempt.

She swung herself up into Reuben's cab.

"Hi." Her voice was too low.

Reuben studied her face. "What's wrong?"

"Little run-in with Roscoe." She slammed the passenger-side door decisively. "My fault."

Reuben reached out and patted her knee. "Sorry to hear it. Hope it blows over."

She choked and coughed. Reuben pounded her back.

"I'm okay," she said at last, and pushed him gently away.

"Sure?"

She shook her head affirmatively.

"Buckle up."

"Oh, right. I was thinking of something else."

"Three-oh-two's clogged with tourists doing eighty to get someplace and wait for their vacations to be over. Then we have to go over to New Hampshire, and there's no telling what'll happen over there. They got this lane up the middle for people to turn either way, and sometimes there's two vehicles trying to turn opposite ways in the same space. And the tourists from Massachusetts pass in that lane, as well as on the sidewalk."

She giggled until she realized he was serious.

"Maybe we should take the backhoe?"

He snorted.

"How's Karen?"

"Okay. She says she's going back to the trailer."

"Oh. I was thinking when she bought that car, I'd never want to be her age again."

Reuben nodded. "She thinks I never was. Fact is, I lived in the horse barn for the last three years of high school because my old man threw me out of the house."

Pearl clapped her hands and laughed. "Any particular reason?"

"He hated the music. I bought myself a record player and then an old second-hand Gibson. Knew all of Creedence backward and forward." He smiled at the memory of himself.

"You did?"

"I did. The old man gave me a choice, thinking I'd never be able to take the cold in the winter, and besides, there was nothing but electric bulbs for wiring in the horse barn, so I wouldn't be able to use the record player. I wired the barn and bought myself some amps. But that barn was cold as a witch's tit in the winter, I'll tell you."

"A witch's tit?" She giggled. "How cold is that?"

"Give you frostbite, I hear. I'll ask somebody's felt up Belinda Conroy and let you know."

"Three years?" She shook her head.

"My father was a stubborn man."

"Your father was stubborn? Sounds like it was a dominant gene."

"It is. I come from a long line of pigheaded Irishmen."

"Your folks still alive?"

Reuben looked ahead at the road but she thought he might be seeing something else. "No. My father had a hunting accident. Somehow managed to get the business end of a Winchester shotgun in his mouth and blow a hole out the back of his head."

She was stunned. "Oh, Reuben."

"It was a long time ago. My mother told me he had bone cancer and wanted to keep her from being beggared by the medical expenses. She might have been telling it to herself too. She died four years ago of heart disease."

"I'm sorry to hear it." Pearl touched his arm gently. "Sometime I'll have my dad, Norris, come visit. You'd like him."

"I've got a soft spot for any father whose children love him still. I'd like to ask him his secret."

She nodded. "Norris was a wonderful father to me, but he and my brother Bobby never got on."

There was sudden flash of something huge and fawn-colored and unlikely. Reuben jammed his brakes and they jolted forward against the seat restraints. So extraordinary even Pearl was able to identify it as a young moose, the beast flowed past the truck's nose, over the road, and back into the woods. It was as tall as a drafthorse but had the delicate ankles of a thoroughbred racer and something of the Arabian's nobility in its carriage as well. Snapping at its heels was a familiar black retriever pup.

"Belinda's loose again," Pearl said.

Reuben shook his head. "Roscoe's not going to be pleased."

"No."

Thirty-five minutes later, he pulled into the parking lot of a closed luncheonette just west of North Conway. He turned off the ignition and got out and came around to open her door. She was just sitting there.

"Why, Pearl, you're *pale*."

She smiled weakly and slid out, letting him catch her and prop her up against the truck.

"Never take me here again, okay?"

"It wasn't that bad."

The booths were almost worth the harrowing trip, exactly what she wanted. She paid a little bit too much but she'd waited a long time for them and was losing money they could have been earning. They'd pay for themselves, anyway. The dickering took an hour.

Afterward, Reuben cast a considerate eye over the booths. "Can't fit but two of these things in a pickup. You'd have to go back and forth half a dozen times. You want a carter."

He lost her there; Pearl heard it "kahtah."

"Pardon?"

"Somebody to haul 'em all at once. Same as the former President. Jimmy."

"Carter?"

"That's what I said."

He knew somebody. In five minutes he had it all arranged.

"Done."

She shook hands with the man who had owned the booths.

Outside, she was overtaken by a feeling of anticlimax.

Reuben put his truck on the track back home.

"Thanks."

He patted her knee. "I'm going to let you buy me a beer."

"That's nice of me."

"Sure is."

But he didn't. He bought it himself, stopping at the Stateline store, and came out with a six-pack in a bag. When he came out, he stopped at the public phone and made a brief call.

"Checked the kids," he said, getting in. "All's well."

Pearl opened her purse to take out money. His hand closed over hers and the open jaws of the bag.

"My treat," Pearl insisted.

He shook his head. "I was kidding. You brought supper last night."

She sat back and rolled her head on the back of the seat, discovering how tight her shoulders and neck were. All worked up over her booths. She laughed at herself, low in her throat.

"Pop one of those Miller's, will you?" Reuben asked.

"Driving with an open beer's illegal."

"I'm sober as a judge, I'm thirsty, and I've just driven in New Hampshire, Pearl."

She laughed, popped the can, and handed it to him.

"You too. You've earned it."

He waited for her, then tapped his beer against hers. "May your benches always be well-upholstered."

"Hear, hear."

A little while later she said, "Reuben, we have to talk."

He took his eyes from the road to glance at her. Then he knocked back his beer and passed her the empty. "I'm going too fast for you, aren't I?"

They weren't talking about his driving. She took a deep breath and kept her eyes on the woods at the side of the road. Every house and farm and little business was a patch cut in the trees. She could imagine it from the air.

"Yes."

"Pass me another, will you?"

Silently she passed him another and he popped it.

"I'd like to take you someplace," he said.

"Where?"

"It's a secret."

She laughed. "Irresistible. Now?"

"I told the kids I'd be a while."

She helped herself to another beer.

Eventually they turned off the main road onto a secondary strip and then onto narrow, ill-paved, and sometimes unpaved roads she had never before traveled. She was quickly lost. Catching glimpses of the lake and cottages and camps, she realized they were following on a camp road. There was a final turn and they passed from dirt road to drive, came down an embankment and into a clearing. Blackened timbers and a cellar hole scarred the lot. Enormous old pines around the burnt-out house were scorched but appeared to be flourishing. Even a lilac close up against the foundation was green and healthy, its flowers past but its leaves full and lush.

"Where are we?" she asked.

"Nodd's Ridge."

She bumped her hip into him in a mock tiff.

"This is the old Russell place," he said.

"One of your customers?"

"No. Walter's. But I was fire chief when the place burned. Nothing we could do. Place was fully engaged by the time we got a truck down here. It was winter and we'd had a bad storm."

"Then the place was empty. Nobody got hurt?"

He shook his head. "Liv Russell and her boy were here. She got hurt, some other people got killed. Jeannie McKenzie's son and stepsons. I'll tell you about it sometime when I want to tell you an ugly story. Right now, I'd rather not."

He took her by the shoulders and led her past the debris of the house fire toward the lakeshores. It was suppertime and the lake was abandoned. The low cloud ceiling made an early twilight, and the lake, like everything else, seemed sodden. It was the color of slate but very still, reflecting back watery light here and there.

Deliberately Reuben began to unbutton his shirt. Their eyes met and they both laughed.

"Nobody here," he said. "Go ahead."

They stripped quickly and dove into the water. It was as cold as she'd expected. The rain had, if anything, made it colder. But it felt wonderful.

He came up behind her and took her by the waist. She leaned back against him. He cupped her breasts with his large hands and rolled her nipples under his thumbs.

"Cut glass with these?"

She elbowed him and he went for her throat. He took hold of her waist again and gently tugged her downward, beneath the surface. She went under with a low gurgle of laughter. They sank together, moving very little, letting their eyes adjust to being underwater. It was an eerie moment, hanging there in the water. Her hair floated around her face and Reuben caught a strand in his mouth and held it there a few seconds. Their body hair fluffed out and Pearl saw tiny bubbles jeweling it. Reuben nodded toward the surface and they both thrust upward at the same instant, breaking the surface together, eager for the air. They pulled ashore, where he drew her down onto the sand. It was dark now and they were invisible.

He looked around and listened carefully. "Do you hear a dog?"

She shook all over, part shiver, part laugh. "No. But maybe we should wait for one. It adds something."

"Just growl a lot and scratch my back."

He slipped his tongue into her mouth and she welcomed it, feeling him thicken against her leg.

Breaking away, she said, "Is that a goose bump?"

He laughed and opened her legs.

"You're as warm as the lake is cold. Where you touch me, you're as fluid as the lake, and as dense, you give but you push back, just the same."

She was surprised. Reuben had some poet in him too. He sounded like he'd been taking lessons from David. Went to show you shouldn't take anyone for granted. But she was distracted from following the thought.

"Row, don't drift," she murmured.

Low and sweet, they laughed together and he moved in her as if she were the lake.

THIRTEEN

1

Pearl drew herself a fragrant bath and had an indolent soak. The kitten, apparently lonely, followed her into the bathroom. Pearl tossed her a dry sponge and she batted it happily over the tiles. Her nails made a clittering noise on the plain old-fashioned ceramic octagons. Pearl moved her hand through the foam on the water.

How do you tell a man you're seeing (*truth, now: balling*) someone else on the side when he's just finished telling you his father was a suicide and you know it still hurts? Does something like that ever stop hurting? She still ached for her mother, didn't she? Insensitive, to say the least. Nice way to say thanks for locating the booths she wanted so much, too. That little tussle out there in the rain was a bit excessive for a thank-you-kindly, but it wasn't meant that way. She was beginning to feel a lessening of urgency, a feeling that she was in even less control of the outcome than she was of her emotions. Why couldn't one of them just for once be a shit and make it easy for her? It was all very tiring.

Buying the booths had had an odd effect. She felt as if she had recovered her focus. Her mind kept pulling back to the booths, instead of skittering, like the kitten on the bathroom tiles, after her divided emotions. There were insistent little questions demanding her attention: could she get the summer out of the old cracked leather upholstery, go for ambience and a quick return on the booths, or should she splurge on reupholstering? New leather was a luxury item. She had a comfortable margin, she could do it. And she wouldn't consider anything but leather—it wore the best, despite the initial cost. It was all so comfortably material, or at least leathereal. She managed a tired giggle at her own pun.

The booths would require someone to wait on them, and she and Karen were straight-out on the counter, even needed Roscoe on Sundays. She'd need another hand, unless Roscoe wanted to work every day, part-time. It would be a mischief to offer him a split-shift. No, she'd have to watch her step with him; he was mad enough at her. She'd made some bad moves. She didn't want to think about them. She wanted to think about leather and metal studs and the satisfying thunk of the stud-gun driving brass into the wood.

The kitten chased the sponge into the hallway. The water had become tepid. Pulling the plug, Pearl reached for her towel.

She rang David from her bedroom, tucking the receiver between her shoulder and neck to free her hands to do her pedicure. It took him a while to answer.

"Me," she said.

"Get your booths?"

"Yes. Well, I made the deal. They'll be delivered tomorrow afternoon."

There was a brief silence. "You'll be tied up."

"Have to be there."

He groaned. "All right, then, when may I tie you up?"

"I love it when you talk dirty. Not tomorrow. It's supposed to be clear tomorrow and my garden needs some work."

He proposed going to the movies Friday night and she agreed.

She went downstairs in her wrapper and flopped onto the daybed. Because of the rain, it had been a while since she'd watched the day go by. Not entirely her fault. It had been stealing away in secret, behind the clouds that were now being torn apart, the sun breaking through them even as the rim of the mountains tipped up to cover it.

The kitten popped up into her lap and curled up. The smell of green was heavy in the moist evening air. Her untended garden was growing rank. Tomorrow, she promised herself. The phone rang. Sighing, she got up and answered it.

"What are you doing home?" Bobby asked. "White folks give you the night off?"

She listened to him laughing for a few seconds, then dropped the receiver into the cradle.

He rang again.

"I don't need your jive tonight, Bobby, thanks anyway."

"Okay, be as good a boy as I can." He was still giggling.

"Try."

"I be calling all the time, never get nothing but your goddamn machine. You never home."

"So leave a number, I'll call back."

"I don't talk to machines."

"You mean you 'don't be talkin' to machines.' That's your choice. I put a machine on my phone. You talk jive at me to remind me what color your skin is, in case I forget. I figure we're even."

He stopped chuckling. "Why don't you come to Philly and see me? I'd like to see your face. Then I'd know you was okay."

"I'm okay, Bobby. But I can't get away right now. Maybe in the fall. You could come here and see me."

"You used to tell me you were okay when you were married to Johnny."

"I was, most of the time."

"Sure you were."

"I'm taking care of myself, Bobby."

"Sure. Work yourself to death, is what you mean."

"Bobby." She was exasperated.

"I worry about you, is all."

"I worry about you. But you don't like it, do you?"

He laughed. "You always did talk back."

"Call Norris," she said. "It wouldn't kill you and it would make him happy."

"Don't be too sure of that, sis. I'm outta change. Take care of yourself, little sister."

2

New day. Clear, clean air, soothingly cool. She felt more rested. The booths would be in place before the Fourth. All she needed was another hand.

Roscoe was waiting for her. "Pearl, I mighta gone too far yestiddy."

She shook her head. "You were right. If I'd been working for me, I would have fired my butt right out of here."

He shook out a cigarette and stuck it in the corner of his mouth. His match sucked the air and he nodded over it, a justified man.

Karen drove in.

"What are you doing here?" Pearl asked.

"I'm working today. Doctor said I could."

"Are you sure?"

She was sure. Stubbornness, Pearl remembered, was a dominant gene in the Styles clan.

At three-thirty the booths arrived and Pearl flipped the OPEN sign to CLOSED. When Reuben and Sam rolled in to help unload the booths, Karen's smile closed up as if it were a sign somebody had flipped.

"You don't need me, do you?" she murmured.

Pearl shook her head and the girl slipped out the back as the men came in the front door.

They both saw her go but said nothing, simply looked at each other and then joined the man who had hauled the booths from New Hampshire (the *carter* Pearl reminded herself), putting their backs to the job. Roscoe stood around and offered advice that was both unneeded and unheeded.

It was a quarter after five when Pearl had the booths arranged to her satisfaction. She passed out beer to toast the accomplishment. The carter shook hands all around and accepted a discreet tip from Pearl on leaving.

As the carter bucketed his big moving van onto Route Five, a funereal old gray Lincoln pulled in. The big car breathed a visible sigh of relief when the fat man driving it got out. The man wore a black suit with a black string tie and round rimless glasses. Moving around on a warm summer day, he was beaded with sweat from his almost bald pate, where a few very long hairs were crossed from side to side over a sunburnt, peeling scalp, to his damp palms. He was perspiring as heavily as if he had joined them in their labors.

Pearl became aware of an unnatural silence. Sitting on stools on the public side of the counter, Reuben, Sam, and Roscoe were all watching the effortful approach of the fat man in black with the total absorption of those who know what is going to happen next.

The fat man waved limply at them and mounted the steps. He had the demeanor of an undertaker. Even as he reached into the breast pocket of his suit, Pearl realized he was a process server, someone who always brought bad news.

"Reuben," the man said with a hollow heartiness, "Jonesy said I'd find you here."

Wearily Reuben held out his hand and the man delivered the papers.

The fat man turned on his heel and exited as quickly as he had come.

A professional, Pearl thought. No condolences, no pass-the-time-of-day, just scuttle your fat ass back to your Lincoln and vamoose before someone gets cross and takes the bad news out on you.

Reuben looked at the envelope in his hand distastefully, snapped it against one palm, and opened it.

Pearl noticed the bottles were empty and fetched another round.

Silently Reuben handed the papers to Sam. The boy put down his bottle and looked at his father and then at the paper. Reuben put his arm around Sam's shoulders and tugged him closer. At last the boy could no longer not look. He unfolded the paper but read only a few lines before suddenly crumpling it up and throwing it down.

"I'm not going through that shit again. I'm not." He glared at his father. "Someday I just want to know"—his breath hitched, and his voice shook—"just what the fuck you did to her, she hates us all so much."

He walked out.

Reuben went after him.

Roscoe picked up the papers, glanced at them, and then handed them to Pearl. Laura was suing for custody again. Pearl folded them back into their envelope.

Reuben and Sam were in the parking lot. They didn't raise their voices, but the body English was bad. Sam was rigid, his fists clenched. Reuben had his hands on the boy's shoulders. Sam was going to hit Reuben, Pearl realized, because he couldn't hit Karen or his mother. Then Sam seemed to erupt, throwing off Reuben's restraining hands. The boy was hot and furious and off-balance. Reuben swayed and blocked the boy's swing easily. He grabbed the boy by the shoulders again and thrust him back onto the side of the truck, pinning him there. Sam struggled a moment, then wilted abruptly. Reuben stepped back and let him go. The boy turned his face to the truck and his shoulders heaved. Reuben left him and came back in.

Pearl handed him the process server's envelope. "I'm sorry for your trouble."

"Talk to you." He indicated the storeroom.

"Excuse me," she said to Roscoe, and followed Reuben into the storeroom.

She went into his arms and he held her tightly for a few seconds. They were there for only a moment. She watched him drive away with Sam.

Roscoe was finishing the beer Reuben had abandoned. "Waste not, want not."

He had had a few while they were shoving booths around too, and it was starting to show.

Pearl's throat was tight and dry. A good slug of beer helped loosen it up.

Roscoe sat there watching her. "You fucking him too."

It wasn't a question. Pearl didn't answer. She finished her beer and slipped the bottle into the returns box.

Roscoe cackled. "What the hell, Pearl, you oughtn't to give the boy a miss. Liven things up for 'em, they ain't got enough trouble."

"Roscoe, watch your step."

"Oh, my step's real steady. You're the one dancing on cow patties in your high heels."

"Go home, Roscoe."

"Aw, shit. Can't I wait around and see who you take out in the storeroom next? It was just gettin' interesting."

Pearl slammed the front door closed and snubbed the lock.

Roscoe slid off his stool, picked up his brace of open beer bottles, and strutted out the back way, through the storeroom, cackling as he went.

Pearl sat down on one of the counter stools and surveyed her diner. The empty space was gone, filled up with the booths that doubled the number of seats. She loved the smell of the old leather upholstery of the booths. But the place seemed suddenly smaller, filled up, like her life, in a way she had imagined but not quite like this. Reality was always unexpected; it was impossible to imagine all the details. She hadn't, for one, expected the tables to look so empty. She ought to have been very happy. Instead, she was tired and troubled. She took a final look around, so she would remember just how it was when she described it to Norris.

3

The garden was growing a lush crop of weeds. Determined to whip it into shape before dark, Pearl attacked the weeds and found her humor improving. Intoxicated at being out-of-doors, the kitten hopped and strutted around her, chasing butterflies and dragonflies and occasionally pouncing on the thinnings and weeds Pearl tossed to one side. Whenever Pearl stopped for a mouthful of iced tea from a thermos or for a stretch, she checked around for the kitten, not wanting her to wander off into the woods or down to the road. But the kitten stayed close. An evening breeze came up and Pearl felt the air cooling. She stretched, took another mouthful of tea, and admired the progress she had made.

The kitten was digging a little hole in the loosened soil on the far side of the garden from her. Suddenly a wild belling erupted from the graveyard. The kitten yowled and stiffened, the fur along her backbone straight up. Pearl dove at her but the kitten was already in motion, a ball of fur shooting off into the bushes. Pearl belly-flopped among the new peas and knocked the wind out of herself. The retriever bayed and yelped. Groaning, Pearl rolled over and stared up at a serene sky. The bitch scrabbled directly over Pearl after the kitten, catching her in several places with her claws as Pearl rolled to one side in instinctive self-defense.

"Shit!" Pearl cried into the soil, and got dirt in her mouth.

Then the retriever was gone.

Spitting muddy saliva from her mouth, Pearl sat up and watched the bitch going hell for leather into the woods after the kitten. She stood up, brushing herself off. Hearing the swish of the grass behind her, she whirled around to see Evvie Bonneau striding from the graveyard.

"You okay?" Evvie called.

Pearl nodded.

Evvie was wearing a gun in a hip holster. She had a leash looped over her arm and carried some kind of long-barreled gun as well. All that Pearl knew about guns was which end whatever loaded it came out, but there was something hygienic and unthreatening about the one Evvie Bonneau was carrying that made her think maybe it shot tranks instead of bullets.

The little woman shook her head ruefully in the direction the cat and dog had disappeared. Close up, Evvie cast an appraising glance over Pearl and seemed satisfied that she was not hurt.

"Did you see it?" Pearl asked. "That dog chased my kitten into the woods."

"Bitch was running from me. Just got distracted by the kitten. Kitty'll likely find her way back okay. But if I see her, I'll fetch her home for you."

"Thanks." Pearl noticed Evvie was perspiring and looked tired. "Would you like some iced tea or a beer or something?"

Evvie smiled at her. "Don't mind it I do. I'm not going to catch that goddamn bitch tonight, the rate she's moving."

"Come on in, then."

Pearl rinsed her mouth at the sink and then got a couple of Miller

Lites from the fridge. The two women opened the bottles and drank directly from them.

"Here's to crime," Evvie said.

Pearl raised her can. "Amen."

"You want me to put some Mercurochrome on those scratches?"

Pearl looked at her arms where the retriever's nails had raised welts and barely broken the skin. "Guess I'd better put something on them."

Warm soap and water wasn't too bad, cleaning the scratches, but the disinfectant stung as it was painted on, and she couldn't help wincing.

"Shit," she muttered.

Evvie was unperturbed, humming unmusically as she painted red stripes on Pearl's arms. "Off with the shirt. You got a nasty one across your collarbone."

"So I do."

With a light touch, Evvie cleaned a pair of longer, deeper welts that started at the collarbone and went down Pearl's left breast into her armpit. "Gonna be sore in the morning."

"I know." Pearl grimaced as the disinfectant did its work.

Evvie stepped back and admired her work. "Don't fool around with them scratches. They could get infected and be a real pain in the ass."

"Well, tit." Pearl pulled her sweaty, dirty shirt back on.

Evvie laughed and picked up her beer. "I'll get her, sooner or later. Me and the Mounties. I'm going to have to shoot her and I'd rather do it close up."

Pearl almost dropped her beer. "Shoot her? Do you have to?"

"She took a lamb down at Partridge's. Once they start that, there's no going back."

"Oh." Pearl sat down suddenly and kicked out a chair at the table for Evvie. "I'm sorry to hear it."

"Me too." The woman sat down and stuck her legs straight out. She admired the creases in her uniform pants and twitched them. "Part of my job. Sometimes I have to destroy an animal." She shrugged. "I don't like it, but better someone who knows what they're doing."

"You think the bitch might hurt the kitten?"

Evvie chuckled. "Kitty's up a tree by now. Way up. Probably won't come down until tomorrow."

"She's not used to being out. I keep her in the house."

"Cats are tough. Don't worry about it." Evvie frankly examined the kitchen. "Nice place. Nice garden you got out there. Rain brings on the weeds something awful. I don't grow nothing but tomatoes and peas anymore, myself. And some pot." Evvie looked into the top of her beer bottle. "Actually, I'm glad to see you. I've been wanting to tell you, you can rest easy in your mind. I'll keep my lips zipped about seeing you and Reuben out there in the berry patch. I ain't no gossip."

Pearl laughed. "Thanks."

Evvie shrugged. She looked up directly into Pearl's eyes. "I don't have much use for men, but Reuben's a decent sort. I do have one use for 'em, though, and sidelining that one for as long as he's been outta the game is a criminal waste. He wouldn't look twice at me, I ain't anything special, and besides, he knows I did in my last old man and that tends to make a man wilt. But I'm glad somebody's getting it and he's finally put paid to that dreary bitch he usta be married to."

Pearl realized her mouth was hanging open and slugged a healthy quantity of suds. She was all gooseflesh and wanted to shudder, but suppressed it.

Evvie drained her bottle and laughed. "I shock you?"

Pearl shrugged. "Never heard a confession of that kind before."

Evvie stood up. "I ain't got away with it, honey. I've lived in hell ever since, and I'll burn for it when I'm dead. But don't kid yourself I'm the only murderer walking around loose. Plenty people get away with it, if you mean they don't go to jail."

Pearl finished her beer. "You want another one?"

Evvie laughed. "Sure."

Opening the second bottle, the woman went on. "Been to Roscoe's several times about this goddamn bitch."

"Must be why he's in such a good temper lately."

"Maybe. I've fined him once, and that's it. It's outta his hands now, on account of the lamb killing."

"I've heard there are coyotes around here. Are you sure it's the dog and not one of them?"

"Ansel Partridge saw the bitch feeding on the carcass. It's always possible the bitch didn't do the actual killing and was just scavenging, but she's had a taste of lamb now and will want more."

"Oh." Pearl sat down again, tiredly.

"Anyway, Roscoe's drinking a lot." Evvie made a dismissive motion with her hand. "Always has drunk fairly steady, not so's it kep' him from working or anything, but the way these old farts do once their wives die or leave 'em for the last time. But I think he's getting worse."

"I didn't realize. He seems okay at work."

Evvie shrugged. "Maybe he just misses Jack and he'll steady down in a little while."

She drained the second beer quickly and stood up. "Thank you kindly. You ever want a pup?"

Pearl shook her head. "I've never kept a dog. Don't want to put a chain on anything."

Evvie's weathered ferrety face lit up with open admiration. "You are a rare breed, lady. Most people can't resist either wearing one or choking someone else with one. Good luck to you and thanks again for the beer."

Pearl leaned against the doorframe and watched the tough little woman walk away. She'd just had two beers with a murderess. And never felt safer. There was more than one odd specimen in this place. She didn't know who was odder, Evvie Bonneau or herself for taking a liking to this strange woman who was the town's animal-control officer.

Pearl went back to the garden to finish up, keeping an eye out for the kitten, but she didn't come home that night.

4

She was half-asleep in her bath when a rap on the back door startled her awake.

"Pearl," Reuben said from the bottom of the stairs.

Sitting up, she reached for her towel. "In the bath."

He took the steps two at a time and peeked in at the bathroom door. "I had to see you." By his loose-jointedness, the slur in his voice, the hops on his breath, he was unmistakably oiled.

She liked that smell of beer. "You looking at me."

"My pleasure."

He took the towel from her and held it out for her and she stepped into it. He wrapped it around her and picked her up.

It made her feel like a little girl in her father's arms. But she had never been carried from her bath by her father. By the time her mother married Norris, she was much too big a girl. She closed her eyes and snuggled up against him.

He turned her out onto the bed and sat down next to her to towel her hair. She was all goose bumps.

Catching one arm, he examined her scratches. "What happened?"

Pearl laughed. "Roscoe's retriever. Jumped me in the garden, chased my kitten into the woods."

"Useless beast. Did you disinfect them?"

"Evvie Bonneau did. She was tracking it. Apparently it got a lamb or dined on one a coyote killed."

Reuben nodded and gently traced the scratch over her collarbone. "She'll have to put it down, then. Hurt much?"

She shrugged. "What about you?"

He was taking his shoes off. "Pardon?"

"Hurt much?"

He smiled and swung his feet up onto the bed and gathered her in. "Like a mad bastard."

A few moments later he rolled away. "I've had too much to drink. I'm sorry, I really want you."

He went downstairs, came back with two bottles, which he proceeded to open. He offered her one; she shook her head.

"I've succeeded in protecting Karen for exactly as long as it takes for Spearin's bone to knit. Too little, too late. And I've given Laura just what she wanted."

"Spearin hasn't made a complaint. Surely the court can't take your kids away on the basis of an incident without a formal charge against you?"

"I don't know. I guess the court can do what it wants. Fun thing about divorce is, you find out your kids aren't yours. They belong to your ex and the court."

"Are they really ever yours?"

He kissed the nape of her neck. "Of course not. I mean you find out how many people have a say in your life and theirs that you never imagined when you were making the babies."

"Why does she want them?"

"She doesn't. She's scoring points. Anyway, she won't get them. Lawyer says I can manumit Karen—say she's independent and responsible for herself. I lost her a long time ago, Pearl, anyway. Laura'll get Sam but he'll be gone, as soon as the finding's handed down. He's big for his age, he can pass for eighteen. A strong kid can always support himself. He'll run."

Pearl twisted around to look Reuben in the eye. "How do you know?"

"His buddy told me. Josh says he'll go with him."

"You can't stop them?"

"How? I'm just glad Sam's got a good friend. Josh is a year older, he's got a driver's license. A couple years on the road'll be a hell of a lot of fun for them and they'll come back grown up, maybe ready to go to college."

"What about you?"

"I'll miss the hell out of him." Reuben put his arm under her breasts and tucked her up against him again. "Any way it comes out, I've lost my kids. You heard Sam today. He's sure in his heart I must have given Laura just cause to keep this war going."

"Reuben, why don't you tell him his mother"—she thought of what Evvie Bonneau had called Laura—"is a sorry bitch who can't help herself?"

He was quiet a moment. "I won't play that game of running down my ex. She's his mother. We made him together, made Karen and my oldest boy, Frankie, all in the same bed in the same house. I won't lay it off on her. She wouldn't have left me if I'd been the husband I should have been."

"You're as hard on yourself as Karen and Sam are."

He held her more tightly. "Mind if I'm hard on you? Guess I'm not as far gone as I thought."

She laughed and snuggled into his arms.

5

"Wake up, Pearl, you've overslept." Karen was shaking her awake.

Pearl sat up in a panic. Reuben was gone but there were empty bottles on the floor. She bolted from the bed.

"I'll open up," Karen said.

"The keys are on the kitchen table."

Karen smiled brilliantly and disappeared down the back stairs.

Another hasty shower, dress in whatever clean thing came quickest to hand, slip into a pair of sandals. She stopped to dab on a little perfume and in the mirror of the vanity she saw the pillows on her bed. There were two clear impressions on those pillows. Reuben had apparently not been too drunk to keep in mind the possibility that Karen would call first thing in the morning and had taken himself away, but at what hour, she couldn't say. Her memory was vague, only of a cessation of warmth.

After gobbling a quick breakfast, Roscoe put on an apron. He would be working full-time until she hired another hand, so that Karen could work the booths.

Pearl stuck a sign in the window that said HELP WANTED.

The midmorning lull came and the place emptied out, except for Sonny Lunt, who was working out a hangover, and the McKenzies. When Walter got up to go, Jean hung back.

"I'll be right out, Dad." Jean McKenzie gripped her handbag firmly. As soon as her father was out the door, she leaned over the counter and whispered, "Pearl, I'm interested in the job."

Pearl almost dropped the plate she was handing off to Karen.

Jean fluttered and blushed violently. "I don't have any experience, but . . ." The tips of her fingers, nails chewed to the quick, dented and smeared the patent leather of her handbag. "I could learn." She looked up and met Pearl's gaze directly. She had painted her thin lips beyond their margins, creating a little Cupid's bow where there was none. Her eyebrows were entirely plucked away and she had drawn new ones, the width of the pencil, in surprised arcs well above the natural arch. But there was a defiance in her, a stubbornness that counteracted her ludicrous outdated makeup and dignified her. "I'm an awful hard worker, Pearl."

Pearl nodded and wiped her hands on her apron. "Can you come back at three-thirty? We'll talk about it."

Jean's nerve was going fast. She was already backpedaling toward the door. "Oh, yes. Oh, yes."

Roscoe stared after her. "Mother of Jesus." He rolled his eyes at the ceiling. "A menopausal moron."

Sonny Lunt snickered. "Here's your last chance, Roscoe."

Pearl gave Sonny a stern look and he straightened out his face. A lot of schoolteachers had seen that transformation in Sonny, she thought.

"Yours, Sonny," Roscoe said. "I give all that jiggery-pokery up."

"You're mean, Roscoe," Karen put in, passing by. "Jean's had a hard go."

"So's everybody else come here," Roscoe said cryptically. "Now I think on it, be a blessing to have a spayed old pussy in here."

"Match you, eh, Roscoe," Sonny gibed. He leaned over the counter. "You musta gone woods-queer, old man. If I was behind that counter, I wouldn't be bitchin' about it, I'll tell ya. I wouldn't be able to get out Pearl's and Karen's way for not being able to walk. Be applying for all the overtime I could get."

"If that's a compliment, Sonny," Pearl said dryly, "I thank you."

Karen stuck her tongue out at him.

"Oh, Jesus," he moaned. "Do that some more, Karen. I can't stand it." Laughing hugely, he rolled toward the door.

Outside, there was a screech of brakes and the black retriever shot by the front of the diner.

"Speakin' a bitches in heat," Roscoe said.

Pearl snapped a towel at him. "That's enough out of your foul mouth."

"You ain't got nothing to say about what comes out of my mouth, considering what you put in yours!" Roscoe shouted.

Sonny came to a halt at the door. He stood there with his mouth fallen open, staring at Roscoe and Pearl.

Karen nearly dropped the dirty dishes she was piling on a tray.

Roscoe was in full rage, purple of face and foaming curses.

Pearl's hand came down over Sonny's last cup of coffee, which had grown cold. She threw it at Roscoe.

As the cold coffee cascaded over his head, he blubbered to a stop.

Pearl threw her arms around the old man. "Oh, Christ, Roscoe, I'm sorry."

He pushed his way out of her arms. "Fuck you. You ain't no better than a whore."

Snatching up a towel and swiping at the coffee running down his face, he stormed out past Sonny.

Sonny hesitated, then walked up to Pearl. He took a large cotton neckerchief out of his back pocket and dabbed at the tears on her face. "Here, don't let the old bastard get to you, Pearl. His ass is so tight he has to shit out his mouth."

Pearl snuffled into his hankie and then burst out laughing. "Oh, Sonny, I'm the bastard."

He didn't know why she thought that was funny, but he laughed with her anyway.

Pearl went to the rest room to wash her face. When she came back, Karen was loading the dishwasher.

"I've never seen him so angry," Karen said. "What *was* he talking about?"

"It doesn't matter. I'm just sorry I lost my temper."

"Give yourself a break. Roscoe's always had a rotten temper and a worse mouth on him. You oughta fire him, talking to you like that."

Pearl shook her head and went to mop the coffee off the floor.

"Tell you something else," Karen said. "The peckerhead's been stealing my tips."

6

When Pearl finally locked up for the day, she had hired Jean McKenzie to start work the next morning. That left her still short a hand. She would have to go see Roscoe, but first she was going to stop home and shower and change and read her mail.

The kitten was waiting for her on the steps. One leg was opened in a bloody gash nearly to the bone. There wasn't a square inch of her fur without a burdock stuck in it.

Crooning "Poor baby," Pearl picked her up gently. Fetching a towel from the kitchen, she folded it under the kitten and held her in her lap as she drove to Greenspark.

The vet's office was empty but still open. Belinda Conroy was not in sight. Another woman, LEEANN by her name tag, came out and admitted Pearl and the kitten to an examining room. Dr. Beech appeared immediately.

"Lock the door, Leeann, will you?" he said to the woman. "We were just shutting up, my help's all left for the day." He shook his head over the kitten. "What a mess. What happened to her?"

"Dog chased her into the woods."

"Close call, sweetheart," he murmured to the kitten.

He opened a cupboard and took out an electric shaver. "Well, it looks worse than it is. She won't like it, but it'll grow back."

A few minutes later, the kitten was furless and shivering as he stitched up her leg.

"There. She'll have a sexy scar."

Pearl laughed. "Thanks."

Dr. Beech stepped to the sink to wash his hands. "I'll bill you, Miss Dickenson."

The kitten slept all the way home. Pearl was carrying her into the house when she remembered what day it was. She was supposed to go to the movies with David.

On the phone recorder was a laconic request from Reuben that she call him.

He couldn't see her that evening. "I spent most of the afternoon with the lawyer and I've got a big old Connie on the lift I promised for tomorrow. And if I don't do my books tonight, I'm tax man's meat."

"That's okay," she said. "I'm going to the movies."

"Have fun. I'll call tomorrow, maybe we can do something."

"Sure."

She went upstairs to change for David, unable to stop thinking about how she was going to manage the diner with only Karen and Jean. Well, she would just have to do it somehow. Necessity was the mother of invention and all kinds of other virtues. Necessity would make a nice name for her female kitten. Now she would have to find a complementary name for the male. A minor distraction and a welcome one. There. If you didn't force a thing, it would solve itself. The male ought to be called Distraction. She laughed as she shucked her clothes, and felt strangely freed of worry as she stepped into the shower.

FOURTEEN

1

Necessity was washing herself when Pearl left the house.

Pearl concentrated on the idea of a night out. It would be nice to sit in the cool dark of a movie theater and not think about anything else. It wouldn't be any kind of hard work at all. The anticipation had a calming effect on her.

As she parked the truck, she realized she had decided to tell David about Reuben. She felt sure David would understand; he didn't have a monogamous cell in his body. He'd probably be amused. It seemed a bit silly that she hadn't told him already.

He pulled that trick of his again, emerging out of the darkened hallway as if condensed from its shadows, to fling open the door. Wearing only a pair of running shorts, he was glossy with perspiration. He picked her up bodily to kiss her, and his strength and vitality went through her like a shock. He put her down.

"A white sundress," he murmured, tracing the sweetheart neckline. His voice was full of bemused wonder and then concern. "How'd you get those scratches?"

"That awful dog. She went after one of my kittens too and I had to take her to the vet to have her leg stitched. Poor thing came out of the woods all full of burdocks and the vet shaved her naked."

"A naked cat's a shocking thing." He was enormously pleased with the image. "I want a photograph."

Suffused with an excess of energy, he grabbed her hand and led her through the house to the deck at a lope, explaining as they went, "The time got away from me. I worked later than I should have and I have another ten minutes' workout. Come on."

So much for his pose of indolence, if he'd let himself be carried away by his work. She wondered if he meant the poetry or some other sort of writing, or perhaps he'd been chopping wood or something.

There was a Tunturi rowing machine, like a big mutant chrome insect, on the deck.

"So that's what you do. I knew you did something."

He folded himself back onto it. "I'm addicted to it. Don't feel right unless I do it."

Pearl sat down to watch him. The fluidity with which he moved, the human part of an odd temporary cyborg made of his conjunction with the machine, had an immediate and disturbing effect on her, but she couldn't take her eyes away.

"Didn't notice it here before."

"Make myself put it away every day. I know what I'm doing. I don't care what anyone else thinks about it, I'm just hiding it from myself. I figure a good kink is worth preserving."

"It looks healthy to me."

"Really, Pearl. One of the world's most beautiful lakes is a hundred feet from my door. And my sister's body's in it. I thought it was a bit too obvious, myself."

Pearl sat back on the chaise and put her feet up. It was lovely to sit in the sun again and feel its warmth. She watched him now through half-closed eyes. His pace was slowing gradually. He wasn't moving so much as flowing from one position to the next. She found herself wishing she were a rowing machine.

He kept on talking.

"I rowed in college. Swam too. I do that in the winter at a club. Summer's the only time I don't swim." His eyes, fixed suddenly on the lake, were blank and unreadable. "It's only this place."

"Why do you come back here?"

He took his eyes from the lake long enough to meet her eyes and shrug. "Can't not come back. If I don't come back, then it's beaten me." Another easy, fluid stroke. "It's the only place I'm even half-alive. I come back here, I always feel as if I had forgotten it, and now all of a sudden I'm remembering and wondering how I could have forgotten, except I know I forget because I want or need to forget. This place is a secret and I have to come back to remember what the secret is. India's here and that's part of the secret, and I can't find her, she's beyond my reach, wherever she is. In my heart I know she'll come back if I'm faithful to the place, if I'm here, where I'm supposed to be. She'll show herself the way she used to when we were kids and we'd dive and swim a long distance and tease each other by staying under long enough to scare the other one. She'll be laughing but I won't be mad at her. I think she might not tell me where she's been, that'll still be a secret. But the place itself has some mystery in it, something I'll never be able to comprehend, even though I know it inside and out, where the roads go, and who owns what, and what grows where, but I don't really know it. All these years, and still I don't know it and I know I never will. Even the people, I know them by face and name and family history, I know things *about* them, but I don't know them and they know it. I think they know *me.* And I'm just part of the scenery to them, less than that really. Somebody who comes and goes and leaves no mark upon the place, like five feet of snow in the winter. You can't find it when it's gone, can you? I think I'm almost, but not quite, invisible to them. I don't know if I could stand being real to them. It's so goddamn strange. I keep this place in my heart, or it keeps my heart in it, whatever, and I creep back here and hide here and think to myself: The rest of the world doesn't know about it, it's another place. And then you, Pearl, you come out of the world outside and"—he snapped his fingers—"like that, you're part of this place, you got it in your heart, it's like you come from here. Of course, you did, in a way. Your mother took this place with her and slipped a map of it into your DNA, maybe, and whispered: You own all this, it owns you, you belong here, you'll never be happy anywhere else. Will you, Pearl?" He stopped moving, stopped talking.

She was nearly as damp with perspiration as he was, her stomach churning and tight. She felt as if she had been listening to someone recite impassioned poetry in another language, a language she didn't know. Something was happening to David and she didn't know what it was or what to do about it. She nodded yes to his last question and he bolted from the rower.

"Whew," he said, "I stink."

"I love a sweaty man." The storm of words seemed to have passed. She was melting with relief.

He smiled and pulled her to her feet. "Take a shower with me?"

She shook her head. "I'm clean."

"Then come watch me. Thank God the rain stopped. I was going to lay a keel here pretty quick and start rounding up breeding pairs."

He stopped in the kitchen and took a bottle of wine out of the refrigerator.

"I forgot I bought this for you."

He uncorked it and poured a glass, gave it to her, and headed for the bedroom.

She picked up the bottle, looked at it, and called after him, "Did you really pay forty-four dollars and ninety-eight cents for this?"

"No. I bought some of those little stickers and put one on to impress you."

She put the bottle back in the fridge and followed him to the bedroom. He was already in the bathroom. The shower erupted and he stuck his head out the door.

"Of course I paid it. Hasn't anyone ever bought you an expensive bottle of wine before?"

"Well, I admit to having tasted pricey stuff before, but I think the guy was buying it for himself, you know what I mean?"

"A fool. But if he hadn't been, you'd probably be changing diapers somewhere, or shaking the voters' hands and wishing you were dead."

He flung his running shorts on the bedroom floor, grabbed Pearl's hand, and pulled her into the bathroom. "Before I stop being sweaty, is there anything you want to do?"

She laughed and pulled his face down to hers and ran her tongue lightly around the edge of his lips and let him go.

"God damn, I love your mouth," he said, and ducked into the shower, not bothering to close the glass door.

Pearl perched on the counter. A fine mist of steamy water dewed her skin. She could almost feel her hair curling up with the moisture, pulling itself strand by strand out of the pins that were supposed to hold it in place. Reaching up, she pulled out her big old-fashioned hairpins, one by one, holding the freed ones between her lips as she did it. She was conscious he was watching her, his eyes fixed on her as he lathered soap in his hands. He took his eyes away long enough to cast an amused glance at his own tumescence, as if it were happening at its own behest, and then soaped himself deliberately. He let the shower rinse away the soap and then stepped out of the shower and put his wet hands directly into her hair. He twisted it around his fingers.

She picked up her glass and laid it next to his skin. He shivered at the touch of cold.

"David," she said, "what *are* you on?"

He bellowed a huge, delighted laugh and then sobered abruptly. "You. Me."

Water was running off him, dripping on her dress, puddling on the floor. He picked up a towel and began drying himself. "You went to college, love. Longer than I did. I bet you know all about it."

"No. What are you talking about?"

Dropping the towel on the floor, he pushed it around with one foot, mopping up the water. "Ruby'll be pissed as hell if I ruin the tiles."

He snatched the towel from the floor and flicked it into the hamper decisively.

In the bedroom he pulled on a pair of lightweight cotton trousers, not bothering with underwear. "Come on." He took her by the wrist. "I want to show you something."

"I've seen it," she said, and they laughed together, but he was already herding her out of the bedroom.

He stopped at the fridge and took a quart of milk and drank half of it, straight from the carton. "Low blood sugar," he murmured, putting the milk back with one hand while hooking out the bottle of wine with the other from the refrigerator. He picked up her glass to refill it. But he stopped suddenly, the bottle poised over the glass. A thoughtful look came over his face. He put the bottle down and, to Pearl's astonishment, carefully inserted the empty wineglass into the disposal in the kitchen sink.

"David!"

He clapped a thick rubber lid over the pie-cut rubber diaphragm and flicked the disposal switch on the wall. There was a heart-stopping shriek from the machine as it chewed the glass. Pearl stared at his hand holding down the lid, expecting to see slivers of glass erupting through the rubber lid to shred it, and the lid shook but held. The disposal stopped with a noise that suggested it found the glass ultimately indigestible.

"Remind me to get that disposal fixed," he said, taking down another glass and filling it for her.

Stunned, she opened her suddenly dry mouth to say "David" again, and he whirled around and kissed her urgently.

When he let her go, she was barely able to gasp for breath before he was hustling her into the living room, up the stairs to the open upper stories of the room. The faded and dusty found objects in their niches seemed suddenly ominous. Pearl was breathless when they arrived at the top of the stairs, three flights up, and faced a wall of books. David pushed the end of the bookcase and it slid silently to the left, revealed a room behind it.

She clapped her hands in delight. "A secret passage!"

David laughed with her. "Well, a secret room. Reuben built this bookcase wall for me."

"Reuben?"

"He thought it was amusing. Don't you?"

"Well, yes."

He took her hand and they stepped into the secret room.

It was a long narrow room, sparsely furnished with a button on a platform and a desk with a word processor buried under unstable dunes of papers. The walls and floor had been lacquered Chinese red and gleamed like stained glass in the light from a skylight and a single small porthole. Except for the lurid color of the walls, it would have been strikingly monastic. He didn't need to tell her this was where he wrote.

She was still trying to take it in when he put one bare foot between her feet and threw her skirt up at the same time. She cried out in surprise, trying to pull her skirt down with one hand while scrabbling with the other at his hands, which were pulling her underpants down.

"I always wanted to throw a woman's skirt over her face," he said as they unbalanced onto the futon. "Cotton panties," he howled.

"It's summer," Pearl said, losing the struggle for the panties.

"Let's pretend you're a Catholic virgin." He undid himself one-handed.

"Slow down," she said.

"No."

"Please, I'm not ready."

"Good. Let's pretend I'm raping you."

She gave him a good whack on the side of his head but he only laughed.

"Not funny. You're not raping me."

"No, but we all need our fantasies, don't we?" he murmured, and entered her abruptly.

She gasped and clawed at him but he only laughed happily.

"Come on, baby," he crooned, "I need this, you can't imagine how much I need this. I'm drowning, you have to save me."

This man is crazy, she thought, *seriously crazy. Broken as that glass in the disposal, shards and dust.* She held him tightly because she couldn't think what else to do. She believed what he said. He was drowning.

The struggle wiped away all but the most fragmentary thought as she was caught up in the response of her own body to his. Everything except the urgencies of the instant slipped away from her. In the first moment of release she felt a fierce joy, as if they had, mouth to mouth, somehow learned to breathe water. But then she forgot how, and the breathlessness nearly suffocated her before she gave up and let the water flood her lungs again. Surfeit yielded to fatigue, and fatigue to exhaustion, but David went on, spilling words that only occasionally made any sense to her. A deep sense of resignation welled up in her, the recognition that orgasm was delusion, she was not saving him from whatever fearful waters he was treading, nor even herself: they were both drowning, as he had written.

They both slept intermittently or were intermittently conscious. She lost any ability to feel a response, yet he seemed only briefly satisfied. She kept waking up in the middle, not remembering when they had begun or knowing when they ended.

She had one clear memory of his waking in the dark and saying quite clearly, "Oh, Christ, I've finally fucked myself blind," and laughing, even as he reached for her again.

Gradually she came awake to a lightening of the night sky and realized the night was nearly finished. And then she realized how like it was to the second night they had been together, only this time there had been a magnitude of increase in the intensity and fury. When she looked at him, he was sleeping so deeply he was barely breathing and she knew he had come to the limits of his strength at last, and (his word) drownded.

2

You knew better, she reproached herself wearily. This is what comes of going to bed with someone before you know him. A fine mess you've gotten yourself into. She crept home, feeling beaten, and still felt that way after a lengthy shower, aspirin, a brave attempt at eating some dry toast. A minor blessing was that Karen didn't show for a wake-up cup of coffee. It was going to be hard, Jean's first day.

When David came into the diner, he looked decidedly shaky, hiding his eyes behind his shades. He ordered a huge breakfast in a subdued voice, took one bite, and bolted for the rest room.

Pearl followed him. "Not my cooking, I hope."

He wiped his mouth and shook his head. "I'm sorry. I need to talk to you. Later?"

She nodded. "Go home. Go back to bed and get some sleep."

He leaned against the doorframe with his eyes closed. "I don't think I can." But all at once he threw back his head and shoulders, grabbed the lintel and swung on it easily, dropped to his feet, and strode out through the back way.

Karen stopped Pearl in the doorway to the storeroom to whisper, "What's wrong with David?"

"Bad night," Pearl said, and kept on going.

Bad nights were something Karen understood. "Too much blow," she murmured sympathetically.

"For Christ's sake," Pearl snapped, "Jean's about to cry. Again. See what's wrong, will you?"

Reuben called.

"Sam tied one on at a dance last night," he told her. "First time he's ever gotten drunk. Josh got him home in one piece. He's sick as a dog. I'm going to stay home with him tonight and watch a ballgame. Do you mind?"

"No, no. Things are crazy here, I'll need a quiet night."

Later on, Karen confided that they hadn't seen Walter because Jean had shown some iron and ordered him to stay away. "She's worried he'll settle in and spend the whole day taking up a space."

It saddened Pearl to think of the old man avoiding the place. He'd be lonely and she'd miss him. What could she do? No Roscoe, twenty more places to serve.

After work, she found David sitting on her back steps, his hands closed between his knees, waiting for her.

She slumped down next to him.

"I wanted to say I was sorry," he said without preamble.

She had a headache the size of Mount Washington. "I'm so goddamn tired, David."

"Me too." He held out one hand and it was shaking. "So now you know."

"I don't know *fuck*," she said, and was surprised at her own anger.

He wasn't. "I scared you, didn't I?"

She nodded.

"It's fun for me too," he said ironically. "I think of it as scar tissue." He reached for her arm and traced the healing scratches the dog had made on it. "Scar tissue's smooth, almost silky. It's both tougher and more sensitive than virgin skin. A plastic surgeon can debrade scar tissue or fill it full of silicone where it pits below the surface of the surrounding skin, but it's still there, however faint it may become. Do you understand what I'm saying?"

"A little, I guess."

He laughed. "Now for the hard part, as the politician said to the actress. Another wise man said, This is an age of miracles and wonders. There's a cure, a cure for poetry, Pearl. And I won't take it." He laughed incredulously. "Shit."

Her headache moved into Mount Saint Helens country and threatened to blow the top of her skull. She could imagine her brain cells snowing down over the Ridge.

"I don't know anything about poetry or whatever it is that's wrong with you, David, any more than I know anything about nuclear fission or astronomy. I'm not qualified to make any judgments. How often does this take you?"

He put his arm around her and drew her closer. "Not often enough, when it's going on. I really do like it when it's happening, you know. Ah, Pearl. 'Take me as I am,' as the assholes say." He added quickly, "I don't mean that."

She pushed him away and unlocked the door.

"I can't keep my own head above water. How'm I s'posed to keep yours above?"

Necessity looked up from her basket in the corner, leapt out of it, and skittered under the table.

David was delighted. "That cat's embarrassed."

Pearl smiled. "It's a viable position."

"*Don't* take me as I am," he said. "Never. Fight me all the way. I can make it if I've got someone who won't give up on me."

Pearl leaned against a cupboard. "Somehow I hadn't planned on becoming someone's therapy. And if I don't go to sleep soon, I'm going to pass out."

He hugged her impulsively. "God, yes, of course you're wiped out. I didn't mean I wanted you to become the equivalent of a course of primal screaming. I've spent my life looking for the right word and I hardly ever find it, do I? I would love, sometime, for you to stay with me all night. I wake up and you're gone, every time."

And then he went away, seeming in perfect health, the frailness he had briefly shown this morning vanished. He was some kind of vampire, she decided, and fell onto the daybed into an exhausted sleep.

3

Sam was still pallid but he made some popcorn and sat down in front of the tube with some of the anticipation with which he'd once watched ballgames with Reuben when he was younger.

Along about the bottom of the third inning, Reuben came to a decision. He pointed the remote at the tube and lowered the volume.

Sam, draped over the couch, turned to look at him.

"Sam," he said, "I've been seeing Pearl Dickenson."

Sam sat up straight. "I was up in the night a couple nights and I saw you weren't home. I figured you were tomcattin' and I thought it might be Pearl."

"Oh, you did?"

"You've been awfully pleased with yourself lately," Sam said, and they both laughed. "Lucky man. Really. You going to get married?"

"Just waiting on Pearl. She needs some time, she's new here, just started her business and all. She's been single awhile and has to get comfortable with the idea."

"Karen know?"

"No. I'm worried about how she's going to react."

"The hell with her."

"It isn't that easy, Sam."

"Yeah, well, she never wants anyone else to tell her what she oughta do, she's got no say what you do with your life."

"What she wants won't change my mind, but I'd like her to be happy about it."

"She hasn't got sense enough to be happy." Sam had a further thought. "Will this make any difference about the custody thing?"

"Doubt it. It won't hurt, but I doubt it'll help."

"Mom know?"

"No."

"Well, she'll be pissed off too."

"I've pissed her off before, I can handle it."

"I won't let on to Karen," Sam said. "She's so anxious not to be part of this family, she can hire a detective to find out what's going on."

"There's two more things, Sam."

"What?"

"One is Bri Spearin's going to be looking to get his own back, once his casts come off. He'll get you if he can't get me. Watch your back, you and Josh both."

Sam grinned. "Gotcha."

"The second thing is, I wanted to answer your question. I don't know what I did to make Laura so angry. Maybe all I did was marry the wrong person."

Sam nodded. "Josh told me I was an asshole about it. He said she was angry at herself for leaving us, so she has to think up a good excuse."

Reuben smiled. "Josh is a perceptive fellow."

"Yeah." Sam raked his hair with both hands and laughed. "I wisht he'd *preceived* how bad this hangover was going to be and thrown me in the back of the Maverick about a six-pack sooner."

"That was your job, not his."

"Yeah. Yeah. You want some more popcorn?"

Reuben turned the volume on the ballgame back up. The Sox weren't having a good evening, let alone a good summer. He couldn't feel very distressed about it, all of a sudden. He just felt a huge relief. Finally, he thought, I've made a right move with one of my kids.

4

Karen's gentle shake woke Pearl the next morning.

She stretched and yawned, realizing she had slept right from dusk to dawn.

"There's time for you to have something to eat. Go shower and I'll start coffee and make you some toast," Karen said.

A few minutes later, fully awake and feeling much more herself, she sat down at the table with Karen.

"I saw Bri," Karen told her.

"What for?"

Karen blushed and chewed a fingernail. "I guess I had to be sure it was over."

Pearl choked down a mouthful of dry toast and was once again thankful the girl wasn't her daughter. "Is it?"

Karen nodded. "He says he's going to get back at Dad."

"Wonderful. Better and better."

"If I tell my father, he'll know I went to see Bri."

"Reuben's a big boy, he can look out for himself. My money's on him."

After work Pearl called Norris.

"Daddy, I've been meaning to call, but it's been so crazy."

"I thought mebbe," Norris said. "You got your hands full, don't you?"

She admitted she did.

"Sounds like you could use your old pop to come and give you a hand."

Pearl laughed. Just listening to the soft slur of the South in his voice was comforting. "Oh, Dad, I'd love to have you come visit. But it wouldn't be very nice for me to invite you here and then put you to work."

"Oh, poop," Norris said, "I'm sitting here growing cobwebs. I can bus tables for you and sit on my butt when I'm tired. Ad in the paper says I can fly to Portland for less than a bus ticket, be there tomorrah evening."

"Let it be my treat. I'd just love you to be here for the Fourth. I've been wishing you'd come see me for a long time."

"I've been wishing too."

He promised to call with the flight information as soon as he had it.

The sense of relief was so strong, she wondered why she hadn't called him before, just to talk, never mind him rushing up to give her a hand. It would give her a breather, having him here. People be keeping to their own beds for a while. Maybe she'd be able to sort out what she should do if she had a few nights' sleep and Norris' cheerful company. It would be like putting a plant to soak its roots. She didn't have to discuss her love life with him, but maybe if she were lucky, some of his wisdom would rub off on her. She was so high with the anticipation of his arrival that when he called to say he hadn't been able to get a seat on the next evening's flight but did have one on Monday evening, she couldn't find it in her to be disappointed even a bit.

David called and she told him about Norris coming to see her.

He was quiet for a moment, let her bubble some about the old man.

"You must be relieved."

He didn't miss anything. Well, she hadn't really expected he would.

He sighed and asked her to have a drink with him at the Dog.

"Safety in numbers," he said, "but we'll have the time driving there and back to talk."

He seemed very much in control again, which was as much a relief as Norris' visit was going to be.

5

Roscoe was asleep in the hammock on his porch when she drove into his yard. Up close, she realized he wasn't sleeping but was passed out. Beer cans littered the porch floorboards under the hammock and were flung under the lilac bush like bad fruit. The odor of beer and piss competed with unwashed drunk. Mouth wide open, unshod feet in dirty socks with ragged, overgrown toenails protruding through large holes, Roscoe looked ten years older and twenty pounds heavier. She suppressed the desire to drag him into the house, fill a bathtub, and heave him into it, the way you'd wash a filthy mutt.

As Pearl closed the door of her truck, the black Labrador bitch loped around the corner of the house. Scavenged lamb and woods critters had been sufficient to support a growth spurt; she was twice the size she had been when Belinda Conroy had foisted her on Roscoe. Watching Pearl with her glittering malevolent black eyes, she snarled and began to trot toward her, picking up speed with every padded step.

Pearl responded in kind, diving back into her truck. She considered for a moment whether it was safe to leave Roscoe unattended with the retriever apparently hanging around the yard.

Pearl pounded the truck's horn. The bitch barked and bared her fangs but Roscoe did not respond.

Pearl wished for a baseball bat or a tire iron. She waited. It was hot, and after a while the retriever circled around herself and settled down to apparent sleep. Pearl waited a long time, then opened the truck's door very slowly and carefully. The dog remained asleep.

Never taking her eyes from the animal, Pearl minced across the yard to the porch. She put a foot on the bottom step and a hand on the rail. As her weight came down on the step, the wood creaked. She froze.

The bitch twitched in her sleep and then was still again.

Pearl crept up the stairs, finally reaching Roscoe. She spoke softly into one dirty ear.

"Roscoe."

He went on silently reeking.

She shook him gently.

He mumbled something that sounded like "Fuck off."

She shook him a little harder, to no avail.

The hell with it, she decided. If he wanted to get his ass chewed by a feral dog, let him.

She stood up and looked at the retriever. It was gone. While she had been concentrating on Roscoe, it had snuck away. Maybe it had gone off into the woods. Maybe it was around the corner of the barn again.

Looking left and right, she crept down the steps. No sign of the beast. She started across the yard to her truck. It was only a few long strides, taken as light-footedly as possible. In half a minute she had a hand curled around the truck door handle and the bitch came our from under the truck and got her by the ankle.

Pearl screamed and grabbed the dog around the throat. It snarled even as it bit into her. Frantic with pain, she choked it and there was an immediate loosening of its grip. She drew one hand back and punched the retriever between the eyes. The bright stupid eyes glazed satisfactorily and the teeth that felt like spikes in her ankle let go.

She kicked the semiconscious dog away with her good foot and flung herself into the truck, slamming the door behind her. Sobbing and gasping, she collapsed over the steering wheel and nearly passed out herself. She heard the dog scrambling and blinked tears away enough to see it staggering toward the woods. She wished she had a gun.

Evvie Bonneau's place was a neat small house of no distinction at all. It needed a coat of paint. There was a kennel, and Pearl was greeted with a din of barking and yelping. It was as good as a doorbell. Evvie came to the door, saw who her visitor was, and called out hello.

Pearl slid out of the truck and Evvie caught her.

"Jesus," Evvie said.

"Goddamn dog," Pearl said through clenched teeth.

"Bitch has got something against you," Evvie said, and helped her into the house.

When the blood was washed away, Evvie grunted over the wound. "You're lucky, bitch didn't chew much."

"I don't feel lucky."

Evvie laughed and fetched Pearl a beer.

"Little anesthesia," she said. "I'll drive you to the doctor's."

"I don't need a doctor, do I?"

"No, I guess not. Bone's not broke and I can't see anything deep enough for stitches. You said you were okay for tetanus. Doctor probably give you some painkillers, though. Sure you don't want a good knock of codeine or something with a punch to it?"

Pearl shook her head.

"Let me bandage it up for you." Evvie took out some gauze and tape and went to work on Pearl's ankle. "How's your love life, lady?"

Pearl choked on a mouthful of beer.

Evvie pounded her back.

"That bad, huh? Well, you don't have to tell me nothing. Hope you don't mind me being interested. I ain't got much to do with myself except mind other folks' business."

Pearl coughed and shook her head. "I wish somebody'd mind my business for me. I'm not doing a great job of it myself."

Evvie laughed. "If people knew what they was doing, most of the time they wouldn't get outta bed in the morning." She straightened up. "You want me to take you home?"

"No, I'll manage. Automatic drive, I can do it with one foot."

"Where'd this happen?"

"Roscoe's."

Evvie took her holster down from a big brass hook in the wall. "He okay?"

"Was when I left. Passed out. I couldn't get him to come to."

Evvie nodded. "Miserable old sot. I'll get him inside before I start tracking the dog."

The animal-control officer helped Pearl back into her truck. "You take care of yourself. I'm sorry about the trouble you've had with this dog."

"I was a fool to ever get out of the truck," Pearl said. "You're the one needs to take care of herself, out looking for that beast. Maybe you ought to have help."

Evvie laughed. "Don't worry about me. Go on home and take care of that ankle."

Pearl didn't have much choice, so she did.

FIFTEEN

1

Pearl limped wearily into the house and upstairs. A glance at the clock on her bedroom mantel reminded her of David. She had better clean herself up.

While she was in the shower, he let himself in, bounded up the back stairs, and strolled into her bedroom as she limped out of the bathroom wrapped in a towel.

"I knocked," he explained, "heard the water, figured you were in the shower, so I just strolled in. What happened to your ankle?"

She sat down on her bed and examined her wounds. "That dog of Roscoe's."

David sat on the bed like an Indian chief and cradled the ankle in his hands.

"Looks sore. Seen a doctor?"

"It is, and no, I don't need one."

"Want me to bandage it for you?"

She relaxed on her bed and let him. He wrapped it tighter than Evvie had and then one hand slid lightly up her calf to her knee.

"That beast hates you."

"Seems to, and don't you be starting something."

He laughed and took his hand away.

"You'd better stay in bed. If I don't get to the Dog tonight, I won't miss it."

She thought staying in bed might lead to the usual complications. Getting back on her feet was the first step to clearing up her life.

"Be damned if I let that dog keep me home. Probably this ankle will just stiffen up if I sit all evening." She gave him a quick kiss. "Let me get dressed."

2

Perhaps it was only because the Dog was a down-and-dirty little roadhouse of a bar that Pearl was immediately depressed and apprehensive on entering it. Perhaps it was emotional hangover from the dog's attack, but she could not escape the foreboding that retribution was imminent.

She was almost relieved to see Evvie Bonneau there, in the company of Sonny Lunt. Sharing their table was Lurch Mullins and his date, a woman Pearl knew by face and habit—always took her tea unsugared, without cream, and was partial to plain doughnuts—but not by name.

Karen Styles was at another table, with half a dozen kids her own age. One of the boys, a dark-haired boy with a winsome Irish face, was clearly courting her, holding her hand and whispering in her ear.

Belinda Conroy was also there, at a table with several people who looked from the cast of their features to be family. It was as if nearly everyone on the Ridge had adjourned to the Dog for the evening. Pearl felt uncomfortably as if she were looking at her jury of her peers.

Evvie Bonneau waved them to her table.

"Pearl," Sonny shouted. "You come dancing with your ankle all chewed up? You got the balls of a tiger."

"Hush," Evvie scolded him, and then Pearl, "You oughta be off that ankle."

Pearl sat down.

"Now I am."

David went to the bar to buy her a beer and himself a ginger ale.

"The bitch was gone," Evvie confided, "time I got there. I rousted Roscoe, though."

"He's been lying up, drinkin'," Sonny filled in the others. "Tell 'em what you told 'm, Evvie."

She shrugged. "Told him to get his head outta his ass. Nobody gives a shit if he wants to drink himself to death, he's got a constitutional right, but he's attractin' flies. He oughta take a bath or join AA."

"Meetin's Mondays, Wednesdays, and Fridays at the Congo Church and the resta the week at the Churcha Christ," Sonny said. "I went twicet last week, but I dunno."

"You're too far gone," Lurch advised him. "Me too."

Sonny contemplated the beer in front of him. "It's a hard row to hoe. I dunno if I can do it. Lifetime's a long time to go without a drink."

David, coming back, patted his shoulder.

"Haven't had a drink in years, Sonny, and I don't miss it."

Sonny looked at him in a jaundiced way. "You got money, looks, and your youth. What d' you need booze for?"

David laughed. "Nothing."

Pearl listened closely to hear that was being said over the noise of other conversations. It wasn't as noisy as it was going to get, but it wasn't quiet either. Someone tapped her shoulder and she looked up at Belinda Conroy.

"I understand you had to get your pussy shaved," Belinda said.

Lurch sprayed beer across the table. David pounded him between his shoulder blades.

"Next time I'll call ahead," Pearl said, "and you can watch."

Belinda simpered and twitched off, triumphant.

"Rabid bitch," Evvie muttered. "Like to put a hypo of animal trank up her—"

David explained to Evvie, Sonny, Lurch, and Lurch's date that Pearl's kitten had required shaving after becoming entangled with burdocks. They were loudly amused.

Pearl wished she had stayed home and let her ankle ache.

The waitresses were straight-out, so David went to buy another round. He was gone awhile, waiting his turn at the bar.

Evvie pulled her chair closer to Pearl's. Under the cover of the others' banter and joke-telling, she murmured, "You get around, woman."

Pearl was not offended. She liked this gritty, eccentric woman and felt a sympathy for her she did not entirely understand.

"Can't blame you," Evvie said. "I wouldn't throw him outta bed either. You ain't in over your head, so to speak, are you?"

Pearl just looked at her. Evvie nodded.

"Come see me again," the woman said. "Sometimes you talk somethin' out, it helps. I don't charge to listen."

"I might just do that."

David came back with a new round. His mood had changed. He was subdued and uneasy.

"Let's go," Pearl said.

She caught the fractional instant of relief in his eyes and then he was suddenly cheerful again. He shook hands all around, remarking it had been real.

"Sorry," he said out in the parking lot. "Your ankle's hurting you, isn't it?"

"Never mind."

"Shoulda stood in bed." He fingered a lock of her hair that had escaped its pin at the nape of her neck. "What's Belinda got against you, anyway?"

"I don't know, exactly. Bad chemistry, I guess. We just took one look at each other and it was instant hate."

He smiled. "She has some kind of negative charisma."

They were on the road before he spoke again. He glanced at her and she could see he was working up to something.

"What I told you about my mother and Reuben? I should make it clear she was the aggressor. He was this sweet innocent, I'm telling you. It wasn't exactly seduction. It was more like she molested him."

Pearl shook her head. "And how do you know that?"

He grinned at her, and she saw the shadow of the curious and difficult little boy he must have been. "A preternatural talent for being invisible when I wanted."

She laughed. "You've outgrown it, then. But why do you want me to know?"

Some darkness overcame him. "My point is, I've known Reuben Styles a long, long time, and in a way, I know him intimately. So when I tell you what I heard at the bar, you'll understand how angry it makes me."

Pearl's mouth went dry. Somebody'd told him, seen Reuben leave her place too late at night or too early in the morning, Roscoe had speculated out loud, or Evvie Bonneau hadn't kept her word about keeping mum. The farce was over. She braced herself.

Again he hesitated and then said, with a sigh, "There's no delicate way of putting it. The story making the rounds is that the real reason Reuben put Bri Spearin in the hospital was payback for Bri cutting into Reuben's territory. That Reuben's relationship with Karen is incestuous."

Her stomach contracted painfully. She closed her eyes and groaned.

"It's not true," David said, "it can't be. It's something Bri and his brother Ryan are putting around to get even. But Karen and Reuben and Sam'll be hurt by the lie, just the same. The damage'll be done."

She felt shrunken, far, far away. "You know, I think I hate the human race."

David pulled her close to him. He sighed again.

"I'm sorry. I know you have strong feelings for all of them."

She nodded.

The calm point and counterpoint of his heartbeat was audible and reassuring. He smelled good, like a newly bathed infant. What an enigma he was, with his rich boy's assurance, his line of chat, the physical strength and beauty, so like the shell of the nautilus. He hid himself inside all that, the living man, subject to tidal forces upon his very sanity, and did so by choice. All her anger and fear, generated by his extraordinary demands upon her body and emotions, melted away. His forearm under her breasts held her tight against him, as if he were bearing her ashore.

They didn't speak again until they were at her place. Seeing her to the door, he gave her a chaste peck on the cheek. But eye-to-eye she could not hide from him, nor he from her, and they fell into a more passionate embrace.

It was David who withdrew, with a quick laugh. "If we don't stop now, I'll be here when your stepfather arrives and he'll be scandalized. Besides, I want you to know I can stop."

"I'm not sure I can get behind a total reformation."

She kissed him again and let him go with a smile.

The house was dark and empty. Even Necessity, the naked kitten, was asleep. She limped to her desk, turned on the lamp, and sat down with her books. But she couldn't concentrate. Her ankle hurt miserably and nothing added up right.

3

She turned off the lights and crawled onto the day bed on the sun porch. Necessity hopped up to curl in her lap. Pearl dozed off, tense as she was.

A high-piped meow as Reuben lifted the kitten from her lap broke the thin veneer of her doze. He settled the kitten gently on the floor. Necessity meowed a complaint, yawned and stalked off, stretching her legs behind her.

"What happened to the cat? It's naked."

Pearl was not exactly awake. Her voice sounded to her as if she were whispering a secret, perhaps the time of the break-out, through a prison wall. Her head was thick with curdled dreams. "If I died and this is the resurrection, it's too late. My brains have moldered too much. My head aches, to say nothing of my ankle."

His interest in the cat evaporated. "Your ankle?"

She tried to laugh but it came out rusty. "Roscoe's bitch got me."

He was all concern. After unwrapping the bandage and shaking his head over the ankle, he brought her aspirin and water.

She squinted at the tablets in his palm. "I was hoping for Tylenol, with the cyanide booster."

He settled down next to her and hauled her, unresisting, onto his lap. "I know another cure," he said, slipping one hand under her tee shirt. "Some people say more than a handful's wasted. I'm glad my hands are big."

But he was slow, patient with her, waiting for her body to become fully conscious again.

Her body seemed to her to have grown heavier and more sodden, more resistant to wakefulness. The center of gravity was within her and the night seemed thick and heavy.

"What's wrong?" he finally asked directly.

She bit her lip. "Not in the mood, I guess."

"That ankle's bothering you, isn't it? I'm sorry. I guess I was just thinking of what I want. Maybe you ought to see a doctor tomorrow."

In the silence, the nightsounds—cricket, mosquito, swishings of leaf and grass of nocturnal hunters—were loud. She closed her eyes, fighting tears.

"There's something else, isn't there? Tell me now," he said.

"There's a story going around . . ." She stammered. Her insides felt as if she'd been eating stone soup. "It's awful."

He chucked back her chin, made her look him in the eye. "I'm a big boy. Tell me now."

She turned her face away and gagged on it. "You and Karen."

He sucked in his breath as if someone had grand-slammed on his kidneys with a lead pipe, a two-by-four, a Louisville Sluggger.

She burrowed against him, holding him tightly. Time passed like a freezing shock wave and she thought: *Somebody's going to get killed.*

At last he asked, in a distant, rather academic way, "I feel like that bitch has been chewing on me, considerably higher up. Where'd you hear this?"

"I had a beer with David at the Dog. Somebody said something to him, he told me later."

Reuben sighed. "David. How's he doing?"

She covered his hands with hers. "Not great. Up and down."

"You're kind to look out for him."

She demurred, feeling her face heat.

Then, casually, "What do you think?"

"I love you," she said with more misery than she had ever imagined such a confession could contain.

Throwing back his head with a remarkably sweet laugh, he tightened his hold on her and made her gasp.

"You know where it's coming from, don't you? Somebody's paying me back."

She nodded and he smoothed her hair. "I don't know what I'd do without you," he murmured.

But it wasn't that easy. The evening was cool and greenly fragrant, the new moon transparent in the sky. The quiet deepened as the road emptied of even the odd late traveler and the creepers and swoopers and night feeders fed or were fed upon and came to the end of their day. She and Reuben fell asleep together in an unexpectedly peaceful mood.

4

The following morning, Karen was sitting quietly in the kitchen when Pearl came downstairs from dressing. The girl had started coffee. Her skin had lost its translucence and she had shadows under her eyes as deep as bruises. She could not have had much sleep.

Pearl put her arms around Karen and the kid burst into tears, her whole body shaking with her distress.

At last, gasping, Karen wiped her eyes and said in a shaky voice, "Oh, Christ, I miss my mother."

Pearl winced and her own eyes filled. She turned hastily away. Just when you thought you were all healed up, somebody bumped your old wound and you found how much it still hurt.

Karen spoke dully. "Bri's going around telling people my father . . ." She broke down again, burying her head in Pearl's bosom. "I can't believe it," she sobbed. "I thought I was in love with that shithead. What if Sam hears it?"

"You stick together, you Styleses," Pearl reassured her, "you'll get through this."

"Sam and Dad'll never forgive me. If it wasn't for me, none of this would have happened."

"Our acts have consequences," Pearl said. "We can't foresee them all. But you can be sure of this: they love you. Maybe you better go see them right now."

"Dad'll be gone to work. I . . . I can't talk to him in front of Sam of Jonesy or who knows who might be there. It'll have to wait until tonight." Karen blew her nose vigorously and returned Pearl's hug.

"Go wash your face," Pearl advised.

Karen did and then hurried away. The Plymouth smoked and rattled, leaving a trail of blue pollution behind it.

Pearl shook her head and went to work. Her ankle troubled her all day, slowing her down, flaring up whenever she put the slightest pressure on it. She found herself counting off the hours until she could dose herself with aspirin again. She tried not to notice whenever one customer spoke to another in a low voice, not to jump whenever there was a faintly lewd laugh, not to cringe when some woman gasped at a whispered confidence from another. It can't have gotten around so quickly, she told herself. But her heart churned when over and over again she witnessed one of her locals look at another and then look away, shocked and embarrassed and distressed.

Sonny Lunt never did show, a relief in a way, but she worried a bit about whether he had drunk so much that he had gotten into trouble or was still laid out from it.

Jean McKenzie had her worst day yet. It was beginning to look as if she was going to be forever worse than useless, but Pearl kept the thought to herself and tried to be patient.

And David did not come in. Or call. A good thing, she thought.

Closing came as a huge relief. She turned a deeply discouraged Jean over to Walter. In the course of the day, Jean had wept her way through a couple of boxes of tissues, but when Walter asked how the day had gone, his daughter assured him shakily that it had been fine. Pearl patted Jean's hand. The older woman grinned painfully and clambered ungracefully into Walter's Jeep.

"There," he said. "You see, you can do it. I tol' you." And then, with exquisite tactlessness, "Hope she didn't bust no more dishes than the last time, Pearl!"

As she was dismounting her truck in the yard, she braced herself for a poem or something from David in the door. She found her door unlocked and the kitten gamboling on the porch, when she was quite sure she had snubbed the lock and left the beast inside. It made her wonder if she were finally losing her mind, either from weariness or from dissipation. But the shirt on the back stairs and the cut-off shorts on the landing informed her she had been invaded, and by whom.

David was on her bed, reading an old *Newsweek* magazine and only casually cultivating a handsome erection. "Hi. Christ, it's hot in this room. Why don't you buy an air conditioner? How's your ankle?"

She dropped his clothes on his head. "I don't have time for your bullshit today."

He made a show of picking up the bedside alarm clock and peering at the time display. "You do too. It's going to be a long week, Pearl."

She stood over him with her arms crossed, trying to maintain a straight face. So improbable, the male tumescence, it was not surprising it made her laugh. "*Newsweek* that good? Is it George Will's picture or Jane Bryant Quinn's?"

"Oh, no, it's all for you, love. Maybe a little bit for George. The bow tie."

She laughed. "What about stopping?"

"It's a sacrifice, but I have to think of you."

He caught her hands and tugged her down.

5

Pearl did not so much leave as flee Nodd's Ridge. The long ride alone was calming, an opportunity to think without interruption. She glanced in her rearview mirror and saw the mountains receding into blueness. Behind her was a monumental mess, a disorderliness in her private life of a degree which she had never before imagined herself capable.

She thought she was an accident in David's life, in the sense philosophers once used the word to mean a nonessential attribute. But it was clear from the way he spoke that he did not, that he was weaving her into his life the way a weaverbird works a bright-colored string into its nest. There was something primitive and frightening in the way he found numinous significance in what seemed to her to be incomprehensible details, and worse, that the nature of that found or assigned significance seemed so ominous. In his long, priapic ramblings he had spoken constantly of *it*. She was not sure what *it* was, or even the same thing all the time, except *it* was an obsession that had become central to his existence. It was a peculiar nexus, a knot of geography and emotion that was as much inside him as outside him. He was turning himself inside out to contain it, like one of those holes in the walls of his house where he kept his fetishes. Now he had entangled her in the knot of symbols he had woven. All her adult life, even during her marriage to Johnny, she had been her own woman. Yet there were times, like today, when David seemed the essence of sanity, as if she were a puzzle and he was her missing piece.

Pushing almost physically against the flow of rush-hour traffic exiting the city, she groped her way to the airport. Mere yards east, the continent plunged into the sea. People who lived on this peninsula faced the water as the people who lived in Nodd's Ridge faced the mountains, as if one or the other were a lodestone, a magnet for a particular kind of person, a water soul, a mountain soul. She didn't know what her lodestone was, an infinite quantity of water or an immeasurable quantity of rock, any more than she knew what part of her was white and what black. Black and white were meaningless. Most folks were various shades and tints of beige. There was no DNA code that made a person one or the other, the way there was for blood type. She supposed she meant culturally one or the other. It seemed to her to be something inborn that could not be nay-said or denied. There was a pointer inside her that couldn't find true north, at least when David was around.

The sight of the sign directing her to the airport was a relief. At least she could find that. The sign said PORTLAND INTERNATIONAL JETPORT. She giggled, thinking of old science-fiction stories from her adolescence—*Lucky Starr Blasts Off*, with a cover painting of Lucky's rocket flaming upward from among shiny domes and needle spires.

It was a shock to see Norris, but a familiar shock, among the passengers deplaning through Gate Two. He was always so much smaller and older than the image of him she carried around with her. When he put his arms around her, she felt like a little girl again.

A little while later, she wiped her eyes and laughed.

"Must be something in the air, or the stars have gone bad. Everybody I know has spent the day crying. I guess it's my turn."

Chuckling his deep old-man chuckle, he hugged her again. "All that crying musta made you thirsty. How about I buy you a drink. You tell me what happened to your ankle?"

Suddenly she was *so* dry, she did need a drink. They went off to the bar, where she let him buy her a Pepsi and she told him about the dog. When she finished she was in a cold sweat. She hadn't realized how frightened she'd been when it happened.

A half-hour later, his bags claimed and stowed in the truck, they drove sunward. The horizon was flame-stitched with celestial light. The sunfire blazing in Pearl's eyes while the world around was blurring into darkness ignited a pounding headache. Her ankle throbbed but she ignored it as she had all day.

They crested hills and came around curves and Norris kept saying, "Oh, my, my Lord. Isn't this something?" He stared into the dark walls of trees and shook his head. "More trees than people here. Never seen so many big trees." He looked at the sky's reflection in the ponds and lakes they passed and laughed. "Nice, nice. Don't it look like quicksilver. Glad I came already."

By the time they reached the Ridge it was too dark for him to make out much of it. She pointed out the diner as they passed it and he beamed. The house delighted him.

"You get off that ankle," he said. "Just tell me what to do."

So she played with the kitten while he made dinner under her direction.

When they pushed back their chairs, she said, "My compliments to the cook."

"I didn't do anything but what you told me."

She looked at him sitting across from her at her kitchen table.

"You know, Daddy, this is the first time this kitchen's felt like home."

Norris laughed. "Good. That's good." He looked her up and down appraisingly. "You look a little thin for you, like maybe you're working a little too hard, maybe forgetting to eat once in a while. But you look like you belong here. It would make your mother happy to know you'd made a home in this place."

Pearl reached across and squeezed his hand.

Norris took a cigar out of his pocket. "Okay if I sit on the steps and make a stink with this thing?"

"I'll take iced tea out and sit with you."

He settled onto the steps outside and nursed the cigar alight. A satisfied little grunt signaled success.

"So tell me. You got a boyfriend?"

Pearl choked on her tea.

Norris patted her back.

"I take it you do. I hope he's an improvement on that jumped-up corporation lawyer you had the good sense to show the door. Sometimes it's about impossible for a father to see what his daughter sees in any particular fellow, but you *always* had better taste than that. I figured he must have blindsided you, then you felt obligated. Hope he was less selfish in bed than he looked to be."

"Daddy, you're scandalizing me."

Norris snorted.

"It's true. Fellow's mean outta bed, selfish, tight, he'll be selfish *in* bed."

He rolled the cigar a little, admired it in the moonlight, stuck it back in his mouth, and talked around it. "I'm too old to beat around the bush, Pearl. Ain't got the time to waste. And you're thirty-five, going on thirty-six. Time you settled."

Pearl leaned back and propped herself on her elbows on the steps. Her ankle was stiff and swollen from the drive. She would rewrap it tightly before she went to bed.

"I'll wait as long as I have to wait. You know I won't be rushed."

With a slow shake of his head, Norris admitted that was true. He sighed. "I suppose, Pearl, I'd like to see your children before I die."

"Listen to you! You're going to live forever, Norris."

He chuckled softly. "Doubt it, honey, I sincerely doubt it."

It had been a long day for him. For her too. The jaunt to Portland had been a hundred-twenty-mile round trip. Too bad Lucky Starr's Commuter Jetservice out of the Portland Jetport wasn't yet operational.

"You tired?" she asked.

"Finish this poop-leaf. Expect we're up with the sun."

"You sleep in," she said. "You sit around all day if you want. There's the wagon here, you know where the diner is, drive down when you feel like it, want lunch or company or something."

"Kind of you, darlin'. I be up with the sun. Might's well go with you, see if I can't make myself useful. Maybe if I bust some plates, that Jean of yours'll feel like she ain't the world's *worst* fool."

6

Karen went straight home from work and made a phone call to Sam's friend Josh. He was cooperative. As she drove toward home, Josh passed her in the Maverick, with Sam in the shotgun seat, headed in the opposite direction. The boys waved and she not only waved back, she grinned.

Reuben came out of the door at the sound of her car. It suddenly seemed offensively noisy to her. She realized how it must sound to him and was ashamed of it. She ought to have done better, waited longer, saved more.

He came to her. "Hi, button."

She was seized by a sudden shyness as violent as a physical cramp.

He opened the Plymouth's door for her as if she were a lady.

"Daddy, I just wanted to tell you how sorry I am."

He picked her up by the waist and swung her around in a complete circle, exactly as he had done when she was very small.

"Come on in. I've got things to tell you."

His hand was on the doorknob when the baying suddenly erupted and they both turned to see the black retriever hurtling at them from the woods.

Karen was paralyzed.

Reuben stepped between her and the bitch just as the retriever launched herself with a blood-freezing snarl.

Feeling as if she were moving in slow motion, Karen dove aside. Going for Karen's throat, the bitch was unable to correct her trajectory.

Reuben took the retriever's weight in the solar plexus. Her hind-paw nails, seeking some kind of purchase, raked his torso and his arms, which he was raising instinctively to protect himself. Her forepaws missed his face and came down on his shoulders, tearing through his shirt. Teeth bared and slobber spraying, the triangular head was driven by the weight of the body behind it into the hard musculature of the big man's chest. The bitch flipped over and rode the steps back to the ground on its back, where it lay unconscious.

Reuben was driven off his balance and backward through the screen door.

There was a sudden startling near-silence in which all Karen heard was the heaving breath of the dazed bitch and the clunk of falling hardware torn from the doorframe.

Then Reuben rolled over and retched.

Karen staggered into the kitchen and fell on her knees next to him.

He wiped his mouth with the back of his hand and shook his head. "Has your mother been here?" he mumbled, and then he laughed raggedly.

A shadow fell over them both, and when they looked up, Laura was there, her car keys in her hand.

"What's that supposed to mean?"

Reuben laughed again.

Karen jumped up and looked out the door. The dog was gone.

"You're bleeding, Reuben," Laura said, as if he were doing something antisocial.

"It's gone, Dad."

Laura's displeasure was increasing at a geometric rate. She had never been able to tolerate being ignored.

"What's gone?"

Karen filled in the missing detail. "The goddamn dog that just almost ripped his throat out, okay?"

"Karen!" Laura exclaimed.

Reuben picked himself up. "Never mind. What do you want, Laura?"

"Karen. And Sam. Where's Sam? Do you even know?"

Karen turned on her heel and ran out.

As Reuben and Laura stood looking at each other, the Plymouth ground to life and gravel spurted angrily from beneath its wheels as Karen peeled out.

"Catch her, if you think you can," he said, "You can't catch her, she's the gingerbread man," and then amended the rhyme. "Woman. Doesn't scan. The hell with it."

He opened a cupboard to take out a mop and pail. He dropped the pail into the sink, squirted in detergent, and turned on the faucet.

"Where's Sam?" Laura shrieked at him. "You tell me right now!"

Reuben winced and closed his eyes. His stomach was hauling back for another spew. The bright scent of lemon exploded from the detergent foaming in the pail.

"Keep on screaming, Laura. Maybe he'll hear you over in Greenspark."

When he looked up, Laura had gotten some control of herself again. Her arms were crossed tightly over her nominal breasts and she was rigid with fury. "I got a phone call last night."

Reuben wrung out the mop and flopped it onto the floor in front of her. "Excuse me. Friend of yours?"

Her mouth twisted in an ugly way that made him feel strangely desolate. "You know what it was about."

"Price of broomsticks going up?" he ventured.

That did it. She pointed a shaking finger at him. "If it's true, if you ever laid a finger on Karen, I'll see you in jail for it."

"You forget to ask me about Sam? Or hasn't anybody called you yet to tell you they heard around I'd been molesting him too?"

Her eyes widened and she covered her mouth with her hand.

"This is turning into a habit," he said, "but get the fuck out, Laura. You don't live here anymore."

"You never used to talk like that. You never used to be a foul-mouthed man."

Reuben laughed rustily. "I never knew why men used the word 'fuck' the way they do until you left me, Laura, that's all."

She kicked a fallen chair regally out of the way and stalked out.

Reuben finished cleaning up the mess. He removed the broken door from its frame and broke down the pieces, one by one, into small fragments. Then he went to his bedroom, unlocked the gun rack on the wall, and took down his Winchester 410. He broke the shotgun open and loaded it with buckshot. A flick of his wrist snapped it closed. He tucked it under one arm, picked up the phone, and dialed it. As he listened to the phone ring, he saw himself in the mirror. His shirt was torn and bloodied, but the welts on his arms and shoulders were clotted now. There was a dull ache where the bitch's weight had hit him, a tenderness in the meat, and he thought tomorrow he would have a sunrise of bruise on his chest.

"Hi, Evvie," he said. "How'd you like to go bitch-hunting?"

7

Evvie Bonneau jumped out of her truck in Reuben's yard. "Jesus. You're a mess."

Reuben laughed. "That beast of Roscoe's was here. She went after my daughter. She's chewed on Pearl, and this is the second time she's had some of my skin. She's been in the woods awhile now, might have had herself a little rabid raccoon."

Evvie sighed. "Come on, then. Light'll be going soon."

But after they had beaten the bush for two and a half hours, nightfall forced them to give up. The dog had been easy enough to track but had been moving fast and had successfully stayed in front of them, teasing them with frequent volleys of barking and baying. They had gotten several miles away from Reuben's.

"Shit," said Evvie, lighting a cigarette. "You know where we are?"

Reuben stood quiet for a moment. They could both clearly hear a distant thump of music.

"About a mile from a beer," Reuben said.

The Dog was surprisingly full. It was hot and the doors were propped open. Someone had jacked the sound on the juke to thunderous levels, so it was impossible to make oneself heard. Nevertheless, Evvie and Reuben were greeted with glee by Sonny Lunt and Lurch Mullins and other regulars. David Christopher was helping Sonny and Lurch hold up the bar.

"What the hell," Sonny shouted. "The fuckin' Sandinistas landed or what?"

David laughed happily.

The proprietor's face gleamed wetly with nervous perspiration.

"Leave them guns outside," he roared. "You want me to lose my fuckin' license?"

"Oh, shut up, Fudgy," Evvie said. "Give us a couple beers before we die a thirst."

"Gimme them guns," Sonny volunteered, "I'll lock 'em up in my truck."

Reuben and Evvie gave up their weapons and Sonny staggered

out with them to general catcalls not to shoot himself in various parts of his anatomy.

"I feel left out," Lurch said. "If you guys gonna go out night-hunting, you don't wanna leave me and Sonny outta the fun."

"We've been bitch-hunting," Evvie explained.

Lurch looked around elaborately and then said, "Well, Belinda Conroy ain't here." He slapped the bar and roared.

"What are you doing hanging out with these reprobates?" Reuben asked David.

David raised his glass of ginger ale toward his boon companions. "Gaining perspective. You look like you've run into a little rough trade, Reuben."

Reuben smiled as the proprietor thrust a beer at him and David passed it along.

Sonny had come back to the bar.

"That goddamn runaway of Roscoe's attacked Reuben," Evvie told him.

Lurch dug his elbow into Sonny. "Don't ya see he's bloody."

"Don't faint now, David," Sonny teased. "David can't stand the sighta blood. Comes of being teetotal. Ginger ale takes the sack right outta ya."

David laughed and shoved a fresh beer at Sonny. "That's why I'm hanging out with you Real Men, Sonny."

Sonny grinned and admired Reuben's war wounds. "This the retriever Belinda or the one you failed to nail the other night?"

"Have a beer," Reuben said. "It might be the last one I'll ever buy you if that bitch's rabid."

"In that case," Sonny shouted, "Fudgy, gimme two, quick."

"Say, Reuben."

Reuben turned from the bar to discover Ryan Spearin, Bri's brother, right behind him.

David Christopher twisted around to look at Ryan.

"Say, Reuben," Ryan said slowly, "you get them scratches from Karen when she was coming? She do like to scratch, don't she?"

That's when the fight started.

8

Tom Clark gave Reuben a hard shove in the small of his back. Reuben wasn't resisting. He stumbled forward into the side of the sheriff's cruiser. It rocked a little. He hoped Tom Clark was satisfied by that.

"Hands on the roof," the deputy said. "Spread 'em."

Reuben did as he was told.

Jeff Deluca shoved David Christopher up next to him.

"You have a good time tonight, Reuben?" Tom Clark asked him as he stopped to run his hands up and down Reuben's legs.

"Are you?" Reuben asked.

David Christopher laughed. Jeff Deluca was frisking him.

"Hey, Reuben," David said, "at least I got a cute one feeling me up."

This got David a sudden, much harder shove into the side of the cruiser, but David didn't stop laughing.

"Both of you listen up, I'm only gonna say this once," Tom Clark barked. He recited the formula of their rights, then tried to snap a handcuff on Reuben. "Shit. This is gonna hurt you. They don't make 'em any bigger."

Reuben shrugged.

The deputy grabbed David's right hand and manacled the two men together. He opened the back door of the cruiser. "Get in, gents, this is your limo."

David suddenly swayed and jerked against the handcuffs. Reuben grabbed him and held him up as he spewed violently onto the parking lot.

"You gotta look out for that ginger ale, David," Reuben said, and David laughed.

Tom Clark stepped daintily backward.

Two more sheriff's patrol cars and a state-police cruiser swung into the parking lot of the bar. Two deputies who had arrived simultaneously with Clark and Deluca had most of the rest of the combatants facedown on the ground.

Jeff Deluca had picked up the radio microphone and was talking with the dispatcher.

"Where's the goddamn ambulance?" Clark demanded.

"The ambulance volunteers are on the ground, sir," Deluca said apologetically. "They're all under arrest too."

"Lovely," Clark grunted. "What about the paddy wagon?"

The county maintained a paddy wagon for just such barroom melees and the occasional outbreak of labor troubles among the millworkers. But it didn't move as fast as the cruisers and had to be deployed from Greenspark.

"Ten minutes, sir."

Tom Clark leaned in at the open window, "You gents sit tight. He has to puke again, Reuben, get his head out the window, okay?"

David found this very funny. He tucked his legs up to his chest and laughed until tears started in his eyes.

SIXTEEN

1

Karen reached for the phone on the second ring. Her head felt thick and curdled, her mouth muzzy.

" 'Lo."

"Karen."

A man swore loudly in the background.

She propped herself up and shook her head to clear it. "Daddy."

"You awake now?"

"Unhuh. Where are you?"

"Under arrest. There was a little disagreement at the Dog. The cops are sorting it out."

"Oh, God."

"I won't be home until morning. I want you to go home and tell Sam and stay the night there. I don't want him to worry or come here, either."

"I'm supposed to go tell Sam you're in jail?"

"He's going to find out about it anyway, might as well tell him right out."

Karen spoke slowly. "Daddy, how'd you get into another fight?"

"Stupidity."

There was silence between them.

"Mine or yours?" Karen asked weakly, but despite the attempt at a joke, her eyes were suddenly watering.

Reuben laughed. "Go home, Karen, please."

2

The warder led David back to the holding cell.

He was pale, bleeding from several cuts, one eye swollen shut and lip swelling too, but he was notably lively.

"I haven't had this much fun in years."

"Shut up," the warder said. "Mr. Styles."

Reuben stood up and followed the warder.

"You okay?" he asked David as he went out.

David slumped onto the bench Reuben had been occupying and laughed.

Reuben was led to a cubicle where Tom Clark was conducting interviews.

"Siddown," the deputy said, and pushed back his chair to take a long drag at a cigarette that already had half an inch of ash dripping from it. He changed the tape in the tape recorder at his right hand. Then he turned a page in a book in which he was making shorthand notes. "Name and address, please."

Reuben gave it.

"For the record," Tom Clark said, "Mr. Styles and the interviewer are well-acquainted. Now, of those arrested tonight, four were sober, as attested by blood alcohol analysis. One of the four was injured and is at the hospital. I am interviewing the three who are sober and have only minor injuries. Photographs have been taken by the warder of all injuries, and histories will be taken of how they were received. Evangeline Bonneau has already told me how you happened to go to the Dog, but I'd like you to start there and tell me in your own words."

"I was on the back porch of my home," Reuben said, "with my daughter, Karen."

"Identify your daughter for the record, please. Full name, age, residence."

Reuben did.

"Your daughter, Karen, is sixteen years of age and she does not reside with either parent? Is that correct?"

Reuben nodded.

"Her mother and you are divorced? And you are the custodial parent?"

"Yes, sir."

"So you have effectively emancipated Karen and abrogated that part of the custody agreement?"

"Yes, sir. Lawyer's doing it now. Karen's also dropped out of school."

"She's working as a waitress? Do you give her any financial support?"

"She won't take any from me."

"How would you describe your relationship with Karen?"

"Until recently, we were estranged."

"Why?"

"She is angry at both of us over the divorce. I believe she has been punishing us by misbehaving."

"Let's go back to the dog's attack."

"We were just going to the house when the retriever came out of the woods and went for my daughter."

"You know this dog?"

"She's a black Labrador bitch, about eight months old. She's been running loose, killing sheep, for a couple of weeks. She's attacked other people."

"Do you know who owns her?"

"I don't think she's licensed to anyone. I know she was bred by Belinda Conroy. Mrs. Conroy gave the dog to her uncle, Roscoe Needham, who didn't want it. The dog's been uncontrollable from the beginning."

"Go on with your account of the dog's attack."

"Well, she went for my daughter, got me instead. She hit me hard enough to knock me off balance, scratched me up some."

"Which injuries of yours does the dog account for?"

"Scratches on my arms and shoulders, bruises on my chest."

"Go on."

"Then she took off again. I called our dog officer, Evvie Bonneau, and the two of us set off to catch or kill the dog."

"Did you?"

"No. It got dark and we stopped. We were close to the roadhouse, so we went in to have a beer."

"The proprietor, Mr. Perry, has already indicated you and Mrs. Bonneau were armed when you entered the bar and he requested that you take your firearms back out at once."

"That is correct. Mrs. Bonneau's weapons were ones she is authorized to carry as the town animal officer. I have a license for the shotgun. Sonny Lunt locked them up in his truck."

"For the record, Sonny Lunt is Sanford Harold Lunt the Third, whose testimony will be taken later, as he is still inebriated. Now, was Mr. Lunt inebriated when you handed over your weapons to him?"

"Yes, he was."

"But you trusted him to lock them up for you?"

"Yes."

"Tell me about what happened in the bar, what started the fight, Mr. Styles."

"I was at the bar, drinking a beer, in the company of several people I know well."

"Names, please."

"David Christopher. Sonny Lunt. Lurch Mullins, that's Melvin Mullins, Evangeline Bonneau."

"What condition were all these people in?"

"Sonny and Lurch were well-oiled. Evvie and David and I were sober. David doesn't drink, Evvie and I had just arrived."

"Then what happened?"

"Ryan Spearin came up and made an offensive remark to me."

Tom Clark looked up from his note-taking.

"Would you tell me exactly what you remember him saying?"

Reuben shrugged.

"He said, 'Hey, Reuben, you get those scratches from Karen when she was coming? She does like to scratch, doesn't she?' "

"The Karen whom Ryan Spearin referred to is your daughter?"

"Yes."

"It's the inference of this interviewer that Spearin was accusing you of committing incest with your daughter. Is that how you took it?"

"Yes."

"And then what happened?"

"I picked him up and threw him across the room."

"And?"

"And a general fight broke out. Spearin's friends and mine."

"A riot ensued?"

"Yes, sir."

"Let's go back a bit. Why did Spearin make this public accusation?"

"To start a fight. Grudge match because I beat up his brother."

"A week ago you were involved in another altercation with Ryan

Spearin's brother Brian. My report on that incident is appended to this interview."

"Yes, I was."

"What was that about?"

"Brian Spearin beat up my daughter, Karen."

"Can you give me the date, time, and place when that occurred?"

Reuben did.

"So you beat him up?" Tom Clark asked.

"Yes, sir, I did."

"Did your daughter see a doctor after Brian Spearin allegedly beat her?"

"Yes." Reuben gave the doctor's name, and then, after a slight hesitation, said, "There was more to it than a beating. It'll be in the doctor's records. Spearin forced Karen to swallow some coke. It was his coke. He'd left it at Karen's place and it had been sun-damaged."

Tom Clark frowned. "You didn't tell me this last week."

Reuben sighed. "I didn't want Karen involved in a drug investigation."

"Karen been doing drugs?"

"I imagine so. Spearin's a drug user; I assume she did drugs with him."

"What's her relationship to Brian Spearin?"

"He was her lover."

"How long were they sexually involved?"

"For a little over two years."

"You're saying Brian Spearin began having sex with your daughter when she was below the age of consent?"

"Yes, sir."

"For the record, Brian Spearin is twenty-four years of age.

"What about Ryan Spearin, Brian's brother? Has your daughter had a sexual relationship with him?"

"I don't know."

Tom Clark looked up from his notes. "I'm sorry about this, Reuben. I have to ask you these questions."

Reuben nodded.

"Have you in fact had sexual relations with your daughter, Karen?"

"No."

Tom Clark nodded.

"You got anything else you want to say?"

"No."

The deputy turned off the tape recorder. "Lawyer'll be here shortly to bail you and Evvie and young Christopher out. Their stories match yours. You'll all be arraigned by the grand jury when it sits next week, for felonious assault and rioting and telling jokes about the pope, I imagine. The prosecutor'll throw the book at the lot of you, Spearin's gang too. I don't know whether you're looking at jail time, but I do know you're in a world of hurt, Reuben. No way to keep it outta the papers. And Karen's gonna have to come talk to the grand jury about the cocaine and the beating and the statutory rape."

Reuben nodded.

"Go on," Tom Clark said. "I'm dead on my feet. You boys have had your fun. Spearin's got three busted ribs and a concussion. Go back and sit in the holding tank now and enjoy the smell of the drunks."

David was stretched full-length on the bench with his hands folded on his chest, as if he were laid out in a funeral parlor, except his feet rested in Reuben's lap. He was asleep.

Reuben pushed David's feet off his lap. "Wake up, the lawyer's here."

David opened one eye. "I was just starting to like it here."

Reuben laughed.

3

Karen was late.

Pearl introduced her to Norris as the girl tossed her handbag in the closet and snatched up her apron.

"Pleased to meet you, Mr. Dickenson," Karen said. "Pearl, Dad's in jail."

"What?"

"He and David and Sonny and Lurch and Evvie broke up the Dog last night, fighting Bri's brother Ryan and Bri's buddies."

Pearl winced. "How did that happen?"

"Long story. I'll tell you when we get a break."

Norris watched Karen scurry away to start taking orders.

"This is going to be an interesting week," he said softly.

David came in shortly thereafter, at the same time Walter McKenzie did.

Jean shot her father a nervous glance, then looked anxiously at Pearl, who smiled reassuringly.

"Pearl," Walter cried delightedly, "look at this boy. Has he bin ta the wars, or what?"

David's dark glasses hid some of the damage, but it was still extensive. He took the shades off and displayed the full glory of a black eye. Other bruises and cuts distorted his face. His lower lip was notably thickened and split. There was an ironic gleam in his eye, but an attempt at a smile turned into a wince.

It made Pearl feel queasy to look at the damage. She took a deep breath and worked up a weak smile. She got busy. She didn't want Norris noticing anything. She introduced Walter and David to Norris.

Norris announced he was going to wait on them so he wouldn't miss any of the story.

David and Walter both laughed.

Karen bustled.

David glanced at her and then put his shades back on.

"It was just a brawl. Somebody said something to somebody else and all hell broke loose."

Walter was disappointed. "Here I thought there was hope for you, boy. I said to myself: There, that's not too bad for a teetotal—he got himself into a good fight. Then you tell me the story, and goddammit, it's a teetotal's story of a barroom brawl. Flat ginger ale, boy, is all that story is."

David was properly apologetic. "Sorry, Walter."

Norris winked at David. "Some girl behind it, I imagine, Walter. Probably this young fella's protectin' some lady's honor."

That perked Walter up. "That so, David?"

Karen blushed furiously and bustled a little more intensely.

David smiled over his coffee at Pearl. "That sounds right."

He left the leather case for his glasses next to his plate when he left. Pearl picked it up and went after him. His car was out of the line of sight from the diner. He was leaning against it, waiting for her.

"You forgot this," she said.

"No, I didn't."

She laughed. "I didn't really think so. Are you all right?"

He nodded.

"What the hell happened?"

"It'll take some telling. I'll call you later."

Walter settled into a corner booth and opened a one-stop gossip shop to all and sundry. People stopped to chat with him, the old and retired lingering over coffee or tea grown cold. The previous night's goings-on at the Hair of the Dog were the major topic.

"Karen," Walter exclaimed, "I must be gettin' soft. You're the cause a all that ruckus, a course."

"I was not. It was just a bunch of drunks."

Walter ignored her. "Shoulda married you off couple years ago. Couple, three yowens and a big belly and there wouldn't be no fightin' over ya in bars."

Karen burst into tears and ran to the rest room.

Pearl watched her go with an unexpected sense of resentment. Reuben was in trouble, Sam was likely to have to leave home, and David, who wasn't even a family member, had been injured, all because of Karen. Maybe it was a good thing if she felt a little guilt, if Pearl didn't rush to the rest room after her to tell her not to feel bad because it wasn't her fault. It wasn't *all* her fault, but some of it was. And if it stopped here, she would be very lucky. Things had gotten nasty, and Pearl had a foreboding they would get a lot worse.

Eventually Karen came back, noticeably subdued, blowing her nose and sniffing.

Pearl sighed and patted Karen's bottom as she passed, and the kid looked over her shoulder and put together a weak grin.

The day went on. Pearl's ankle bothered her but she ignored it.

Whenever she prodded Norris to take a break, he went over and sat down with Walter.

After the first couple hours, Jean stopped craning anxiously at Walter and gradually relaxed about him being there.

"I hope he ain't being a nuisance," she whispered to Pearl while wringing a damp tissue to death and staring at the floor.

"Not a bit of it."

Jean heaved a huge sigh of relief.

Pearl intercepted a look of anger and distaste from Karen, directed at Walter.

Karen colored and turned away to open the dishwasher.

"Old people. I hope I die young."

Pearl wiped her hands on her apron and spun the girl around by the shoulders. "I like old people. They know more stories."

Karen bit her lip.

Pearl let go of her. "I hope if you do live to be old, the world's not full of young people who feel the way you do now."

The girl swallowed hard.

"Excuse me." She plunged past Pearl toward the rest room again.

Jean was in difficulties again, weeping over some confusion. Norris patiently began sorting her out.

My whole female crew is weeping, Pearl thought. *And I would like to cry too.*

Reuben called to say tersely he had to see her and could he stop by the house after work?

"Good a time as any," Pearl assured him. "Are you all right?"

"Better than that, considering the shit I'm in."

4

They were in the kitchen, chopping vegetables together, when Reuben drove in.

" 'Nother one of your warrior friends," Norris said.

"Karen's father." Pearl dried her hands on her apron. She wondered how long it would take Norris to pick up on Reuben and her. "Come in, Reuben."

Though scratched up and with a few lumps and bruises, he was nowhere near as spectacular as David.

She made introductions and added, "My trade was off his morning, with so many of my regulars at the county jail."

Reuben threw back his head and laughed. "My fault."

"That's why I brought it up to you."

"You folks do this sort of thing often?" Norris asked.

"Just lately," Reuben admitted, "too often."

Pearl handed him a glass of iced tea. "Karen said that foolish dog marked you up again too."

Reuben touched his chest gingerly. "Had a rabies test at the hospital last night. Find out about it next week. If it's positive, everybody the cops arrested at the Dog will have to be tested in case I bit 'em, bled on 'em, or spit on 'em. I figure Spearin was rabid before he came in and could have infected me too. Evvie's got to get the dog now. Wardens'll help her hunt it."

"Oh, my." Pearl pulled out a kitchen chair. "Sit down."

"You say 'Oh, my,' " Reuben said, "it makes me think of Dorothy in *The Wizard of Oz.*"

Pearl laughed and then realized Norris was looking from one to the other of them. So it had taken him maybe thirty seconds.

"The worst part of these punch-ups I've been having is how much time I've spent lately with the lawyers. The state's going to revoke my custody of Sam and hand him back to his mother. You know he doesn't want to go. So sometime in the next couple of weeks, Josh is going to drive Sam to my sister Ilene's in Oregon." Reuben stared at the tabletop, reached out to finger the asparagus fern in the vase of wildflowers there. "I always thought the way people stole their kids from each other was shameful. I've done a number of things lately I never thought I'd do. The kid doesn't want to live with Laura, he hates the Reverend Dick, and the man hates Sam. How could that be good for Sam?" He looked up at Norris. "Pardon me, Mr. Dickenson, for spewing my private trouble on you when we've just met."

Norris shook his head. "Never you mind. I know you come to talk to Pearl. I'll make myself scarce, if you like."

He started to push back his chair from the table.

Reuben rose. "No need. Stay. You look natural there."

Norris laughed and settled back down.

"I've got to go home, having supper with my kids while I got'm."

Pearl stood too. "I'll see you out."

The two men shook hands again, with an exchange of pleased-to-meet-yous.

On the porch, Reuben's hand stole around Pearl's and he put an arm around her waist.

"You okay?" she asked him.

"I'd like to see you tonight. Suppose your dad's like most old folks and never goes to bed."

She laughed.

They drew a little closer and he winced as she came in contact with his chest. She made a little concerned sound and then touched his clavicle with the tip of her tongue.

"Oh, my," he said.

Norris was grating carrots onto the salad when she came back in. "Don't be shy around me," he said. "You wanta kiss the man, kiss him."

"He's the one that's shy." Pearl picked up a celery stick, looked at it, and thought better of it. She put it down to pick up her glass of iced tea.

"Oh," said Norris. "That explains everything. Excep' what about the other fellow?"

Pearl choked on a mouthful of iced tea.

Norris patted her back. "You okay?"

She got out a yes between coughs. She collapsed into a kitchen chair and Norris pounded her back.

She looked up into his eyes and complained, "You see too much."

"That's the least of your problems." Norris sat down across the table. "You must be under quite a strain. This is an awful small town to be stepping out with two fellows at the same time. Did you ask me up here so as to get a rest?"

Pearl burst out laughing. "No, not really. I've wanted you to come visit since I got here. Honesty compels, though. I don't mind any beneficial side effects."

"Well, it's none of my business."

Pearl folded her hands in her lap and thought carefully before she spoke. "Maybe we'll talk about it sometime. But right now, I need to sort things out in my mind."

Norris slapped the tabletop. "Good enough. Let's eat. I'm hungry. Been workin' all day. I'm not used to that. Been in the leisure class too long."

5

The next day, Walter did not come to the diner until lunchtime. "I'm sitting outside," he announced. "Gettin' out from under your feet, Pearl."

Pearl glanced at Jean, whose cheeks were suspiciously pinking. "I don't mind you stopping awhile."

Walter waved his fedora around. "It's so goddamn hot, be cooler out there."

He was not to be dissuaded, but went out and parked himself on the bench of one of the picnic tables.

"Take your lunch break with your dad," Pearl urged Jean.

She and Pearl brought two chicken baskets out to the table Walter had chosen.

The old man squinted up at her. "Pearl, you're looking well."

Pearl laughed. "Hard work and a good night's sleep."

"I used to be full of piss and vinegar," he complained. "Now I ain't got no poop at all." He gestured toward the diner, where Karen could be seen waiting table. "Look at that Karen, she's up half the night dancing and running around with some fella or other and making trouble for everyone, and she works all day and looks as fresh as a peach off'n the tree."

"She could use my help. Talk to you later." Pearl hurried back in.

"Karen's been distracted," Jean said to Walter. "I notice her making mistakes she never made before. I think she must be upset about all the fighting."

"Never mind the goddamn gossiping, Jean."

"Well," Jean sniffed.

Walter worried a chicken leg for a few minutes and then put it down.

"Having trouble with your teeth, Dad?"

"I must be turned around again." His eyes were cloudy.

"How's that, Dad?"

He turned to her. "Why do women do that?"

"Do what, Dad?"

"Get that glow."

Jean gave way to exasperation. "Dad, what are you talking about?"

"Shoulda married Karen off two years ago," he mumbled.

"In the old days, maybe, but you can't do that anymore, Dad." He was just confused again, she thought. He was getting awfully old. But it was a very pleasant day and the chicken was just delicious. "Isn't this chicken just delish?"

He wasn't paying any attention.

After lunch, he left her and drove straight to the service station.

Reuben came out of the garage bay to greet him.

"Reuben," Walter said without preamble, "you better get Karen married off quick."

Reuben laughed and patted his arm. "Easier said than done, Walter."

Walter shook his head and wrung his fedora. His nose was running but he didn't seem to notice. "Be the best thing."

"I don't know about that. Spearin's not my idea of son-in-law material."

" 'Course not. Find somebody else."

"I'll get right to work on it," Reuben said.

"Good." Walter started to shuffle away, and a further thought arrested him. "You best get married too."

Reuben laughed again. "I expect I should."

"Pearl'll make a good wife, you'll see," Walter told him. "Be a fine mother for your children."

Reuben looked at the old man in surprise.

Walter pointed a shaky finger at him. "You ain't no goddamn pepper-pants teenager no more. Children need a mother *and* a father."

"I know." Reuben flung an affectionate arm around Walter's shoulders. "I know."

Walter punched feebly at his fedora. "Don't mean to pry, but things are going to hell in a handbasket. I gotta say something."

"Walter, you old cuss, pry all you want."

Walter peered at him for a long moment, wiped his runny nose with the back of his liver-spotted hand, and then shook his head with satisfaction. "Good." He waddled away.

Sam came out of the garage bay. "What'd Walter want?"

"Pass the time of day."

Reuben rolled himself underneath the elderly and mistreated LeBaron that belonged to the man who owned the Dog. Part of the fallout of the last fight at the bar was that the deputy had discovered Fudgy Perry had sold liquor to Ryan Spearin, who wouldn't be twenty-one until the following month. Never mind Ryan looked twenty-five, had two hundred muscular pounds attached to his six feet of height, and had to shave twice a day, or that he possessed an altered driver's license. While Fudgy's business had picked up dramatically and he was selling a great deal of beer to people who wanted to hear all about the bust-up, he was still sweaty over the deputy's angry remonstrance. Tom Clark knew his man, knew a warning would be more effective than a prosecution. Fudgy was relieved but unnerved and querulous. Reuben had offered an overhaul on Fudgy's swaybacked old LeBaron. Fudgy, who couldn't turn down anything free, not even the most diseased bar bag, took him up on it.

But Reuben's mind kept turning back to it. Walter'd been so wound up. Wasn't anything to be done about Karen. Everything he'd tried to do had backfired. She'd find a husband eventually, with or without his assistance. Not that getting a husband was the same as keeping one.

Funny how Walter had known or guessed about Pearl and him. Maybe they hadn't been as discreet as he'd thought. Probably it just showed. He wasn't any kind of actor, probably gave himself away all the time. Never had a good reason not to do so. If Pearl was showing it too, then it was a hell of a good sign, as far as he was concerned.

Old man had failed a lot in the fast few years. He'd leave a hole when he left, old Walter would, and that was as much as you could say about most of the folks for whom Reuben had dug holes in the graveyard next to Pearl's house. Of course, you could never consign these old birds to eternity until they were cold. They had a way of hanging on for years while people shook their heads over how this or that old fart had failed of late.

He looked forward to getting the old man tiddly at at least one wedding, come fall. Walter was indiscreet when he was sober; with a few beers in him, he broke out in bawdy songs and tried to dance. It made a person realize how much there was to be had out of life at any age.

The bell chinged outside and Sam's big feet in their high-tops shambled out to meet a decrepit old Pacer. Reuben recognized it and the owner's ankles and the tip of her cane too. First-class ankles, but a bum knee made Olivia Russell's cane a necessity. He slid out from under the LeBaron and went out to say hello.

Liv had put on some weight, maybe as much as twenty pounds. She was wearing a shabby man's shirt over grubby clam diggers and her hair was falling down from a clumsily pinned chignon. Her eyes were hidden by mirrored sunglasses. The obliteration of her eyes made her high cheekbones stand out; you could see there was an Indian in her woodpile. A few years ago, she had taken a beating that had damaged a nerve in her face, so her smile was crooked. He had come to like the vulnerable crookedness. It relieved the fierce, almost stony stillness of her expression. She had beautiful teeth, all store-bought, but she rarely smiled.

They shook hands cordially.

She tapped her cane against one of the Pacer's tires. "Old stinker's still running. I'd like to leave it and have you overhaul it."

"Be a pleasure. There's so much under that hood, it's like doing a jigsaw puzzle. But I won't be able to get to it until after the Fourth."

"Fine." They made arrangements for her to drop off the Pacer after the Fourth and pick up a loaner.

"How's Walter?" she asked.

"About the same."

"Good. I had a note from him saying he was retiring. I'll be needing a new caretaker, come fall. Can you take another client?"

"I'll put the rate card in the mail, you can let me know if it's okay."

She nodded. "Needham's has changed hands, I see. I stopped for breakfast this morning and saw Karen was still there. And Jean McKenzie was there, that was a surprise. The food's much improved. I was there awhile, reading my newspaper, heard you'd been disturbing the peace."

"Something like that."

Olivia Russell burst out laughing.

He laughed too.

She shook her car keys out. "It's good to be back," she said softly.

She tucked herself into the car and he closed the door for her and leaned in at the window.

"How are you, Liv?"

"You asked me already."

"You didn't answer then either. How are you?"

She turned the silvered mirrors over her eyes away from him, to stare straight ahead. "Glad to be back. Isn't that good enough?"

"Liv, if I can do anything, if you need anything, you let me know."

"Thank you, Reuben." She wasn't cold, just sad, somber.

Watching her drive away, he remembered cutting the snowsuit off her leg, in the aftermath of the gang rape and the fires that had taken her old summer place and old Miss Alden's house. It had been like gutting a fish, slicing through the tough slick nylon. A mess inside. Ironic that the fabric of her snowsuit was made of the same stuff as artificial joints. Liv had had her choice of a nylon knee right away or a nylon knee and a nylon hip in twenty years. She had a zipper scar and never wore shorts or skirts anymore, just clam diggers and slacks or jeans. The scar on her leg and her mouthful of expensive, almost jewellike false teeth, the way her mouth was forever twisted, were the visible scars of being raped and nearly murdered. The worst damage was inside, hidden away like the grit in an oyster that becomes the heart of the pearl. He could see Liv was still building her pearl, still accreting the layers of scar tissue. He shook his head. There was a deal of trouble in the world.

SEVENTEEN

1

Pearl took Norris to North Conway for dinner and a movie. Driving by Reuben's on their return, she noticed lights on in the garage bay.

As soon as they were home, Norris yawned hugely and announced he was dog-tired and ready for bed.

"I'm so tired, I'll be asleep before I get my shoes off."

"I worked you too hard today."

He laughed. "Naw. I don't do enough most days to warrant a decent night's rest. Probably be the soundest sleep I've had in a month a Sundays." He examined a cigar thoughtfully and put it away. "Guess I won't. It's so hot, honey, I think if I were you, I'd take a walk or go for a ride or something, wait for it to cool down before I went to bed. You forget," Norris went on breezily, "I come up from the Keys. This isn't real heat to me. I'm cool. It's all relative."

Flabbergasted at having her stepfather urging her out the door late at night "to cool off," she didn't know what to say. What most bemused her was, Norris had never given her bad advice. She kissed Norris' cheek and watched him stump his way upstairs, picked up her keys, and left the house.

When she turned the doorknob, she found the garage office door was open. She let herself in and walked through the office to the service bay.

"Braking like that's bad for your tires, and your brakes don't like it either, Pearl," Reuben said from underneath a nasty old Chrysler LeBaron. "You in a hurry?"

"How'd you know it was me?"

"Sound of your engine. Confirmed sighting of the Pearlbird when you walked in. Ankle's still bothering you, isn't it? Nothing I like better than white high-heeled sandals with ankle straps, and one taped up like a sock with gauze, unless it's the tolerances of Mercedes-Benz engines. The Germans fit 'em together like jets."

She laughed. "You coming out from under there?"

"If I can look under your skirt. Be right there."

He trundled out from under the LeBaron.

"I can't believe you've got a secret letch for German machinery. Took you for a Detroit or Die man."

"Winter after I got divorced, I took a course. Had a job offer to take over the maintenance-and-repairs department at the Mercedes dealership in Augusta. Decided I couldn't live in town. Not enough of 'em around here to live off. Mercedes won't certify you unless you work for them, want to service their own vehicles. Only see one now when someone has an emergency or lets me play with one. But yes, I like German machines. You would too if you had to work on what Detroit's been turning out for twenty years. Suppose I should be grateful. Keeps me working."

"I like the way garages smell," Pearl said. "You get high from the fumes?"

He laughed. "Let me wash up."

"Don't you dare."

He grabbed her wrist and led her across the bay to a back door.

The door opened behind the garage to where half a dozen vehicles were parked. The only light was from over the stoop and what spilled from the back windows of the garage. A huge old funereal black Caddie sucked up the light like a black hole.

"Nineteen-fifty-nine, Eldorado Biarritz," he said. "With the V-8 from a sixty-three Sedan under the hood. Zero to sixty in ten seconds, zero to eighty in sixteen. It's mine. Been restoring it. It's ready to go on the road except for the shocks. Thought maybe I could get some more mileage out of the old ones, but they're shot."

Pearl touched the cool rigid metal flanks of the machine. Open, its black roof collapsed like a cowl, it looked like the dead hulk of a 1950's rocket ship on the cover of a pulp science-fiction magazine. Could be blasting out of the Portland Jetport.

"I forgot cars were ever built this big."

He laughed and put his arms around her. "Back then, they built 'em big enough to get laid in the back seat."

"And how would you know that?"

"Knew a woman once liked it in the back of a Cadillac. It's good for the leather, that's what she said."

The Caddie's back door even sounded heavy when he opened it.

"You knew her, did you?"

"Taught me all I know about taking care of the leather on the back seats of Cadillac automobiles."

"Tell me about it, I'm interested."

The back seat was like a long cradle, as narrow as the daybed that had been their first bed. It didn't seem possible to accommodate a man of Reuben's size in such a space, any more than it seemed likely that a woman of her size could manage his weight, yet the fact of it was, it was comfortable, even cozy, she liked it fine. The leather upholstery had aged as soft as skin and had its own perfume, complicated and dark. It blended with the salt taste of Reuben's skin, the oil-and-grease smell of the garage and the vehicle, the night air with its burden of water and fecund forest. The whole vehicle rocked gently. She imagined herself as part of the back seat, part of a mechanical beast so perfectly tuned it was alive.

She wondered if he were remembering that woman as he made love to her. How could he not? It was so strange that he had been David's mother's lover, so strange. He was only a few years older than she was, as she was to David. But it was enough to bridge a generation. He didn't know she knew about it. But the touching and tasting and moving, they were all the same, weren't they? She felt as if a spirit, some ghost that had resided in the leather of the back seat, had entered into her with Reuben and now she was possessed, there was more than just Pearl living inside her skin, there was some woman she had never met, a woman who wore David's face, had borne David out of the same body that Reuben had loved, who had gifted David with his wordiness and his madness and maybe his bed-wildness too. Perhaps that was how it had been for Reuben, the way it was with her and David. Perhaps David's mother had reached out for Reuben, looking to be saved. If it hadn't worked, at least the woman had had something, those moments in the woods and in the back seat of some other Cadillac, when Reuben did what he was doing to Pearl, the moment, the moment.

When they were finished, he shifted them around so she was on top. He did not withdraw from her. They were slick with perspiration and half-glued together.

"I would like," he said, "to fuck you all over this town. Draw a map and give it out to the guests at our wedding. And I'd like to keep on doing it, adding to the map and passing it out on every anniversary. Maybe by the time we're dead, we'd have fucked on every square inch of the Ridge."

She laughed so hard she got hiccups. He got hard and they did it some more.

2

Creeping into the house at around two, she fell into bed like a tree crashing down. It seemed like five minutes passed and the alarm went off. *So this is how the dead feel when they get a space virus and have to get up and eat living flesh,* she thought. Her ankle felt as if the dead had been chewing on it. She tried to shower herself awake or at least to the point where she knew she was conscious and didn't like it. Next came aspirin and a whole glass of water. Poking her fingers into the corners of her lips, she pushed her mouth into a parody of a cheerful smile and went down the back stairs, into the perfume of fresh-brewed coffee.

Norris turned around with a plate of toast in one hand. "Good morning, darlin'."

"What you grinning about?"

He pokered up his face. "Such a pretty day. I slept like a top."

The toast helped. She discovered she was ravenously hungry and hurried Norris off to the diner to make them a full breakfast. She had eaten most of hers by the time Sonny Lunt started banging on the door.

"Finish yours," she told Norris. "Day Karen and I can't handle Sonny, I might as well quit."

"That an offer?" Sonny asked. "I'm kinda old for the both a ya, but I'd give it my best Boy Scout try, Pearl."

"Drink your coffee and be quiet."

"Yes, ma'am."

Karen doled out doughnuts to Sonny to hold him until his breakfast fry-up was ready.

"You're a rainbow today."

Sonny had stitches lacing one eyebrow, and the black thread bristled among his own blond hair.

"I got a bruise on my butt where one of the cops booted me looks like sunset in Margaritaville."

Karen shuddered. "I don't want to see it."

"Wimmin," Sonny said. "That's the kind of appreciation you get when you try to do something for 'm."

"You didn't do a goddamn thing for me," the girl said angrily. "You just wanted to get into a fight."

Pearl snagged Karen. "Watch your language in here, lady, you represent the management."

"What's your problem? You heard every word of it before, and say it yourself. Didn't you get your beauty sleep again last night?"

A stiff little silence like a cheap partition formed between the two women.

"Go back to work, Karen."

Pearl turned away.

Norris watched Karen stalking off to take orders from the first customers in the booths. He shook his head.

Pearl laid a reassuring hand on his arm.

The day went by. Queasy, she regretted the huge breakfast she had bolted, never mind the stupidity of tomcatting half the night. Every time she came down with her full weight on her ankle, she had to grit her teeth against the pain. Her priorities, she chided herself, had gotten mixed up. She crutched on, gobbling aspirin when no one was looking. Just before closing, she stumbled to the rest room and vomited.

Norris clucked and insisted on driving home.

They hardly got through the door before the second round started. Her mind was preternaturally clear. *Well, well. Intestinal flu. Roto Rooter enteritis. Haven't had that in five years. Won't I feel great when it stops.*

Norris was hovering when she came out.

"Flu," she said, "some kind of intestinal flu."

"Maybe." He took her by the elbow. "You're feverish. I wanta look at that ankle."

She wasn't strong enough to resist. He was very careful unwrapping the ankle but she had to grimace anyway. He grimaced right back at the sight of it.

"Damn," he said. "You goin' to the doctor."

The trip to Greenspark took twenty very long minutes. Waiting for the doctor in the emergency room took another age.

"My goodness," Dr. Hennessey said, "textbook septicemia. Probably should have had your tetanus shot renewed right after you got bit, just to be on the safe side."

She hardly minded the indignity of having a shot of antibiotics in her bottom. More antibiotics to take by mouth, and if she wasn't better in the morning, he wanted to know about it immediately.

They stopped at the pharmacy to pick up the antibiotics and another prescription for Darvocet. With one of the latter in her, she was only semiconscious for the ride home. Norris tucked her into her bed. She knew he came in several times in the night to check her.

3

In the morning, Norris checked the ankle and seemed relieved.

"Karen and Jean and I'll take care of the diner today. You stay off that ankle and sleep."

She didn't fight it. Shaking with chills one minute, she was throwing off the blankets and trying to cool off the next. More diarrhea, no doubt turbo-boosted by the antibiotics, until she was as wrung-out as last night's dishrag. It was all she could do to get from one Darvocet to the next.

Jean looked in at midmorning, woke Pearl up, fussed over her, and then, thank God, she went away.

David stuck his head in the bedroom door and Pearl pitched a glass at him. She heard him clearing it up.

He came back in with a new drinking glass and a vase of wild roses.

"Go away," Pearl said.

"In a little while."

He began doing things to the bed, to the sheets. He hauled her nightie, as she protested weakly, over her head. Then he bathed her with a sponge, tsking over her ankle. More doings with the sheets, and suddenly she was lying between clean linen and he was buttoning her into clean pajamas.

"Make a good nurse."

David laughed.

"Learned to do it for my mother, last few months. Forgive me if I kiss you someplace strange."

He rolled her gently up and kissed her left shoulder blade, gently eased her back down, and then he was gone. She heard the screen door slap after him.

4

Reuben woke her up, dragging up a chair and turning it around to sit on, next to the bed.

She opened one eye, her stomach woke up, and she surged out of the bed and into the bathroom.

He followed her and held her while she regurgitated bile that felt like maybe it was her stomach lining coming out into the toilet. Afterward she broke out in violent shivering and he bundled her back into the bed.

"I hope it wasn't the sight of my face made you sick up like that," he said, washing hers for her with cool, damp terry cloth. He went away and came back with another one. "Suck on that."

She wanted to laugh but couldn't. She did as she was told. The terry-cloth loops tasted wonderful, the water a sweet, cool nectar.

Reuben went away, Norris drifted in and out of the room, and she drifted in and out of sleep and sickness. *I'll be okay tomorrow,* she thought. *If I don't die. Dying. What a good idea. Finally meet my Uncle Ghost. Go wrestle the roots of that wild rose with him.*

She didn't die but she wasn't okay the next day. She was drained, weak. She felt as if she had battled a giant. Norris still wouldn't let her go back to work and she was too woozy to fight him too.

5

Pearl woke to the sun coming in the window, beautiful and warm, like Danaë's loving shower. It made her raise her arm to shield her eyes until they were used to it. The angle and strength told her it was already midday. Another day, but she wasn't sure which one. The house was inordinately quiet. She was weak but she wasn't sick anymore. She realized Reuben was sitting in the chair next to her bed.

"Hello," she croaked.

He stood up and came round the chair to sit on the bed. He looked as if he too had been ill. He took one of her hands and wove his fingers into hers.

"What day is it?"

"Fourth of July."

She struggled to sit up. "What's wrong?"

"Walter's dead."

She closed her eyes.

"He was dead this morning when Jean got up. Guess his heart just gave out."

She cried. She tried not to but she couldn't help it.

"Jean called me first. She wasn't as hysterical as you might expect. I have to take her to Greenspark to pick out the coffin and make the final arrangements."

After Reuben left, Norris brought her clear soup and dry toast and the newspaper. All day long, she could hear firecrackers going off. It was like the smell of the turkey dinner wafting up to her bedroom that long-ago Thanksgiving, when she was eleven, that she had been sick abed. She had never imagined how sad and lonely firecrackers could sound.

David came calling, with fresh wildflowers and a stack of books and a folder he said casually he had stuffed a few poems into that she didn't have to read if she didn't want. He held her hand and said, "I'm out of words."

"Me too."

He nodded.

She blubbered and he held her awhile until she stopped, and then she made him go away. She slept and slept.

6

The next day, Pearl went to work over Norris' protests. Jean wasn't there and he and Karen were carrying the whole load. She sat down a lot but she was there. It was a strange experience to spend so much time sitting down, at one of the booths or on a stool. A new and interesting vantage point, and she tried to get out of it what she could. She went home early and went right to bed.

The next day was better. Still shorthanded without Jean, but then, there was less breakage, so it wasn't entirely a loss. She couldn't face the wake at the funeral home in Greenspark so she and Norris went straight home after work. He was visibly tired and she was worn out trying not to show she was still weak. When she suggested he take a nap, he went right off.

Pearl went out to sit on the back stoop to enjoy the sun and think about things she hadn't done. Weeded her garden, for one. Read any of David's poems.

He'd called; she'd said she was still taking it easy. He seemed subdued, affected by Walter's sudden demise and perhaps by her illness.

The yellow backhoe passed by, going into the graveyard.

Reuben waved at her.

She limped under the elms and sat down on the rock wall. Her ankle was tender but she could walk on it again. With her arms crossed, she watched him maneuvering the machine, squaring his hospital-neat corners. When he was finished, he backed it off and she went to him. He took her hand and they walked slowly through the graves and toward the woods.

"Thinking about burying Gussie?" he asked.

She nodded.

"Me too."

He was broody, somber.

"I don't know how it happened, I wound up taking care of this boneyard. When I started, I never had any idea I was going to know everyone I buried. Going to have to bury everyone I know, I mean the old people, my parents' and grandparents' generation. Dug holes for their children and grandchildren. Bury 'em like a dog buries a bone. Scratch out a hole, put 'em in, cover 'em up, go start at a new hole. I'm tried of it. I don't want to do it anymore."

She clung to his arm and he held her a moment.

"You're nothing but skin and bones. Don't you melt away on me."

She leaned into him, savoring the way he smelled, his incredible solidity. In the shade of birches they swayed together, found their footing again, and kept it.

7

She looked at herself in the mirror. From the way the black dress hung, she had dropped maybe ten pounds. She pinned up her hair and fastened the string of pearls around her neck. The bedroom was close, and the smell of the flowers nauseated her. Suddenly she could not abide them, and pitched them violently out the window into the garden bed below.

As they drove by the diner, she read Norris' neatly hand-lettered sign in the window: CLOSED IN RESPECT OF MR. WALTER MCKENZIE. The bleak realization that the old man really was dead overcame her and she fumbled for her handkerchief.

The crowded parking lot of the white church on Route Five bespoke a full house. A minor shock was seeing Reuben's restored Eldorado among the cars. It was less a vehicle of transportation to her than a kind of monument. He hadn't mentioned to her that he was ready to put it on the road.

David waited at the door, in blinding white linen with a plain navy-blue tie. It was startling to see him fully and formally clothed. She hadn't ever seen him wear anything but cut-off shorts and well-aged, open button-up shirts with half their buttons missing, or a pair of khaki trousers and a sport shirt, and had taken his natural state to be barefoot and sockless. This was an entirely new mode. He was wearing his sunglasses against the brilliance of the day. She had forgotten how they emphasized the planes on his face.

He took her hand without a word, leaned across her to shake Norris' briefly with the other, and led them inside. The church was somehow more full than the parking lot, people sitting shoulder to shoulder, both air and places to sit in short supply. Evvie Bonneau was there, in uniform, and Sonny Lunt, and other familiar faces who had been strangers only a funeral ago. Walter would have been amused to fill up a church, Pearl thought, for she had heard him say he was a godless man. It was Jean who had prodded him into an occasional Sunday-morning snooze at the Congregational service.

All the old people who had come to Gussie's interment were there, some of them wearing the same somber suit or dress. The church was full of flowers. Pearl's stomach turned but she mastered it. David brought them to a pair of seats on the aisle, whispered something to Norris, and left them.

"He wants you to be able to leave if you feel ill," Norris murmured.

She wondered where David had gone but then the organ music began and they brought Walter's coffin up the center aisle. Reuben and David were both pallbearers, and so was young Sam. Behind them, Jean wasn't the lone mourner. There was another middle-aged woman who must be the sister Reuben had mentioned, who lived very far away, Alaska it was. The sister was nearly Jean's double but her posture was fiercely erect, and she had an air of competence. It was good Jean would not have to cope alone.

Pearl tried to pay attention but she just couldn't concentrate. Norris took her arm gently, indicating it was time to rise and leave.

They went home, David following them. He walked to the graveyard with them. He was more than subdued. He was pale. Pearl realized all this business was far more trying for him than she had ever expected or imagined. His touch was tense and desperate. And he was diverting the stress into his favorite channel. He touched her briefly, quite circumspectly, in the small of the back, and she had all she could do not to tremble. Ophelia, she thought. He's going to have an Ophelia fit again and if I'm not careful, he'll throw me down on the coffin and jump me right there. If he gets through this, he'll be wild for it, he'll be wanting me to come to him tonight, or he'll crawl up the walls of my house.

There were nearly as many mourners who had adjourned to the gravesite as had filled the church. Norris, saddened despite his brief acquaintance with Walter, as they had taken a strong liking to each other, stayed at her side. Norris was of an age in which the reminders of death are too frequent, a constant goad about his own proximity to it. And he was tired, awfully tired from the week he had put in, nursing her, working the diner. She squeezed his arm, and he squeezed back.

David had to rejoin the other pallbearers, and she was grateful that he had something to do, but the part was too quickly played.

In the middle of the interment, Pearl noticed suddenly that Roscoe Needham was at the far edge of the crowd, a little separated from them. He had made a bad job of shaving, and his fly was but half-zipped, but he was there, with a hat in his hand, paying his respects. He looked up at her and she saw his eyes were red with boozing or grief or both. He cringed from her glance.

The brief service was ending when the bitch began to howl.

Myriad faces turned toward the edge of the woods where the black retriever bayed like a banshee.

Evvie Bonneau, standing only a few feet away, said, "Shit," in a low voice.

Then the animal turned tail and was gone, having effectively spooked everyone.

The mourners began to depart. Reuben had somehow inherited responsibility for Jean and her sister. Helping them into the Eldorado, he glanced up and met Pearl's gaze.

The pressure of David's hand on the small of Pearl's back suddenly changed. He looked from Reuben to her. She couldn't see his eyes but his touch was full of his discovery. Nor could she help tensing in reaction. Then she realized he was stifling a grin.

None of this passed unnoticed by Norris.

David caught her arm and drew close enough to murmur, with great amusement, "Pearl, this is too rich. Do you realize Reuben Styles is in love with you? I think I'm jealous, but I'm not sure of whom."

Pearl rounded on him and said through clenched teeth, "Please, we are burying Walter."

He was properly abashed.

She stalked, or tried to stalk, but it was more like a stumble, on her wobby ankle, away from him. Norris hastened to catch up with her.

So did David. "I'm sorry. It was just such a surprise. I mean, it's perfectly understandable. Any normal, healthy, even part-time heterosexual male would find you attractive. It just never crossed my mind that Reuben might. Something oedipal, I suppose. It just seemed droll, Reuben as a rural Romeo to your Juliet. He'll probably fantasize about you for the rest of his life. Lucky him. But imagine what you could talk about with him, or do you have a secret passion for manifolds and mufflers and torque? If you like the type, I'll be happy to get some overalls and use Pennzoil for after-shave—"

"Shut up." She lengthened her stride toward her house. "Leave me alone."

Glancing back as she gained the porch, she saw that David had come to a stop and was still standing there, his eyes hidden behind the blankness of his sunglasses. His hands were in his pockets. Something dejected, kicked, perhaps a little panicky was expressed in the curve of his shoulder, in the slight twist of his mouth.

Norris was approaching, concern on his face.

Out of breath and light-headed, she fled to her bedroom as to a refuge.

Norris set himself to guard the door of the house, like a dragon with a hoard of gold coins, for she heard David's voice, and others, Karen's, much later, Reuben's, but no one gained admittance. She felt like gold, hard-edged and two-faced. And spent. Spent. But the pun was a bitter one, like biting a coin to see if it was base or real.

Falling into bed in what she thought was exhaustion, she found herself restless, sleep elusive. She gave up on it and picked up David's folder of poems. The first poem had no title.

Watch
the blank snowfield that lies
where lies the lake in summer.
There is a body in that lake.
Most likely
it will surface
late spring or early summer,
floating
like a snowflake on the skin of the water.
Now it is the secret of the ice,
a raft of nougat
studded with rocks and yellow boatlines,
broken oars, beer cans, and that
body.
The ice may break like a feud
with a roll of cannons, break up
in huge tarnished chunks,
come crashing onto beaches,
to break the backs of young trees,
bash in the footings of docks
with foot-treading ponderous humor.
I watch
for a bloated hand reaching
from the pocked ice
(the fingernails, rime-frosted
like a tissue of lace),
a purple knee half-bent in curtsy,
come to rest
on my patch of sand
like a deceit.
The snowfield that lies out there,
that is the lake in summer,
cannot hide that false place from me.

Watch
and never forget where it lies.

She shivered and thrust them all aside.

Finally she did not fall asleep so much as sleep crept up and claimed her, like a tide across a coastal causeway. In the muggy night, her dreams flowered, gorgeous and exotic. She was in the kitchen, cooking. Stirring a big pot fragrant with filé gumbo. She realized she was naked and laughed, happy as a child in her bath. In fact, she was a child in her bath, the pot transformed into the tin-cup measures her mother had given her for tub toys. Her mother, alive again, and younger, as young as she herself was now, trailed her hand through the bathwater and provoked, as if she had bruised it, the soporific perfume of lilies. Pearl's breasts and body hair had vanished and between her legs was the charming naked keyhole of a little girl again. The smooth white walls of the tub grew up around her like one of the giant teacups of the Mad Hatter's Tea Party at Disney World, and then bigger still, until she had no sense of what contained the water. The water pleasantly warm at first and growing colder and colder, rose higher and higher. Like a cold needle, a horrid panic of the water rising over her head pierced her through, but her limbs, her whole body, were weighted as if the very water in her cells was thickening to ice. Then she was beneath the surface of the water. The light still spilled diffusely into it, like the sun in an overcast sky. The panic dissipated, or was frozen, and she floated, like an ice cube in a drink, her weight and the water's nearly equivalent. Teeth chattering, she felt herself growing blue as her blood thickened in her core, trying to preserve her vital organs. The water began to thicken around her, and draw her down again, sinking inexorably into the darkness and away from the diminishing skin of light. Now she could not move. She was contained within her frozen body as the xylem, heartwood and sapwood, of a tree is held within the dead rings of its years, the callus of its bark. She was Daphne, in her green silence, changed to wood. She cried out but no one heard. The water held her. She held no one and this made her weep. Someone put his arms around her neck, someone shed and comforted her, and she was sure, for an instant, that David had come to her, had crept into her bed and her dream and held her close. David's face was in her mind, his face as a child. How had it grown so pale, so colorless? But then she realized she was still cold, there was no warmth in these strange arms. They were, white tinged with iris blue, and icy, a child's limbs. She felt their mournfulness, their loneliness. She heard a whisper like a draft under the door. *Come play with me. Come play with me.*

She woke tangled in sheets that were soaked with a cold perspiration. Sick to her stomach, she staggered into the bathroom to whoop up bile.

She rinsed her mouth with tepid water and stood shivering while the shower grew tepidly warm. Fixing it at that temperature, she let it just wash the sweat away, dried herself roughly, and put on a clean dry nightshirt.

With a hard-edged angry strength, she tore the linen off the bed. The kitten leapt out of her way, and then stalked off, offended. She threw the sheets in the hamper and remade the bed. The clean linen soothed her.

EIGHTEEN

1

Walking in the morning again, not much earlier than she needed, it was with that sense of surprise she had slept at all that often comes at the end of a bad night. She had a little energy, but not much, and faked more for Norris.

What was chiefly on her mind as she drove them to the diner was how she was going to get through the day shorthanded and hobbled by her still-tender ankle. No Jean, as she was sorting out the remnant details of her father's life. It was almost a mercy not to have to deal with Jean's incompetence. She was thunderstruck to see Roscoe's truck in the parking lot, the old man sitting inside it, staring at the diner. She gave Norris her keys and went to talk to him.

"Hello, Roscoe."

His head turned slowly, like a turtle's, to face her.

" 'Lo."

This morning's shave had been more successful. He smelled of Ivory soap. There was a long pause before he cleared his throat.

"Thought you might need a hand, Jean out and all."

"I'd be lying if I told you I don't."

He thrust his head forward as if trying to escape a too-tight collar.

"I guess I went too far. I'd like to 'pologize."

"I owe you one. Let's call it even."

Roscoe nodded and thrust his hand out the window.

Smiling, she shook it.

Karen's Plymouth rolled into the parking lot. The girl's grin when she saw Roscoe and Pearl convinced Pearl that Karen had had something to do with Roscoe's appearance at the diner.

"Let's go fry some eggs," Roscoe said.

Karen's good humor quickly dissipated. She worked steadily but silently. At first Pearl thought Karen was having an attack of the sullens, then decided the girl was simply more distracted than usual. There was something furtive about Reuben's daughter, a sense of something held tightly and secretly.

They got through the day. And the next day. But like an athlete who cannot find her stride, Pearl's strength and courage eluded her. It was disheartening to be a mere dishrag by the time three-thirty rolled around, and then to find the energy to try to kid Norris that she felt otherwise. He knew better; she caught a few of the anxious glances and felt the rest. She was at least able to put off both Reuben and David when they called. For once she was telling them both the truth, admitting she was still wrung out and needed to rest.

The phone was ringing as she unlocked the door to the house, and she managed to catch it. It was a voice she didn't know, asking for Norris.

Bobby something's wrong with Bobby.

Norris' face sagging as he listened to that unknown voice told her she was right.

When he hung up, she hugged him.

"I'm sorry," he said, "Bobby needs me. I've got to go to the hospital in Philly."

"I'll book your flight. You go pack."

It was late by the time she got back from delivering Norris to the Portland Jetport. He wanted to come back to Maine after Bobby's crisis was over. The house seemed empty without him. The light was on her phone recorder but she didn't play back the tape.

Showered clean, she slipped into a nightshirt and flopped onto the daybed on the sun porch. Necessity hopped up and Pearl cuddled her. She heard the Eldorado before she saw the sweep of its headlights, a whisper of something peaceful, like a wave in the ocean.

Reuben rapped on the door, let himself in.

"Norris had to leave." She held her arms out to him. "I just got back from Portland."

Reuben picked her up. "There's a Cadillac waiting outside. You like to go for a ride?"

He knew the answer, the way he knew when she'd be home.

2

Pearl came downstairs the next day as Karen's Plymouth shuddered to a halt in her driveway.

The girl's posture as she entered was tense, her smile jittery, but her nervousness only served to emphasize her beauty. The summer was nothing to her skin, the lushness of her body, the fullness of her lower lip. Karen looked around nervously.

For Norris, it came to Pearl. She wants to impart some confidence but would prefer not to have him share it.

"Norris had to go to Philadelphia," Pearl told her.

Karen seemed relieved.

"You feeling better?" Karen asked, a shade too solicitously, as they sat down at the table with coffee.

"Yes."

Pearl realized she was lying. She felt about the same as she had the previous day: drained, as if she had sprung a leak and her substance was slipping through it, churning like bathwater funneling out of the tub.

Karen took a deep breath.

A circuit tripped over for Pearl. She stared wide-eyed at Karen.

"You're pregnant, aren't you?"

Karen nodded. A small hysterical giggle escaped her, like a bubble blown from a loop by a child's breath.

Pearl closed her eyes briefly. "You sure?"

"Yes. I did one of those home tests and then I went to the doctor."

"What are you going to do?"

Karen shrugged. "I can't have it, Pearl."

Pearl leapt out of her chair and started to pace. "What about having it and giving it up for adoption?"

The girl leaned toward Pearl and said intensely, "I can't have it. There's sure to be something wrong with it after what he did to me."

Pearl was overtaken with nausea. "I didn't think about that. Is that what the doctor said?"

"Well, he said almost certainly it would affect the baby."

"Oh, Karen." Pearl hugged her.

"Hey," the girl said. "I can handle it. I don't want to have this kid, believe me."

Pearl let go of her, stepped back, tried to get Karen to look her in the eye. "No. That's not what I meant."

Karen's gaze dropped to the coffee mug in front of her. Her lower lip trembled. "I suppose you think abortion's murder."

"Karen, my mother didn't abort me. That's all the answer I've got."

"I'm not your mother and this kid isn't you. I'm going to get rid of it. But I need some money."

Pearl didn't know what the hell to do or say and it made her panicky. "Karen, I'd do just about anything to help you, but paying for an abortion, I don't think I can handle it. I've got to think about it."

The girl's face set stubbornly. "I'll pay it back."

"Karen, you're a minor. You've got parents who need to know about this, who'll help you make the right decision. Please talk to Reuben."

Karen shuddered. "He'll kill me. You may have doubts about abortion, but I know where he stands on it, he'll kill me."

"No. He won't. I don't believe that."

Karen stood up.

"I think I know him better than you do. I should have known better than to ask, I guess. I thought you were a liberated woman. I'll figure it out myself, somehow. I've been taking care of myself for a long time now, I guess I'll just have to keep on doing it."

Liberated, Pearl wanted to shout after Karen as she stalked out. *Where'd you get the idea the slaves were free, baby? Where'd you get the idea anybody was?*

Karen drove away in the direction of the diner. Maybe she'd actually be there when Pearl arrived, maybe she'd keep on going.

Pearl picked up the phone, started to dial Reuben's number, bit her lip, and hung up. Her hand went to her handbag, hanging on the back of a chair. Deliberately she extracted her appointment book and opened to the back page, where the twelve months of the year were arrayed. A single glance was all she needed to confirm that she was herself a full week late.

"Shit. Oh, shit, shit, shit."

Liberation. So much for liberation and free lunches. God doesn't serve any free lunches at Her diner, does She? No deal, no favors,

God was having Her little joke on Pearl. *Liberation.* Did that mean the dull resignation one feels when every premonition of impending doom proves true?

"Uncle Ghost," she said aloud, "you have left your house to an idiot, a woman with no more sense of self-control than a sixteen-year-old hellcat."

Uncle Ghost didn't answer. Probably too busy laughing his skinny old man's butt off at her. He must be getting a gut cramp by now from laughing so hard. Maybe Uncle Ghost would intercede with God and grant her a reprieve. *Let me be late, please, God, let me be just late.* She pulled herself together and went to work.

3

Hiding behind a tight smile, Karen was waiting for her at the diner. It was Pearl's day to be distracted.

David turned up, wearing reassuringly David clothes, shorts and an open shirt and sneakers old enough to have lost all color and shape and their laces as well. He ate breakfast and left his sunglasses by his plate.

Snatching them up, Pearl hurried out after him.

"Thanks," he said as she gave them back. "Take you out for a drink at the Dog this evening?"

She hesitated. "Will there be a fight?"

He laughed. "Only if you want one."

He was radiantly sane today. The finely planed intelligence in his features, the fluency of speech and body, announced such rationality, such comprehension, he seemed a refuge from the messiness and pathos of her life. It was as if he had pendulumed to an opposite pole. So strange, to perceive him as a safe place, when only a little before he had been a maelstrom. Maybe he was the eye of a hurricane. Everything moved, somehow, around him.

Reuben she frankly fled. She didn't know how she could face him and not give away what Karen had said or what she suspected about herself. She might not need to say anything. It was possible he would look at her and know about her little secret just by serendipity.

David was another cup of tea. For one, his daughter wasn't pregnant too. If he stayed in this steady state, she might actually be able to talk to him, to tell him what the situation was.

"Yes. Yes, I'd like that."

David swayed toward her slightly, then pulled back. He held himself just beyond touch. "I'm sorry I was snotty about Reuben. I know you like him. So do I."

She nodded, her throat suddenly tight. She crossed her arms, felt the rougher skin of her elbows with the tips of her fingers. Maybe it wasn't going to be so easy to talk to him, after all.

David's face was somber. "I'm okay now, you know. You don't have to be frightened of me." His breathing hitched. "I can't bear you to be frightened of me. I'm just me, just David, that's all. A little bit crazy, maybe, but I can be okay as long as you're with me."

"I have to go back to work."

He reached out suddenly and touched her lower lip, then the hollow of her throat, with two fingers. The jolt of desire that tightened her core was so strong it made her nauseous. Or maybe it was only her little mess, her little oopsy-daisy, her little bitty broken egg, burrowing somewhere inside her, dividing and dividing and dividing into dizzying multiplication of new being, not yet the homunculus, still only a crinkly lump like a crumpled map yet to be unfolded and read, stirring up her guts.

He barked a laugh that was all edges. "The alarms just went off. The pile's heating up too fast."

He ducked away from her, into the little car, and goosed the thing out of the lot as if he were fleeing the devil.

She watched him go, wondering where he was headed, down what back road, what untraveled route.

Reuben called to ask how she was. She was busy and thankful for it. He said he would call again later.

4

Wherever David went, he came back later in the day, slugging the little car up the hill of her driveway. She stood up straight, pressing the small of her back, admired the heap of weeds she had torn out of her garden, and went to meet him by her back steps.

"Nice sweat you've worked up. How's the ankle?"

"Better every day. Have a radish."

By the time she had put away her gardening gloves and a couple small tools, he was in the kitchen running water over the radish she had given him. It crunched nicely between his fine teeth when he bit it.

"Stop that."

"What?"

"Sexy biting," she said over her shoulder as she double-timed up the back stairs. The sound of his amusement followed her.

Deafened by the water pouring over her, and with her eyes closed against the soap as she washed her hair, she was startled by his touch, not just his hand, but the sudden collision with the whole length of his body as he stepped into the shower with her. Instinctively she cried out and leapt away from him, and opened her eyes, which the soap promptly attacked. But he had his arms around her and she did not escape. Her racing heart settled a bit, then found a new rhythm. She forced herself to stop blinking against the burning of the soap in her eyes and let the clear water flush them. He held her so tightly it hurt, and thrust one leg between hers, entwining them. Then, as she held her face to the force of water, his mouth found the nipple of her left breast.

Hours later, the vague realization penetrated her doze that it had gotten dark outside. She hauled herself up. David was sprawled half-asleep, still entangled with her. She grabbed the alarm clock, blinked at the time, and poked him. He burrowed closer and she put the clock down again.

"David, I've got to work tomorrow. You have to go home."

He rolled over and picked up the alarm clock to peer at it near-sightedly. "Yeah." He kept on rolling, over the top of her and right off the bed. Like a cat, he caught himself as he started to fall, and landed neatly on his feet. He pulled on his clothes. "That was better than a fight at the Dog."

She felt a laugh percolating up from the sleep that was pulling her down into itself. She wondered if he heard it, if she really did laugh or just thought she did. He kissed her very gently on her forehead and tucked the sheet around her, the way he had when she had been sick. Distantly she heard the little car spurting away.

5

As Pearl stood on the stoop with one hand on the doorknob, she realized the key to the diner was not on her key ring. She fanned the ring for it again. She couldn't believe it. She reached for the knob and it turned. Silently, the door opened. With a dreadful sinking feeling she went inside. The cash register's lock drawer, in which she kept the day's receipts, was open and emptied. She hurried into the office and her small safe was also open, the week's receipts in the bank sack gone too. Slowly she sank into her desk chair and sat staring at the open safe.

The thief had had a key, had known the combination of the safe. The key must have been her own, removed from the key ring she had left on the kitchen table while she was dallying with David the previous evening. The back door of the house had also been open. There was only one deduction to be made. Karen.

Roscoe stuck his head into the little office. "Why's the register emp—" The question answered itself before he could finish it. "Jesus High-hat Christ. We been robbed."

Pearl spun the desk chair around to face him. "Roscoe, go out and close that drawer and come back, okay?"

Roscoe's stare flicked from the safe to her and back again and then he did as she bid. When he came back, she indicated the door and he shut it behind him.

"Roscoe. I'm pretty sure Karen took the money."

The old man's mouth dropped open, and he made an unintelligible gabbling sound.

Pearl told him her theory quickly.

"I can't believe it." He shook his head. "No."

She waited for him to work it through himself.

"I just don't understand." He slammed his hand against the door.

"I'm not calling the cops."

He looked up at her. Tears were running down his face.

Pearl stood up and seized Roscoe by the forearm. "I know why she did it."

Still dazed, he could only shake his head.

"She's pregnant and she wants an abortion. She asked me to lend her the money yesterday."

Roscoe barked a horrified bitter sound that was only nominally a laugh. "Shit-a-goddamn." He looked at Pearl with a deep loathing that made her flinch. "You proud of yourself? You set her a hell of an example, didn't you?" he lashed out at her.

Pearl bolted for the rest room. As she was washing her face, staring into the mirror, there was a faint rap on the door.

"You okay?" he asked. His voice was subdued.

She sucked in a shaky breath and opened the door.

"Go sit down. I'll bring you a cup of coffee."

She heard him making the coffee, letting Sonny Lunt in.

Then he came back. "You're right. You shouldn't call the cops. We'll handle this private." He patted her hand. "I apologize. Christ, I been doing more 'pologizing lately than I ever did in my whole life. You understand it was a hell of a shock."

She nodded.

The coffee he brought her gave her enough of a boost to get going.

Jean arrived and was told Karen had taken the day off.

Pearl whispered where she was going to Roscoe and hurried out. She raced over to Karen's trailer on Pigeon Hill, and even though the Plymouth was not there, pounded the door and shouted for her. No answer. Disconsolate, Pearl went back to the diner, trying to think what else she could do. She had no idea where Karen had gone. It might be Greenspark, or Lewiston or Portland or North Conway, New Hampshire, just as easily. Even if Pearl rushed to tell Reuben, there was little hope of reaching Karen before it was too late to stop her.

It was another day she endured rather than enjoyed. Too many of those of late. Roscoe patted her shoulder as they locked up, but it was of little comfort.

6

Karen stepped out of the elevator into the lobby of the hospital in Greenspark. She was so relieved she felt a little high. The discomfort was bearable. Her stomach was shaky, in part because she knew there was another hard thing to do. She had to go see Pearl and ask for her forgiveness. Her increasing apprehension distracted her and she almost didn't see Bri Spearin's mother, just coming through the swinging door marked CAFETERIA, with a personalized mug (DEBRA) in one hand. A tall woman, intimidating in her nurse's uniform, Debra Spearin went rigid at the sight of Karen.

"Hello," Karen said. "You've switched to day shift, have you?"

The look Bri's mother gave her was poisonous. "You rotten little whore," Debra Spearin hissed. "I hope you've got cancer."

Karen shrank from her, then hurried past her, almost running. Suddenly she hurt, much more than she had ever expected.

7

There was a message on Pearl's phone recorder from Norris about how well Bobby was doing. He promised to call the next day. Messages from Reuben and David. She called them both and begged off seeing them for the perfectly truthful reason that she was exhausted. It was too early to go to bed. After a long relaxing bath, she put a casserole in the oven and curled up on the sun porch to wait for it to be ready.

She dropped her paperback at the sound of Karen's car.

Karen saw where she was and came to the screen door of the sun porch. The girl hesitated.

"Come in."

Karen stepped inside. Shaking and so pale she looked on the verge of fainting, she held out her hand. The key lay in her palm.

"I'm sorry," she said in a little high voice. "I'll pay you back."

Pearl picked the key from her palm and silently replaced it on her key ring.

"Oh, I almost forgot." Karen pulled the bank money sack from her handbag and handed it to Pearl.

It had some weight, there was still money in it.

"I didn't need all of it. Please don't tell my father."

Pearl dropped it on the daybed and reached for Karen. The girl burst into tears and allowed herself to be enfolded. Pearl held her, smoothing her hair, unable to think of anything to say that would be any comfort. Eventually they both cried themselves out. Karen fell asleep on the daybed and Pearl covered her up.

Then she called Roscoe and told him what had happened.

"Good thing she didn't come to me first," he said, "I'd've given her a good whipping. You tell her for me, I'm disgusted."

But Pearl knew his outrage hid a real relief that Karen was in her hands for the night.

"You gonna tell Reuben?"

"I don't know yet."

He sighed. "Well, get some sleep. You've had a shock yourself."

Her bed was empty. It seemed so luxurious to sleep, and sleep alone. As she fell asleep, she heard the retriever bitch baying from the woods. The long howl cracked the quietude and hung in the air, empty and idiot as the moon, the echo of day cast back upon the shadow of the sun.

8

Karen was gone in the morning, leaving a piece of notepaper on the pillow of the daybed saying *Thanks. Gone home. Will be in to work tomorrow.*

Stripping and remaking the daybed seemed like a decisive act, a gesture of order in the midst of chaos. Lately every little thing seemed significant, metaphorical, a habit of mind she seemed to have caught from David. Today's metaphor, Pearl decided, bundling sheets into the washing machine, was dirty linen.

After work, she found Karen sunbathing behind the trailer. The girl was positively cheerful. Pearl thought she too would be cheerful if her own little problem was so handily solved. Karen wanted to treat her to pizza at the Dog. She accepted, in part as an unobtrusive way to keep an eye on the kid, in case Karen developed some kind of complication. And it was a way to duck both her men. The two women agreed to meet there.

Pearl proceeded on to Greenspark.

When she dropped the home pregnancy test on the pharmacy counter in front of the lady clerk, the woman peered over her glasses at Pearl. Briskly ringing up the purchase, she whisked it into a paper bag and handed it to Pearl.

"Guess you didn't buy enough of them other things," she said down her rabbity little nose.

Pearl grabbed the sack from her. "This isn't for me. It's for Mrs. Conroy."

Though she regretted it as soon as it was out of her mouth, it was worth seeing the woman's lips making a perfect little O, her birdy eyes widening. Not a wise remark, just a wise crack, or an unwise crack, to be literal about it. And then she burst out laughing at her own inadvertent pun. She knew an unwise crack or two, and one of them was named Pearl.

But it appeared Uncle Ghost had successfully intervened for her. The little tube contained a pair of yellow beads, one of which would turn blue if she were pregnant. The second bead stayed yellow. Negative. She was so relieved she found herself blinking away tears. She decided the smart thing to do would be to give up sex altogether. It seemed like a perfectly reasonable decision.

9

With lifted spirits, Pearl set off to meet Karen at the Dog. Business began to bustle while they were trying to eat the mediocre pizza. The current hot spell had gone a long time. The farmers were haying, the woodcutters were in the woods ten hours a day, road and construction crews were drawing their longest hours of the year, and they were all both hungry and thirsty at the end of the day.

Sonny Lunt lumbered in and parked at their table, generously helping them consume the pizza. Evvie Bonneau arrived and finished it off. All at once, combatants from both factions of the last brawl were present—Bri Spearin's brother Ryan and some of Bri's biker friends holding up the bar. On the other side was Lurch Mullins. Pearl tensed. A glance at the proprietor at his till caught his habitually pissed-off expression shifting to apprehension. She whipped around, and there was David coming through the door. No wonder Fudgy was nervous. Her own stomach fluttered; perhaps it hadn't been wise to come here.

Sonny greeted David noisily, giving Pearl some cover in which to compose herself. For too long a time, she had been tense and depressed. It wasn't natural to her, it tired her out. She determined to ignore everything and just enjoy herself. The irony of forcing enjoyment quickly became obvious.

David pulled up a chair next to her, with a quick squeeze of her knee under the table. The only other overt thing he did was to lightly flick a wayward wisp of her hair from her cheek. It was as obvious a declaration of intimacy as a kiss, but it was so quick and cool that anyone not looking right at them could have missed it. He joined in the general conversation without missing a beat.

When Sam and Reuben walked in, both Karen and Pearl started nervously. They were not alone in their reaction. But then, the two Styles men were hard to miss and tended to attract gawkers.

Pearl hoped David would take her sudden nervousness as wholly a reaction to the possibility of another outbreak of hostilities. Her stomach knotted fiercely. The thought of another dash to the rest room with the whoopsies was a dismal one; she had been doing too much of that lately. How could she have ever imagined she would never be in the same place with the two of them in so small a town? The inevitable was happening. The truth was about to erupt.

David scintillated into a new mode, lively to the point of edginess.

Evvie Bonneau looked worried.

Spotting Karen and Pearl, Sam came directly to their table to sit down with them. "Since we had to come here anyway to deliver Fudgy's car, I talked Dad into picking up pizza."

Reuben went to the bar and handed Fudgy the keys to the LeBaron even as Sam was telling them.

"Might's well eat it here," Sonny told him, and directed the waitress not only to send whatever Reuben and Sam had ordered by phone to their table but also to bring over some beer for Reuben too. And another one for Sonny, while she was at it.

Pearl was trying not to look at either David or Reuben too often or too intensely, while wishing her mother *had* aborted her. She turned to say something inconsequential to Karen and the girl was staring at the door, suddenly pallid and sick-looking.

Just coming into the bar were Belinda Conroy and Debra Spearin.

The bite of pizza that Pearl had been swallowing scraped at the walls of her abruptly constricting throat. She swigged a mouthful of the beer Sonny had bought her, and the obstruction cleared.

Belinda and Debra swiveled like compass needles and stood staring at them. A buzz among the regulars, already alert to the potential for confrontation, was immediate. For a fraction of a second the two overcoiffed heads dipped together, some confidence was exchanged, and then the women advanced upon Pearl's and Karen's table.

"Shit," muttered Evvie Bonneau, "here comes trouble."

Reuben arrived simultaneously with the two women. Around them, the bar had quieted, the better to hear what might be said. It was not a long wait.

"Karen." Belinda Conroy posed, one hand on her hip, playing to her audience. "How are you? I hear you had a little scrape yesterday."

Pearl went numb inside.

Evvie Bonneau came to her feet, her eyes blazing. "You loud-mouthed bitch."

Reuben looked first at Karen, then at Pearl.

As Pearl watched the shock explode in his eyes, she started to rise, to say something, but all that came out was a choked gurgle, as if she had been struck. David grabbed her by the waist to restrain her.

Karen looked ill. With a low cry she stood up and tried to leave.

Reuben caught her by the arm. She jerked away from him and he let go. She bolted from the bar.

Belinda Conroy and Debra Spearin wore expressions of triumph.

Pearl's stomach churned at the sight.

Reuben was following Karen, Sam after him.

"You witch," Pearl said, and punched Belinda Conroy in the mouth.

It hurt like hell. She thought she might have done her hand as much damage as she had Belinda's mouth. And it wasn't even very satisfying. She just wanted to hit her again, preferably with a tire iron.

David hooked her by the armpits and hauled her off.

"Okay, baby," he said in a low amused tone. "You got it out, it's okay," as if she were a small child having a splinter removed from under a fingernail.

Belinda's mouth was bleeding and she was weeping. Glaring at everyone, Debra Spearin had encircled her with a protective arm.

Pearl shook David off and hurried after the Styleses. He trailed after her.

Reuben had caught up with Karen in the parking lot. He held her by both arms. Her head was twisted away from him, as a child might try, by avoiding the parent's eyes, to somehow evade the parental wrath. Sam was at his side.

Pearl threw her arms around Karen from the other direction and Reuben let go of his daughter. Karen, sobbing, buried her head in Pearl's bosom.

David positioned himself at an angle to Reuben, just this side of ready to come between the big man and his daughter.

"What did that bitch mean?" Reuben demanded of Karen.

"Please, Reuben." This plea from Pearl seemed to give him pause. The bewildered hurt in his eyes wounded her.

The sight of her father responding to Pearl's request and calming down seemed to provoke Karen. Suddenly the girl was defiant.

"You know what she meant," Karen shouted at him.

He flinched.

Karen pushed out of Pearl's arms and stood straight and angry. "You tell me, did you want your first grandchild to be Bri Spearin's kid?"

Reuben closed his eyes.

"Oh, Christ," David muttered.

Karen stalked past her brother toward her car.

"Nice going, Karen. Just when I think you've pulled your worst stunt yet, you top it," Sam said to her as she passed, reaching out to grab her arm. His voice was thick and shaky with tears.

She twisted away from his touch so he came up with thin air.

Pearl put her hand on Reuben's forearm. He seemed not to know she was there.

They watched Karen peel out.

Sonny Lunt and Evvie Bonneau caught up with them.

"Get the hell outta here," Sonny urged Reuben.

"Fudgy's calling the cops again," Evvie said.

Reuben and Sam looked at each other.

"Go on." The urgency in David's voice made them all start.

Reuben suddenly came back into focus. He put an arm over Sam's shoulder and the two of them headed for the truck. They were as quickly and completely gone as Karen.

David took Pearl by the hand.

"You've got a nice right. I wish you'd been here the other night."

She managed a weak smile.

"The cops'll be here soon," Sonny said. "Didn't I hear Belinda call Pearl a nigger bitch, Evvie?"

Evvie Bonneau agreed. "Heard her myself."

"Me too," David said.

"I swear I did, I'll have to tell the cops, it's my duty as a citizen." Sonny grinned happily in anticipation of perjury and put his arm around Evvie. Then he thought of something else and slapped himself on the forehead. "Shit, I forgot to give Reuben his Winchester again. And I'm working outta town all week. Oh, hell. Have to take it to his place later, I guess."

Inside the bar, Debra Spearin was holding an ice pack to Belinda's mouth.

"Oughta shove it down her gob," Evvie murmured to Pearl.

A pulsing siren announced the imminent arrival of the law. Pearl hastily quaffed a beer, which at least settled her stomach. But it didn't make much of a dent on the Breathalyzer.

" 'Fraid you're legally sober, Miss Dickenson," Tom Clark said. The deputy was a hearty breakfaster and often came in for coffee while on patrol.

"Wish I weren't." Pearl essayed a smile.

Tom gave her a big grin in return. They were sitting in the back seat of his cruiser while he interviewed her. "We calling this a racial incident?"

Pearl shook her head. "They're trying to protect me."

Tom sighed. "I thought so. What'd she really say?"

Pearl told him.

He winced. "My God, I'm glad that girl's not my daughter. Look, I've taken Mrs. Conroy's statement and she's lying about what she said too. Far as I'm concerned, that cancels everything out. I'm going to tell her if she wants to have you charged with assault, I'm charging her with breaking the peace, verbal assault, and provoking a riot. That oughta shut her up. I'd really appreciate if you folks would stay outta this goddamn roadhouse and if you'd just head the other way when you see this particular bitch. I'm losing my patience."

"No argument from me."

He tipped his hat to her. "Think of it as my compliments to the chef."

Feeling suddenly rocky again, Pearl went back into the bar to go to the ladies' room. Evvie Bonneau followed her. Bodyguarding her, Pearl suddenly realized.

"You and Reuben get married, I wanna be invited to all the fights, okay?"

Pearl laughed. "What makes you think I'm going to marry anyone?"

Evvie was instantly serious. "You don't marry someone pretty soon, babe, there's two friends a mine who're gonna get hurt. Shit, far as I'm concerned, you can live with both a them, if you can work it out. I don't doubt for a minute you can handle two men easy. For all they say men are naturally polygamous, I know more women can do that than men."

"I got in over my head before I realized it."

Evvie grinned. "I never thought otherwise. Now you got to either start swimming in one direction or another or drown."

David was just closing the trunk of his car. Sonny was with him, running his mouth as usual. Evvie hooked a finger at Sonny and Sonny heeled amiably. David came with him and walked Pearl to her truck.

"Don't forget," Sonny bawled before allowing Evvie to lead him back into the bar.

"I won't," David told him.

"What doesn't Sonny want you to forget?" she asked.

"Reuben's shotgun. Sonny's working an out-of-town job, he's on the road by four in the morning, so he won't have a chance to return it to him. He keeps forgetting it, anyway. So he gave it to me. I'll take it to Reuben tomorrow. Or maybe not. Maybe I ought to keep it awhile. He might decide to use it on somebody, the way things have been going."

She couldn't disagree with David. On the other hand, she wasn't crazy about David having a firearm handy, either.

"Are you okay?" he asked her.

She nodded.

"You don't look it."

"Been a difficult week." She filled him in.

"It gets worse and worse," he said. "Well, come to my place and swim. You need to be distracted."

She grinned at him. "You're always inviting me someplace to do something that never gets done."

He laughed. "This time I'll throw you in the lake myself."

NINETEEN

1

Pearl dove into the lake without his assistance. Once in, she did not want to come out and went on swimming until she no longer trusted her strength and had to stop. It was fully dark when she emerged. The night was cool and crisp, the sky roofless to the stars. It was easy to believe in the planet as spaceship. Some kind of vessel, anyway, maybe a pirate ship.

David lounged on a blanket on his beach, alternately staring at the lake and the sky.

As he wrapped her up in a big towel, she told him through chattering teeth, "I almost feel human again."

"Let me tell you how you feel to me."

He pulled her down next to him on the blanket and held her close, giving her his body warmth. He peeled her out of the bathing suit. It all seemed natural and reassuring. When it was her turn to look at the stars, she searched them for some pattern, some map, and found only a brilliant chaos.

Though she left him fairly early, she was replete, savoring the taste and feel of him all the way home. She slipped into a nightshirt and curled up with the kitten on the daybed, wondering what Reuben was doing, how he was, how Karen was. Sam. She let her thoughts meander toward dreams.

Reuben's unsteady rap at the screen door startled her out of her doze. She groaned inwardly. It was all starting again. She didn't need to smell his breath to know he was drunk, as drunk as she had yet seen him. Drunk enough to come to her on foot. He was trying hard not to fall apart.

She dumped the kitten. It skittered under the bed.

He didn't say anything. He stood over her for a few seconds, weaving, then picked her up and carried her upstairs.

2

Out of an exhausted sleep, she sat bolt upright at the sound of Karen's Plymouth in the driveway.

"Oh, my God," Pearl said.

Next to her, Reuben stirred. He opened one eye.

"It's Karen."

He started to roll toward the side of the bed.

Pearl was already out of the bed, pulling a robe on. She jerked back her palm, cautioning him.

"Be quiet. I'll go down and tell her I overslept, which I have, and send her on ahead to the diner."

She hurried downstairs.

Karen was just coming in. Her eyes were swollen and red with crying.

"I overslept," Pearl said, and then halted. "Are you all right?"

Karen shrugged.

Unmistakable sounds of someone else moving around came down the back stairs after her.

Karen grinned weakly at Pearl. "I'll open up for you."

Pearl plucked the keys from her handbag and started to separate the diner key.

Behind her, from the stairs, a zipper closed. She whirled around and Reuben was ducking down the passage, threading his belt through his pants.

Karen and Pearl both froze.

He was deliberate and calm, unmistakably at home.

Karen looked from Reuben to Pearl and laughed jaggedly.

"Oh, this is cute."

"Enough of that," Reuben said. Addressing Pearl, "It's time she knew."

Karen backed toward the door. There was hysteria in her voice. "Did you tell him yet whose money paid for the scrape?"

He flinched and so did Pearl.

Karen slammed through the door. In the silence between them, they heard the Plymouth erupt into noisy life and peel out.

"Did you, Pearl?" he asked. "Pay for it?"

"Not exactly." Pearl shoved the question aside. "She didn't have to find out this way. It was like throwing somebody in that damned cold lake. Why didn't you stay put, why'd you have to come down here? Did you do it on purpose to piss her off, to get even with her?"

Reuben's eyes clouded. He thought he'd known his own reason and it hadn't been anger, a desire to shock the kid as she shocked him. Now Pearl was suggesting something to him he hadn't suspected of himself. He turned around and went back up the stairs.

She sat down at the kitchen table and listened to him finish dressing.

When he came back downstairs, he had the aspirin with him. Silently he offered her some. She took it. He drew water for them both and knocked his back.

"I'm hung-over as hell. There's a brick on top of my head. You going to tell me what she meant?"

"She asked me for the money. I said I had to think about it. Then she just took it from the diner."

"She stole it." He sounded as if she'd punched him. "But you knew about it, she told you she was pregnant and wanted an abortion and you never told me. That's hard for me to accept, Pearl."

"It all happened so fast and I didn't know what to do. Then she took it out of my hands."

"Would you have done it that way if you'd been her mother?"

"No. But I'm not."

He stared at the glass he held in one hand. Then he put it down. It was as if she weren't there anymore. There was a disturbing stillness in his expression.

"Have to think about this." He walked out the door.

She hauled herself to her feet. It was time to go to work.

3

Karen wasn't there.

"I don't expect her," Pearl told Roscoe.

He looked at her sharply but left her alone.

Her stomach was a mess again. Twice she had to whoops; nerves, she supposed.

After work, she again went to Karen's.

The girl was sunbathing, just as if the past twenty-four hours had never happened. Karen opened her eyes and saw it was Pearl.

"You've got a nerve to come here." Her voice shook with anger.

"Karen. I've protected you. I didn't tell Reuben when you told me you wanted to get an abortion, I didn't call the cops in when you stole from me. You have no good reason to be angry with me."

"How about you're fucking my father, is that a good reason?"

"Isn't that between Reuben and me?"

"No, it's not. It's bad enough you've got David. I've seen him looking at you, you've got him twisted round your little finger. You haven't got any right to take my father away from me and Sam too."

Pearl crossed her arms under her breasts and resisted the sudden filling-up of her eyes, the tightening of her throat. How stupid of her to have underestimated Karen's jealousy over David, never mind the girl's possessiveness of Reuben.

"I'm not taking him away from you and Sam. He's still your father. Whose bed he's in doesn't change that. Don't you think he's as entitled to his life as you are yours?"

Karen looked as if she had a mouthful of something nasty.

"I thought you were my friend," Karen cried.

"Me too." Pearl went away.

She drove to Greenspark again and bought another pregnancy test. The clerk's mouth pursed.

"This one's for my mother."

The woman glared at her.

"Have a nice day," Pearl said.

At home, there were several messages on her phone recorder to return.

Norris, staying at a Ramada Inn, was out of his room. She left a message she would be home this evening.

David was slightly breathless.

"Babe," he said delightedly at the sound of her voice. "Want to do to dinner in North Conway?"

"Maybe tomorrow. I'm beat."

"You work too hard."

"Something else I've been doing too hard too."

He was amused. "Can't do it too hard."

"Be good. Talk to you tomorrow."

Maybe by then she'd have things halfway straightened out.

She played back the last message.

Reuben's voice: "Pearl. Please call. I need to see you."

Jonesy answered and there was a pause while he summoned Reuben.

"Tonight?" he asked.

"Yes. I tried to talk to Karen this afternoon. I don't know if it did any good. But she seems to be okay, physically, I mean."

"That's a relief. I've called her but she hangs up when she hears my voice. Going over there as soon as I lock up here."

She wished him good luck. He said thanks and was gone.

She went out to attack the garden.

4

The trailer was locked and Karen was gone. Reuben left a note tucked into her door and went home.

Sam was in the kitchen, making biscuits.

"Went to Karen's," Reuben told him. "She wasn't in."

"Wasn't there this morning either. Josh and I dropped by because she wasn't at the diner. Thought we ought to see if she was okay."

"Pearl told me she saw Karen this afternoon and she seemed to be all right. Physically."

Sam rolled his biscuit dough out of the bowl and onto the floured marble slab. "Water over the dam. Maybe it's all for the best. Josh and I have been talking about it. He says she's too young to have a baby, she's too screwed up to be anybody's mother."

Reuben put an arm over Sam's shoulders. "Probably true, but she could have put it up for adoption. I'd have raised it myself, no matter who the father was."

Sam grinned. "You and Pearl?"

Reuben turned away. "Maybe."

The boy remembered what he was doing. The dough was sticky. He sprinkled flour over it. "Something wrong between you two?"

"I was there last night."

Sam cocked an eyebrow at his father. "I know."

"Karen stops at Pearl's early for coffee sometimes. Always made myself scarce before. But I thought it was time she knew, so I came downstairs. Karen was furious. Maybe it was a bad time for her to find out."

"Tough," Sam said unsympathetically. "She doesn't ask your approval of who she screws, does she?"

"Whom she screws," Reuben said. "Do you have to be so crude?"

Sam laughed and punched the biscuit dough.

"Crude is appropriate for certain people, like my bitchy little sister. Her taste in men sucks."

"Always wanted to have conversations like this with my kids." Reuben gave the kid a casual hug and left him to his biscuit making. He wanted a long shower, he needed to get clean.

5

Reuben came to Pearl just before sunset. He was on foot again but judge-sober.

She opened the screen door to admit him to the sun porch.

"Needed a long walk," he said.

"Did it help?"

"Yes."

"I worked in the garden. It helped. Iced tea?"

He nodded and she went to fetch it. They sat down together on the daybed and he put his arm around her.

"I still haven't seen Karen. I hope she's okay."

"I think if she weren't, it would have been apparent by this morning."

This seemed to unsettle rather than reassure him. "I don't know anything much about abortion or the possible complications."

When she said, "Me either," it seemed to relieve him.

"Done my thinking."

"And?"

"You're not her mother, never been anybody's mother. You've done more than you needed just keeping the theft quiet. I want to make that up to you right away. Karen can pay me back, if she's going to pay anybody back."

"There's no rush. Maybe she should pay me back directly, Reuben."

He thought about it, nodded. "I see the point. Anyway, I want you to marry me. Then you'll be her stepmother and if it ever comes up again, you'll be in a position to tell me."

Pearl chortled. "That the only reason you've got?"

He shook his head. "I was just teasing you. I hope to God she's learned something from what's happened. She'll come around about us eventually."

His hands were caressing her breasts.

"You're distracting me," she said, "I can't think."

"That's the idea." He boosted her into his lap.

"We have to talk," she whispered.

"Later," he said, and carried her upstairs. But they didn't talk later, they fell asleep.

6

The sound of a car in the driveway woke her. *Not Karen* was the first thought in her head. She was still in Reuben's arms. He was already awake, just lying there, holding her.

"That's David's car," he said.

Of course. She jumped out of bed and grabbed her kimono. Fumbling into it, she felt as if she could fly, planing on thermals of sheer panic.

"What's he doing here at this hour?" Reuben asked.

"I don't know. Be quiet now and I'll send him on his way."

She stumbled down the back stairs.

David was just coming in, taking off his sunglasses and putting on his clear lenses. He smiled serenely and put his arms around her. When she tried to evade his kiss, he took it for teasing and laughed. She struggled harder. Suddenly he let go, looking past her. She turned around slowly.

Reuben was at the bottom of the back stairs, threading his buckle through his belt loops. He had come down, she knew, to make clear to David who was in possession, almost exactly as he had to Karen the day before, but with no idea that David had any claim on Pearl. Ironic amusement, an edge of personal triumph, was giving way in Reuben to something else, darker emotions, wariness, anger, and pain.

" 'Morning, David," he said coolly. "What's this all about?"

We've played this scene, Pearl thought dismally. It was bad enough the first time.

David was very still. Then quietly he said, "Pearl, this is very naughty."

Reuben started forward protectively.

Pearl shrank from David but his grip on her wrist was painfully strong.

"How long has this been going on?" David asked her. "Since Walter died?"

"What business of yours is it?" Reuben interjected.

Irritation flashed in David's face. "She's been balling me too, you fool."

Reuben flinched. "Pearl?"

She nodded.

"Why?" he whispered.

"Well," said David, "if I had to make a guess, I'd say she was a greedy little hotbox, but perhaps that's uncharitable. Tell me, Pearl, what compelled you to seduce Reuben? The challenge? It must have been like shooting a moose. You still haven't told me how long you've been doing us both."

She backed away from them both.

"David," Reuben said, "since June fourteenth."

It was David's turn to flinch, and then he laughed harshly.

Reuben turned to her. "What happened between you two, Pearl? Tell me about it, maybe it's something I can understand."

"There's nothing to understand," David said. "That's the same day she and I got started. Must have been a big day for you, Pearl. When, Reuben, I'd love to know. I think maybe you got seconds."

Moving so quickly David never had a chance to evade or protect himself, Reuben punched him in the mouth.

David reeled back against the cupboard. His glasses flew off onto the counter.

With an anguished cry, Pearl thrust herself between the two men.

David wiped the back of his hand and it came away bloody. He grabbed her around the waist and held her tightly against him.

Reuben reached past Pearl to touch David's mouth. David did not flinch away.

"I'm sorry, David. I'm sorry."

David laughed again.

"Sure, Reuben. I know you are. What's a little poke between friends? You know, you've gotten good at roughing people up lately. But I forgive you. You're practically a member of the family. Fucked my mother, fucked my Pearl. Maybe I should fuck Karen."

"Stop it, David," Reuben said.

And he did. Suddenly the tension went out of him the way a sheet on a clothesline or a flag goes slack when the wind fails. He took a deep breath. With shaking hands David reached for his glasses, folded them up, and exchanged them for his sunglasses, blanking out his eyes.

"If you're going to punch *her* out now, I'll stay to watch, but otherwise, I'm gone."

"I'm not going to hit her," Reuben said.

David nodded, turned abruptly, and strode out. The sound of his little car being gunned out of the yard ripped through the silence between Pearl and Reuben.

"You'd better go now too." She started past him to go up the back stairs.

He caught her arm. "I'm not finished here. We're not finished yet."

His hand around her arm was unbelievably hard, as hard as David's around her wrist had been.

"Let me go."

"I could understand if you did it once because you were drunk or he seduced you. I know David. You're not the first woman he ever talked into bed. But why did you go on with it? Why? The fucking's bad enough, Pearl, but the lying, the lying I just don't understand."

"Take your hands off me."

He didn't. He seized her other arm and tipped her backward onto the stairs. He thrust one leg between hers. Her kimono fell open and he brought his knee slowly up between her legs.

"You don't understand what you've done," he said softly. "I can take the hurt. But David, he's brittle. He's been skating on the edge of suicide since he was ten years old."

"So you punched him. I can see how much you care for him."

"I love David," Reuben said. He ran his hands down her arms and gathered her wrists into one, like a manacle. "As much as I do my own kids. Don't you see, Pearl, it's like you've been sleeping with Sam. I've known David since he was a baby, thirty-two years, longer than I even imagined you. You've been in my life for ten weeks."

She shuddered and pleaded with him, though for what, she did not know. "Please, Reuben."

"Tell me about it." His voice was soft, crooning. "Explain it away."

He shoved her against the treads of the stair. It hurt her back. She went limp, exhausted. He shoved her harder against the wooden risers. He was like stone, bar the part of him against her leg. David, she thought hysterically, would have had an erection. He'd be fucking her by now. Suddenly Reuben let go of her and she collapsed on the stairway. He reeled back and then past her, going slowly up the stairs.

She gathered her kimono about her and went upstairs after him.

With the concentration of a man who is late for work, he was finishing dressing.

"I'm going after David," he said. "You understand why. Better come with me, I might need someone to call for help."

The urgency in his voice galvanized her. She didn't bother with underwear, just pulled on jeans and a T-shirt, slipped into sandals. She realized he was watching her, with a weary irony. Then she remembered Sonny Lunt's message.

"He's got your four-ten."

"What?"

"Sonny gave it to him to return to you the other night because he kept forgetting it."

Reuben bolted down the stairs, grabbing her keys from the table.

It was a short, fast, tense drive.

"You've been closer to him than I realized," Reuben said, his mouth twisting sardonically. "What kind of shape was he in, before this came down?"

"He's been better the last week. A while ago he had some kind of manic phase."

David's car was in the driveway, the trunk standing open. It was empty.

7

The cavernous living room with its three-story window wall was like an aquarium containing a body of light instead of water, in which the three of them, mute and stunned as fishes, seemed to float. David perched on the back of the couch, the shotgun cradled in his arms. One hand possessed the trigger. Its dark lustrous wood stock was the color of Pearl's skin. Though his mouth was swollen, the bleeding had stopped. He still wore his sunglasses, like a blind man. He seemed relaxed.

Pearl and Reuben hovered just inside the room.

"Hello," David said, "long time no see."

Reuben was both gentle and wary. "Hello, David."

"Pearl. Come to me, baby, I wants you."

Reuben caught her wrist as she moved forward in response to David's request.

"Let her go, Reuben," David said. His voice was flat, his eyes unreadable behind the black mirrors, like the lake's water, of his sunglasses. "I'm not going to hurt her. I'm not going to hurt anybody."

Reuben looked at David, then at her. He let her go.

She crossed the room to David, who came down off the back of the couch. His eyes never left Reuben until after she was there. He caught her by the waist and pulled her up against him until he could rest her head on his shoulder.

"If you'd just told me the truth, it would have been okay, you know. I'm not that fastidious."

She held him carefully, as if he might break if she dropped him, but his left hand tightened on the shotgun. His right drove into the small of her back harder, so hard it hurt, and she bit her lip rather than cry out. He tipped her head and found her mouth and kissed her hungrily. She tasted the blood and knew it must have hurt him.

Reuben moved a step toward them.

David reacted immediately, jerking back from her without letting go. "Stay where you are, Reuben."

In the corner of Pearl's right eye, a shadow moved on the other side of the window wall and barely had a chance to register.

Suddenly David swung the shotgun upward and pushed Pearl at Reuben. He pivoted casually toward the glass wall and pulled the trigger. The shotgun roared and the huge panes of glass revealed, like secret writing before a flame, an intricate lacy blue-green map, unnamed roads to unnamed places, another country. For an instant the crazed glass hung there as if by habit, and then it came down. Even as the window wall exploded like a dam bursting, Reuben's big hand caught Pearl on the side of the head and she went down, distantly aware he was coming down on top of her. The full weight of his mass knocked the breath out of her. The thunder of the shotgun, the disintegration of the glass wall with a sound like a waterfall, became only the sound of all that man landing on her. She felt the stinging of glass needles on the backs of her ankles, her feet, one hand that had remained exposed. For a long moment the glass came down like hail being blown by the wind.

Then it was over. Reuben lifted himself carefully off her and she could breathe again. She reached up to touch his face. He seemed to be all right, though bleeding here and there. Glass sparkled evilly in his hair. Moving cautiously because of the glass that was everywhere, they helped each other up.

David was curled up against the back of the couch, hugging the shotgun, his free arm raised to protect his face. He was cut and bloodied but not much worse than Reuben. Uncoiling slowly, he hauled himself upright and looked around calmly.

The center of the glass wall was gone. The frame still held corners of crackled glass. On the deck, the runaway retriever was a crumpled dune of black fur. The room was now open as a porch to the out-of-doors, the house itself cracked open like a dollhouse with a removable wall. The scents of pine and spruce and hemlock, of all the green forest, of soil and lake water, of sun-warmed sunlight flooded in. Pearl thought she had to be imagining the metallic smell of blood. After the noise, it was preternaturally silent. The sound of the shotgun and the glass breaking must have carried out over the lake.

David put down the shotgun and brushed himself off. "That was sort of fun, wasn't it?"

Reuben seemed to find it amusing too.

Pearl wondered how it was she had gotten herself involved with two crazy men.

David picked his way through the glass to Reuben. "I'm sorry. I wouldn't have hurt you for the world."

He put his arms around Reuben. Reuben closed his eyes and sighed and embraced David in return. The two men held each other for a moment.

Then David turned to Pearl again. Tipping her chin up, he kissed her lightly on the lips, this time wincing at the pain, and then he laughed.

He walked back to the couch, picked up the shotgun, and tossed it to Reuben. "Yours, I think."

Reuben caught it.

David smiled at both of them and then walked quietly out of the room onto the deck.

Pearl let go of the breath that until then she hadn't known she'd been holding. Reuben drew her close. He looked at her searchingly for what seemed a long time, as if he were seeing her for the first time or possibly the last and wanted to remember everything about her. Absently he picked a few flecks and winkles of glass from her hair. Then he kissed her, fully as passionately as David had.

"I don't want to leave him here alone," was the first thing he said. "I'd like him to come and stay with me for a while, or you, or someone. He can't stay here, in this mess, and he shouldn't be alone."

She nodded.

But when they went out on the deck, he wasn't there.

TWENTY

1

It was in the hiatus when the early-morning fishermen have given it up and the boaters and skiers are still lingering over coffee and newspapers. It did not appear that the sound of the shotgun blowing out the window wall had attracted anyone's attention. Perhaps those who heard it took it for a dynamite blast; such things could be heard when people took it into their heads to build new cottages or put foundations under old ones. The trees tossed and rustled in a light wind and there was a steady chop to the water.

David came out of the boathouse and dropped a cobweb-patinated canoe of a faded rose color onto the water.

"David," Reuben called, vaulting the deck rail.

Pearl followed him.

David didn't look back. Throwing an oar into the canoe, he hoisted himself into it from the water. He had taken the first powerful strokes and was shooting away from the shore by the time Reuben reached the water.

Reuben stopped to kick off his shoes.

Pearl shed her sandals and they both dove into the water. Stinging in the many small cuts made by the disintegrating glass, the cold water shocked her, doubling the surge of adrenaline powering her. The rough chop made every stroke a maximum effort.

David kept his lead despite their best efforts. When he reached the bend that protected the bay on which his house was built, he dropped his oar and stood up. He looked back at them, only yards away. His face was blank. Taking off his sunglasses, he let go of them nervelessly. The twin mirrors tumbled into the water and disappeared. For a second David blinked in the full glare of the sun and then deliberately, dove from the rose-colored canoe, tipping it turtle with the backward thrust of his momentum. He went under and didn't come back to the surface.

In synchrony with Reuben, Pearl covered the last hundred yards to where David had been, filled her lungs, and plunged after him.

When her eyes adjusted to the water, she could see David below her, floating downward without active resistance into darker water, like a snowflake from a cold sky. Reuben was closer, descending upon him like a huge predatory bird. Pearl's lungs burned in her chest and she struggled to the surface.

She sucked in breath and went back down. It took precious seconds to locate Reuben trying to bring David up, David struggling away from him. Then it was Reuben who had to let go, to seek air at the surface. She got behind David and got her arms around his chest.

Struggling still, he turned toward her. His face was distorted with pain and terror. His hands flailed through her hair and then he recognized her and seized her, first by her hair, and then around her waist. She realized then he meant to take her with him, wherever he was going, and that she was again in desperate need of air, as David must now be. He must be exerting the most extraordinary willpower to successfully resist the body's demand for oxygen. She didn't know if she could last until he lost consciousness.

Then Reuben's big hands hauled her free and he brought her to the surface. He stayed there long enough to hear her gasping and then was gone again himself. She trod water and screamed for help, though she did not see anything upon the lake by way of watercraft. With her lungs refilled, she followed Reuben down.

This time they had to return to the surface for air without having found David. Her screaming had provoked something, there were boats in the water now, headed their way, toward the overturned rose-colored canoe that still rose and dropped upon the chop a few yards away. She did some more screaming to orient the rescuers to their location and then dove again.

She found Reuben but not David. They touched, signaling each other, and looked frantically for any sign of him. At last they glimpsed him, ghostly, farther down than they had yet been.

He floated, no longer moving of his own volition. She was sure he was unconscious. But his color had changed, he was pale and bloated. Coming closer, she saw she was wrong. He wasn't, didn't look like that, so like a corpse; he looked like himself, asleep.

The pale and bloated part of him was something too human in its shape but with the lifelessness of a mannequin. Its arms and legs entangled his in a grotesque embrace. Pearl's hands reached for David and touched it. Moon-colored and waxy, it was the size of a child but doll-like in its deadness. There was no face, only a blank, protofetal head that looked like one of those odd bulbous stalks on a tropical fish, wobbling on a neck that was mostly exposed spinal column, some evolutionary elaboration more carnival curiosity than well-fitted puzzle piece in a complicated but mechanical Darwinian universe.

Her own consciousness wavered and her chest began to burn for air. David's hand clamped suddenly upon her wrist and jerked her into his ghastly dance with the awful thing. Now his eyes were open but glazed, dead man's eyes, seeing her but not seeing her, open wells into which she would be compelled to plunge against her will. He was cold to the touch, but the thing in his arms was colder, fish-cold and scaly.

Strands of Pearl's dark hair, drifting in the water like the trailing fins of high-bred koi, were caught by the scurfy texture of the thing. Terrified, she fought it, fought David, to free herself. The weight of the water made every move slow motion. She lost all orientation, any sense of which was up or down. Then it was as if an iceberg had opened a hole in her side and she wallowed, helpless, suddenly strengthless. The world had turned into a banana peel under her. All the terror and fear and even the explosive pain in her chest was gone. The only thing she felt was curiosity and surprise, surprise at not being afraid anymore, at how simple it all seemed, and what a relief it was to be dying.

Then, with equal suddenness, she was freed. Reuben was guiding her toward the surface with one hand. She saw he had David by his collar with the other one. There was no resistance, David seemed finally to have passed out. Yet David still clung to the terrible thing or it clung to him, for it was trailing to the surface with them. Pearl could not help her body coming into contact with it or David as they rose like a pod toward the air. She felt a revulsion that brought tears to her eyes. It broke the surface of the water just after her and floated there.

"Oh, my God," she heard a man cry out. "Jesus Christ, will you look at that."

There were boats around them, with people in them reaching out to them. Reuben lifted David's body into the strong hands of two men in a large cruiser. Then he seized her and she was taken from the water like a sportfish and huddled next to David. She slipped beneath him, to hold his head in her lap. His lips and fingernails were blue. She stared at his chest in terror but it did not rise or fall. In seconds, Reuben was over the side and crouched next to her, the tips of his fingers on David's throat, searching for a pulse.

"Gun it to shore to Christopher's landing," he said to one of the two rescuers. The sudden violent forward movement of the boat jolted them. "Got a radio?" They did. "Call the rescue unit to meet us there.

"I'm not getting a pulse," he said to Pearl. "Do you know CPR?"

"No." Pearl shook her head.

Suddenly he bent over David, seeming to kiss him. Then she realized he was blowing breath into him. She jumped when Reuben clenched his fist and struck David's chest for the first time. It didn't get any easier. Every time he did it, she felt the blow herself, transmitted through David's body to hers. The boat juddered over the water, rattling her bones. She shivered with a newly felt cold. One of the two men slung a thin nylon jacket over her shoulders.

Then they were at the dock. One man jumped onto the dock and the other picked up Pearl and passed her to him. Reuben remained as he was, trying desperately to resuscitate David. A woman came from somewhere and put her arm around Pearl's shoulders.

"Get some blankets," the woman said, and Pearl looked at her again and realized it was Liv Russell, whom Roscoe had pointed out to her. There was something very comforting in the woman's solidity. She was like a pillar, only warm.

Pearl swayed back and forth, trying to take in everything going on. Some of the boats had followed them to shore. There were a lot of people shouting and yelling and running to and fro, and a fair number just standing around and gawking. Someone came down from the house with blankets and Liv Russell slung one around Pearl.

Her skin burned from the cold of the water and her limbs were so heavy she thought they would fall off. Her ankle was screaming.

"What the fuck happened?" she heard someone say. "The goddamn glass wall's been blown out."

"I heard it," someone else said. "Figured someone was blasting."

When she looked back at the lake, she saw the boats that hadn't followed them to shore were circled around the place where they had been, marked by the reddish pointer of the canoe. The people in the boats were taking something out of the lake. She did not want to see what it was.

"You see it?" an anonymous voice asked someone else.

The response was a heartfelt, "Jesus. It can't be, can it?"

"Fucked if I know. All I know is that every other kid that drowned in this lake in the last twenty years, we've recovered the body. It is a body, isn't it?"

"What else can it be? Mother of God."

"Hey," Liv said to the conversationalists, "shut up, will you?"

"Sorry," one of them said, abashed.

The siren of an ambulance rose in the distance and then it arrived. Pearl recognized Ansel Partridge at the wheel. The farmer puffed up to them.

"You want me to spell you?" he asked Reuben.

Reuben waved him off.

Everything started to move fast. Unceasing in his effort, Reuben moved with David from boat to ambulance as if the two of them were bonded together like Siamese twins, Reuben's heart and lungs keeping them both alive. Liv Russell tucked Pearl into the front seat of the ambulance with Ansel. Pearl closed her eyes, the back doors of the ambulance thudded closed, the siren bleeped and then began to shriek, and Ansel floored the accelerator.

She kept her eyes closed to keep from being scared of the speed at which they were moving. In less than fifteen minutes they were at the hospital, where a reception committee of people in hospital greens stood around a gurney. Someone flung open the big doors on which the word EMERGENCY was stenciled. As they were all swept inside, she had the sensation that the hospital was sucking them into itself, as a magnet draws iron filings.

Once inside, Reuben and David disappeared around a corner. Disoriented and weeping, Pearl was thrust into an empty examining room and left to herself until the arrival of Ansel Partridge, even more out of breath than she had last seen him.

A few minutes later, Reuben came in. He took her in his arms and Ansel disappeared so quickly he almost went poof.

"David?"

Reuben held her tighter. "They haven't given up yet."

It was scant comfort but all they had.

2

Reuben was haggard, close to exhaustion. It was hard work, breathing for someone else, forcing an extra heart through its motions, the suck and pump of the tidal change of the river of blood. Sitting there, in the lee of the hospital's activities, with her in his lap like a child upon her father's knee, he talked. "It was India."

Pearl winced. "It couldn't be."

"Couldn't be anyone else. We dragged the lake for a week and never recovered so much as a sneaker or her cap. We've recovered every drowning victim since. Has to be her."

The tears flowed again. She didn't know where they were coming from anymore.

Reuben stroked her hair. "Something else. India was Joe's kid."

She was stunned. "Uncle Ghost?"

"Uncle Ghost." Reuben smiled. "Your Uncle Joe. I've never told anyone else, not even David. She was your cousin, Gussie's niece on the wrong side of the sheet. If she'd spent more time here, other people would have tumbled to it, but her mother, Torie, traveled a lot during India's lifetime. People around here just never had a chance to notice the family trait coming out in India. That flaw in the color of the eye."

He touched her cheekbone under her flawed eye. "That little wedge of tarnish that's copper in your eye was gold in hers. Same place, eleven o'clock on the iris. Gussie had it, you have it. How closely do people look at other people's kids? Especially if the kid's a summer resident."

"So the trait's expressed in the female, while the male's a silent carrier. The opposite of hemophilia. What about David?" she asked.

Reuben shook his head slowly.

"No, no. I won't swear David is Guy Christopher's son, but he's not Joe's. And he's not mine either, not by blood. I wasn't that precocious. David might be a changeling, though."

She leaned against him. They were both still soaking wet but not cold. The warmth of one human furnace is more than doubled by the close proximity of another, the most obvious exception to the law of thermodynamics that no more energy comes out of a system than goes into it.

"I know who shot India, known a long time," he said. "Joe's wife, Cora, did it, for revenge, on him and Torie."

"Does David know?"

Reuben shrugged. "I don't think so."

"Somebody should tell him," Pearl said.

"You think so?"

"Good God," Pearl exploded, "he's been living in a world where his sister was murdered apparently at random, Reuben. Don't you think it would be easier if he could make some sense of it?"

Reuben nodded. "Maybe. Maybe not. Maybe it would make him hate his mother for giving India to Cora for a target."

Pearl sighed. "Maybe."

He spoke again, after a quiet moment.

"I know how it happened between Joe and David's mother because it happened to me too. At the time I wasn't thinking about why, I was a horny kid making it with a woman who seemed like the most sophisticated woman in the world. She was everything the girls I knew weren't. Been everywhere, done everything, twice. I wasn't capable of wondering what she was getting out of laying a clumsy kid. Later, I figured, well, she was an alcoholic, it was the drink, it didn't matter who she went with, she could and did bed men just because she was drunk. Wasn't flattering to either of us but it seemed like the truth. She was dying before I began to wonder if there wasn't something more to it than a drunken fuck. By then my own marriage was coming apart like that window wall. I thought maybe Torie wasn't looking for sex or companionship or love, maybe she was trying to make me David's father, after the fact."

Pearl, curled up against him, listened to the thudding of his singular heart and thought if it was not true, it ought to be.

At last Dr. Hennessey came in.

"Reuben. Miss Dickenson. He's comatose. We've stabilized him on the respirator. He's a healthy specimen. The machines will keep his heart and lungs working for decades if necessary. God forbid." He said it as if he were mentally crossing his fingers against a vampire. "I take it you two saved him."

Reuben nodded. "We tried."

"You did the best you could. The CPR was really important. What's the story? Couldn't he swim? Or was it a boating accident? Alcohol a factor?"

Reuben squeezed Pearl's hand. "He's a fine swimmer. It was a suicide attempt."

The doctor paused. "You sure? That's a very fit young man and it's tough for a good swimmer to drown himself. There are more certain ways to do it."

"There was logic to it," Reuben said. "It's a long story."

The doctor nodded.

"But he's been despondent, making threats and so on?"

"He's got a history, yes, and he's been under a lot of stress just lately."

"Okay." Dr. Hennessey made a note. "Any family?"

Reuben shook his head. "I'm as close as there is."

"Okay. You'd better get out of those wet clothes. How are you two?"

"Just wet," Reuben said. "Tired. I'll take the lady home and come back."

"If you like. Or you can let us call you if there's any change. Frankly, there may not be any for a long time. Unfortunately the healthy and strong can survive in this state far too long."

"I'd like to see him," Pearl said.

Dr. Hennessey nodded and led them down a corridor.

David was in a room full of machines, the human component for which the devices pumped and beeped. Tubes ran into him and tubes ran out of him. One particularly cruel-looking one was thrust into his mouth. He had traveled into the alien depths of the lake and now he was in some other alien place, some place of unbreathable, inhuman atmosphere. His hands on the hospital linen were naked and vulnerable, in the context of the machines. She fitted her own right hand over his. It was reassuringly warm and alive.

"He's not flat-line," Dr. Hennessey said, "he could come out of it anytime. Or not." Then, suddenly, "Look at that," and he ripped a sheet of graph paper from one of the monitoring machines. "Delta waves. I'll be goddamned. He's dreaming." The doctor went away with his strip of paper to consult with someone more experienced in the reading of such codes.

Reuben made her come away with him. Ansel Partridge was waiting for them outside the emergency bay. Reuben told him how it was with David and Ansel tucked them into the front seat of the rescue-unit ambulance to drive them back home.

In a state of hyperconsciousness, Pearl watched the road unreel. The trees, the greenery, the raw rock, and the dull, amorphous pavement pressed in upon her, insistent in their material substance. They assaulted her nose with chlorophyll, dusty bark, sun-heated tar oil. She felt as if she had been flayed of her skin, and the light was falling directly upon her lidless eyes, boring into her nervous system, electrifying it. She did not think she would ever sleep again.

3

Passing the diner, Pearl was amazed to see it was open. Karen's Plymouth in the parking lot next to Roscoe's truck. How that had come to pass, she could only speculate.

At her house, Reuben sent Ansel away, saying he would walk to his place of business. Then he turned on the shower and proceeded to strip her of her wet clothing.

"We both smell like the lake," he said. "I don't want to smell like that right now."

Fatherly again, he came into the shower with her, washed her hair for her, though she could have done it herself, and toweled her dry. She took his wet clothing and put it in the washing machine while he finished his own shower.

Then, from her bedroom, he made phone calls. To Sam. To Jonesy. To Roscoe at the diner. To other people. He arranged for someone to sheet the destroyed window wall with plastic to keep the elements out of the house until the glass was replaced. A window company had to be called out to measure the expanse so that the glass could be ordered and custom-cut. He talked with someone in the sheriff's office, then the attorney general's office and the state medical examiner in Augusta. It was as if he were spinning a web to which they could all cling.

She brought him a mug of tea and then breakfast, which he ate from a tray between phone calls. He ate a lot. She brought him more tea and a stack of toast. He called the hospital but there was no change. David was still dreaming.

"Called Norris, took the number off your notepad. He'll be in on the late-afternoon flight from Philadelphia. Josh and Sam will pick him up."

"You didn't need—"

"You're not going to be alone. You need him."

Chilled by the implication that Reuben would not be with her, but too frightened to ask him outright if that's what he meant by it, she took up the completion of necessary tasks to hide and ease her distress. She brought him his dry clothing, neatly folded and stacked.

He put down the phone. The presence of his clothing reminded him of his nakedness. He laughed. "Fig-leaf time." Patting the bed next to him, he pulled her down next to him. "How did we get here, Pearl?"

She didn't have an answer. Mouth to mouth, body to body, the hard work of resuscitating love itself was the only answer they could either of them articulate. There was so much rage in him, so much desperation in herself, she thought: This is it, there's nothing after this, we can't go back to where we were.

4

Rapping at the back door alerted them they had visitors. Neither of them had heard the arrival of any vehicle. Pearl slipped into her kimono and hurried downstairs. It was Tom Clark and his partner, Jeff Deluca, on the other side of the screen door.

"Miss Dickenson." Tom Clark took off his hat. "Would Reuben be here still?"

She let them in. Reuben was coming downstairs, buttoning his shirt. She turned away quickly so they couldn't see her trying not to laugh.

"Tom. Jeff."

"Had yourself quite a morning," Deputy Clark said.

Blushing, Pearl propelled herself past them and up the back stairs.

When she came down again, the two deputies were sucking up coffee and taking a statement from Reuben. They wanted one from her too.

Reuben had told them David had come to her house early in the morning in a distraught state. She told them no more. He had not elaborated on the scene that had taken place or the nature of her involvement with both David and himself, and somehow, Tom Clark had tiptoed his way around it.

Then Clark punched off on his tape recorder and sighed. "The body's on the way to the state medical examiner's office."

Reuben moved a spoon next to his emptied mug. "Think it's India, Tom?"

"Can't be anybody else." Tom Clark shook his head. "Goddamnedest thing. I talked to Henry—that's the state medical examiner, ma'am—long distance, on account of he's out west prospecting for dinosaur bones, he does that every summer, he's all excited. Excited for Henry, I mean. Henry doesn't actually get *excited.* 'Interested' is maybe a better way to put it. Says he had a case once before of some remains that might be five times as old as these. Apparently a deep cold anaerobic lake is better than a freezer for preserving soft tissue. I figure she got stuck down there, under something big, like a rock ledge, and just come loose all of a sudden, who knows why. 'Course we may still not be able to get a positive ID." He stood up abruptly and seized his tape recorder. "I hope David makes it. Maybe this'll be the end of it. Maybe if he knows she's safe in the boneyard, he can finally accept it."

"If he ever knows it," Reuben said.

5

Directly after the deputies, Reuben left her, urging her to sleep. She knew he didn't believe she would, and she didn't.

She was just going out the door when the phone rang. She came to a dead stop and her mouth went dry. Full of dread, she made herself go back into the kitchen and pick it up.

"Sister," Bobby said. "Sister sister."

"Bobby." She was relieved.

"Norris is on his way, thought you'd want to know."

"Thanks. How are you?"

"Gettin' by. You havin' troubles, sister?"

"My share." She didn't feel like elaborating for him.

"Don't want to tell me about it, do you? Norris said you got two boyfriends, both of 'em white. No brothers up there good enough for you?"

"No *brothers* up here, period," she said shortly. "Anyway, I don't pick my men by their color. In case you've forgotten, I married a *brother*, and he was an asshole."

"So he was. But you wants to live up there in Whitebread Holler and sling hash. Coupla expensive college degrees and you happy being a waitress."

"It's honest work and it's my choice, Bobby. Are you ever going to get it into your head I'm not going to live my life according to what somebody else's idea of what a 'politically correct' black woman ought to be? Who is it that decides what's 'politically correct'? Lincoln freed the slaves, Bobby, why don't you free your mind?"

"Don't give me that shit, sister. We ain't none of us free, sister, now or ever."

"You speak for yourself, Bobby. Not for me."

But he'd hung up.

She sat down and buried her face in her arms and wept. Why couldn't they ever talk to each other like normal people? She blew her nose.

Bobby wasn't normal, of course. Probably she wasn't either. Wasn't the whole concept of "normal" a delusion? Didn't "normal" mean "average," and who actually was average? Average was a stereotype, just like Uncle Tom and Aunt Jemima and Big-Black-and-Mean.

One of the reasons she liked her work so much was the sudden revelation, on a daily basis, of some unique quality in one of her customers. She remembered her pleasure the day a brutish-looking logger had spontaneously sung a few lines of an old ballad. It turned out he was a locally famous tenor, much in demand for church socials and dances. An elderly woman, a church pillar and chair of the local Republican party, blue-haired and corseted, overhearing the word "faggot" used, remarked that she knew of at least one homosexual couple in the summer community she would trust over nine-tenths of her neighbors. Evvie Bonneau, self-confessed murderer, spent her days looking after stray animals. People hardly ever turned out to be just exactly what they looked or what their circumstances might lead you to believe.

But Bobby really was a stereotype, a crippled, drug-addicted Vietnam vet. Maybe he knew it, maybe it hurt like hell to be boxed in that way. It couldn't be a fate he desired. Mentally, she turned a wheel. Now it seemed obvious that others were also what they seemed to be as well. Reuben was a stolid, often terse country man, capable of punching out the man who had wronged his daughter, almost incapable of admitting he needed to be loved unless he was drunk. David was an urban intellectual, born to wealth, who had never worked a day in his life, a manic-depressive, bisexual, and suicidal—the perfect profile of a poet. Yet even as Reuben was a romantic, David lived an intensely physical life and was as obsessed and possessed by this rural place as Reuben, to whom it had never occurred to leave. And the others—Roscoe *was* a rotten old sot most of the time, though he had genuinely loved and grieved for his old dog. For all his rough chivalry, Sonny Lunt was a drunk and a rowdy. Evvie Bonneau was the willing executioner of animals when she deemed it necessary, as well as preferring the beasts to people.

And what was she herself? The truth was, when she found herself in a morally questionable situation, she had let things drift, she had not done thing one to rectify the situation. In the eyes of Belinda Conroy and perhaps others, she made herself the picture of the black woman as whore. Her perception of herself as no more or less than another woman with a divided heart, overmastered by circumstance, would never occur to the Belindas of this world. How did she explain that she only wanted not to be defined by accident, by the color of her skin, by her job, by someone else's lazy labels? Her thoughts turned back to Bobby, who, after all, had so little when she still had so much. Her health, her strength, the legs that carried her.

She called him back.

"Bobby, I wanted to tell you I love you."

There was a long silence.

"Bobby?"

He cleared his throat and she realized he was crying.

"Okay, sister. I love you too."

6

She washed her face, took some aspirin, and went to the diner, arriving as the luncheon crowd was tailing off.

Karen put down a tray of dirty dishes and threw her arms around her. Jean hovered and fluttered.

Ansel Partridge had been in and informed them of David's condition.

"Good thing I had an old spare key," Roscoe told her with nervous heartiness. "Jean and I opened up, no trouble at all, and I called Karen in."

"You oughtn't to be here, you ought to be home resting," Jean scolded, and then broke out into blushing and nervous giggles at her temerity.

"I couldn't sit still right now if you cemented my sit-me-down to the stool." Pearl gave the woman an affectionate hug.

"Then let's do some work," Roscoe declared.

After they had shut up the diner for the night, she drove back to Greenspark. David was unchanged but they let her stay with him for a while. In the hours since she had last seen him, he seemed to have grown thinner and younger, as if the machines were sucking life out of him instead of keeping it going.

She stopped Dr. Hennessey in the hall as she was leaving.

"Excuse me," she said, "if you could spare a moment, I think there's something you should know. One of your staff has committed a breach of ethics."

7

Reuben drove Liv Russell's Pacer into David's driveway, parking it next to the Chevy Citation he had loaned her.

She came to the door as he approached it. She had a big push broom in one hand.

"Reuben," she said. "How's David?"

He shrugged. "Could go either way."

"Too bad." She let him in.

He gave her her car keys.

"Thanks. It'll be nice to drive the old bomb again."

They went directly to the living room. Against one wall, she had pushed a dune of broken glass. It twinkled and shone, a crystalline comber frozen in mid-curl.

"I hope I got all the slivers out of the sofa. The vacuum cleaner sounded sick, like it was gargling."

"Lot of work," Reuben said.

"I didn't mind. Felt like I was doing something."

He looked at her curiously. "How are you, Liv?"

She laughed. "You're gonna have an answer, one way or the other, aren't you, Reuben?"

He smiled and hugged her casually. "No, you don't have to tell me everything. Guess I'm just saying if I can do anything, speak up. You don't have to gut anything out, you don't want to."

As she looked up at him, he saw the brightness of tears in the suddenly rapid blinking of her eyes. Then he became aware of the warm body in his arms, against him. For an instant they breathed in synchrony, and it felt like floating in some buoyant medium. And he wanted her, and it hurt to want, hurt like a sudden immersion in freezing cold.

She swayed backward slightly, but it was enough to break the emotional connection. They both took deep breaths and then she laughed again.

"You've rescued enough people today, Reuben. You must be tired."

He nodded. He was shaken by his sudden desire to bed Liv. Even the backing-off, the knowledge he was going to do nothing of the sort, made him uneasy, for it might as easily be cowardice as fidelity to Pearl. Was this how it had happened between Pearl and David?

But there was something else to be done, some other matter yet unsettled. He looked around the room, anywhere but at Liv again. She seemed to understand. With her arms crossed under her breasts, she rocked from one foot to another, her eyes a bit too bright.

"I thought I'd take the dog's body to Evvie to bury."

Liz looked puzzled. "What dog's body?"

Reuben went out and looked at the deck. There were spatters of dried blood and fur, but nothing else where the retriever had been.

"Was that what David was shooting at?" Liv asked.

Reuben nodded.

Liv shuddered. "I'm just as glad if it dragged itself off."

8

Tom Clark and Jeff Deluca came into the diner and sidled into a booth. Karen approached with her notepad in hand.

"Karen," Tom said, "siddown a minute, will ya?"

For a second she hesitated. She glanced at Pearl questioningly. Pearl nodded.

Karen slipped onto the seat next to Jeff Deluca, who pawed at his Smokey hat and blushed.

"Jeff and me, we thought we'd ask you if you don't want to help us with a little law enforcement," Deputy Clark said.

Karen's eyes widened.

"We hear some people you know have been dealing," the deputy continued. "Like you to help us set up a buy."

Karen covered her mouth with one hand.

"If we can put those fellas behind bars," Jeff Deluca said softly, "they wouldn't be able to go after your dad and your brother."

Karen sighed. She looked around at Pearl. Pearl smiled reassuringly. The girl took a deep breath.

"Okay," she said.

9

Dr. Hennessey stopped at the nurses' station, where Debra Spearin was doing paperwork.

"Mrs. Spearin," he said, "if you'd just step into my office, I'd like to have a word with you."

She gave him a curious look.

"It's about medical ethics," he said.

She stared at him a moment.

He turned his back on her and walked away.

"My office," he said.

She stood up uncertainly and followed him.

10

The day was whispering away as Pearl returned home, the colors fading, a breeze picking up. She called Reuben and got a recorded message. Waiting for Josh and Sam to arrive with Norris made her twitchy. She remembered something she hadn't done.

She found the kit she had tucked away and did a second pregnancy test. The second bead promptly turned blue; she was. Like plucking petals off a daisy—she loves me, she loves me not—only it was yes you are, no you aren't with little yellow and blue beads.

The long summer day took its time expiring. The sun was just setting when the boys finally drove in with Norris. He had flowers for her, a sheaf of gladioli, spears of white and yellow and red, bought from a roadside vendor. Her throat tightened up and she sniffled but managed not to weep in front of Sam and Josh, who politely made themselves scarce.

"Funny thing was, I had the flight information all ready, I was going to come back anyway tomorrow or the next day. Bobby's okay for now, don't you worry about him. I was looking forward to getting out of the city heat again," Norris said.

Pouring out iced tea, she sat down with Norris on the sun porch. They stared at the sky. The day in its glory was departing. A rising tide of green-black pushed bands of lavender and gold over the edge of the mountains, upward toward a concavity of darker blue-black closing down from above.

Slowly, stumbling, she told Norris what had happened since he left. With his arm around her shoulders, he listened closely, not saying anything, only shaking his head once in a while.

"And," she finished up with the hardest thing of all to say, her throat tight enough to mold cement in, "I'm pregnant."

Like a startled turtle, Norris jerked his big old head backward.

"Pearl, didn't you know any better?" he blurted.

That did it, the dam burst again. She was furious with herself for dissolving into wronged-maidenly tears. "I think sex makes people stupid."

Norris squeezed her hand. "You might have something there."

Jumping up, she went into the bathroom and bathed her face in cold water. When she came out, she was composed again.

"I'm sorry."

"It's been a tough day," Norris said. "I don't suppose you know which fella's the father?"

She shook her head and dabbed at her eyes.

"What are you going to do?"

"Go to bed. Get up and go to work. I don't have to do anything right away."

He nodded. "That which is sufficient unto the day. Best thing for you would be some sleep."

Astonishingly, she did sleep, an exhausted sleep.

11

The bed moved under her, like a boat in the water adjusting to a swell, and she came awake to Reuben's presence, the way he took up room. She opened her eyes. He was sitting on the edge of the bed, an old cap occupying his hands, watching her.

It was getting light out. The clock said five-thirty. She covered her mouth with the back of her hand and yawned. It was nice, Reuben being here.

He reached out, touched her hair on the pillow. She spread the fingers of her right hand over his forearm.

"Pearl," he said softly, "we better stop all this foolishness right now and get married."

"Now you're in for it," she whispered.

Norris, sitting at the kitchen table with a mug of coffee and chicory, heard a hoot of male laughter from Pearl's bedroom and grinned. He leaned over and turned on the radio.

"Damn," he said. "Hardly hear the weather, must be gettin' deaf."

He turned the volume up until he was sure it could be heard upstairs.

". . . already seventy," a thickly accented Yankee voice declared, "gettin' hotter every minute. Only five weeks to the first frost, 'cording to the *Farmer's Almanac.* Ain't it lovely?"

TWENTY-ONE

Pearl closed the strand of pearls. They glowed richly against the soft dark skin of her throat. She touched the comb in her hair, tugged at her new black dress. The old black dress, the one she had worn to Gussie's interment and to Walter's funeral, would have constricted her swollen and tender breasts and emphasized the slow rise of her belly. When she glanced out the bedroom window, she saw the yellow backhoe in the cemetery.

Norris clucked approvingly when she came downstairs, and Bobby, in his wheelchair, reached out to pat her bottom. She blew them both kisses and hurried out across the lawn and under the turning elms. It occurred to her sadly that the leaves of several of the old giants might very well be dying for the last time. She stopped there in their shade, watching Reuben in his shirt sleeves manipulating the backhoe's claw. It was tearing at the farther roots of the white rose, which were not coming up without resistance. He looked up at her and smiled distantly, his thoughts on the hole he was digging and for whom he was doing it.

She leaned back against the trunk of one of the old elms and crossed her arms underneath the new fullness of her breasts. The rose shuddered under the assault of the backhoe. Some of the roots were already exposed, thick as cables, and even the thin ones tough as wire. The roses were long gone, of course, their hips like drops of blood among the green leaves and the tiny thorns.

When Reuben was done, he parked the machine in the shade at one side of the cemetery and dismounted.

She walked to the hole he had dug between the Nevers and the Christopher plots.

He looked at his watch and then rolled down his sleeves, shrugged on his jacket, and took a tie from one pocket. He turned up his collar and knotted the tie around his neck. She turned the collar down over it and patted it.

"Okay?"

"Okay."

"Funeral hack should be here soon."

"I know. Don't fret. It'll be here soon enough."

She slid off the seat and they wandered through the graveyard, holding hands, looking at the stones.

The long black Cadillac hearse swung silently into the cemetery drive and climbed the hill toward them. It came to a stop and the undertaker emerged. Reuben conferred with him, the hole was inspected, the elevator placed to lower the coffin into the ground.

"A great tragedy," the undertaker murmured.

Other vehicles were now entering the driveway or coming up Pearl's driveway to park there. Karen, pale and wan, with Sam and Josh, tugging at their ties. Roscoe, a little shaky from a recent binge. Jean McKenzie, fluttering and nervy, clutching a damp hankie. Evvie Bonneau in her uniform. Sonny Lunt. Lurch Mullins. Ansel Partridge and his daughters, solemn and smelling of horses. Norris came from the house, his bald head shiny in the autumn sun.

Reuben looked at his watch again and squeezed Pearl's hand. His fingertips settled on the gold band on her third finger and shyly traced its circumference.

The undertaker opened the back of the hearse, revealing the mahogany box, the color of her skin. A sheaf of lilies glowed like pearls upon its lid.

It had all come round again. Three times lucky, she thought.

And David, in white linen, came through the gapped line of the elms, thin and serious, his eyes hidden behind sunglasses. Taking them off, he met her gaze and smiled and walked toward them. He took her other, ringless, hand and the three of them turned to watch the undertaker remove India's coffin from the hearse.